Breaking Free...

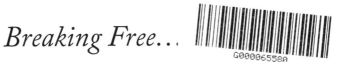

BOUND
for
BARCELONA

MARCELLA STEELE

Published in the United States by Red Hot Years Press
ISBN: 978-0-578-60518-0 eBook
ISBN: 978-0-578-60519-7 Paperback

www.marcellasteele.com
Book Cover Design by ebooklaunch.com.
Book layout by Sarco Press.

A Note From The Author

I THINK IT'S SAFE to say that each reader will take away something different from this story, based on where you are in your own journey. The book is a blend of genres, and because of its many facets, some will be attracted to the compelling story of a woman's struggle to reinvent herself in midlife. While others will be drawn to the steamy and daring romance, the passion that life can bring us. Any woman who has tried her hand in the treacherous world of dating will resonate with the peaks and valleys in the road. Finally, if you are among the many women of 'a certain age' who have challenged societal norms and found an unconventional love, this book will speak to your heart.

Wherever you are on your path, the story will sweep you away to experience foreign lands you long to visit or make the magic of the places you have loved, come to life.

It is my hope that you will in some way be inspired. Possibly to step out of your comfort zone, dare to dream, or take that leap of faith. To defy the odds, no matter the number of years you have. And most of all, to open your heart to the one person who matters most—YOU. Only in being true to yourself, will you find the answers.

A word about age, my peeve. Those of us living in English speaking countries know that age defines us in a direct way. That is, I *am* twenty, I *am* fifty. In Spanish, the translation is: I *have* twenty years, or I *have* fifty years. To my ear, the latter sounds more fitting. Just because you have a particular number of years residing on this planet, it doesn't have to define you. Whether you are a twenty-five-year-old who is judged to be without wisdom, or a sixty-five-year-old who is perceived to be "over the hill"—shine your own light and blast through the labels.

One of the things that most inspired me about Barcelona during my first visit, was the way in which the culture encourages people of all ages to prioritize play. The dance of life is for everyone. Join in, and dance like nobody's watching (and judging). Lay claim to your own internal age and watch the possibilities blossom.

Is this book a memoir? Although the story is based on my memories and life experiences, I chose to design it as a novel. As such, it is a work of fiction. Names and details have been changed to protect the characters' anonymity (as well as my own), to ensure the flow of the story and to provide the reader with a thrilling ride.

With that said, there are a few characters who've given permission for their real names to be used, and they are seen in brief, cameo appearances. A shout-out goes to my salsa teacher, Salsa with Juan, whose identity is portrayed in the story. He welcomed me into the *"familia"* and gave me a new home in his classes. Without him, I wouldn't have realized my dream to become a dancer, and because of that, I began a new chapter in my life. He was truly an influence in my journey to break free.

And now, the story begins. I look forward to taking you all on this two-part journey. My hope is that after you break free from being Bound, you will look forward to joining Elena as she discovers her Destination.

Chapter One

F<small>ATE. *W*HAT *WOULD*</small> *my life be like if I'd never met him? If I had never boarded that plane to Barcelona?* So much had changed in the last year, since that morning I had set out for Spain. *I* was changed.

I grabbed my overnight bag and paused, capturing the image of his bedroom in my memory. The bed we'd shared was still warm. I breathed in the scent of him and the rush almost halted my steps at the door. Wild, passionate scenes of our lovemaking played through my mind like multicolor pyrotechnic explosions. Last night's celebration of his birthday was filled with surprises, I had made sure of that. But this morning's 'surprise' had me reeling.

"Elena," he called to me from the top of the stairs as I exited through the iron gate of his Victorian flat. "I'll see you soon, okay?"

I turned and looked into those beautiful brown eyes that could see right into my soul. He knew. He could always tell when I was filling with emotion.

I nodded and raised my hand in a silent gesture of goodbye. I tore myself from his gaze, but the image of him didn't leave me. *Damn, why does he have to look so irresistibly gorgeous?* Even in sweatpants and a t-shirt, his tall, dark and muscular body tortured me. He was my kryptonite.

The morning was shrouded with the San Francisco fog that lay like a wet blanket over everything. It hung over Coit Tower, usually so prominent from my view as I trudged down the hill to find my car.

Thankfully, the traffic across the eastbound Bay Bridge was light on Sunday. I pulled into the driveway of my Oakland house with my mind set on a long hot bath. Suburbia didn't *exactly* hold the same excitement as San Francisco, but there was comfort in the refuge of my home.

Alone, again, I sighed. It was always so difficult to leave him, but this time I welcomed the solitude. Stripping off my clothes, I slipped into the bath, my pale knees bobbing above the lavender-scented bubbles.

The hot water soothed by my ragged nerves as I lay soaking in the silence with only the *tick* of the small clock on the shelf to remind me of time passing. My stare was fixed on the sun's rays radiating through the skylight, and I lingered, reflecting on our night together. I could still feel his silky, dark skin against mine, his powerful body on top of me as he brought me to a screaming orgasm. At once, I inhaled sharply with the rush of sensory memories. My back arched, and my belly tightened. He was ingrained in my cells. Just the thought of him could ignite intense desire.

I couldn't imagine what my life would have been like if I'd never met him. My life had taken so many turns—it never was a straight trajectory. But in the middle of the journey, came this most delicious twist. I had never expected to see him again. I definitely couldn't have anticipated that he would be anything more than another fleeting fling. Against all odds, I had found the greatest passion I've ever known.

I desperately wished I could stop time. The clock seemed to be ticking faster since I passed the dreaded fifty mark. It had been several years since then, but I'd stopped counting. Since, I'd taken a crowbar to beat back the hands of time. I had become my mother. She also looked much younger than her age. No one knew her real age or her natural hair color. Even she'd lost track, having changed both so many times.

But unlike my mother, who gave up dating around my age, I was in the most active time of my life.

I had come to understand that every moment must be lived to the fullest. Time was finite, and I was sliding down the other side of the slope. At thirty-six, he had all the time in the world to find his path and was only beginning to take life seriously. I knew I had to make my own decision at this crossroad. A crossroad that was more complicated than the love affair, though my heart was positioned squarely in the center. The course of my life, my career—*everything*—hung precariously on the direction I was about to choose.

I sank my head back into the water. My long brown hair floated to the surface as I submerged. Sounds muffled, my voice was eerily distant as I spoke out loud the words that kept ringing in my head.

Why the hell did the universe throw us together? I didn't know if it had been a blessing or a curse. But two divorces and living through the endless maze of midlife dating had taught me one thing. That heady, euphoric combination of great passion and love—it doesn't show up more than a couple of times in your life, if you're lucky enough to find it at all.

My mind ran in circles, desperately seeking direction in the chaos. The time had come to face the dilemmas that had been haunting me.

As I drew myself from the water, I tried to draw on the reserves of my strength. My body felt far heavier than 120 pounds, the weight of so many decisions hanging from every limb like anchors. But then, the thought of returning to Barcelona poured through me with a rush, tingling the synapses in my brain. It had become my happy place and there was no telling what new adventures might be in store.

Fate had changed my life in ways I never could have imagined. It led me to my journey and the beginning of a love affair. Barcelona had begun a new chapter, and nothing would ever be the same.

Chapter Two

Eighteen months earlier

I LAID ON THE horn. "Hey buddy, put down your phone and drive!" I shouted from the relative safety inside my car. Not that he could hear me with the windows closed, but I needed to yell at someone—anyone except the one person who was the cause of my anger.

The drive from my house to the downtown Oakland office was less than thirty minutes. Fifteen, in fact, if I hit the traffic lights just right. A fraction of the time of most Bay Area commutes. It wasn't like me to fly into road rage, but lately, I jumped at the sound of a toothpick dropping.

Pulling into the parking lot adjacent to the government buildings, I paused before turning off the engine. My hands locked onto the steering wheel. When I let go, they trembled. *Dammit.* Adrenaline shot through my body at the thought of facing another day in the office.

Steadying myself on the edge of the car door, I grabbed my briefcase and slung it over my shoulder. *Just breathe,* I told myself as I rode the elevator to the third floor. Before exiting through the parting doors, I peered down the hall to make sure it was empty. With a few dozen quick steps, I reached my office and closed the door. Firing up my computer, the fog that clouded my brain began to clear. The two dozen emails that had come in since yesterday grabbed my attention just as an alert reminded me of the day's supervision meetings with my staff. I steeled myself for another hectic day.

Since it was the end of another school year, it was my job as a counseling supervisor to tie up all the loose ends. This year, *I* was one of the loose ends, according to my boss. As if her tone of disapproval wasn't enough warning, gossip was rumbling through the department and co-workers had hushed as I'd walked by their desks in the last few weeks. The signs were about as subtle as flashing neon lights.

For the last seven years, I had been managing the school counseling program within a division of this local government agency, along with my partner, Emily. In fact, we had founded it—built it from the ground up. After spending so many years on the front lines of the helping profession as a therapist, it was a joy to be able to teach others. Especially the eager new college interns, but also my clinical staff. I never ceased to be in awe at how each one of them gave their heart and soul to help kids and families.

I stared at the computer screen and checked my schedule. Meetings in the office and all over the school districts dotted the grid. Despite the daily challenges and the crises which always seemed to pop up, I loved my job. That was, until a new regime took over in the last year. She became known as "Hitler" in the underground culture of the department. A power-hungry boss who was clawing her way to the top, crushing anyone who didn't submit to her slightest whim. One by one, she had built her inner circle of loyal servants and ruthlessly discarded those who got in her way. And somehow, I had gotten in her way.

From my desk, I saw her nearly six-foot frame stomp down the carpeted hallway, and my jaw clenched. Her thudding footsteps would have told me she was near, even if I hadn't seen her. *Great. That's all I need this morning.*

"Elena," she called, pushing open the door to my office. "I need to talk to you." Without invitation, she sank into the armchair situated on the other side of my desk. The hairs on the back of my neck bristled at the icy tone in her voice.

"I have a supervision meeting in fifteen minutes," I said, glancing at my watch.

"This will only take a few minutes. In fact, that's what I wanted to talk to you about. I've laid out the changes for next year. In your meetings with the staff, I want you to find out who's on board with the new job description I've outlined. Everyone—and I mean *everyone*—must be in alignment with my goals," she spat.

She rose from the chair and loomed over me, pointing her large index finger as if it were a threat. The trembling began again so I hid my hands under the desk, out of her line of sight.

"Which of your staff have been complaining about the changes? I want the names." She leaned in, glowering. "You must know."

Beads of sweat misted on my forehead and the pit of my stomach clenched. There was no right answer.

"I honestly don't know who's made complaints. And as I've demonstrated in the reports, they are meeting the target goals that you've outlined." I wasn't about to throw my staff under the crushing blow of that bus.

"Really?" She cocked her head and with shrewd eyes, examined my face as though I was on the witness stand. "If you don't know what they're thinking, then you can't be doing your job. Find out," she barked, then stormed out of my office, leaving me rattled, yet again.

After her footsteps trailed down the corridor, Emily's round face popped around the corner of my doorway. "Couldn't help but overhear."

"I would imagine, since these walls are paper-thin, and her voice is like a bullhorn. Come in, have a seat, but close the door. While you're at it, close the blinds."

"I heard the same speech the other day." My partner's plump hands were trembling, and she'd developed a twitch in her eyelid. One eye blinked incessantly. "She thinks we are responsible for poisoning their minds—undermining her."

"She's clueless. She's done a fine job of making them hate her all on her own." I grabbed the bottle of antacids sitting on my desk and popped three in my mouth, chasing them down with several gulps of water. "But she needs scapegoats and we are the most likely targets. You and I, my friend, are in trouble."

"I hate to say it, but I think you're right. Have you noticed that she's holding management meetings without us? I saw them on her calendar."

"Not a good sign. But honestly, it's better than having to attend those meetings and endure the berating. I'm having panic attacks every time I walk into a room with her." I slumped in my chair, sinking my head into my hands. "I don't know what we're going to do, Emily."

"Look, at least she can't fire us on a whim. It's one of the few perks of being a government employee." She chuckled, but it wasn't her usual bubbly laugh. "However, rumors are floating around that she's planning to restructure the department. As in, 'design a plan to dump our asses'." Her fingers twitched with air quotes.

"What is she thinking, though? I can't figure out her strategy. We're the only two in this department who're qualified to do clinical supervision."

"She just wants us out, no matter what the cost."

"So, where does that leave us? And the staff?" My eyes met Emily's blank stare and we froze for a second, absorbing the weight of the question. "Now, I wish I would have joined the management union. Although, my staff went to their union reps and it only made things worse."

"I didn't get that news bulletin. What happened?"

"She threatened to fire all of them. She doesn't care about the rules." I glanced into her eyes glazing with tears, "We aren't going to win this one, you know that."

Through the slats in the blinds, I saw our team coming down the hall. As I headed for the door, I stopped and pulled Emily into a hug, her thick mama-bear arms engulfing me. "Let's focus on getting through these next couple of weeks, then we'll figure this out, okay?"

Emily managed a weak attempt at a smile and nodded. "I guess it's showtime. Get your poker face ready."

I took a deep breath before stepping out into the hallway. Emily followed behind, then veered off, gathering her group in the conference room. I heard her laughter in the distance. We both knew we had to maintain the illusion that all was well.

Ushering my staff into the smaller windowless meeting room, I forced a cheerful smile to camouflage the anxiety gripping my gut. After the usual chatter quieted down, I read through the agenda and listened to their site reports, but my mind was barely present, and they knew it. All eyes were on me, worried eyes that looked at me for an answer to some unspoken question. But I had no answer—yet. Despite the awkward tension hanging in the air, we dutifully slogged through the two-hour meeting.

No one paid any attention when I slipped out of the office at four. Under this regime, I was expected to be on duty seemingly 24/7, but at least I could come and go as I wanted. To me, the freedom was worth the extra responsibility. My shoulders began to loosen on the drive, and my thoughts drifted to the dirty dishes waiting for me in the kitchen. I wondered if I could procrastinate one more day.

But there was something else... I ticked through my mental calendar and then it hit me. *Dammit!* The flat of my hand pounded the steering wheel with the realization that Beth had bought tickets to a wine event for tonight. It had totally slipped my mind, but then I was losing track of everything these days. I thought of every excuse to explain why I couldn't make it. I practiced saying each one out loud, but short of being diagnosed with an incurable disease, my friend wasn't going to buy it. We'd planned this weeks ago and I couldn't let her go alone.

Resigned to going through with yet another hunting expedition, I walked through my front door and straight into the walk-in bedroom closet. *Out of all these clothes, how could I have nothing to wear?* It had to be a dress, or maybe a skirt. The dating manuals all had chapters that professed to give the best advice on what a woman should wear when stepping out into a social scene. I'd poured through all of them during my steep learning curve in the world of dating, part two—post-divorce and child-rearing. But still, I stared vacantly into my closet. I wondered how I was going to gather the energy, not to mention the motivation to keep trying.

I heard my phone ping an alert and I glanced at the message from Beth. She wasn't going to let me off the hook.

> Hey girl, you ready yet? We should be on the road by 6:00. The traffic going into San Francisco will be crazy.

> I'm a little brain dead, but I'll make it. What are you wearing?

> I'm dressing to impress. The event is at a classy hotel, so I expect the guests to be more upscale.

> Got it. Dress and heels. I hope this is worth the effort.

> Dude, you always meet some guy.

> 'Some guy' is not what I need. I need the right guy.

> Stop complaining. Be ready in 30, I'll swing by and pick you up.

She had a point. I'd been running a marathon of men in the past few years since I'd started to date again. Beth and I had met in the salsa community, and we'd bonded over our passions. Topping the list was dancing and sex. But I couldn't expect my thirty-three-year-old friend to understand that from where I was sitting, time was not on my side. More of the same just wasn't enough.

Without much thought, I pulled my usual black dress from the closet and trudged through the routine of makeup and hair revival. Considering the endless stream of dating disappointments, it was no wonder my motivation had tanked. I faced the mirror and forced a practice smile. *Oh God. Perk up!* I patted my hands against my cheeks, hoping it would wake me up or at least give me a rosy glow. *You love going to the city, and who knows, maybe tonight will be different.*

Chapter Three

LATIN MUSIC BLARED from the car's speaker as Beth and I drove across the Bay Bridge to San Francisco, inching through the usual traffic. Beth chattered about her latest dates, but I wasn't in the mood to listen. Instead, I took in the glorious sight of the sun's ribbons across the water and the brilliance of the reflection on the windows of the skyscrapers. Exiting the bridge, we wound our way through the busy streets teeming with people leaving work for the day. Due to sheer luck and the tiny size of her car, we landed one of the rare parking spaces, only several blocks from the wine event on Geary Street.

Entering the grand hotel, we found ourselves in a sea of people, most already had a wine glass in hand. The rich wood walls spiked up toward the high ceiling. Gold chandeliers cast a dim light in the windowless elegant room. Long tables draped in red cloth were topped with wine bottles labeled by California vintners while servers in black jackets stood by to explain the merits of their particular label.

The San Francisco vibe perked up my energy. The city had always had that effect on me. Its vibrancy resonated inside that part of my brain which craved the high of something more exciting. Something the suburbs couldn't give me.

As my eyes scanned the room for the shortest line, they landed squarely on the face of a man who emerged from the crowd halfway across the large hall. *Wow...* I was instantly riveted. *Gorgeous...* immediately came to mind. As far back as I could remember, I had always been drawn to beautiful black men, and this guy had exquisite skin, not unlike the color of dark caramel.

He stood tall, towering over the man he was talking with, and then I saw it when he turned his head—his big, radiant smile. It lit up his face, twinkling in his eyes, making the cutest dimples in his cheeks when he laughed.

I was suddenly glad I'd made the trip over the bridge.

The dimples were like punctuation marks on the strikingly handsome face. As I scanned his form from top to bottom, I noticed his kind brown eyes, set against perfectly defined features. His black hair was shaved on the sides, giving him a slight faux hawk look. *He's got edge. Nice. And class.* The black collared shirt and sport coat he wore were tailored with a European cut, which revealed a surprisingly muscular frame. When he crossed his arms, the fabric stretched across a broad back and over the outline of defined biceps. I quieted an involuntary moan from escaping my lips as I took in the sight of him, casting my eyes lower. Designer jeans fit snugly on his narrow hips and down his impossibly long legs.

His presence drew me in as much as his looks. He carried himself in a way that oozed confidence and stood as if he was comfortable in his own skin, straight and tall with perfect posture.

I didn't know what came over me, but I couldn't tear my gaze away. Like a voyeur, I followed him with subtle eyes as he moved through the crowd. He walked with an easy grace, his expensive-looking leather shoes gliding against the tile floor with each step. I saw him survey the room then bring a wine glass to his lips. He caught my stare, and I froze. *Damn. Busted.* I held his gaze for a moment, then casually averted my eyes. I knew the game—hold eye contact for three seconds, then slowly look away. I had no idea what I'd do if he got the message that I was interested in him. The pit of my stomach began to lurch at the thought of actually talking to him.

While Beth and I maneuvered through the sea of bodies, I never lost sight of my target, though I was careful to be less obvious.

"You see that gorgeous guy over there? The tall one." I nodded my head in his direction. "It looks like he's with a friend."

"Yep. I have my eye on him, he's hot." Beth's eyes pointed a laser-sharp gaze in his direction. "I'm definitely interested."

"Yeah, he's hot, and he's exactly my type. He certainly does stand out from the crowd," I added, as my jaw dropped slightly and my lips parted.

"Elena!" Beth snapped her fingers a few inches from my face, jolting me out of my trance. "I'm going to take a look around. I really need a drink. God this place is packed. You coming?" she shouted over the noise.

"In a minute."

Her tone set me back on my heels, but maybe I needed the reality check Beth so blatantly provided. I was competing in her territory. I didn't belong in the competition for a thirty-something guy. What was I thinking?

Just when she left me standing there alone, I saw my target winding his way through the crowd, getting closer to me. My heart stopped. A sudden surge of panic struck me, and I turned, looking for an escape route, but bodies blocked me in every direction. *Why am I running? What am I, in high school? Get a grip.* Squaring my shoulders, I turned and found myself face to face with Mr. Tall, Dark, and Dazzling.

"Hello. Are you enjoying the event? I hope I'm not intruding."

His deep, velvety voice flowed over me, disarming me completely. I took in the view of him at close range. He was tall, over six feet by the look of him. A lean, well-defined build that would make any woman weak in the knees. The kind that cuts from broad shoulders like a V to the waist. His perfectly etched lips flashed a smile at me. Not an ordinary smile. A gorgeous, sexy, dazzling smile that made my pulse race. I struggled to find my voice.

"You aren't intruding at all." I paused to catch my breath. "And the event, it's crowded, but I love the venue."

"Pretty good selection they have here, right? I'm on the Cabernet, which tasting are you on?" He extended his long arm in offer of introduction. "Oh, by the way, my name is Ethan. Ethan Pierce."

Our hands folded together in a firm grip. The sheer strength of his magnetism pulled me in with the force of an invisible rope. His touch was electric. A surge ran through my body, and I felt the heat pulsating at the apex between my legs. That tingle, the one women talk about feeling with the first kiss. I felt it, with just the touch of his hand. My face began to flush, betraying my undeniable response to him. If he noticed, he had the courtesy to keep it to himself.

His hands were soft, his fingers long and slender. I imagined that they were the hands of a musician or artist. But the handshake was firm and with intention. *Impressive.*

"Good to meet you, I'm Elena Vidal," I stammered, not at all on my game.

My observations had been dead-on, he had a powerful presence. He looked even hotter up close—exquisitely masculine and dangerously seductive. I found myself captivated with his eyes, they were bright and intense. It felt like he was looking right through me, stripping me bare. It was as intimidating as it was exhilarating.

"Actually, I'm not so sure, but I think it's a Merlot. Do you have any recommendations?" I asked, in my best attempt to sound unruffled while straining over the noise of chatter in the room.

As he talked about the wines, I realized he was a connoisseur, of sorts. His sophistication was impressive and quite unusual for a younger man, but clearly, there was nothing typical about this guy.

"I'm going to check out some other varietals. Care to join me?" Ethan invited.

I managed to conceal my enthusiasm with a charming smile. "You can be my guide, lead the way."

At first, we stayed on the obvious topic, discussing the merits of each tasting as we wandered over to the next table and sampled some full-bodied reds.

"Do you live here in San Francisco?" Ethan asked.

"No, I live in Oakland, just came over for the event. What about you?"

"Yes, I have a flat in the Marina, been there for years. I'm originally from the Caribbean though. I grew up in North Carolina but moved here after college."

"I know that area of town. Lucky you, except for the parking situation, it's impossible over there."

I tipped my nose to the glass, pretending that I had some expertise in discerning a wine by its aroma. "What do you for work, if I may ask?"

"My business is in investments. I help the wealthy to increase their assets. When it comes down to it, it's about client services. It helps that I'm a math guy though."

The boxes were ticking off one by one. Intelligent, good looking, cultured—and the sound of his voice was undoing me. No hint of a southern accent but smooth as Tennessee whiskey.

"And what about you? Tell me about yourself."

"I'm a California girl, been in various parts of the Bay all my life, but I'm ready to start traveling again. I definitely need a change of scenery."

"And what does your husband/boyfriend/partner think of that?"

"Divorced/single here."

"Surprising," he said, with a raised brow and a glint in his eyes.

He leaned toward me, giving room for the crowd to pass, his torso brushing against my breasts. At once, my breath hitched, stopping in my throat. I tilted my head and our eyes locked.

"*Umm...*" I stammered. "So, do you travel?"

"I'm on the road a lot, been traveling all over the world, but Barcelona is still the place I choose to spend most of my time. You really have to visit there."

"That's what I've been hearing from everybody, it's become very popular. I guess that should be my next destination. It's been way too long since I've been in Europe and I'm dying to go back."

"If you're interested, I'm always looking for a travel partner to share these experiences, it would be fun." Ethan's eyes flickered with a hint of seduction. I felt like a schoolgirl being asked out to the prom by the hottest guy in the senior class. I hoped it wasn't just a casual remark to get my attention.

"That sounds like an intriguing proposition. I do have a lot of vacation time stored up, and I'm not crazy about traveling alone. I might take you up on it." I played it cool, but in my mind, I was screaming, *Hell yes! When do we leave?*

"So, Barcelona it is," Ethan proclaimed. "By the way, you look like you could be Spanish." He took a step back and his eyes swept over me. "Maybe it's the combination of your long dark hair, petite figure, olive skin... and there's something exotic about your eyes. Your eyes are... smoky... intense," he paused, looking away into the crowd. He hesitated, then shifted toward me with a piercing gaze, "You are stunning—but you've probably heard that before."

This gorgeous hunk of a man thinks I'm stunning? I stumbled over my words, shifting uncomfortably in my high heels.

"I guess my Latin looks come from my father's side. I have Portuguese blood. Good to know I will look like a local in Barcelona. You have me excited about Spain."

I offered my glass in a toast, "Cheers, here's to new adventures."

With the glass tipped to my lips, I glanced up at him through my lashes. The look in his eyes stunned me. Hot, smoldering eyes bored into mine. Holding me in an intractable beam, seducing me as if we were the only two people in the room. Sparks sizzled in the air between us, neither of us tearing away until Ethan got out his phone and asked for my number, "Done, got it, more wine?"

"I'm here with a friend. I should check in with her. She's around somewhere." We both scanned the room.

"I lost my buddy as well. Let's go check and meet back here in ten."

When I found Beth, she backed me into a corner. "Well, did you close the deal?"

There was a distinct sarcastic tone in her voice. I hadn't noticed she'd been watching us, but then, I was preoccupied. Her inquisition kicked my insecurities into high gear.

"I don't know... well... we talked about travel and he took my number. Not sure if he will follow through," I stammered.

Beth gave me the *look*, with one hand on her hip, her eyes blazed into me. "Whatever," she scoffed.

I bit my bottom lip, holding back the words I would blurt out to put her in her place. Beth could be difficult, but her friendship was important to me.

My hopes for Beth finding a diversion in Ethan's friend were instantly extinguished when we found them in the crowd. Casting a glance at Beth, I cringed as I saw her face fall. The reason was clear. Abe was seriously lacking in all areas including height, looks, and personality. A trifecta that wasn't going to work for her. I knew that look on her face. The forced smile she wore when she tried to be polite. But her eyes darted at me with daggers.

She held the facade when Ethan proposed the four of us go to dinner at a restaurant across the street. Following the host to a table, Ethan caught my eye and motioned me into the chair next to him. Beth made sure to sit directly across, placing herself in the perfect position to strike up a conversation with him. Her skills were well-honed, though utterly transparent—to me, at least. There was no mistaking that perfectly timed giggle and toss of her head, throwing her long auburn hair over a shoulder. If I was keeping score (and I was), I had to admit that the game was about to turn in her favor. By a two to one margin, I suspected. No longer emboldened by Ethan's initial advances, I began to shrink.

I lost count of how many bottles of wine we went through. After dinner, we staggered up the street to a club on Geary. As we made our way into the packed club, Ethan stayed with me, despite Beth's attempts to draw him away. We inched our way into the crowd, and he reached for me, his arm pulling me into a dance. My breasts moved against the sinewy muscles of his chest as we swayed to the beat. The pop music blaring from the speakers elicited my sexy dance moves, but I refrained from turning it into an obvious hip grinding opportunity. He drew me in close with his hand on my back, sending an electric charge straight down to my groin. I caressed his rock-hard biceps, sliding my hands up his arms and locking them around his neck.

His scent drew me in with a powerful rush. It wasn't cologne, he smelled fresh, maybe of body wash. More than anything, there was something in the aroma of his pheromones that I couldn't resist. I found myself having thoughts of being taken by him right there on the dance floor.

The DJ spun another song and I used the break to head for the bathroom. It wasn't like me to be falling all over a guy. I faced my image in the bathroom mirror. *I have to get myself back under control.* Taking a deep breath, I wound through the crowd to find him again. Rounding the side of a couple lip-locked in what was clearly more than just a dance, I saw them.

Beth was in Ethan's arms, grinding on his body and seducing him to the beat of the music. I froze in my tracks. Clutching my stomach, all the air left my lungs. Immobilized, I stood there awkwardly gawking at the two of them. They didn't even notice me; the bodies moving in all directions kept me hidden.

How could she? With a stabbing pain of disappointment and betrayal, I pulled myself away from the train wreck, but my escape route was blocked by the crowd. I felt another set of arms pulling me into a dance. I obliged him, pretending to be unaffected, but nothing could distract me. I watched as Ethan and Beth headed to the back of the club. Like a crazed stalker, my eyes traced their movements until I saw Beth raise her lips to meet his and was rewarded with a kiss. My heart sank and my feet sprinted for the exit. *What can I expect? She's cute and much younger, why wouldn't he be into her?*

Moments later, Beth appeared at the doorway, wearing the expression of a dog who'd just shredded someone's prized flowerbed and had been busted. Ethan's gaze was poised at the sidewalk where I waited, and Abe didn't seem to have a clue. Ethan's offer to let us crash at his place did little to ease the awkward tension hanging on the mumbled words of goodbye. Beth and I barely said a word to each other all the way home as we pretended to ignore the elephant in the back seat. The air crackled as the fibers of our friendship unraveled and disintegrated into something unrecognizable.

As for Ethan, I couldn't help but wish he would come to his senses and pick me. For some reason, this man got to me. While I would never buy into the idea of "love at first sight," it was rare that I was inexorably drawn to a man. Ethan embodied the kind of man I was looking for. It had taken countless dates and failed attempts, but I had come to recognize what I wanted when I saw it. If only he'd felt the same.

Chapter Four

Emily and I had always thrown a party for the staff at the end of the school year. They chose the place, and we sprang for the picnic supplies and token gifts. This year, it helped to have the diversion. I busied myself with planning and shopping, in an effort to stay away from the office.

Under the shade of the redwood trees in the Oakland hills, I greeted the staff as they arrived on their last official day of work before summer break. I didn't let them see the anxiety that had my insides in knots. But a few looked at me with questioning eyes. They knew something was up. My boss and her inner circle were scrutinizing my every move, listening to every conversation. I had to wonder if it was the last time that I would celebrate the end of the year with the people who I had come to appreciate. Most of them had reported to me for seven years. I knew their deepest fears, their strengths, and their dedication to the clients they served.

When it came time to stand before the group and give a person-alized speech for a year well done, my voice cracked. I looked from one face to another, each one had a pained expression in their eyes. *Oh God, they must be seeing right through me.* I was never good at hiding my feelings, but I had to keep it together. Though my chest tightened, and the pressure of tears threatened to explode, I finished my speech and even managed to throw in some humor. Thankfully they all laughed. It was like a machete cutting through the cloud of tension.

Arriving home before five, I hauled bag after bag of food and gear up my front steps. The couch was tempting me to sprawl out and park in front of the TV for the mindless diversion of old reruns but sweat had congealed dirt and charcoal smoke on my skin. Grabbing a pair of yoga pants and a t-shirt on my way, I heaved my sore and tired body into the shower. While I was drying my hair, a text alert pinged and I glanced at my phone. *Thank God it's Anna.* My best friend always seemed to have a knack for knowing just what to say when I was down.

> Hey, Elena, we are all meeting at Jack London Square for some salsa tonight. Will you come?

> Oh Anna, I'm having a hellish week. Not sure I'm up for it.

> C'mon girl, what better way to improve your mood?

> I could think of one other thing. But men aren't lining up at my front door.

> That should be my next business plan. Men on delivery... LOL.

> I think that might already be a business. Not sure if it's legal in California though.

> Just come. You never know what you'll find if you don't leave the house.

I tried getting out a few weeks ago in San Francisco. I met someone. Someone I really liked. Went nowhere. But you're right, nothing improves my mood more than salsa, so I'll be there. See ya soon.

I arrived at the Latin restaurant and noticed the sign out front.

Taco Tuesday
$2 tacos
Happy Hour Margaritas

RESTAURANTS MUST HAVE invented the tradition in California, I mused. It was a way to get the crowds in on an unpopular weeknight.

My salsa peeps were out in force that night, mostly to support our friend Inés and the band. I gave her a nod as I passed through the crowded space, her hands rhythmically pounding the bongos while her melodic voice filled the room with the irresistible salsa song. My hips instinctively moved with the muscle memory of the dance I had begun to learn some three years before.

"Elena!" Anna called. "I'm so glad you made it." Her enthusiasm was infectious.

"How could I miss it?" She grabbed me by the arm and pulled me into a hug. A rush of warmth poured through me. I soaked up her affection, desperate to let down my guard and be myself.

My voice rose above the music, "This is so much easier, to hit a place in Oakland rather than make the drive to San Francisco. Although I miss those Tuesday nights at GlasKat."

"Oh my God, that place had some of the best dancers. Remember when we started out in Juan's classes? He took us there on a group dance night, and I was so intimidated I couldn't get my timing right." Anna scooted up onto a barstool, her high heels dangling in the air.

"I remember that feeling well," I snorted. "Thank God I found his classes though. I'd probably still be sitting at home every night alone. Dateless in the suburbs."

"Same here. It got me out after my divorce. We've come a long way for a couple of middle-aged ladies." She looked anything but middle-aged, with her flawless porcelain skin and sexy dress that clung to every curve.

I hopped up on the stool next to Anna, my petite frame topping hers by a couple of inches. I pulled at my short skirt, tugging it down my thighs.

"By the way, did you sign up for the bachata performance team?"

I bent, slid my feet into the black satin dance heels, then cocked my head up at her.

"Yep, and it's kicking my ass. We practice every week in San Francisco, and I have to run through the choreography every night. It's not easy being the oldest girl on the team, and the rest have far more dance experience than I do. But the workouts have been good for my figure. I don't think I've ever been this toned and lean."

"You've got more guts than I do. I don't think I could stand the pressure, let alone perform."

"I'm not sure that I'll perform, but I love the dance and I get such a thrill learning the dips and tricks. I feel like I'm on *Dancing with the Stars*, but without the gorgeous hunks."

I took a glance around the dimly lit restaurant. "I love our guy friends, but honestly, there's no one here I'm interested in. Sometimes I think I get more of a high from dance than sex. Considering most of my encounters have been less than memorable."

"No luck with the online dates?" Anna asked.

"*Nada*. I never dreamt it would be so hard to find someone after the divorce. My mother keeps saying 'You have to kiss a lot of toads before you find the prince.' I've definitely been kissing, but I think the concept of a 'prince' is as dated as the old adage."

"What about Ron? I thought you two were starting something?"

"We were, very briefly. But my lack of fertility sent him running in the other direction." Despite the infectious sound of the music, moisture glazed my eyes. The weight of those piling disappointments threatened to pull me down a path I didn't want to go. It took a few mental bench presses to push back. "You'd think a forty-five-year-old would have figured out that he wanted a kid long before then." I bristled with the sting of rejection. "Besides, he fit the social norm. A forty-five-year-old guy looking for a thirty or thirty-five-year-old. He wasn't about to date a woman eight years older. Unfortunately, he figured out my age only after I had fallen for him."

"Oh girl, I'm so sorry." She had that sympathetic look on her face. *Not now, not here. I can't fall apart.* I straightened in my seat and averted my eyes.

"What about you? How's your love life?" The back of my hands swept inconspicuously over my cheeks.

Anna exhaled a long sigh, "I'm not doing much better. Online dating is pointless, the guys are mostly looking for a hook-up. I keep trying to find someone for the long term since Kevin has gone back to his wife again."

"Let's see... how many times does that make this?"

"I've lost count." She leaned on the table, perching her chin against her hand. She looked as frustrated as I felt. "He comes in and out when it suits him. I'm not sure what I can do. Just let him go?"

"I can give you advice and tell you to take care of yourself. Don't let him take advantage of your sweetness. But don't look at me as an example. It's damn hard to let go, even when the hurt keeps on coming."

The suede soles of my shoes hit the floor as I stood. "C'mon, let's shake this off. What we need right now, is a great dance."

"Let's hit it!" Anna exclaimed.

The sound of one of my favorite salsa songs emerged from the speakers. The DJ took control as the band set down their instruments. I turned to watch Inés step off the bandstand and felt a hand take hold of mine.

"May I have this dance darling?"

"Juanito!" I threw my arms around his shoulders, which were positioned only a few inches above my own. "Thank God. I desperately need to dance to this."

"I know." He cocked his head and an affectionate smile lit the corners of his mouth. "That's why I asked. Ready?"

I assumed the dance hold position he had so carefully taught me. Straightening my posture, I placed my left arm on his shoulder and my right wrapped around the palm of his hand. I tested the connection between our hands with a subtle nudge. His hold was gentle, with just enough pressure to guide me but not so much as to yank my arm out of its socket. He was a pro, and I knew the pleasure would be mine.

His fingers tapped gently on my back, preparing me for the first move. I watched him for the signal and stepped back on my right as he moved forward on his left. The romantic salsa song "Tu Amor Me Hace Bien" swept me into the smooth rhythm, and I flowed effortlessly across the tiled floor. Juan kept a delicate hold on my fingers, subtly leading every intricate pattern in perfect timing. The music ignited my body. With each step, with each sway of my hips, I came alive. I had failed miserably at every sport I had ever tried. But dance—it was in my blood. My worries disappeared as I swirled and spun across the floor with Juan.

While it always made me nervous to dance with my teacher, he never failed to compliment me at the end of a song.

"Thank you, my dear. That was fantastic, as always."

Our hands met in a double high five, just before a *salsera* hooked Juan's arm and pleaded for a dance. I got in a few more dances with my friends, before I noticed the food was served.

I didn't realize how hungry I was until I lined up at the buffet table, and the mouth-watering aroma of herbs and spices stimulated my palette. I piled my plate as if I hadn't eaten for days, concocting tacos filled with fish or meat and topping them off with salsas which by their outward appearance, didn't threaten to burn a hole through my tongue.

"That's an ambitious plate. It's nice to see a woman with an appetite."

The voice distracting me from my buffet table mission had come from the man standing next to me in line.

"I'm not sure if that was a compliment or a dig." My lips pouted in a smirk as I quickly sized him up. It was clear he wasn't one of the usuals at the salsa nights. There was nothing impressive about his attire. Jeans and a colored t-shirt did not scream class. The gray in his stubbled beard and fine lines around his eyes gave me reason to believe he was in his late forties. Though he had a full head of hair, wild and curly, with just enough product to keep it under control. I wouldn't have called him extraordinarily handsome, his nose took a prominent place on his face, but he was cute. In a rugged sort of way.

"Take it as a compliment, please. I'm Sicilian, and in my culture, food is something to be passionate about. Enjoyed, savored. Every. Last. Morsel."

Each word was enunciated with intentional precision. He spoke without a trace of an accent, but the glimmer in his eyes and the obvious seduction in his voice convinced me of his heritage.

Holding his plate in one hand, he reached with the other to shake mine.

"Hi, I'm Thomas."

Juggling my plate, I met his large hand in a grasp, and his fingers folded over mine as if he was inviting me into a dance. It was one I recognized, and it definitely wasn't salsa. He didn't tug or grip, nor was his hand too soft or limp. It was a caress, more than a handshake. The muscles on his broad chest expanded under the thin material as he moved. My eyes followed the line down to his bulging biceps.

"I'm Elena, pleased to meet you."

"I'm sitting at the bar, and there's an empty seat next to me, would you join me? I hate to eat alone."

There was something about him that intrigued me. Confidence with a subtle tone of suave always worked for me.

He held a chair and waited for me to sit before taking his own seat.

"Old school Sicilian. You are impressing me, Thomas."

"My mother was old school, and she raised me with a tough hand. I was educated in the ways of a gentleman. Mostly with a wooden spoon against the side of my head." He turned his head just slightly, enough to glance my way. His full lips pressed into a wry smile.

"You see, Sicilian families are always in the kitchen, so a spoon was never far from her hand. And I must admit, I usually gave her good reason. I was a mouthy kid. I guess I never managed to outgrow that."

I returned his smile and chuckled. "I can relate to that. While my mother didn't resort to a wooden spoon, even as a child I argued with her constantly. I nearly drove her crazy. She used the "Dad" card. 'Wait until your father gets home, he'll take his belt out on you.' But he never did. He got me. He knew that reasoning was the best way to handle me. Even at age five."

The smile on his face lit up his eyes. "So, you're a handful, are you?"

"I guess you could say that. Always been a rebel, always questioned things."

"Now you are impressing *me*, Elena. I've made a living out of questioning authority figures. I'm a journalist, and apparently quite good at making politicians angry."

My interest in food was waning with our conversation. I managed to eat at least one of my carefully constructed tacos before it became cold, but his wit and intelligence drew me in. We debated politics and the societal issues that impacted heavily on Americans, such as gun control. He had been on the forefront of reporting when the Columbine school shooting occurred, having spent many years living in Denver.

"I didn't expect to come out for Taco Tuesday and find such an intellectual conversation. You intrigue me, Elena. So, who are you? Tell me about yourself. Other than being a great dancer and a good sparring partner, I don't know much about you."

Having been on so many dates where a man never got around to that precise question, he instantly earned my attention.

Thomas politely called over the bartender and gestured at me with an open palm.

"What are you drinking?"

"Margaritas."

"Two margaritas, please."

He rotated his body and placed his elbow on the bar, propping his cheek against a knuckled hand.

"Go on, I'm listening."

"'Who I am,' involves a very long story, but I will give you the short version." I sucked in a long breath, preparing to launch into the all-too-familiar introduction spiel. I must have had a hundred opportunities to hone it after so many first meets from countless dating sites.

"I've lived most of my life in various parts of the Bay Area. I spent my whole adolescence in a small, conservative suburban town. I hated it. I'm more city than country. Oakland has been my home for the last twenty years, but I'd be happier living in San Francisco. Except for the cold weather."

"Do you have family here?"

"Both my mom and dad live in California. They divorced when I was twenty, but they had gone through multiple separations since I was ten. Those years were not easy ones, for me or my brother. I was the oldest, so I took on most of the worry."

I looked down at my fingers knotting in my lap. "That probably had a lot to do with my career choice. I knew I wanted to help kids and families since I was a teenager. I have a master's degree in social work and I'm a licensed therapist. I've been working in my field since I was in college."

"Interesting. My ex-wife was a psychologist." His face grimaced like he'd tasted something bitter. "Have you been married?" he continued.

"Divorced too, quite some time ago. Actually, twice divorced. I was only seventeen when I met the first one. I have one son who will be graduating from college soon."

"Me too. I have a grown daughter. She lived with her mother after the divorce, so I didn't spend as much time with her as I would have liked. But she is the light of my life." His eyes brightened with the thought of her.

"In my case, all my time went to my son. While we shared custody, I was 'Mom.' That meant I handled everything. I even put my life on hold for eight years while I raised him. Adding a man into the mix would have complicated our lives, so I've only been dating a little over three years since he left for college."

His mouth gaped open in disbelief. "Are you saying that you were celibate for eight years?"

I shook my head in disbelief at my own life. "Yes," I squeaked out. "I began dating when I began salsa classes. Dance changed my life."

"I'm sorry, but it's hard to believe. You?" His cheeks scrunched upward against his eyes. "You are attractive, sexy, and... have a smokin' hot body. That must have been some coming-out party when you let loose."

I shot him a sly smile and rattled the ice in my glass. "You could say that."

"How old are you anyway?"

"THAT is not a subject I discuss, especially with a man I just met. A gentleman doesn't ask that question."

His eyes narrowed in shrewd examination. "I think you are near my age, and I'm forty-seven."

My expression was unrevealing, but he pressed on.

"Are you older?"

I scowled. How dare he.

"Please, don't take offense. I think mature women are hot, but I usually date much younger women."

Now he'd pushed all my hot buttons. I fired back at him.

"What a coincidence because I usually date much younger men." I crossed my arms and challenged him. "Out of curiosity, why date younger women?"

"Because I like sex. Younger women are usually more into sex, from my experience." He rolled the sentence off his tongue so casually. It was bait, and I reacted like a mouse racing toward the cheese.

"Well then, you have not experienced the joys of sex with a real woman. A woman who knows what she wants and has the confidence to claim her sexuality. Not to mention a woman with an advanced intellect. Someone who can hold a meaningful conversation," I scoffed.

"So, I take it *you* are an example of such a woman?" His expression twisted into a triumphant grin. "I have to admit, a woman like you might change my mind. I've really enjoyed your company. One more drink for the road?"

He'd done a good job of stirring things up, but his demeanor was cool and collected. I sensed his intense sexuality. It oozed from his voice and from the way he moved his body. He smelled of subtle cologne, like delicious vanilla and spice. He was an alpha male, playing it smooth. Despite my irritation, I was drawn to him.

"When we're done with our drinks, would you be so kind as to drop me off at home? I just live about seven blocks away, but I'm dead tired."

I hesitated, getting into a car with a man had always meant trouble.

"Sure, but I'm just dropping you off." I tried to sound like I had some semblance of resolve, but there was no denying he'd made me hot.

Thomas settled the bill, paying for my dinner and drinks. I wondered when the point would come when he would cease to be a gentleman, but I was betting it was a car ride away.

I found Anna on the dance floor and told her I was leaving. She glanced at the bar and saw Thomas waiting. She waved at him with one hand and gave me a secretive thumbs-up with the other. I shrugged my shoulders, "Hey, you never know unless you try, right?"

Chapter Five

WHEN WE ARRIVED in front of Thomas's apartment building, he invited me up to see his place. No surprise.

"I don't think so, another time."

"Just for a few minutes, I'd like to show my new apartment."

I was already parked just outside. In the moment, that rationale made sense. I blamed the tequila for the downfall of my resolve (if I had any to begin with).

"Alright, but just for a few minutes." I wasn't naive, but I was conflicted. He turned me on, but I knew the way things usually went down. If I gave into my sexual urges on the first date, very often I was viewed as a throw-away. Someone who wasn't real dating material. Yet, as a man, it was expected that he would try to lure me into bed. It was a trap, and I had never quite figured how to take the bait without feeling the sting of the metal springing back on my ass.

"Please forgive the boxes. I haven't finished unpacking yet." He threw the keys on the kitchen counter, then hung his jacket in a closet that held little more than a few pairs of jeans and t-shirts.

"This looks like a brand-new apartment. They seem to be springing up all over this part of town. When did you move in?" Setting my purse on the counter, I glanced around the sparsely furnished, industrial-style studio. A large bed filled the entire space of an alcove, and a lone desk chair was positioned in front of a translucent computer table.

"I've only been here for two weeks. I moved from Denver to start my new media business in San Francisco."

The walls were bare apart from a few carefully hung photographs in black frames. I stood close, inspecting the photos for clues.

"Is this your daughter?"

He moved in behind me, grazing his arm against mine as he pointed to the images. "Yes, that's her. And that's her husband. And these little ones, are my grandkids," he said, beaming with pride.

"You? A grandpa?"

He chuckled, "Yeah, I can't quite believe it myself. They are adorable, aren't they? They live in Florida. I don't see them as often as I'd like."

"And this is your dog?" I pointed to a photo of a regal German shepherd. Thomas was crouched on one knee, his arm wrapped around the dog's neck.

"That's Max. He and I were inseparable. While everything fell apart in my life, he was there for me. He made the trip with me when I moved here." He held the frame between his fingers, and I saw a flicker of pain in his eyes. "He got sick just a few days after we arrived. I had to put him down."

I felt that familiar wound in my own heart break wide open and bleed. His pain was fresh and raw. "I know exactly how you feel. I lost my golden retriever last year. It was unbearable."

His eyes glazed for a moment, then he squared his shoulders and stepped into the kitchen. He reached for a bottle of wine on the counter and cleared his throat before he spoke.

"Would you like a glass of Merlot? I just opened it last night."

I had felt his heart. That rugged, scrappy Sicilian heart. He had melted me without even trying. In a few steps, I was behind him. I wrapped my arms around his broad shoulders and laid my head on the curve of his neck.

"I'm so sorry," I whispered.

I heard the breath rasp from his lungs and at once, he turned into me with ferocious need. With his hands grasping through my hair, his soft lips devoured mine. I kissed him back, sliding my tongue along the ridged edges of his. His hunger stirred in me something deep, something primal.

He broke away just as suddenly as he'd started. His shrewd eyes studied me, widening with surprise. Silently, he held my gaze and in those few moments, I saw the walls he had built over time. He allowed me only a glimpse of a vision into the man he was.

A smile creased his round cheeks and he led me by the hand to the only sitting area, conveniently located on the foot of the bed.

"I'm tired and in need of some cuddling. Join me?"

Before I could respond, he peeled off his shirt, then his pants. After the socks came off, he promptly jumped into bed, arms beckoning me. My mouth gaped open, only in part due to the sudden disrobing. Muscles rippled under his smooth olive-colored skin. He had the derriere of a perfectly formed piece of Italian sculpture. My eyes took note of the impressive package between his legs, and I felt the delicious twinge dart down to my sex.

I weighed my options. I could walk out the door with an imagined sense of propriety and rely on my trusty vibrator at home for some relief. Or, I could indulge in what promised to be a wild ride with the real thing. His coaxing pushed me over the edge, into the latter.

From the moment his sleek body hovered over my naked flesh, his lips kissing every erogenous zone, I knew I'd made the right decision. His mouth descended to the apex between my legs. The flat of his broad tongue stroked the inside of my lips, then flicked relentlessly over my clit, sending exquisite waves of pleasure to my core. My hips rose off the bed and my thighs quivered, his expert skills driving me to the brink. He moaned into my trembling sex, and with the most perfect technique, his lips puckered and gently sucked while the tip of his tongue flicked the hypersensitive bundle of nerves. My body exploded as wave after wave of the intense orgasm spasmed through my core. I screamed out incoherent sobs of pleasure, mindless of how my voice might carry through the apartment walls.

He rose and climbed my body, meeting my lips with a satisfied smile and a kiss.

"You have *some* skills!" I panted.

He cocked his head, "So I've been told."

I was still gasping for air when I reached for his thick cock, grasping him hard around the base. Mounting his muscular thighs, I stroked the full length of him with both hands until I had him writhing under my touch. Before he reached his peak, I bent and lowered my mouth to the crown. My tongue teasing the cleft, then taking him in, down to the root. His fingers fisted the sheets, his chest heaving for air, I sucked harder and pumped him with my hand. Seamlessly sliding up and down his cock, I felt him engorge and his thighs stiffen against my legs. I stopped just in time, leaving him on the edge. A hoarse moan left him in a gush of air, and he caught the smile on my face as he rose.

With a powerful sound, his hands gripped my waist and flung me onto my back. Poised above me on strong arms, he slid along the slick entrance to my body. With a steady, easy pace, he began rocking his hips. He sank into me at the perfect angle. Each stroke sliding against my clit, then deepening to that sweet spot within my walls. My neck arched against the pillow, and with closed eyes, I absorbed every luscious sensation.

"You look so beautiful."

I opened my eyes to see him gazing down at me.

"That's it... feel me. Let me make you come again."

He bent his head and took my nipple in his mouth, electrifying the sensations. The pad of my finger rubbed against my clit, hastening my climax. Everything tightened and I spasmed around his cock, crying out as he slammed into me, sending me over the edge into another mind-blowing orgasm.

The rush of pleasure still pulsing in my walls, I wrapped my legs around his buttocks and bucked into his feverish thrusts. His body misted with sweat, and his breath came hard and fast with each stroke. Every muscle strained and tensed as he raced toward his release. At once, he pulled out and stroked his cock, hovering over my breasts. With a gentle grip, I reached my hand and massaged the tightening sack between his legs.

He moaned, "Yes, that's it," and a low rasping sound escaped his lips as he spilled on the mounds of flesh and puckering nipples.

With the last of the spasms that tore at his body, he fell limp at my side, his breath gusting in my ear. Groaning out a satisfied sound, he rolled over and reached for a towel near the bed.

"You certainly made a mess on me."

"My version of safe sex. Let me clean you up."

"I like your manners," I teased, blowing an air kiss his way.

Thomas's invitation to cuddle had been a transparent ploy, but now, satiated and satisfied, he settled against my body for some well-earned snuggle time.

"Hey, sleepyhead, I have to go to work in the morning, so I have to go."

His eyes closed and he mumbled a feeble "No."

I leaned in and kissed his cheek, then gave him a playful slap on his backside. "Please get your very cute ass up out of bed, put on some pants and walk me downstairs?"

He mumbled a sleepy protest but raised from the bed while I got dressed.

"So, Thomas, do you still want to know how old I am?"

He nodded, barely peeking at me through half-closed lids.

I pulled on my jacket and paused while he took a pair of sweatpants from the closet. "I'm older than you. Early fifties."

Suddenly he was awake. His slitted eyes flew open and he shook his head. "Seriously?"

I nodded, and cocked my head, flashing him a wicked grin.

"Damn. That's a first. You keep impressing me, Elena."

I gave him a slap on the ass and a look that got his attention. "Darlin', don't ever underestimate me."

He stumbled into the elevator and kissed me goodbye at the door, promising to be in touch. I hoped he would. That Sicilian had impressed me, and I was not easily impressed. I liked him, and he was certainly closer to my age than Ethan. Besides, Ethan hadn't contacted me. Not that I expected he would.

But with a quick assessment of the odds, it didn't seem likely he would be the boyfriend type. His new business was going to be all-consuming. Besides, he'd already told me, he dated younger women. I didn't expect that I had impressed him enough to change his pattern. Still, I held onto a glimmer of hope. Maybe this time…

Chapter Six

I PACED IN THE small space of my office, closing the blinds on the door to hide from the peering eyes of co-workers bustling down the hallways. The knock at the door nearly sent me jumping through the ceiling.

"Elena, how are you doing?" Emily peeped around the door. "I know, dumb question." She stepped into the office and closed the door behind her.

Emily's eyes had the same deer-in-headlights look that she must have seen on my face. Although she was the Zen in our dynamic duo, even she couldn't maintain the facade that all would turn out well. As I'd suspected, after we had said goodbye to our staff for the summer and prepared to settle into the task of planning for the next school year, we received a notification. The head of the Human Resources Department was requesting our presence at a meeting. One which would include our boss. It was starting to look official.

"So, they have you scheduled to go first?" I asked.

Emily's round hands shook. "Yes, I guess we'll meet up after?"

I nodded. "Hey, I feel like I have to apologize. If I hadn't submitted that complaint to HR about workplace harassment, maybe she wouldn't have taken things this far."

"Elena, are you kidding? She has been planning to get rid of us for a year. She set us up, there's no way we had a chance. And besides, I'm the one who went above her head to talk to the director. I'd hoped to head this off. He knew exactly how she treated people. Her abrasive personality even earned her complaints from city officials. But, still, she's a good negotiator. She brings money into the department."

"We had a case, you know. But she holds all the cards. If there is one thing I should have learned through all my years, it's that the sacrificial lamb is never the one at the top."

Adrenaline pumped through my body as I walked the path to the next building in the warmth of the summer sun. My career was at stake. A career I had worked to build since the age of eighteen.

No one has got my back. I'm hanging out here on my own and I'm going to get crucified. My sweaty palms reached the door handle of the office, and as I entered, I saw the lineup of power figures seated at a long table. A hand motioned me to have a seat, a lone chair situated across the all-female management team that held my fate in their pens.

This might as well be a firing squad.

Their words blurred together as the panic raged in my head. I heard terms like "budgetary constraints," "restructure" and "suitable transfer." "Hitler's" pencil lips and beady eyes softened in feigned compassion. An Oscar-worthy performance.

The head of HR handed me a document to sign. I put on my glasses and scanned the paper. The budget for the department had been reduced, and our management positions were cut. Technically, I wouldn't be demoted and there would be no change in pay. I would remain in the current position, sans function, until HR could find me another assignment. There was no guarantee it would be in the management classification.

I signed the paper, with only a feeble attempt to express my disappointment.

Nothing I could say mattered. "Hitler" put on a show for HR's benefit, expressing her regret at the unfortunate circumstances. Through my sadness, I glared at her. *Bitch.*

With the last of my strength, I held it together until pushing open the outer door of the building, then the tears began to flow. My worst fears were confirmed. It seemed like my body weighed a thousand pounds as I walked to the cafe and sank into a chair across from Emily. Both of us shaking, as we compared notes and wondered what was next. Neither of us could bear to go back into the office that day. Defeated and unsure of our future, we pulled our cars out of the parking lot and headed for home.

I DIDN'T KNOW which comfort food group to tackle first. I opened the freezer and retrieved a pint of Ben and Jerry's Chocolate Brownie ice cream while balancing the phone in the crook of my neck. It was my special reserve for occasions like this one.

"Yes, Mom, I know. Somehow things will turn out alright."

Mom was my rock. I could always turn to her for support. But the anxious tone in her voice was making me more panicked than less.

"Mom, thanks, but I have to go. I have another call coming in. I'll keep you posted."

I hung up the cordless landline phone and picked up my cell. Thomas had tried to reach me. He'd texted a few times in the last week, but I'd been too preoccupied with work to communicate much.

Before I could return the call, his text popped up.

> Can you meet me at the Latin place where we met? I'm at the bar.

I paused for a moment to think. It couldn't have been worse timing, but I needed a drink and a diversion.

> Be there in 30

I made it down to Jack London Square, having freshened my make-up and changed clothes in record time. My mood instantly perked up when I walked in the door and heard the music. After greeting a few friends, I found Thomas and plopped down on his lap. My hands wrapped around his neck and I spoke into his ear. "You have no idea what a day I've had."

Giving him the synopsis of recent events while the music was blaring was difficult enough, but his attention seemed to be lacking. When he answered, his words were slurred.

"What do you want to drink?" He waved to the cute, young waitress and she didn't hesitate. "This is Maria. She is a very, very good waitress."

She saw me—straddled on his lap, arms clinging around his neck—and she smirked. "Yes, Thomas? Will you have your usual?"

He ordered two Margaritas and flashed her a sloppy smile.

"How long have you been sitting here drinking?" I asked.

"A while," he said evasively, cocking an eyebrow over a slit of an eye.

"And what's up with Maria?"

"Ah, Maria. She's been very friendly. I've been back here a time or two."

I saw the look in his eyes, and it wasn't hard to read between the lines. "You're sleeping with her, aren't you?"

"Well…" His cheeks cringed up against his heavy eyes. "We're not technically 'sleeping'." Through his drunken haze, he did seem to notice my face falling. "Look, Elena, there's something you need to know about me. I'm not good boyfriend material. In fact, I suck at being a boyfriend. Many of my ex-girlfriends would corroborate that fact."

I planted my feet on the floor and pushed off his chest with the palms of my hands to stand.

"Goodbye, Thomas."

I have no idea why I took pity on him when he asked me to

drive him home. When I was hell-bent on fighting for someone else's injustice, I was as formidable as a bull. But when my own feelings were at stake, I clung to being nice like it was ingrained in my DNA.

"Aren't you coming in?" he asked, the key still in the ignition when I pulled to a stop at the curb.

"Nope."

"Really? Why not?"

Adele's song "Set Fire to The Rain" was playing on the radio and tears began to stream down my face. "Because I've been down this painful road before, and I can't do it anymore. I won't."

Silence hung in the air between us, both of us staring out the windshield of the car with only the song filling the empty space. Thomas finally turned, and with one last look, he reached for the door handle. "I'm sorry. I can't be someone I'm not."

"You don't know what you're missing out on with me, you know. Too bad," I called out, in what sounded like a pathetic attempt to validate my worth.

He gave me one last look before he shut the car door and walked away.

The last notes of the song trailed off, and I pulled away from the curb. *Just when I thought a day couldn't get any worse.*

THE FOLLOWING WEEKS were torture. I found myself trapped in employment purgatory. Each day began and ended the same—shut in my office, waiting for reassignment. There was little to do but pack boxes and surf the internet. I endured countless meetings with HR as we explored other options. Though I went on a couple of interviews, there simply weren't any available positions that fit my qualifications. I wondered how long they would keep paying me to sit around and do nothing.

For some odd reason, thoughts of Ethan continued to drift through my mind. Maybe it was the daily boredom or the fact that he was the only person who had excited me in a very long time, but I couldn't get him out of my thoughts. I sat at my desk, my chin resting heavily on my hand, and gave myself the talk. *Shouldn't you be over him? It was just an evening—stop obsessing.* Beth had texted me that she hadn't heard from him, but I knew that she could make a lie sound just as believable as the truth.

I looked around at the half-packed boxes, my frustration mounting. *I've got to get out of here.* As soon as my hand turned the knob of my office door, it hit me. I needed to get much farther away than the coffee shop downstairs. Ethan's words rang in my ear. "You must visit Barcelona, it's amazing."

Diving back into my desk chair, my fingers flew, pulling up images of the city. First, I looked at the photos of the old Gothic Quarter of the city. Then, the more elegant and modernist inspired architecture of the Eixample areas. And finally, the miles of beaches along the coastline.

I pictured walking through the old Roman ruins and the labyrinth of cobblestone streets and sipping wine at an outdoor cafe. I had an inexplicable feeling that something was drawing me to this place. Barcelona was calling to me. With or without Ethan, I needed an escape. Getting approval for the vacation time would be easy, I was sure they preferred me to be out of sight.

Planning the trip was exhilarating. I'd been to Europe before, twice in my twenties when I traveled with friends. It had opened my mind to a whole new world, and each time, I returned with a different perspective on a direction for my life. Since then, I'd been tied down with a family and a job. It seemed that this was the perfect opportunity to go back.

The diversion made space for my spirits to soar again. Though the thought of embarking on a European trip alone for the first time felt daunting. I pushed back the nagging doubts, rationalizing that I wouldn't be totally alone. My son and his girlfriend were traveling Europe to celebrate their college graduation and I arranged my itinerary to coincide with their arrival in Barcelona. He was the same age as I was on my first journey to Europe. Although he considered me a *cool* mom, still, the last thing he needed was a family vacation at this stage of his life. I had to accept that I'd be on my own most of the time, and besides, I needed the space to recalibrate. If it was anything like my previous trips abroad, it might help me uncover what I truly wanted at this juncture in my life.

The trip couldn't come soon enough. The start of the new school year was impossible to bear. My staff flowed into the department offices for meetings. Meetings and trainings that I would normally be orchestrating. With the door closed, I watched from the window in my office which had a view of the hallway. My co-workers avoided me. I felt like I'd been branded with a scarlet X on my forehead. They either pretended I wasn't there or looked at me with pity. I had become a symbol of the very thing they feared—ending up on the wrong side of "Hitler's" wrath.

By mid-September, I escaped hell. For two weeks I would find relief in Barcelona. I already knew it was a trip from which I wouldn't want to return.

Chapter Seven

O N THE MORNING of the flight, the alarm clock blared at 4 AM. Reaching one hand to slap it into silence, I moaned as my eyelids flickered and fought to open in the darkness of the early hours. *Why do I always do this to myself? I'm going to be brain dead on four hours of sleep.*

A rush of adrenaline propelled me out of bed and into the shower. With deliberate strokes, I applied my make-up, featuring my eyes in a dark smoky gray. Checking the clock, I quickly ran the curling wand through my long brown hair to tame the unruly natural waves. Then, making a dash for the closet, I found the travel clothes I'd set out the night before and pulled on the long, flowy, black skirt. I topped it with a sheer royal blue blouse and matching camisole. With one last look in the mirror, my hands smoothed the skirt and I gave myself a nod of approval. *It will do.*

After running through a quick checklist in my head, I grabbed my purse and new passport, then wheeled my suitcases out the door to meet the shuttle driver. My hands shook as I locked the front door. Travel always made me feel jittery, and this time it was worse. I was headed out alone. The wheels of my suitcase clunked down the porch steps and rolled over the jagged driveway to the curb. With one last look at my house in early dawn's light, I was overwhelmed by the rush of uncertainty and exhilaration. *Well, there is no turning back now.*

We'd just passed the toll booth on the Bay Bridge when the sun began to rise over the bay. It burned through the low clouds as a hot pink ball, sending crisp shards of light across the smooth morning waters. It reflected on the windows of the high-rise buildings in an amber hue, illuminating San Francisco's jagged skyline. My nose pressed against the window in awe of the beauty. It was rare that I witnessed a sunrise, especially from this vantage point.

The seat belt jerked and tightened against my torso as the van came to a sudden stop. Not ten seconds later, the sound of police sirens blared from behind. Cars veered into the adjacent lanes making room for one, then two, then three police vehicles to pass. The van's engine idled, then chugged to a stop. It was clear we weren't going anywhere. A sea of cars littered the roadway, forming a barrier between me and my dream escape.

I assessed the odds. It was still two and a half hours before departure, but I needed to be at the airline counter two hours in advance. *That* was not going to happen. If we could arrive in an hour, I could still make it through check-in and security.

During the thirty minutes that I was trapped in the claustrophobic uncertainty, my stomach clenched into a knot. I checked and rechecked my carry-on with obsessive anxiety. With each examination, I was relieved that I hadn't forgotten any crucial item but still, we hadn't moved an inch.

At minute thirty-five—and yes, I was counting—I heard the sound of engines firing up and cars began to funnel to the right. An officer blew a whistle and waved the traffic past the accident. Even more frustrating was the sight of two cars with smashed bumpers. *That's it? That's the reason for all this drama?*

As the van pulled up to the drop-off zone, I opened the door before the wheels stopped rolling. Ignoring the driver's shouted admonition, "Jeez lady, slow down," I leapt from the van at the curbside drop-off, tugging my suitcases as I ran for the line at the United Airlines counter.

My foot tapped nervously on the tiled floor then shuffled up in the line as the ten or so passengers before me got their boarding passes. When I finally arrived at the check-in desk, I was hot, sweaty, and nerves had replaced excitement. Not at all the image I had in mind as I set off on a new adventure. I passed through security and raced to the gate, arriving just as they announced the boarding call.

I made my way down the aisle of the plane, checking the row numbers as I maneuvered through the narrow corridor. As I approached my row in the back section, I saw the lone empty space at the end, my aisle seat—the rest of the row filled. *Damn.* I'd hoped to have room to stretch out.

Just then, I caught sight of him. He was sitting in the seat next to mine. It couldn't possibly be him—it was impossible. I blinked hard three times, but when I opened my eyes, there he was. For a split second, I considered that I might be having a hallucination due to sleep deprivation. But his dazzling eyes were fixed on me. Like an intractable laser beam, he drew me in.

Instantly rattled, I averted my eyes and nearly dropped my suitcase as I attempted to jam it into the overhead bin. With a flush of embarrassment, my legs wobbled, and the overstuffed bag forced me backward. Before I could regain my balance, a hand lifted the carry-on over my head. My eyes trailed from his long, graceful fingers, up to his cut bicep and finally, his face. Our eyes locked and I breathed in the scent of him.

"It *is* you!" I exclaimed.

"Hello, Elena," he chuckled and shook his head

My mouth gaped open in disbelief. "How could we...?" The stuttered phrase hung in the air.

His hand reached for mine, pulling me into our seats, and instantly, I felt the familiar electricity. Looking over my shoulder, I caught a glimpse of the impatient faces in a line waiting to pass.

I rotated toward him in my seat, my eyes sweeping over his gorgeous face. The one I thought I'd never see again.

"Hello, Ethan. You have impeccable timing."

"I could say the same to you. Your first trip to Barcelona, I assume? And you pick the very flight I'm on? His eyes sparkled with a look of amusement.

Still stunned, I blurted, "I just changed my seat assignment last night. I couldn't decide where to sit for the long flight, so I changed it five times before settling on this one."

"I booked at the last minute and this was the seat assignment they gave me. It's a big plane. If we'd been sitting anywhere else, we might not have met up." He paused, and his eyes raked over me. "I'm very glad I have the chance to see you again. How long are you going to be in Barcelona?"

"Two glorious weeks. I can't wait!"

"I'd love to give you a tour. Barcelona will amaze you."

He scrolled through the contact list on his phone, and to my surprise, my number was still there. He added my email since communication by cell was limited when abroad.

Just then, the flight attendant appeared at my side and leaned in. "Mr. Pierce, we are able to accommodate your request for a seat in business class. If you follow me, I will show you to your seat."

I stepped into the aisle to let him pass. His hand firmly held my shoulder, "Hey, we'll be in touch. I'm looking forward to showing you Barcelona. See you soon." He beamed a smile at me before turning to leave. The smile that made my bones liquefy.

As soon as my bottom hit the seat, I fought the urge to pace the aisle. The unbelievable coincidence had my mind reeling. His effect on me was not diminished in the least. The anticipation I felt about embarking on a new adventure had just taken on a whole new meaning, with one touch of his hand.

Chapter Eight

T HE WARM, MOIST air clung to my skin as I exited the airport terminal. My eyelids scrunched half shut from the glare of the midday sun. Sounds were no longer familiar. The voices I heard from every direction spoke in a language I barely understood. College Spanish classes were a distant memory, unfortunately. A quick scan of the signs led me to the taxi lineup. Luckily, "Taxi" was within the lexicon of universal language. I settled into the back seat and watched with anticipation as the landscape flew by outside the window. The view changed from freeway and undistinguishable suburbia to the architecturally rich facades of the city, a mixture of Spanish and French influences. It was so different from anything I had seen in France, with its clean, white, intricate structures. And not like Italy, where I had noticed red tile roofs and a Renaissance antiquity. Elegant buildings with grand balconies and stained-glass windows lined the streets on my way to the center of town. The character was uniquely old-world charm with a sophisticated flavor.

My apartment was difficult to find as it was located on a busy pedestrian street, just off Las Ramblas, the central tourist area running from Plaza Catalunya in the center, all the way to the sea. The taxi driver dropped me at the corner and pointed the way. As he spoke only in Spanish, I had to trust the hand gestured directions.

I thanked the technology gods as I turned on my phone and found the data to be up and running. After a quick email to the manager, his small wiry frame was at my side. We climbed the large winding staircase, lugging the bulging suitcases up to the flat. The heavy door creaked open, revealing a worn and very simple, furnished apartment. The dingy white paint was cracked on the high ceilings, from which hung simple chandeliers. Their metal had long since corroded.

I worried that it might feel lonely in the large, three-bedroom flat all by myself. But it was bright, with natural light pouring through several large balcony doors. The weathered wood-framed windows opened to a small balcony that overlooked the bustling street below. I hastily threw them open, longing for some fresh air to flush out the musty smell which permeated the flat. The warm breeze swept past me, blowing the long strands of hair from my shoulders. A myriad of fragrances wafted up from the street below. The fresh-baked smell of waffle cones at the gelato stands was the most pleasing. The updraft from the ancient sewer system would take some getting used to.

Exhaustion washed over me with a crushing wave. Suddenly the idea of the siesta seemed like the best way to integrate into my new surroundings. *When in Rome*, I thought.

It was still warm and balmy when I set out the door to explore the streets of the old town. The sky was beginning to darken, so I grabbed a scarf to put around my shoulders. The direction to travel initially seemed easy. Head to the end of the street and turn left onto Las Ramblas. The long, wide street consisted of a center promenade with narrow roads on either side to facilitate the traffic. The center was teeming with people, mainly tourists I supposed. Along the center were outdoor restaurants and vendors of all kinds. Souvenir shops piled one on top of the other. I could resist buying a tacky Barcelona t-shirt, but the richly colored mounds of gelato were beckoning to me. There was nothing like a vacation to entice me into indulging my guilty pleasures.

My mood began to brighten with each step. I felt my shoulders relax and the muscles in my back lengthen as I strolled down the tree-lined promenade. The heavy weight I had been carrying like a load of bricks had vanished. It was exhilarating being back in Europe. The anticipation of unknown adventures that might await stirred something deep inside me. Something familiar, like a distant memory, long since buried.

Everything about Barcelona seduced my senses. My eyes feasted on the stunning architecture of the buildings and drifted to the tapas displayed in the windows of the restaurants. Giant-sized posters advertising flamenco shows and Spanish guitar concerts caught my attention, adding to my must-see list.

I walked in the direction of the sea, magnetically drawn to the coast. The sun began to sink behind the hills by the port as I arrived, and the horizon was flooded with colors. Pinks and yellows against the darkening blue sky. The towers and spires of the Gothic style rooftops took on a magical appearance as they stood silhouetted against the darker colors. The harbor filled with expensive yachts glowed in the golden hues projected by the sunset as they gently rocked in the glimmering waters. Mesmerized by the beauty, I sat on a bench until darkness fell. I felt as if I had been teleported into another world so different from the one I'd left just a day ago.

Reluctantly, I left the waterside and entered the labyrinth of narrow alleyways of the Gothic Quarter. Directionally challenged, I tried to defy my instinct for getting lost by glancing at the GPS on my phone. I was determined to explore the maze of streets, none of which formed a straight line. The five-story buildings on either side made it impossible to determine north from south, not that I could determine my direction anyway without the aid of a compass. I wandered in circles and figured sooner or later I would run into something familiar. Oddly enough, something familiar ran into me.

Ethan's tall frame was easily recognizable even in the narrow dark alleys, and he was headed in my direction. At his side was a petite woman with dark hair and a slim figure. I was struck by the similarities in our appearance. She looked oddly bundled up in jeans and a jacket, considering it was still quite warm out. My mouth hung open in stunned disbelief. *In this labyrinth of streets? What are the odds?* It would have been challenging enough to intentionally find a meeting spot in this part of town, but to accidentally run across the one person I knew in Barcelona?

Recognition flashed across his face as our eyes made contact. A wide smile broadened on his lips and he looked down, shaking his head as he approached. "Twice in one day? Unbelievable!"

He introduced the girl standing by his side. She greeted me with a "*Buenas noches*" but her expression was flat. Like a movie set in slow motion, she faded into the distance and my eyes locked on Ethan. I managed to fumble out a few words before he ended the brief encounter.

"We have a dinner reservation, so we need to get going." Ethan caught my gaze and mused, "I'll see you later, no doubt."

In the middle of the alleyway, I stood frozen in my steps while barely noticing the people passing by.

This is incredible, I head to Barcelona and twice in one day, under astronomically ridiculous odds, the universe presents me with this man. He still gets to me. But I need to be careful, who knows if that chick is his girlfriend or just a date. I tried to put him out of my head and focus on enjoying my first night in Barcelona, but the unlikely coincidences of the day were drawing me in. I couldn't shake the feeling that destiny was about to reshape my life.

Chapter Nine

THE FOLLOWING FEW days were a test of patience. In my case, this had never been a well-developed trait. I checked my message inbox often, but no sign of Ethan.

It was strange, to be traveling alone. Memories of the adventures I'd had traveling in Europe with my girlfriends floated through my mind. I found myself wishing I had someone to talk to, since most of my conversations were limited to a few basic Spanish phrases. I'd rather have been taking silly selfies with a friend, instead of asking a stranger to snap a photo while poised at the wall of the Montjuic Castle. I averted my eyes every time I saw a happy couple locked in an embrace. Sharing precious vacation moments they would remember for years. I'd hoped for another chance after my divorce. Another chance to get it right, to find the magic. But there I was in Barcelona on vacation, alone.

The magic of the city seduced me, nonetheless. I walked for hours with aching feet through the Gothic Quarter and soaked in the atmosphere. Discovering delights around every corner, I made a mental note of my favorite spots, although completely unsure of how to find them again.

When I came upon the Roman walls and structures that were

discovered and preserved from the Medieval Period, I found myself enraptured by the incredible sense of history. The ancient stone walls, partially crumbled over time, formed a circle. As I followed the path, it led me through tree laden plazas. They were filled with tiny outdoor cafes, where people languished over a glass of wine and conversation.

Gothic style apartment buildings surrounded the plazas which suddenly appeared around an obscure corner. Clearly, the city planners of the era must have enjoyed the element of surprise. Always, the businesses and restaurants were situated on the ground floor with apartments stacked four to six levels above. My eyes gazed up at the myriad of balconies and I dreamt of what it might be like to live there with such an awe-inspiring view. Settling in an iron chair under the shade of the lacy tree limbs, I ordered a sangria and let the ambiance wash over me.

Conversations floated in the air around me, most in Spanish but other languages as well. Local artists made their living in these plazas. Acrobats drew a crowd of people around them and amused with their aerial display of talent. But it was the roving musicians who captivated me as they moved from one cafe to the next. The Spanish guitar music, so passionate, so sensuous, almost brought me to tears. It didn't matter that I couldn't understand the words. The emotional, almost pained sound of the singer's voice resonated in a deep, mystical place in my heart. Lightning-fast fingers created stirring melodies, along with an intoxicating rhythm. My body intuitively moved while my hand tapped against my thigh. I felt… like I was home. As if I had found a missing piece of the puzzle that fit so perfectly inside my soul.

It was well after dark when I arrived back at the apartment in a sleepy haze from the sun, sangria, and a full plate of paella. Connected again to the WiFi, my phone pinged with alerts. There it was, finally, on day three. An email from Ethan.

Hey, Elena, I hope you've been enjoying the city. Sorry for the delay. I've been catching up with friends. If you're up for it, let's hit the beach together tomorrow. Meet me in Plaza Catalunya at 1:00 and bring beach gear.

"*YES!* My arm shot up in the air with a celebratory fist pump. We finally had a date planned. Sprawled across the wide bed on my belly, I typed out a response to confirm then drifted off to the sounds of Spanish guitar music on my phone's app and the warm evening breeze flowing in through the balcony doors.

THE RATTLE OF metal gates opening as shop owners began their day was an effective alarm clock. Luckily, the streets were quiet until around ten in the morning. Being a night owl, Barcelona's schedule was growing on me.

Dressed in flip flops and a sundress, I slung my new beach bag over my shoulder and headed out the ancient wooden door into the throngs of tourists. I thought about how Ethan had said I would blend in with the locals, but I'd sabotaged that when I bought the beach bag with *Barcelona* written in neon letters.

Stopping for a fresh croissant and a *café con leche*, I still made it to the center at Plaza Catalunya earlier than we'd planned. The benches were filled with tourists (and maybe a smattering of locals), many with a picnic lunch resting on their laps. The cacophony of pigeons cooing filled the plaza as they competed for the bird food provided by vendors. Families lined up to have their picture taken with several of the creatures on their arm. I shuddered as my feet made a path through the flock and ducked as they narrowly missed my head. Scenes from Hitchcock's *The Birds* came to mind, sending a shiver down my spine.

My eyes scanned the crowd, hoping to catch sight of him. I paced nervously around the center, looking in all directions. It didn't take long to recognize him once he entered the plaza, and I watched as he sauntered across the mosaics in my direction. He was dressed for the beach in plaid shorts and a pink polo shirt. His feet shuffled along the ground in flip flops. I thought to myself, *on any other guy this might look really bad, but this one pulls it off.* He spotted me in the crowd and gave me a quick hug.

"It's good to see you again. You ready? Let's head to a beach just outside the main one in Barcelona. It has better sand and there are good restaurants. We can do lunch before hitting the beach."

"Sure, I'm game for anything. Lead the way."

We arrived via the metro at Port Olympic. Posh restaurants lined the beach and became trendy nightclubs late in the evening until almost dawn. The path bordering the beach led us to Carpe Diem, an exotic Balinese decorated restaurant oozing with ambiance.

Ethan approached the entrance a few steps ahead of me and requested a table from the hostess. The tall, wildly attractive, sexily clad woman who sat us at the table greeted him with familiarity.

"Oh, you come here often?" I quipped, shooting a sideways glance at him.

"Eh, a few times, more or less," he answered vaguely. An answer which left me wondering how many women he might have in this town.

We sunk into a plush couch on the terrace with a view of the sea and scanned the menus. Ethan ordered a liter of cava sangria to start. It was perfection—cool, crisp and delicious. Not recognizing most of the dishes listed on the menu, I acquiesced the job of ordering to him. As we shared tapas, our conversation turned to all things Barcelona. I learned that his Spanish was pretty good, largely due to the fact he'd spent a few months in a language school the previous summer.

"So, is that where you met friends here?" I asked.

He lifted the pitcher of sangria and stirred the fruit with a long spoon, then refilled our glasses. "I was worried that it would be just a bunch of kids at the school, but I found a lot of people there were around my age. Barcelona is very international, so it's not hard to make new connections here."

The realization sunk in that this guy could easily make friends wherever he went. It made me think of the similarities he had with my father, who would stop at a gas station and make friends with everyone there by the time he left.

"I spent the summer last year in class every morning and on the beach in the afternoons. My evenings involved dinners with friends, and of course a lot of late-night partying. Barcelona is a great place for enjoying life. It was an amazing four months, but this year there's a more serious purpose for my visit. I'm thinking of buying property here because the prices are still pretty low, since the economic crisis in Spain."

"It sounds like you have an amazing life. I would love to be able to do that—stay in Barcelona for months learning Spanish. The beach is a given, I need to be by the coast." My eyes drifted to the view of the sand, surf, and the elegant seaside restaurants. What a dream it would be to stay here.

Glancing back at Ethan I asked, "Do you come here a lot?"

"Well, not for months at a time, but I do return every couple of months. I'm getting a little tired of the crowds and the heat in the middle of the summer though. That's why you found me on my way here in September. It's a great time to visit. By the way, I still can't believe we were on the same flight, let alone sitting next to each other."

"I know, I still can't get over the shock."

He leaned back into the pillows. His eyes glazed as he looked out to the sea.

"What? You look like you're deep in thought."

"I was picturing you the night we met, at the wine event. I was so taken with you, so intrigued. It was you I wanted to date."

I propped my elbow on the back of the chair and leaned my head on my hand. I searched his face, but his eyes were avoiding mine.

"So, why didn't you?"

"Since your friend had intervened, I thought it would have been awkward for me to call you. I imagined you might not be too receptive."

"That night did not end well, to state the obvious. But did you date Beth?"

"She texted me after the event, and I saw her once or twice, but we didn't hit it off."

"She lied to me. She told me she never heard from you. I didn't see her again after that evening, but she texted to see if you had been in contact."

I glanced at my lap where my fingers were twisting at a defenseless scrunchie band. "I admit I had a similar reaction to you. I zeroed in on your face in the crowd when we first met. You were... quite impressive to me as well. I wish you would have called me."

I looked up and found his stare—that mixture of lust and warmth, peeking out from the ultra-cool, confident look he always wore. He must have seen my eyes melt under his heated gaze.

Ethan broke the hypnotic moment, "But by a stroke of luck, or fate, we're here now. In Barcelona of all places. So, what brought you here?"

"Well, if you remember, you did mention that Barcelona was the place to visit." I gave him a wink and couldn't help but smirk at his question, thinking back on his invitation.

"It was time for me to travel again. I needed an escape, things were rocky at work. I'm in the middle of some changes, but I don't want to go into it. I'm having too good a time."

"Fair enough," he nodded, "I'm glad you are having fun."

Ethan refilled my glass and brushed against my shoulder. The brief contact with his body heated my skin.

I took a long pull of wine, restraining my desire to squeeze some part of his body. "So how do you manage to travel so much? Can you work remotely?"

"I can, sometimes. I do have clients around Europe and the US, but when I'm in Barcelona, I tend to chill. It's conducive to relaxing and socializing here, I'm much less motivated to work. Don't get me wrong, I work hard, but I allow time for play in my schedule."

"I envy your lifestyle and I'm beginning to see how there could be a better work/life balance here in Europe than we have in the States," I released a long sigh, "I could get used to this."

"You ready to hit the beach?" Ethan asked.

"You might have to carry me. I'm pretty relaxed from the wine."

"I could, you know. Right over my shoulder."

Sweet Jesus, he read my mind.

"It's okay, I wouldn't want you to strain yourself," I said with a hint of a smirk.

Ethan asked for the check and said, "C'mon, let's head for the sand. I'll walk behind and make sure you can make it."

I shot him a satisfied look over my shoulder, "Yes I'm sure that's the only reason you want to walk behind... *uh-huh*, enjoy."

I raced him to the water, weaving around half-naked bodies and the obstacle course of beach blankets. Of course, his long legs carried him there way ahead of me. As we laid our towels on the sand, I couldn't help feeling apprehensive. Not that my body wasn't worthy of wearing a bikini—I had worked hard to make sure it was—but in no way did I have the tight body of a thirty-year-old. Sucking in my tummy a little, I shimmied out of my dress and revealed a pretty, plum-colored Victoria Secret bikini. At the same time, Ethan maneuvered out of his shirt and shorts. Underneath, he wore a tight, black swimsuit of the boxer brief variety. Much classier than those banana hammocks the Italian guys wore, and a whole lot sexier than American swim trunks.

I glanced at his tall, slim but muscular form and gulped hard. *Jeez, could a body get any better than that?*

"So, work out much?" I said, biting my bottom lip.

"Pretty often, hey, if I didn't, I'd just be tall and skinny. I've got that body type. You look like you work out yourself." With a glint in his eyes, he casually scanned my tanned body, pulling down his shades momentarily. I tried to appear casual and not at all worried that he was checking out my body. The body which, despite my best efforts, was succumbing to the forces of gravity. But the look in his eyes reassured me that maybe he didn't see the flaws that glared at me in the mirror.

"Not in the gym much, but I do dance a lot. Salsa is my thing, it's my sport. Do you dance?"

"Ha," he snorted, "not really, but I'd love to see you dance."

"Seriously? A black guy who doesn't dance?"

"Well, I'm from the islands, so I can dance reggae if I have to."

"Funny... but I do seem to recall you pulling off some decent dance moves the night we met," I glanced at him to check his reaction.

He fixed his eyes on the surf. "There was a lot of alcohol flowing that night. So, I'll have to take your word for it. Anyway, *chica*, I'm going for a quick swim. Keep an eye on our stuff, Barcelona is known for getting ripped off."

That was a hell of an exit, strategically timed. My eyes followed him as he walked with large strides through the sand. *I'm in trouble with this one...* I noticed the many other female heads turning as he walked by. I imagined that he must have a ton of girls falling all over him. The thought was more than a little intimidating, but I pushed it away. I was on a quest to live in the moment—and those moments with him were worth enjoying.

My body relaxed into the sand, feeling the warm sun on my back. An unfamiliar sense of contentment swept over me. I hadn't played like this with anyone in a very long time. *So, this is what it's like. To feel... happy.*

Cool water dripped on my back, startling me from my bliss. I looked up to find Ethan delivering the salty water and wearing a mischievous grin.

"That was refreshing, can you bring me back more? I like the service," I teased.

"So, are you enjoying the day?" he asked, lowering himself on a towel next to me.

Propping my chin on my hand, I found his eyes gleaming through his sunglasses. "Yes, very much."

"Good, let's do it again. Next time we can go up the coast to a better beach out of town."

"Sounds perfect." Inside, I was doing a happy dance.

We lay on the sand and soaked up the sun while Ethan coaxed me to practice my Spanish. While fumbling with the language made my brain hurt, I was feeling more and more comfortable with Ethan as the hours passed. Having lost track of time, he finally glanced at his watch and said, "It's getting late. What are you doing tonight?"

"Since my son isn't arriving until tomorrow, my calendar is wide open."

"Oh, you have a kid? How old is he?"

I cringed at that question. Telling a man the age of my son was always met with a look of surprise, followed by math calculations.

"He just graduated from college. He and his high school sweetheart are coming here for the first time." It was all true. I just evaded the actual numbers. I could have added that I'd been a teenage mother, but I left that to his imagination. I waited for a moment, but his face didn't show the usual reaction.

"That's great! They'll have an awesome time here. Do you have a good relationship with him?"

"The best, we've always been close. I made him my top priority, staying in the marriage much longer than I should have. In the end, he was ten when we divorced. I have to admit, there were times I smothered him with mothering, but he knew he could always count on me."

Ethan listened intently. His interest surprised me. "I admire that. It must take an enormous commitment to have a child. What about the girlfriend? That can be tricky."

"I'm not going to lie, it was hard. I'm not number one in his life anymore. But she's an amazing girl, and they're happy together. It's the best a parent can hope for."

Ethan's hand raised in a 'high five' and our hands clasped. "Well done, Elena."

He cocked his head. I saw the glimmer of an idea spark in his eyes. "Let's get showered and I'll meet you at around seven-thirty. There are a few places I'd like to show you later."

My face must have lit up like Time's Square. "I'll give you my address."

I scrolled to the notes on my phone and his eyes popped when I read aloud, "It's near the corner of Las Ramblas on Portaferrissa."

"Damn, girl, you are in one of the busiest tourist sections."

"It was the only apartment I could find in the center on short notice. I'm moving to El Born for the second week."

"Born is my favorite barrio in the city. You'll love it there." He pushed off the sand and sprang to his feet, extending his hand to help me up. "*Vamos, chica*. I'll pick you up later."

I had never been the kind of girl who just popped into the shower and was ready to go in twenty minutes. But the anticipation of spending more time with Ethan propelled me through my usual routine in record time. I was ready before he rang the buzzer.

Chapter Ten

"Y<small>OU UP FOR</small> a walk?" Ethan asked as I emerged from the apartment.

"Sure, got my flats on, I've learned it's pretty impossible to walk in this town without comfy shoes. I'm sacrificing the height that high heels give me, which sucks since I feel so short next to you." My feet skipped ahead as I called out, "By the way, dude, slow down. You have way longer legs than me."

He slowed, turned to look at me and chuckled, "Yeah, you are pretty little—but it's cute."

"Hey, are you calling me short?" I teased, with my hands on my hips. His laughter rang out and I knew we were in for a fun night.

As I stepped out of the elevator on the top floor of Barcelo Raval, a faint whistle blew through my puckered lips. Its 360-degree rooftop terrace view of the city was impressive. Almost as impressive as Ethan. I had to admit, this guy knew how to score points when it came to romantic settings. After taking me on a tour of the cityscape view, we settled on a plush couch to watch the sunset with glasses of cava in hand. Apart from the steady rhythm of house music in the lounge, we sat in silence, transfixed by the golden light dancing across the rooftops. Then, out of the corner of my eye, I sensed his glance shift in my direction.

"What?" I smiled up at him.

His eyes sparkled as he peered into mine. "Do you know your eyes are green? That's actually quite rare."

"They're brown, aren't they? And you are just noticing that now?"

"Nope, your irises are green. And quite stunning."

We held the gaze for what seemed like minutes, heat rising in the space between us. He leaned in, his face only inches from mine. I froze. I was dying to feel those luscious full lips meeting mine, but I waited.

Suddenly he pulled back. "C'mon, let's go get some food. There's a great tapas place I want to take you to, it's not very far from here."

Jesus, he's tormenting me! What is he playing at? I took a deep calming breath and followed him to the elevator. The ride down eleven floors alone with him was agonizing. With each passing floor, I quelled my excitement.

We wound our way through the narrow streets of the old town and finding the small restaurant, we inched our way in the crowd. "Quimet & Quimet," I read out loud the name on the top of the door frame.

"This place seems different from the other tapas places." It was packed, standing room only.

"It's one of the top restaurants in town for tapas, but you wouldn't know it from the looks of it," Ethan explained. "Wait until you taste the food here, you're in for a treat."

While we waited for our order, Ethan struck up a conversation with a French couple who shared our small table. *Why am I not surprised? Mr. Social.*

They seemed so happy and openly affectionate. Envy welled up and bubbled to the surface. The guys began to talk soccer, so they were oblivious to our conversation when the woman turned to me and asked, "How long have you two been together?"

I stammered, "We're not a couple, just friends." The noise in the room obscured our voices. I knew Ethan was engaged in conversation, so I seized the opportunity to confide in her. "I really like him, but he's way younger than I am."

The woman looked surprised, "Oh, you two make a really cute couple. And what does age matter anyway? It's just a number."

"I wish that were true. But when you meet a guy who wants to have a family, age is a deal-breaker."

The woman remained optimistic, "Ah well, you never know, love sometimes wins out over all obstacles."

The French have a refreshing way of viewing love and passion as essential as food and water. But I knew that in my life, love did not conquer all. Two divorces were among the evidence to the contrary.

Our order arrived, Ethan's long arm stretching over the heads of other customers to seize the small plates from the waiter's hands. The small pieces of bread were topped with the most exotic combinations. From the *foie gras* with volcanic salt to the salmon with yogurt and truffled honey, everything was delicious. After I licked the last morsel from my fingers, we said good-bye to our dinner companions and made our way out the door to the streets of El Poble Sec.

Taking it slow, we walked back along the harbor. I looked out to the sea and captured the images in my mind. The twinkling lights of the boats as they rocked in the water, the large modern sculptures that dotted the seafront juxtaposed with the historic monument to Christopher Columbus at the bottom of Las Ramblas. I wished that I could plant myself in a chair at one of the many terraces lining the streets and experience life like a local, never leaving this town.

"I never would have imagined how much I would love it here."

Ethan took my hand in his, and I instantly felt the electricity that ran straight through my core every time he touched me. There it was again, the warm sensation that ignited my body.

"I know exactly what you mean. It's easy to fall in love with this city." He gave my hand a squeeze before releasing it.

I thought to myself, it would be equally as easy to fall in love with him. But also insanely stupid. My heart had enough cracks and scars for a lifetime, and yet, the damn thing kept on beating—kept fluttering for the likes of Ethan, despite my efforts to encase it in a steel box.

When we reached the entrance to my apartment, Ethan faced me and held my shoulders in his hands. I looked up into his eyes and wished the night wasn't over.

"I'm headed to Portugal for a few days to do some surfing. Have fun, but be careful. I'll see you when I get back."

"I'll be here. Just shoot me an email."

And then I waited, hoping for something a little more. But he grabbed me into a quick hug and said good-bye, leaving me with my lips slightly parted and bare.

Thoughts of Ethan ran circles in my mind as I lay in bed, tossing and turning, unable to sleep. I couldn't help wondering what it would be like if he was lying there next to me. Would he even be a good lover? I'd had my share of young lovers who had limited skills in the bedroom. Ethan was young-ish... but I was guessing that he was quite experienced. *I* was experienced enough to know it wasn't just about skills—and size—it was about chemistry. And for me at least, I was combusting like a rocket.

Chapter Eleven

Lᴜɢɢɪɴɢ ᴍʏ ʜᴇᴀᴠʏ suitcases down the stairs, I cursed myself for never having learned to pack light. Luckily, the taxi line was just around the corner, and within minutes, I was on the way to my new apartment in El Born. The cozy, two-bedroom flat had been remodeled with modern furnishings and conveniences. Thankfully, there was an elevator. The location couldn't have been better, situated in a nicer section of town and directly above the pulsing center of activity.

After unpacking yet again, I stepped out in the midday sun to investigate my new hood. Charm oozed from every tiny street. The buildings, fashioned out of large rectangular stone in Gothic style, held trendy, upscale shops. The bars and restaurants had a surprisingly chic interior. Some were set in stone caves while others were spacious, with high vaulted ceilings.

Though I wandered for hours, I had become secure in the knowledge that I would indeed get lost. But this was my new normal. The joy of discovery my new high. After resting my weary feet in a terrace cafe, sipping a perfect cup of *cafe con leche* (from a real cup and saucer—not a paper to-go cup) I turned on my GPS. Surprisingly, I realized I could survive. Alone and directionally challenged, still, my confidence had blossomed.

My spirits were running high, anticipating the arrival that night of my son and his girlfriend. My offer to share an apartment had been met with a definite eye roll followed by raised eyebrows. But they did book an apartment nearby in Born. When Nate texted their arrival, I was out dancing at one of the smaller clubs off Las Ramblas. I shot back a text, then bolted out the door.

I'd already learned to weave in and around the crowds of tourists who seemed to multiply in the evening hours. It was like an obstacle course, but the years of freeway driving in California came as a handy skillset. I power walked to Placa Reial the same way I drove, passing people on the left and right.

Entering the plaza from Las Ramblas, I scanned the terraces bathed in the glow of amber lights in search of Nate and Dana. The plaza was typical of Spain, a large central area with a fountain, surrounded on four sides with restaurants and terraces. The ambiance was palpable, especially at night as it came alive, packed with people dining at the many restaurants or sitting around the fountain. This is what I was beginning to love about Spain. People of all ages were out socializing well into the evening. This particular plaza reflected the unique character of Barcelona, as its 19th-century style buildings were juxtaposed alongside the more cosmopolitan feel of some of the restaurants and clubs which were housed there.

The alert on my phone sounded off an SMS text. Nate saw me first and stood up in the crowd, arms waving.

"Mom, over here," he yelled, greeting me with a broad smile. I grabbed Nate first then Dana into excited hugs.

"Oh my God, look at your beard, it's so long now." Taking a tuft of the wiry hair I gave it a tug. "How it got so red, I will never know. And I'm still getting used to the whole mustache/beard thing."

His sandy brown hair and green eyes didn't quite match the color reflected in the facial hair, but he knew how to pull off the look. Gentleman's haircut, skinny jeans and leather jacket—even when the weather was balmy.

He had his Dad's hard-set jaw and my nose and eyes, but his style was all his own. I swore he was the cutest baby on the planet, and the girls seemed to think he'd turned out to be an equally handsome man. A mom's pride aside, he was damn good looking. He topped out at 5'11, same as his dad. In the last few years, his body had matured, gaining a set of broad shoulders and a muscular upper body.

Hugging Dana, we simultaneously squealed "I'm so happy to see you." But then Dana and I often chimed in with the same comments, we were always in sync. Including our birthdays. I wondered who was more surprised that our birthday was exactly the same day. But I did think there was an initial freak-out moment for my son. They were the image of a perfect couple. They matched each other in every way and glided through all the ups and downs with skills I had never witnessed in a relationship.

She was as strong as she was sweet, of sturdy Scottish stock. Her round eyes shined bright set against porcelain skin. Her bold color choice was a striking red, her long curly locks cascaded over intricately designed tattooed shoulders.

"We already ordered some tapas and I'll get another glass for you," Nate offered.

"I am so excited you guys are here!" I said, clapping my hands together. "There are so many places I'd like to show you."

"This place is already impressive and look at all of the people out at midnight, still eating and drinking," Nate glanced in my direction, "and Mom, you look great. I haven't seen you look so happy in a long time. Barcelona must be agreeing with you."

"It certainly seems to be. I really love it here. It's helping me to forget the hell I've gone through back home."

We sat at the terrace restaurant, soaking up the ambiance while formulating a sightseeing itinerary. I was well aware they would take off on their own, so, I took full advantage of the time we had together. After a few hours, their eyelids began to grow heavy as the day's travel fatigue set in. It was only then, I finally relented and called it an evening.

The next morning, Nate texted me with an invite to dinner at their tiny apartment. I was ecstatic. Not only would I get to spend time with them, but Nate was a culinary genius. He had loved the kitchen since he was young, and while it wasn't his chosen profession, he was a master chef.

As the sun started to set, I tucked a bottle of wine and a fresh loaf of bread in my Barcelona bag and headed out to find their flat. It turned out that their rented apartment was only a few streets from mine in the Born. Although, it didn't stop me from getting turned around, winding through the alleyways several times before climbing the narrow stairs of the third-floor walk-up.

The tiny kitchen held only the basic cooking tools, but Nate was undeterred. Dana and I sat at the old wooden table, sipping from the mismatched wine glasses, relaxing while we watched Nate busily whipping up a gourmet meal.

"I went to three shops until I found all the ingredients, but totally worth it. Taste this goat cheese, I've created a tapa combining it with caviar."

I took one bite and was hooked. "Hon this is delicious. As usual, you don't disappoint."

His face lit up with pride. "So, what have you been up to so far while you've been here." I was sure he anticipated that question to be answered with a simple accounting of my travelogue. But instead, I filled him in on the unlikely coincidences (the G rated version, mostly). Nate had cast me in the immaculate conception version of *Mom*— and according to his psyche, that did not include sexuality. I chose to tread lightly while breaking him into the idea that Mom had a life that included men.

"I can't believe you actually connected on the plane to Barcelona, how random is that? So, when do you see him again?"

"Ethan is in Portugal right now on a surfing expedition, but he emailed me with plans to get together as soon as he returns in a couple days. He's meeting me at the apartment when his plane lands. So, we'll see."

"You're glowing, you know. When you talk about him, you light up," Dana's observation was dead on. I could feel myself beaming and it wasn't just from the third glass of wine.

"It shows, does it? I'm quite sure he sees it too. There is chemistry for sure. But who knows," I brushed it off, preferring to sound less invested than I really was.

As our night came to an end, I walked home through the alleyways, reflecting on all those years I'd devoted to mothering, and I knew I had done right by him. He turned out to be an amazing person, as well as a loving, devoted boyfriend for Dana. Best of all, I was now able to enjoy a great relationship with him as an adult. Whatever sacrifices I had made, it was worth it. Now, he had a life of his own, and while the 'kids' were off to make their own memories, Mom was looking forward to adventures with Ethan.

Chapter Twelve

T HE BELL RANG at 9:00 PM. Ethan was right on time for our date. He bounded up the stairs with those long legs and greeted me with a hug.

"How was Portugal?"

Shedding the large knapsack on his back, he answered, "It rained most of the time, so the surfing was a bust. Good to see you again. You look great!"

I smiled up at him, "Thanks." There was no denying I had dressed to impress.

"I'm desperate for a shower, do you mind?"

"Be my guest, it's down the hall."

The kitchen afforded me a safe distance from the bathroom while I put my nervous energy to work emptying the dishwasher.

"*Chica…,*" he yelled from the shower. The sound of his voice rose above the clatter of dishes.

I tentatively walked toward the bathroom. The door was open, and for a moment, I hesitated, then peeked around the corner. He pulled the shower curtain halfway back so that only his upper body and one leg was exposed.

"Hey, can I have a towel?"

I stammered, "Sure, no problem. Here you go, here's a fresh one," I said, tossing it to him from a safe distance. Gawking at his half-naked body, I froze in the doorway.

"Thanks."

He flashed a broad smile, catching the flying towel in one hand.

Flushed and flustered, I turned on my heels and bolted. *Sure, that wasn't obvious at all! Jesus, could he be any hotter?* I hustled back into the kitchen, wondering if that move was an invitation or a tease.

He emerged from the bathroom dressed in dark jeans and a tailored shirt which clung to his muscular frame, still damp from the shower. "Ready? Let's head for the center of El Born."

"You are talking my turf now. I've been exploring the neighborhood."

The last rays of sun cast jagged patterns of light through the leafy trees along the wide promenade of Passeig Del Born. Unlike Las Ramblas, the cobbled street was short, lined with upscale shops and bars. A well-known strip for bar-hopping, it was there I had found my favorite spot. A small Latin bar I had made my second home. I grabbed Ethan's hand and drew him to the entrance, brimming with enthusiasm to share my discovery.

"Ah, El Copetin. Yeah, I've been here a time or two," he threw me a sideways glance.

Jeez, is there any place he doesn't know here?

The bartender set us up with mojitos, then programmed the sound system. Instantly, the music stirred me. It was impossible for my body not to respond, having danced to the song countless times.

Ethan asked, "You know how to dance to this?"

"Of course, it's a bachata song, one of my favs."

I hopped down from the chair and took advantage of the empty dance floor. Unabashedly, I showed off for him. My hips maneuvered in the sexiest motions, my feet planting against the floor in the precise patterns of the dance, interspersed with dazzling spins—all while holding his gaze. Ethan watched me in amazement, smiling broadly, until he threw up his hands and said, "Okay, okay, I believe you." I returned to my seat at the bar with a satisfied smile. *Well, that worked quite nicely.* With dance, I was in my element. *Payback for the shower dude.*

"I have an idea. Let's take a taxi to the clubs at the beachfront." Ethan leaned into me from his stool. The heat of his skin so close made the hairs on my arms prickle, as if his proximity alone caused static electricity. The look on his face told me I wasn't the only one feeling the magnetic pull. Sexual tension crackled in the space between us.

I cleared my throat and managed to squeak out a response. "Where you took me for lunch? I'd love to see it at night."

Pushing off the seat to stand, he gave me a wink. "We can get some dancing in there because I sure as hell can't do that bachata thing."

When we arrived in Port Olympic, the scene was in full swing. Girls in micro dresses and six-inch high heels were lined up at the entrances to the many clubs. I was relieved that I had chosen a figure-flattering dress and decent heels that I could at least walk in when I stepped out the door for our date. As we waited to enter Carpe Diem, I took note that the crowd looked more mixed in age than the other clubs. I could party like a twenty-something-year-old, but I hated feeling like the old lady amongst the youngsters.

Ethan took my hand and steadied my steps as we descended the stairs into the restaurant that had been transformed into a sultry nightclub. The DJ's blend of hypnotic house music filled the room and bodies swayed with the rhythm. Scantily clothed women performed atop the pedestals which held ornate bronze statues. Their perfect bodies gyrated like Las Vegas showgirls, only slightly obscured by the billowing mist from a hidden fog machine.

"This is some scene!" I yelled into Ethan's ear over the sound of the music. "I've never seen anything like it."

Ethan nodded, his eyes briefly transfixed on the dancers. I couldn't blame him. They were stunning. He found my gaze again and led me through the crowd to the bar. The dance floor blended into every bit of free space in the large room. From the bar to the hanging beds reserved for the VIPs, people free danced with drinks in their hands. A partner wasn't necessary, only a desire to get swept away by the music.

I kept an eye on Ethan as he stood in line at the bar, but I was starting to feel the itch to dance. Then I saw her. A tall, slender, stunning, black woman half my age, who was moving her body to the deep pounding beats. She danced with perfect grace and fluidity. Her hips swayed, her body rolled, and her arms raised, then lowered in elegant maneuvers. She inspired me, and I couldn't contain myself. I mirrored her movements, standing a few feet away. Our eyes met, and I returned her smile. While house wasn't my style, this set had undertones of an African beat with a smooth, sensual rhythm. *That*, I could feel. I moved my torso one direction and my hips in the other. Isolating every body part with precision, unleashing my sensuality and matching hers.

A crowd of men started to form around us, mesmerized by our dance. I looked up to find Ethan among them. He stood wide-eyed with a mojito in each hand. With sultry eyes that locked onto his stare, I danced as if we were the only two people in the room. When there was a break in the song, I slid over to his side.

"Woman, you do have some fine moves," he said, shaking his head. The sexy smile he gave me poured fuel on the fire already burning in my core.

"Let's see your moves." I grabbed my drink in one hand and hooked a finger through his belt loop, pulling him to me.

I heard his laughter and felt the rumble in his chest as our bodies moved together, his one free arm around my waist. I stayed in sync with his steps and slid my hand up the chiseled muscles of his chest to grasp the back of his neck. I felt his hand tighten around my back, bringing me in closer. Heat rose from the places where our bodies touched. It was almost too much to bear.

By the time the song ended, I was breathless, and my panties were soaked with arousal. I downed half of my drink and handed him the glass.

"I have to use the restroom. Where is it?"

"In the back, to the left." Ethan pointed the way. "I'll find you after."

I took my place in line with the other women, giving me time to gawk at the surroundings. Even the bathroom was gorgeous, with its ornate mirrors and a large tub-like sink. It took an awkward minute to figure out how to turn on the water, distracted by the odd stone sculptures whose mouths spewed like fountains.

After freshening my lipstick and running a brush through my hair, I stepped out into the wide entryway leading to the dance floor, when suddenly my body jerked to a stop. A pair of hands pulled at my hips and I whipped my head around to find they weren't Ethan's. A young, dark-skinned man faced me and hooked his arm around my waist. He looked familiar, it occurred to me that maybe he was one of the men who had been watching while I danced.

"*Guapa*! Do you speak Spanish? English?" His breath smelled of alcohol and he staggered into me. "You are so sexy," he rasped.

Pushing hard with both hands on his chest, I tried to break free, but he held me tight in his grip.

I gave him a menacing look and shouted, "Back off! Let go of me."

In the dim light, I saw Ethan's tall frame emerge at the man's side and tower over him. His large hands gripped the guy at his shoulders, digging into his shirt.

"Take your hands off the lady now, and back the fuck off, or I'll throw you across the room." Ethan's voice was deep and dangerous. Not loud enough to make a scene, but strong enough to be heard above the din.

My captor craned his neck up and saw the look in Ethan's eyes. He released me, hands spayed wide.

"*Hombre*, relax. I didn't know she was with you."

Ethan shoved him aside by his shoulders and warned him with a stare.

"Alright, man, I'm going."

When the guy stepped away, he turned to me with a concerned look. "Are you okay?"

"Other than killing my mood, as well as the buzz I had going, he didn't do any damage." My eyes softened, hoping he would relax too. "Thanks for the rescue. I wouldn't want to be the guy who got in your way. You're pretty formidable."

"I hope so," he chuckled. "I have a black belt in martial arts."

Jesus, was there anything this guy couldn't do? I shot him my coy, damsel in distress smile. "Nice to know I can count on you. Now, how are we going to get back into a good mood? I was having such a great time."

He took my hand and led me through the crowd until we emerged at the patio where we had dined at lunch. Up a few stairs, and we were at the edge of the sand.

"Let's head out to the beach," Ethan said, motioning me to follow.

I bent and slipped off my shoes while he waited. The sand squished between my toes as we trudged across the wide beach until we reached the water's edge. The waves calmly lapped on the shore, and our feet made prints in the dampness with each step we took.

"God, this is gorgeous. We don't get these warm nights by the ocean in Northern California. Look at the moon." I pointed to the almost full moon, casting a glow over the dark waters.

Ethan halted in his steps. He turned to face me, closing the distance between us. His body gently pressed against mine, sending shards of heat where he touched me. One hand glided along my cheekbone and he threaded his fingers in my hair. I stood there, waiting in anticipation for what seemed like minutes. With my shoes dangling at my fingers, I gazed up into his eyes. Those warm brown pools shined at me with such intensity, it made my knees almost buckle under me.

In the silence, he bent his head and brushed his lips across mine with a gentle caress, then laid his cheek against my face. I heard a long slow breath in my ear before his head tilted, and those luscious lips poured over mine in soft kisses. My lips melted into his and parted as he deepened the kiss, caressing my tongue with his. It was every bit as sweet as I'd dreamed it might be. I felt the tingle stirring deep in my core and the pulse of excitement in the racing beat of my heart.

When Ethan broke away, I was breathless and dizzy.

He looked into my eyes with amazement. "You're quite a woman, Elena."

My heart did a backflip and nearly burst through my chest. I pursed my lips into a smile and beamed up at him, silently freeze-framing the moment in my memory. I wished the moment would last, but he took a step back and held my shoulders at arm's-length.

"Let's get you home. We have a beach day tomorrow, remember?"

I nodded, reluctant to leave. "I'd better get some sleep anyway. I think I'm coming down with a cold. Not that I'm going to let that stop me from going with you."

"All the more reason to take care."

Ethan dropped me off at my doorstep and bent to kiss my forehead. "Sleep well, *chica*."

The warmth in my heart lit up my face, a smile radiating up at him. I turned and climbed the stairs, full of anticipation at the thought of spending another day with Ethan.

Chapter Thirteen

T HE SUN STREAMED in the tinted windows of the train, blinding me momentarily from my view of Ethan seated across from me. He pulled the Ray-Bans from atop his head and placed them on my face.

"There. You look pretty cute in those." His head tilted. The grin that spread over his face made me think otherwise. I looked at my reflection in the glass.

"Holy crap, these things are huge on me. I look like a giant fly."

"You're adorable," he said, but not without stifling a snicker. Then he flashed me the megawatt smile of his that made me melt.

"I'll take that as a compliment," I said, fluttering my eyelashes. "So where are we going?"

"Sant Pol de Mar. It's about one hour up the coast. We'll catch lunch there at a restaurant I know."

"The spelling of things is confusing here, not like the Spanish I'm familiar with," I said, attempting to make sense out of the names of the towns we passed.

"That's because here, a lot of things are in Catalan, a language that mixes Spanish and French. You'll get used to it, but at first, it does throw you off track."

"That's all I need, one more obstacle in learning the language. Also, I've noticed that they don't seem to like being called Spaniards here. We're in Spain, so what's up with that?"

"Barcelona is part of Catalonia, a region of Spain, and they have their own identity rooted in history. They've been pushing for independence from Spain for many years, but that's a very long story."

Ethan filled me in on the nuances of the Catalan culture as the train whizzed past miles of scenic coastline, stopping at small villages along the way to board more passengers heading up the coast. The beaches were pristine, with white sand and pounding surf.

Ethan led the way as we got off at our stop, then we walked past the quaint village and along the seaside. Clear blue skies reflected on the water, but a chill was in the air, the sea breeze gusting with Autumn winds. The restaurant sat directly on the beach, giving us a close-up view of the pounding surf. He ordered cava to start, followed by a liter of rose, fresh lobster, and a special kind of paella made with squid ink.

Digging out the last of the succulent lobster meat, I raised the fork to my mouth and looked into those gorgeous brown eyes that made me crazy. "Thank you for bringing me here."

Ethan raised his glass, "*Salud*! It's my pleasure. I'm glad you like it."

"The view is spectacular, and the company isn't bad either." I took a sip of wine and with my nose buried in the glass, I peered up at him through my lashes.

"Oh, so my rating is just 'not bad' huh?" He leaned in, his cut torso folding over the table.

"If I told you how much I enjoyed your company, it might stimulate your ego a bit too much."

"Trust me, Elena, my ego is not that inflated. I'm a perfectionist," he said, straightening against the back of the chair. "I was raised with that pressure. So, you can imagine, I have a hard time being anything less in whatever I do. But your company might stimulate other things." A dark brow rose, and his eyes flickered with a promise.

"Oh really? *Hmm...* are you trying to seduce me?"

"Not yet, Elena. You'll know it when I do." He stretched his long legs out under the table, grazing my ankle.

"So, it's not *if*, but *when*?"

"Of course. That's my ultimate goal." The declaration rolled off his tongue so casually, so assuredly. It made my eyes pop open wide. "Now, are you ready? Let's head to the beach."

His abrupt change of topic left me with a gaping mouth and my bottom squirming in the chair. Each moment with him was like exquisite foreplay.

Wind whipped around the jagged rocks on the white beach. I clutched the jacket around my shoulders, following Ethan's footsteps in the sand.

"I've got just the spot for us—over here," he motioned with a wave of his hand, "there's a windbreak."

Ethan spread a blanket, and we nestled side-by-side on our backs in the sandy cove. The sound of the waves crashing on the shore played like a rhythmic melody lulling me into a peaceful sensory haze, fueled by the food and wine in my belly. The world disappeared. There was only the surf and the puffy white clouds drifting against the azure skies—and the warmth of Ethan's body at my side.

"You good?" he mumbled with his face turned up to the sky.

"*Uh-huh…*" I just barely murmured, "It's perfect."

Ethan sweetened the moment. He reached for my hand and interlaced his fingers with mine.

"*Mmm…* so nice." I purred, "*Now* it's perfect," I moved a little closer to his side, brushing my leg against his. I lay there with a giddy grin, staring up at the heavens until I caught his glance from the corner of my eye.

"What?" I asked, perching on my elbow.

"You look happy."

"Happier than I've been in a long time," I sighed.

"You look so beautiful. Happy." The stroke of his finger brushed against my cheek, sweeping away a lock of hair blowing across my face.

The look in his eyes slayed me. "It's getting late, we better check when the train is leaving."

"Okay," I pouted, "But I hate to leave, it's been such a great day."

"I know," he said, leaning in just a little closer. The delicious scent of him mixed with the salty air was a heady combination. "It has been an amazing day." He gave my hand a squeeze, hopped to his feet and pulled my arm to stand.

Sand squished through my toes until we reached the pavement and walked along the path back to the station. Seemingly out of nowhere, a soccer ball came careening toward us through the air and landed squarely in Ethan's large hands. The small heads of two young boys whipped in our direction. With outstretched arms and bright eyes, they scampered up to Ethan, whose face lit up in a wide grin. Dimples and all.

"What are you boys playing? He spoke to them in Spanish, but I managed to interpret the simple sentence. They jumped up and down on sneakered feet and answered simultaneously in thick accents, "*Futbol*," along with some other phrases I didn't understand. But I could interpret their body language and they were anxious to get their ball back.

Ethan's body language wasn't hard to interpret either. His eyes were soft as he gazed at their excited faces. His voice was tender and playful, like he knew just how to talk to children. "Can I play with you for a minute?"

As if they were synchronized, the boys looked at each other and shrugged their shoulders then nodded to Ethan. Stepping back to avoid getting kicked in the shins, I watched as they volleyed the ball between them. Either those kids were extremely talented, or Ethan let them win because it wasn't long before four little arms were in the air, waving in what appeared to be a victory dance. The boys got their ball back and their hair tousled by Ethan's large hands before he said goodbye.

I shot him a playful look. "That was unfair competition, two against one." The smile on his face told me all I needed to know. "So, do you like kids?" I said, keeping pace with his large strides.

"I have a lot of young cousins and I've done my share of babysitting. Yeah, kids are cool. It's just me and two brothers and none of us have had kids yet. I'm looking forward to being an uncle."

"And having kids of your own?"

The piercing whistle of the train stopped us just before we stepped onto the tracks.

"Hey, I think that's our train. C'mon, we can still make it," he said just after the last car passed. We ran across the road and up to the platform just in time.

I stared out the window of the train, relaxing into the rocking motion, the 'click-clack' sound lulling my eyelids to close.

"I have this situation, maybe I can bounce it off you—if you don't mind." Ethan jolted me out of my sleepy, hypnotic haze and my lids fluttered open to find a serious look on his face.

"Sure, what is it?"

"I've been kinda dating this girl here. She's a local, Catalan. I like her, I mean, I think I do."

My mind whirled. *What?* In a flash, I realized why he was holding back with me. The reason he hadn't tried to seduce me, yet.

"But here's my problem. She has two kids. They are great kids and all and I really like them, but I can't imagine myself as a step-dad. I want a family, but I want my own kids. Does that sound wrong?"

I pulled it together and shifted into a neutral tone, the one I used when I talked to clients. "I don't think it's wrong or right. If you want something badly enough, you can find a way. But I do know that step-parenting can be complicated."

"It's just that I have my ideas about the way I think children should be raised, and I have no control when they are not my own."

"Oh, you've thought about that?"

"I think it's because of how I was brought up. My father was strict, I guess. He didn't let us get away with anything. The bar was set high."

"And your mom? What is she like?"

A tender smile flashed across his face, the softness reaching his eyes. "She is all heart. They balance out each other and somehow, it's worked. They've been married for almost forty years."

Ethan shook his head, then paused and stared out the window. "Yeah, the more I think about it, I'm not sure this is something I can do."

His gaze shifted from the passing scenery and looked back at me. "Hey, thanks for listening."

My insides were knotted up and I felt the pangs of jealousy. Of course, it was unreasonable. And yet hearing that he was on the fence about the relationship allowed some room for hope. Blind hope. I knew I should steer clear of him, but there was no denying the strong attraction between us.

We reached the entrance to my apartment, and I fell silent. It was my last day in Barcelona.

"I'll just come up and get my things. I know you need to get some rest since you have a flight in the morning."

I pouted like a disappointed five-year-old. If only I could stay. If only *he* would stay. But his voice was firm, and his hand gestured for me to go first, up the narrow stairwell. Halfway up the climb, he paused on a step below. I felt his smile before I saw it.

"You have great legs. But then you know that, don't you?" His deep voice resonated in the stairwell.

I turned, just a step above him. At once, I was struck with an irresistible impulse. Leaning forward, I tilted my head and pressed my lips against his in a slow, soft kiss.

He looked up at me with his eyes sparkling and the broadest of grins. "Oh great, now you are going to give me your cold."

Teasing him with a smile, I turned and sprang up the stairs.

I stood poised at the door while he pulled the large pack across his back. His arms folded around me in one last embrace. One I didn't want to break from, my arms wrapped tightly around his neck.

"I hope you've had a great experience in Barcelona. I'd love to show you more. Too bad you have to leave."

My pouty face made its return. "I really hate to leave, especially since you're here another week, but thank you so much for showing me your city. I do love it here. No doubt, I will be back."

"I hope so. I really enjoyed being with you. In any case, we'll meet back in the Bay."

His lips grazed mine with a wisp of a kiss. A tease, that left me tingling and hungry.

He called back to me as his large frame disappeared down the stairs, "Have a good flight. I'll see you in San Francisco."

With a heavy sigh, I closed the door and flopped down on the couch. Folding an arm over my forehead, images of him floated through my mind. *Damn. He really gets to me.* I hadn't enjoyed being with someone this much since… I couldn't remember.

Our time together had been light and fun, but I knew that sooner or later, he'd make his move. His ultimate goal was the same as all guys, he just enjoyed the build up more than most, which shed new light on him. Maybe he wasn't the player he appeared to be. It was easy to suspend judgment when I felt that rush of arousal coursing through my body each time he was near—since the very moment I met him. I wanted him—despite the danger signs flashing in neon lights. I tried to put away the dilemma that was playing over and over in my head. There would be time to sort it all out when I returned. But I was certain of one thing, this would not be the last time I saw him.

Chapter Fourteen

The transition back to reality was jolting. Freeways replaced quaint cobblestone streets. Instead of dining on terraces teeming with life, I ate alone at my kitchen table. The daily monotony of my so-called job was mind numbing. This wasn't just the usual post-vacation blues. Barcelona had woken me up to another kind of life. I wanted more of it—travel, adventure. But more than that, to trade in the life that was draining me.

I drove the familiar roadways to my office the week following my return, and each day one persistent thought haunted me: *I need a new life. I just have to figure out how to get there.*

Then the sensible part of my brain would make the argument: *"What? Are you crazy? The life you have is just fine. You have it easy compared to so many people in the world. You could be hiding in your hut, ducking incoming bombs."* I would shake my head, rattling with competing desires and thoughts. Those childhood memories of sitting at the kitchen table and being told to eat all my vegetables because there were people starving in the world who would be grateful to have my lima beans—were apparently lodged firmly in my psyche. If I dared to attempt a change, it was going to be a battle on many fronts.

It had been a week since I'd returned to San Francisco, and there was no word from Ethan. Each day that passed, I sat alone in my office reliving the moments in Barcelona. I wondered what he was doing, where he was traveling. I couldn't get him out of my mind and my usual impatience led to checking emails several times a day.

At the end of week two, my phone rang. I looked up from the computer and saw Ethan's name on my caller ID. My pulse quickened as my hand dove for the phone on my desk.

"Hey, *que tal*, how's it going?" His luxurious voice poured from the speaker.

"Great," I lied. Thankfully, it wasn't a video call.

"How was your flight back?" he asked.

"Way too long. With the stopover time, it was brutal."

"I know exactly what you mean, it takes days to get over jet lag too. My days and nights are still mixed up. If you want, we could get together next week. Do dinner... say, on Tuesday?"

I hesitated, remembering that he had mentioned dating a girl in Barcelona. My mind raced through the pros and cons, but I knew it was an exercise in futility. How could I resist him? I disguised my ambivalence and plowed right through my better judgment.

"Sure, where should I meet you? In San Francisco?"

"That would be great as long as you're cool with coming over my way. I'll text you my address. Park in the neighborhood and we can catch a taxi to the restaurant."

"Where are we going? Just so I have a clue about what to wear."

"I have an idea, but it's a surprise. See you on Tuesday."

My heart began to race as I set the phone on the desk and thought about the attraction I had felt for this man in Barcelona—hell, it was there from the moment I'd laid eyes on him at the wine bar in San Francisco. The excitement I felt at the thought of seeing him again was intoxicating. He was also my link to Barcelona, the city I fell in love with. The magic began there, and I didn't want to let it go.

BY TUESDAY, I was a nervous wreck. It was impossible to focus at work when all I could think about was our date. I glanced at the clock almost every few minutes, counting down the time until the workday ended.

I left the office exactly at five o'clock and raced home, imagining various scenarios that might unfold. I couldn't decide which direction I should take. Keep my distance and secure my guard with him—or go with the flow, wherever that led us.

I changed clothes at least three times. Standing in front of the full-length mirror, I assessed each outfit. *Do I go full-on sexy, or SF stylish?* I had to admit, Ethan's mysterious nature was a turn-on, but in this case, it was causing me some angst. As always, I obsessively worried about fitting in, and there was no doubt that this date ranked a ten on the scale of dressing to impress.

I finally decided on a little of both, and chose a slightly revealing black satin top, with a form-fitting skirt. As it was the end of October, it would be chilly at night, so the boots I bought in Barcelona would finish off the outfit nicely.

The drive into San Francisco was stressful, as always, because of the ever-present traffic on the Bay Bridge, the nightmare of one-way streets, and the impossible task of parking. As I headed to the Marina, a white layer of fog rolled in from the sea and blanketed the city, bringing with it a cold wind.

Finally landing a parking space, I called his cell. "I'm here, found parking on the street."

"Great, be right down in a second."

Waiting on the corner, I scanned the dark street to see which one of the charming two-story Victorian flats he might emerge from.

My eyes fell on his tall frame as he appeared from his apartment door and shut the metal gate behind him. The butterflies in my stomach did backflips at the mere sight of this man. As always, he was well put together, looking tall, dark and gorgeous, clad in a black wool coat and cashmere scarf. With long, elegant strides, he crossed the street to meet me.

"Elena, good to see you again." His deep sensual voice washed over me and tingled my skin as he pulled me into a hug. "You find your way okay?"

"Yes, despite the usual mess of traffic, I did okay. He released me and I wobbled on my heels, affected both by the incline of the street and the usual effect he had on me. Regaining my balance, I covered with the burning question.

"So, where are we going?"

Ethan answered with a mischievous grin, "Let's catch a taxi and I'll tell you."

"*Hmmm*, you do like the element of suspense."

He put his fingers to his lips and whistled for a cab.

"Damn, I wish I could do that."

"What, whistle? You just put your lips together and blow," he said, with a wink.

I cocked my head at him. "Smartass."

The taxi dropped us off at a corner, and Ethan led the way down a cobblestone street.

"Have you been here before?" he asked.

"No, but it looks very European, the way all the restaurants are lined up in the alley with terraces."

"It's Belden Lane. I've made reservations at a Catalan restaurant, called B44. I wanted to commemorate our trip to Barcelona."

I squealed in excitement, "That's perfect!" Since falling in love with the city, all things Barcelona were my new favorites.

Ethan downplayed it, cool and collected as usual, "*Eh*, well, I took a chance. I thought that you would either love it or think, 'Damn, more tapas?'"

I looked straight ahead, mirroring his reserve, "You are charming me you know." I glanced over and caught him with his lips forming into a self-assured smile.

"Am I?" he said innocently and made a sudden turn into a bar. "Let's grab a drink before dinner."

San Francisco had always charmed me too. The *cozy chic* ambiance was exactly what I expected to find in the city. I scanned the blackboards which listed designer drinks written in chalk: "pear drop, lychee martini, raspberry gimlet." Bottles of every kind lined the shelves of the tall brick wall which was lit in subtle tones of orange light that cast a golden hue in the room.

"What did you like best about your vacation?" Ethan slid onto a wooden barstool with one long leg planted against the floor. My eyes gazed up at the high ceiling as my mind sifted through all the experiences.

"There was so much I loved about the trip, but I think the best day was when we took the train to the beach up north."

"You mean Sant Pol De Mar? I know, I enjoyed that day too. I love the pics you sent, the ones of you and me at the restaurant and the beach. You looked so good." His eyes raked over me, from my face down to my boots. "You look gorgeous tonight too."

"Thanks," I said, taking his compliment but not without a measure of that persistent insecurity.

"Where are your photos from the trip? Can I see?" I asked.

"They're on my camera, not my phone, and I haven't had time to do a download," he explained.

"So, you've been busy since you returned?"

"Yes, catching up with work and it was my birthday yesterday, so I've been out with friends."

"Happy Birthday!" I raised my glass and clinked it against his. "We have to celebrate. I'm buying the next round."

"*Aww*, thanks, but you don't have to do that. It's no big deal."

"Birthdays are a big deal. And which birthday is this?"

"My thirty-fifth."

The expression on my face must have looked something like I had just unexpectedly stepped into a pothole. Ignorance was indeed bliss. Ethan seemed to be content with the absence of knowledge as well. He had not asked me my age, thank God. Most people gauged me to be about ten years younger. I preferred to maintain that illusion.

"Well, *salud*, and may this be a great year for you," I choked out, in a tone several octaves above normal and downed half of my cocktail in one gulp.

By the time we'd finished our drinks, I had managed to recover my balance. Ethan had a way of making me feel excited yet comfortable at the same time. It was baffling how he could manage to do both, but he clearly had skills. When he checked his watch and announced it was time to go, I hopped off my stool and followed his lead down the lane.

Dinner at the Catalan restaurant brought back all the sensory experiences from Barcelona. The wine, the tapas, the music... I was transported. The vibe was definitely Spanish, but it embodied the flavor of San Francisco.

My eyes transfixed on him, I watched as he so easily talked with the waiters in Spanish. His gorgeous face, his perfect body, his magnetic presence—he slayed me. I noticed the way his smile lit up his eyes, and the way the space between his brows crinkled when he stopped to think. And the sound of his laughter, deep and melodic, like a song.

"What are you thinking?" he asked, jolting me from my mesmerized haze.

I cleared my throat before answering, "I'm enjoying your company."

His head cocked to the side, and with sharp eyes, he studied me, then smiled wryly. *Why does he seem to know everything I'm thinking?* I took another bite of the *patatas bravas* and glanced up at him. The tables were turned, he was watching me.

"You're not hard to read, Elena. You have the most expressive eyes I've ever seen."

"So... what do you see?" I asked, tentatively peeking through my lashes.

I caught his brows crinkling. "I see a bright, compassionate, sweet woman—who is also incredibly sexy. But there's a lot more to you I'd like to know. You have a fire inside. It radiates from your eyes. It makes me wonder why you are single, but then, maybe that's none of my business."

"Oh God, there's a long list of reasons." My shoulders slumped at the troublesome question. "I'd like to be in a relationship with the right guy, but maybe I want too much. I can't do without passion, great sex, and about a dozen other qualifiers." I had to laugh at the way that sounded. "I know, another woman with a must-have list. I just can't settle for something lifeless and bland."

"I think we have a lot in common. Both of us have a wild side and we know what we want." The smoldering look in his eyes pinned me to the back of the chair. I couldn't break his gaze even if I'd wanted to.

Ethan raised his arm and signaled to the waiter, "Check please."

As we left the restaurant and walked side by side down the street, I burned with anticipation. I'd been on enough dates to know that this was the moment decisions were made. Most guys would be asking me to join them for a drink back in their apartment, and I would already be trying to figure out whether it would be worth my while. But Ethan always left me wondering. It was unnerving, not to be able to predict with him.

Just then, Ethan reached for my hand, "Let's grab a cab and head back to my place before you leave." He shot me a sideways glance, "I desperately want to kiss you."

Swallowing hard, I looked up at him with a coy grin, "Oh you do, huh?" I felt the excitement swell in my chest and trickle down south.

For a split second, I saw his eyes glint with the heat of a promise that tonight, the prolonged foreplay was going to take a new twist.

Chapter Fifteen

My palms were damp by the time we arrived in front of his apartment. With each step up the stairs, the nervous anticipation mounted, and I could barely feel my fingers from the tingling rush.

"You have a great apartment. What a view!" The lights of the city-scape sparkled through the bay windows of the corner flat.

My eyes scanned the apartment and noticed the photographs he had taken from his many travels. "Wow, these are gorgeous. You're really good."

"This is one of my favorites." He pointed to one of an elephant whose eyes looked intensely emotional, almost pained. "It was taken through a night lens, on an African safari."

"That one is stunning! Incredible that you could capture it."

I walked from one photo to the next while Ethan plugged in his phone to the speaker and chose a track of mellow, instrumental music.

"What's this one, of the injured animals? Where did you take this?"

"Oh, that's part of my volunteer work, I help out with animal rescue organizations."

I looked at him in amazement. *This guy just keeps getting better.*

I noticed the family photos as well, and the way he resembled his mother with his refined features. Each photo piqued my curiosity and gave me a glimpse into his life.

As I walked through the living room, I saw a guitar in the corner. "Do you play?"

"Yeah, I play guitar and studied violin for many years. Do you play any instruments?"

"Sadly no, not really. I tried to learn guitar when I was young, but the neck was just too big for my hands. It didn't come easy to me."

He put my hand on top of his, dwarfed in comparison.

"You do have small hands. They're lovely, so delicate and feminine."

He interlaced our fingers, "Come, I'll give you a tour." Following him through the apartment, I was struck by his taste in art as well as furniture. The apartment itself was older, and not renovated, but Ethan had decorated it with style, using pieces from all around the world.

"Sit down, relax. I'll get us some wine," he said, gesturing to the large sofa. Before returning, he dimmed the lights and strode across the room with an air of command that made me squirm in my seat. Everything about this man exuded sex appeal. Not the sleazy kind that makes a girl set up a fake text for an emergency escape excuse. He had a sexy combination of class, intelligence, and the kind of confidence that magnetized everyone around him. A rush of heat poured through me, imagining his body pinning mine to the back of the couch.

He handed me the glass, his fingers elegantly wrapped around the stem. I questioned if I really should have any more alcohol. The numerous cocktails throughout the evening combined with the excitement of finally being alone with Ethan had left me quite intoxicated. Rational thinking would be decimated with one more drink. Though where he was concerned, my brain was already flooded by a tsunami of hormones.

"I just want to let you know that we don't have a lot of time. My cousin is flying in from the East Coast to visit, he'll be arriving by taxi shortly," Ethan's eyes flashed. "This will just be a little taste for tonight."

He leaned in, grazed the sides of my face with his fingers, his thumb caressing the ridge of my bottom lip. His intense eyes explored mine in a way that made me feel like he was already deep inside me. Slowly, he brought his mouth close. His breath warmed my cheek. My lips parted, and my eyelids lowered as I absorbed the heady scent of him. I barely breathed, waiting... his mouth trailed against my skin, heightening the anticipation. The touch of lips felt like velvet, they poured over my mouth so gently, so sensually. My lips softened, opening slightly to bring him in closer. Arousal surged through my body as his tongue swirled against mine. Abruptly, he broke away and whispered, "I love the way you kiss me."

He made a trail of delicate kisses along the sensitive curve of my neck, making me writhe with each one as he worked his way downward. His hands brushed along my shoulders and then to my breasts, caressing their fullness. I heard the long exhale, air escaping through his lips while the flat of his index finger slid into my bra and flicked across my nipple. My chest heaved with a sharp breath, arching into his hand. The first touch of intimacy... I had craved it for so long.

One by one, the buttons on my blouse came undone as he peeled away the fabric. His lips trailed kisses down my breasts, tugging down the lace cups with his index fingers, freeing them from the restraints of my bra.

His pleasure was audible as he lowered his mouth to my nipples and greedily sucked, flicking his tongue over the sensitive tips. Hollowing his cheeks, he drew them in with long pulls.

The sensations, the warmth of his mouth, left me breathless and hungry for him. Tentatively, I reached down and felt the erection bulging in his pants and was not surprised to find my fingers stretching over its generous length and girth.

My mind raced. *Finally... but how far does he want this to go tonight? He said we didn't have much time. How far do I want this to go? Maybe I should be the one to stop? Oh God, why did I wear tights tonight? So not sexy.* Then my body spoke—much louder than the words whirling in my head.

Mindless with desire, I unbuttoned his shirt and brushed my

breasts against his chest. I heard the sound of his breath quickening as the tips glided on his bare skin. There was no denying this was going to move past "just a little taste."

Pressing against me, he deftly removed his shirt exposing his gorgeous dark skin. Lean and muscular, his washboard abs tightened, and his bulging pectorals flexed. His perfect body was my undoing. The broad shoulders led to precisely cut biceps and strong forearms. I visually devoured him, running my hands over his exposed torso, across the silky softness of his skin.

Relieving me of the blouse, he reached around with one hand and swiftly unfastened my bra, letting it fall to the floor. Seizing my swollen breasts in his hands, he stopped to admire the long, erect nipples. He buried his face in the cleft between the mounds and murmured, "You are so beautiful," before lowering himself on top of my body. My inner voice sounded off the alarm of those damn insecurities. *Does he really think I'm beautiful? Will he still feel the same seeing me naked? This is not the body of a thirty-year-old, things have shifted over the years.*

But inside me, was the same roaring sexual desire that had always been my essence. Feeling his skin on my breasts, the heat of his body on top of me, I lost any sense of inhibition. His erection pressed against the lips of my sex and I tilted my hips, grinding on the shaft through the fabric between us.

I rumbled with the vibration of a moan as his mouth sealed over mine, then suddenly he pulled away. Straddling my hips, he sat upright and drew in a long, deep breath. I knew he was trying to make the decision. Whether to go any further, or exercise self-control and stop with "just a little taste."

I didn't have time to wonder before he made his decision. In one swift move, he scooped me into his arms. His mouth hungrily poured over my lips, while his hands frantically reached under my skirt and tugged down my tights. Breaking from the kiss, my chest heaved with frantic breaths.

"I thought this was only going to be a little taste tonight, not the *Full Monty*."

He paused, lips parted and glistening. "Do you want me to stop?"

My body ached with desire, every nerve ending quivered. I fixed my gaze into his questioning eyes and placed his hand on the throbbing, heated place between my legs.

"Does this feel like I want you to stop?"

His only response was a deep, guttural sound as his mouth lunged at mine with a driving force. It was like an explosion, both of us combusting with need and desire. I kissed him back with a hunger, like I had been starving for the taste of him. The intensity was like nothing I'd ever felt before and it had me reeling.

Sliding his hand inside my black lace panties, the pad of his finger stroked lightly between my legs. "Ah, Elena, you are so wet," he breathed as he teased my clitoris with circular motions before sliding his long finger inside. Moans escaped me, following a rhythm that matched his strokes.

I felt his heartbeat on my chest growing faster and his lungs expanding with hard breaths. He panted, "Jesus, woman... I want you... I can't stop."

His eyes were wild as he took control and possessed my body. With one arm, he lifted my hips in the air and tore off the remnants of my clothing, leaving me naked and exposed before him. He planted quick kisses as he moved his way down my body until his mouth reached my apex, sending my hips off the couch, aching for the feel of him.

Teasing my clit quickly with a lick of his tongue, his head slid between my legs. He lavished wet kisses on the soft inside of each thigh, leaving me silently begging for more, while the sound of blood rushing pounded in my ears. My back arched when he indulged my desire. The warmth of his lips poured over my sex, his velvet tongue lashing against the sensitive pearl.

I gasped and muttered, "Yes... like that," the breath gushing from my lungs. He pressed a long finger inside and gently massaged a sweet spot which left me writhing in the sensations. My core tightened, the sweet tension building as he brought me to the brink.

Sensing I was close, he broke away and raised his face to mine.

Teasing my lips with his tongue, he immersed his finger into his mouth, then mine.

"I love the taste of you..." he whispered in my ear.

"I need to feel you... taste you," I pleaded.

My hands blindly reached out and found his erect cock straining against his pants. Fumbling with the buttons, I tried to free him to my touch. He saved me from the growing frustration when he raised his tall frame and quickly unbuttoned his fly. His eyes piercing, never leaving my stare, he stood above me in his tight black boxer briefs. My gaze wandered down to the enormous bulge, and lower to his muscular thighs. *Jesus, could a man be more gorgeous?* The sight of him propelled a long moaning sigh from deep inside me.

It was torture—I needed him naked and I wasn't about to wait any longer. My fingers slid against his skin, undressing him. I took his erection firmly in my hands, sliding up and down the long shaft. This time it was Ethan who inhaled sharply. His head rolled back, and he began to rhythmically move his hips to meet the strokes. My eyes swept over his naked body, admiring every inch of him, relishing his response.

"Stay right there," I commanded as I took control of pleasuring him. I moved under him, holding him in my grasp. Slowly, I ran my tongue around the tip and the sensitive cleft. I licked the salty liquid emanating from the head. He tasted so good, so sweet. His penis was a beautiful work of art. Long and straight, perfectly cut, and thick to the root. The sight of it made my sex clench with anticipation.

Expertly taking his whole organ in my mouth, I sucked hard then popped my lips against the plush head. Gazing up into his eyes, I ran my tongue in circles over the crest and under the carved cleft before I plunged him in my mouth again. I knew my skills, and I was determined to torture him. My hand pumped the thick shaft, together with the rise and fall of my lips. His voice rose higher and higher in response, every muscle in his body tightened. Gasping for air, he pulled himself away from my mouth and the impending orgasm.

Cupping my face in his hands, he looked into my eyes for what seemed like minutes. His eyes were smoldering and intense, his pupils black as night. He searched my eyes for an answer to a question not quite formulated. "Elena… what you do to me…" The look on his face—so raw, so fierce—shot through me, making my sex tremble with need.

At once, his mouth sealed over mine, kissing me long and hard, while deftly lifting my body up onto his lap. He grabbed me into a tight embrace, and I melted into him, my arms wrapped around his broad back. With my face nuzzled on his neck, I breathed in the heady, perfect scent of him. I was overcome with a driving need to feel him inside me.

One hand wrapped around his long shaft, and he guided the head across my clit and down between the folds. Slowly, his hips thrusted, and the crown slid along the slippery entrance of my body, inching his way through the tight, pulsing walls until he was enveloped inside me. I moaned, struggling to accommodate the heavy surge of his penis. With his eyes locked on mine, I watched as a look of ecstasy spread across his face.

"You… feel… so… good… so perfect," he uttered between jagged breaths.

Gripping my waist, he rocked into me with steady strokes. I closed my eyes and absorbed in the feel of him deep inside, exquisitely stretching me to my limit. My hands clung to his broad shoulders for support, while my hips moved up and down the shaft, matching his rhythm.

He plumped my breasts in his hands before lifting one and then the other to meet his mouth. A low, sexy growl rumbled in his chest and reverberated on the sensitive tips, sending waves of pleasure straight to my apex. The sound of him enjoying my body drove me wild. The sensation of his warm mouth on my nipples while he filled me so deeply—the connection between our bodies startlingly intense.

Without warning, I felt his hand hit my bottom with a loud *crack*. I cried out in surprise and as I looked at him with wide eyes, I felt another harder slap, and then another. Finally, wetting his fingers with his mouth, he sent the last blow. My body rose and fell on him in a constant motion, climbing with the fury of pleasure and the sting of his hand. It seemed he was testing me. Testing the boundaries as well as his power. It drove me higher and higher, fueled by the power he possessed to drive me crazy with need for him.

In an instant, his hands were on my waist, raising me in his strong arms. I let out a squeal as he flung me onto my back and a rush of excitement poured through me. His formidable frame positioned over me, every muscle rippling. Awestruck, I couldn't take my eyes off him. He was sexy as hell, and the way he took me was more erotic than I'd ever dreamed. My core clenched as he speared me again, this time hard and fast.

I wrapped my legs around his back and dug my fingers into his firm, round buttocks—feeling his muscles flex and watching him enter me. My bottom rose to meet the roll of his hips. Beads of sweat glistened on his body and I devoured his lips, tasting the salty kisses.

"Don't stop... please... you feel so good," I cried out in a sob. His warm breath gusted against my cheek. He paused between thrusts, then slowly entered the crown of his cock at just the right angle, making me feel every ridge and contour of him. He knew exactly what he was doing. My lips parted with sharp gasps from the feel of him, and the sight of his steeled gaze locked on mine.

I was lost in ecstasy when suddenly, he stood and lifted me in his arms, cupping my behind, his brutally hard cock still deep inside me. My arms wrapped around his neck while my thighs clung to his waist as he carried me to the living room wall. Imprisoned by his body, my back pressed against the hard surface with my feet barely touching the floor. I regained balance just as he pinned my arms above my head, holding both my wrists in one of his large hands. My head began to spin, and my heart thundered at his strength and dominance.

Our eyes locked, he watched my face as I surrendered to him. His hips rolled into me, and the corners of his mouth raised in a wicked smile. He had me right where he wanted me, and I had no desire to resist.

When he released the hold on my wrists, I fell limp into his arms, my hands clinging around his neck. Scooping me up with one arm under my legs, he turned and laid me down gently in the hallway at the top of the stairs, the entry to his living room. Hovering over my body, he braced his elbows against the walls, his long legs angled down the steps. The abrupt changes had my head reeling while my sex throbbed, aching for a release. It struck me as an odd position, but when he pressed himself inside me, I immediately understood his intention. With each stroke, he slid between my lips, and over the nerve laden tissues of my clit. I made a small, helpless sound of need, wrapping my arms around his back, bringing him close.

With a tender touch, his fingers laced through my hair and he cradled my head in his hands, cushioning it from the hard wood. "I've got you," he cooed, rocking his hips and straining against my tight walls into the deepest part of me. A trembling moan left me as his pace quickened, his cock exquisitely filling me and curving against my sensitive cleft.

"Oh, baby," his rasped voice vibrated on my neck, "Are you ready? I'm gonna come, will you come with me?" His announcement pushed me higher toward the peak. I felt every muscle on his hard body stiffen as the powerful release racked his body. As he poured into me, the roar of his voice filled the room and drove me over the edge. The heated roll of an orgasm burned in my core until it exploded, the spasms tearing through me with uncontrollable force. I cried out as he brought me with him to climax, uncertain of where my voice ended and his began.

"Oh—My—God," he panted."

With one hand under my head, he wrapped an arm around my back and held me close. Muscles that bulged and strained just a moment before, relaxed and the weight of his body pressed me to the wood.

Our bellies met with the rise and fall of gasping breaths. I had no time to recover before Ethan announced, "My cousin will be here any minute, so, unfortunately, we have to move."

He caressed my face with the back of his fingers. "I don't want to let you go. I wish you could stay with me. I'm sorry about this, it really sucks. I honestly didn't mean to take it this far. I just couldn't stop with you."

"You don't have to apologize. It took two of us to get carried away." I was jolted, overcome, even stunned—but what could say? I reminded myself that I had known the score even before it began.

The man's timing proved to be impeccable, for as soon as we dressed and walked out the door to my car, his cousin's taxi pulled up.

"Hey, man, how are you? Good flight? This is Elena, I'm just going to walk her to the car and be back in a minute. Let yourself in." As Ethan escorted me, our voices joined in a simultaneous exclamation, "Wow that was close." Laughter broke the tension, my body grateful for the release in an awkward moment. Ethan gave me a platonic hug and a quick kiss goodnight as I got into the car. Quite a contrast to his earlier passion.

"You okay to drive?"

"Sure," I said, although thinking I really didn't have much choice.

"Okay, talk to you soon. Text me when you get home so I know you are safe."

He looked back and waved while walking away, while I sat there all tangled up in a jumble of feelings. The passion was expected from my point of view. But the rest was a surprise, the connection, intensity— and not to mention the sophistication of his lovemaking. My mind was reeling in disbelief at what had just happened. But this was not my first rodeo. Experience had taught me that as suddenly as men made their way into my life, they could just as suddenly exit. *Maybe he got what he wanted and that will be the end of it.* I tried to prepare myself for whatever might be next. But there was something more there between us, and it was powerful. He could either move toward it or run away from it, but either way, it was undeniable.

Chapter Sixteen

"Good morning, Liz."

Liz glanced at the clock on the wall as I walked by the reception desk.

"I think it's officially afternoon now, Elena."

"Don't even go there." I whisked past the desk and waved the back of my hand at her, minus the one-finger salute that almost won the battle to emerge.

I mumbled audibly to myself as my feet trudged down the well-worn pathway of the sterile hall. "What the hell does it matter anyway, I'm just a fixture here now. I refuse to feel guilty for coming in at noon."

Hurrying past the rest of the cubicles I headed to my office and closed the door behind me. *The last thing I need is to run into "Hitler" or her cronies today.*

The night with Ethan was a late one, and it was tough to sleep once I'd arrived home. Memories of the evening would not stop whirling around in my mind. With no real work to distract me, there was nothing to keep my thoughts off him. *Please let him text.* The plea played like a tape set on loop in my mind. *I need to know if he's still in.*

The ring of the cell phone sent me diving for my purse. My heart plummeted when it wasn't Ethan's name appearing on the caller ID.

"Oh, it's you, Anna."

"Expecting someone else?"

"I had hoped it was Ethan. Sorry, didn't mean to sound so disappointed. I'm glad you called. I need someone to talk to."

"He hasn't texted yet?

"No, still waiting. You know the drill. Why are these the rules of the game? The girl has to sit and wait to find out if a guy is really interested or if it was just a one-night thing. Why isn't it the other way around?

"Law of nature, I guess. Men are predators. They need the chase."

"This one needs to be in control. That I know for sure."

"It was that good last night?"

"More than I ever expected. We have amazing chemistry, and you know, all it takes is one screaming orgasm with a guy to get a woman hooked. Now I'm on pins and needles."

Anna snorted, "Yep, been there before. Look, all you can do is trust that he felt it too and that he'll come around at some point. But I know, the waiting sucks."

My breath escaped in a frustrated sigh. "Anna, I've been playing this game since Nate went off to college. Well, trying to play. I've never done it very well. If I'm into a guy it's so hard to be the silent, hard to get type. When I met my ex-husband, I gave him every possible number where he could reach me or leave a message. It became a running joke."

"Elena, if you like this guy, don't scare him off. Have some confidence in yourself. You are a hottie. He would be lucky to see you again."

"Then why have I been single for all these years?"

"Because dating sucks at our age. It's not like the pool of men we had to choose from in our twenties. What's left thirty or so years later is more like a tiny, stagnant pond. Anyway, try to take your mind off him and just see what happens."

"I don't exactly have anything else positive to focus on, but I hear you. I'll let you know."

"Hang in there, girlfriend."

Frustrated, I held my phone in the air and begged it for an answer, as if the magic of *Siri* could solve all my problems in addition to giving me the weather. *Why does this have to be so hard?* I sunk into the big leather chair, and the familiar despair haunted me.

I'm so tired of trying and hoping. It just seems impossible. And yet, here I go again, the only guy I've been seriously attracted to in years, and he's in that impossible thirty-something category.

I looked around at my office filled with boxes. My entire career was reduced to about a dozen of them, filled with books and training manuals I couldn't bear to part with. Between Ethan and the job, the uncertainty was driving me crazy. *I've got to get out of here.*

Tucking my purse under my arm, I bolted out the office door with plans to head to a cafe. Emily and I almost collided in the hall, her face looking just as frustrated as I felt.

"Where you off to?" she asked.

"The cafe downstairs. Join me?"

"Yep. That was my plan too. We should talk."

Entering the cafe, we were careful to sit a distance away from other employees.

"So how are the reassignment interviews going?" Emily's rotund face quivered into a nervous smile.

"HR required me to interview with my old department, right after I returned from vacation. There's a staffing shortage there and I happen to know the job. The job I hated." I tapped a pencil against the lined notebook I'd set on the table, as if I was prepared to take notes on our 'meeting'.

"You mean at the call center?"

"Yep, that's the one. The monotonous, meaningless, mindless job that tied me to a desk and a headset and made me forget why I became a therapist. Each day was the same, sitting at a desk and taking calls for referrals to psychological services. Then I'd spend hours on the computer processing the paperwork. My years of experience were a waste in that position."

Emily's jaw dropped. "No! I thought the agency director took that off the table as an option."

"He did. I had several conversations with Alan. He assured me I wouldn't have to go back there. He told me he was working with HR to create a new position for me. Ideally, developing a new program in another school district. But since our mega control freak boss seems to be calling the shots, not even the director is likely to pull this off."

"What happened when you went for the interview?" Emily glanced up and nodded to a former co-worker passing by with a coffee in hand. I feigned a smile and lowered my voice.

"The woman who is the current director used to be my co-worker. She knew I had hated the job and asked me why I was interviewing. I told her Human Resources required I attend. To do my part, a good faith effort to show I was cooperating with their attempts to find me a reassignment. I told her I had no interest in returning to the position. And furthermore, that HR had reassured me I would not be required to take this 'opportunity.' I swear, Emily, if they force me back there, that will be it for me. My career will be over."

It wasn't until she shifted her eyes to my hands that I noticed they were fisted, my knuckles turning white. Emily wrapped her fingers around one of my fists and patted gently.

"Are there any other options on the table? There has to be somewhere else they can put you."

"I've been to a couple of interviews since the day we were given the ax, but nothing is looking promising. I'm getting worried and damn sick of sitting in the office. But what can I do? Leaving the security of government employment, let alone the pension, is not an option." My voice began to crack as I felt the desperation take over again. But Emily was in the same sinking boat, so I pulled it together enough to climb out of my own pit of preoccupation for a moment.

"So, how about you? Any developments?"

"There's a position in the Public Health department I think I will accept. It's still in process but I need to get out of here, the waiting is torture." Emily looked as strained and tired as I must have appeared.

"I hope it comes through for you, and I'll keep you posted too," I paused, and my eyes welled with tears. "I'm going to miss you."

"*Aww,* sweetie, I'm going to miss you too. But everything will turn out alright for us." Emily leaned in and grabbed me into a tight embrace. I was instantly engulfed by her mama bear arms.

"The eternal optimist! What am I going to do without you?" I choked out, despite the lump in my throat.

I returned to my office and surfed the internet for possible job openings on the government website. Again, nothing. Just as I leaned heavily against the back of the chair, my cell sounded off a message alert and with a Pavlovian-like response, my hands scrambled to grab the phone set close on the desk. I breathed a deep sigh of relief, it was *him.*

Hey, how's your day going? Just wanted to take a minute and check in.

Well, I made it into work, anyway. You kept me up pretty late last night and I think I have a hangover. Totally worth it though. I had a good time.

I did too. I want to see you again, soon. My cousin is here visiting but let's see what we can work out. This is such bad timing.

How long is he here with you?

He's here for ten days and I have to show him around, but he may be visiting other friends too. I will find out. I have to make it up to you, last night was unfortunate. I mean, it was awesome, but I didn't like having to send you home like that.

It was both incredible and awkward. I agree. Let me know what you figure out.

Will do. Kisses.

I had my answer. Game on.

Chapter Seventeen

The days dragged on with nothing special to occupy my time except to pour over Ethan's daily texts: **I'm dying to see you again ... I'm sorry it's taking so long ... I keep thinking about our last evening together.**

His texts brought a smile to my face, but his cousin's visit seemed to be taking up all his time. On top of that, he would be leaving town on business, so our next date was put on hold.

The days blended together in frustration as I waited for HR to find or create a new position for me. There had been no word of late and the lack of communication made me nervous. Without warning, I received an answer in the mail.

Before heading out the front door on Thursday morning, I glanced at the stack of mail on a table. My eyes landed on an official-looking envelope. I hadn't felt like checking the mail for a few days, but this one was on top. My hands shook as I picked it up. Addressed to Elena Vidal, it bore the HR department stamp. I had a terrible feeling in the pit of my stomach. *This can't be good.* I tore it open and tossed the envelope on the floor. It was a letter, signed by Alan Brown, Director in Chief and co-signed by the director of HR. Time stopped, and there was a loud ringing sound in my ears as the blood coursed violently through my racing heart.

A quick scan down the page verified my worst fears. "No! It's not possible. He promised me…. He promised me he wouldn't send me back," I yelled out, piercing the silence of my empty house.

Blood rushed to my head, my breaths shallow and fast as panic flooded my brain and body. I paced the length of the house with quick steps. My fist pounded into the wall and I sent the trash can flying with the kick of my foot. I was oblivious to the self-inflicted pain and ignored the torn knuckles.

My hands hit the sides of my head. *I've got to think… they can't do this to me… what am I going to do?*

Curse words of every possible kind flew out of my mouth in retaliation for all the wrongs I endured. *And now they throw me this curve?* It was the ultimate insult.

I need to call HR. My brain was racing, and I desperately reached out for some reality that countered the one I'd just read. My hands shook, making it almost impossible to dial the number on the phone.

"I need to speak with Janet, it's urgent. Yes, I'll hold." I shouted. Absent was any concern over the tone in my voice.

The hard-driven anxiety surged at the sound of the hold music. I tried to breathe, but tight bands constricted my chest.

"Finally. Janet, I've just received the letter. Alan approved this?"

"Yes, Elena," she said coolly, "The department has been unable to fill the position and they are very short-staffed. It was the only solution. We don't know where else to reassign you."

"But Alan promised me…" The voice on the other end was silent and I knew there was no use in arguing.

As I slammed the phone on the table, I knew my last hope had evaporated. The next call was to my doctor's office, and luckily, I got an appointment that afternoon.

By the time I arrived in her office my pulse and blood pressure had skyrocketed. The tears had made for puffy eyes and one glance in the mirror confirmed that I looked as bad as I felt. I told my doc about the panic attacks and nightmares which had persisted for months since my job was taken away from me. The only relief I had experienced was when I was in Barcelona.

The doctor looked at me with worry in her eyes. "I'd say the cure was to go back to Barcelona, but I guess that isn't going to solve the problem right now."

She had a point, but in that moment, I could barely think, let alone problem solve. I had a million neurons firing in the primal part of my brain that were screaming "Danger! Get a big stick or run like hell." I didn't know which way to turn, but there was no doubt that my brain was interpreting this as a Mastodon sized beast coming straight for me. There was no escape.

"I think you may have a total breakdown if you go back to work right now, so I am putting you on temporary leave. The symptoms you have are the result of repetitive trauma."

"You think?" I managed a weak attempt at sarcasm.

"I'm going to give you a prescription, but you have to find a therapist and a psychiatrist for medication. Come back and see me in two weeks."

The short break from work helped to calm my nerves, but it didn't buy time for the outcome to change as I had hoped. I didn't want medication, and therapy was not going to help me adjust to my fate. I was on my own and barely treading water.

Since Ethan was out of town for a few weeks on business, there was no distraction from the despair. I had way too much time on my hands to perseverate on the thoughts that were spiraling me downward. Family and friends tried to be supportive. Mom offered a time-honored adage, "When one door closes, another opens." It wasn't much consolation. I was spinning out in a maze of endless doorways, and somehow, none were magically sliding open into an alternative world.

The days slid by toward the Monday I was due to report. By Sunday, I could think of nothing else but the impending doom Monday morning would bring. The image of walking back in the door of that office played in my mind like a bad horror movie.

As the minutes ticked by, panic struck my body again. Barely able to sleep, I woke before the alarm and trudged heavily through the morning routine. I faced the rude bathroom mirror. *God, I look like shit.*

It felt surreal as I parked my car in the same lot as I had done before, over seven years ago. I trudged up the staircase to the office, my mind barely registering the steps. Standing aside at the top of the gray stairwell, I watched the parade of employees racing in the door to clock in at the required time.

The receptionist greeted me with an enthusiastic tone. "Elena! Good to see you. What are you doing here?"

"Good morning... "I'm here to... I'm here on a reassignment. I start work today," I replied flatly.

"Oh, I didn't know," her face fell as she grasped the gravity of the situation. "I'll page Beatrice."

My back stiffened against the back of the chair as I sat waiting for my fate. I ticked the seconds, thrumming an index finger on my thigh. Beatrice appeared and graciously smiled as she welcomed me.

"Hi, Elena, we just found out Friday you were coming." She softened with compassionate eyes when she saw the state I was in.

"I'll take you to Jennifer, she will be your supervisor. I believe you met her already at the interview."

Jennifer was clearly unprepared for my arrival and hadn't a clue how I became assigned to her team. She rattled through papers on her desk and found the orientation binder along with those mind-numbing procedural manuals I had dumped in the trash years ago.

"Ah, I found them," she said, placing the heavy binders in my hands. "I don't think these have been completely updated, the procedures have undergone some changes since you were here before. You can start reviewing them and I will give you the latest updates."

She studied my expression which must have looked something like the blank stare of a zombie. It seemed to rattle her. I noticed her hands shaking on the rim of the wood desk, but she had a cheerful look, her face round and cheeks naturally rosy. She wore her anxiety transparently though, and her lips quivered in an effort to smile through this Monday morning curveball she'd been handed.

Motioning me with a wave of her hand, she led the way down the carpeted hallway until she reached an empty cubicle. "The desk hasn't been set up yet for you, and I guess we will have to find a chair."

Jennifer gestured to a dusty desk that sat at the end of a line of cubicles. The desk in the back—the last row away from the coveted window seats. Those in the front occupied the cubicles with the sanity-saving view of the waterways which bordered Oakland. There was more than a modicum of difference in the mood of those afforded the luxury of viewing the outside world, versus those who were encased in three walls under fluorescent light all day.

"I'll introduce you to the staff before you get settled."

One by one, the introductions droned on as we stopped at each cubicle to visit the tethered staff. The length of their leash was only as far as the cord on the headset allowed them to venture. My voice was barely audible as I tried to force some kind of civilized sound to come from my rapidly closing throat.

I had to endure the shock on the faces of those I had known from before, and the repeated exclamations "What? You're back?" I was completely without words to explain what had happened, so I simply responded, "Yes, temporarily." I felt like a prisoner being introduced to the cell block. The words "I'm innocent, I tell you. I don't belong here," kept coming to mind as I shuffled through the office with invisible shackles.

As I made my way through the gauntlet, the unmistakable sound of frustration could be heard in their voices as each call tested their patience. I always wondered how it could be possible to last years in this job, waiting for the release of retirement. The licensed therapists were reduced to paper pushers, more like customer service agents. Memories flooded back, most of the staff had complained that their brain had atrophied. Without real clients to see and feel, their empathetic nature had long since disappeared too.

After finding a leftover desk chair that wasn't patched together with duct tape, I settled into the small cubicle. I could hear the whispers of staff around my desk. There wasn't any doubt they were talking about me and trying to figure out what the hell was going on. It couldn't have been a more awkward entry, but I was not able to hide my feelings of contempt for the job. I kept my head down and pretended to read the tedious manuals. Jennifer came by my desk to bring the staff schedule and go over the rules. As if I didn't remember.

"The lunch schedule is staggered in two increments. You will be assigned a time. You may take your breaks only during your paperwork hours, in order to maintain the phone coverage."

"You won't be answering calls for at least two weeks, but during that time, you can re-learn the job by shadowing workers who are on phone duty." Her cherubic face wore a gentle expression. It was in stark contrast to the hard-edged malevolent look of my previous boss. But Jennifer's eyes looked probingly at me as if she was trying to figure out what kind of hot mess she had just inherited.

All I could do was nod in resignation as the memories of the oppressive rigidity flooded back. I'd lost my freedom. For seven years I had enjoyed complete autonomy. *I* was the boss. Then to be sent back to *this?* Chained to a desk? My voice screamed in my head, but I kept silent. This was not the time for self-disclosure.

The familiar sound of phones constantly ringing resounded from one cubicle to the next, along with the prescribed script. "How can I help you?" was followed by attempts to extract the necessary demographic information needed to laboriously type into the computer-generated forms. "Ma'am, I am trying to help you, but first I need to collect this information. Ma'am, I can't help you if you insist on shouting." Social security number, birth date, number of children—it went on for pages.

Unless it was a life-threatening crisis, the goal was to make the referral and get the caller off the phone as quickly as possible, in order to answer the next call. There was even a quota expected for each day. Only those who were freshly hired or the truly neurotic took it seriously though. The old-timers just scoffed and threw the reports in the recycle bin.

Throughout the day, the bathroom became my sanctuary where I broke down and silently sobbed. Bathroom breaks were allowed during non-break time, but it was expected to be kept at a minimum. Since I wasn't on phone duty, no one was monitoring my frequent trips to the lieu.

When five o'clock came, I knew the drill. As before, there was someone calling out the familiar countdown. *"5, 4, 3, 2, 1..."* I heard the cacophony of phones all sounding the tone that signaled the workday was done, accompanied by loud sighs and a round of "Thank God."

I exited with the herd, nearly running for the door. My feet clomped down the stairs and raced to the car. The drive home was short at least, but dusk had fallen, and the night sky had started to appear. I was already anticipating the long, hard evening.

I fell heavily onto the bed and stared at the ceiling in the dimly lit bedroom. Finally, there was silence, apart from the sounds of cars pulling into nearby driveways. The boys across the street were trying to get in one more round of basketball as their mother called them in for dinner.

Damn it's cold. I shivered and pulled the blanket over me while I waited for the furnace to heat up. There was some comfort in my bedroom. It was my favorite place in the house, my sanctuary.

I settled into the soft mattress with a tissue box nearby to wipe up the tears and occasionally blow my nose. *What am I going to do? I can't do this, I can't last at this job.* I was desperate for a solution.

Opening my laptop, I scanned the entire state of California for possible jobs with government agencies. It had come time to consider moving, something that was incomprehensible just a few months ago. The battle to keep the house after the divorce was hard-won and the buyout cost me dearly. But it had provided comfort and stability for me and Nate. It was the home I had lived in since a year after the marriage began. The home Nate was raised in since the time he was born. Tears streaked my face as the memories came rushing in. *How can I do this to Nate? He loves being able to come back to his home. His childhood memories are all here.*

It seemed the world as I knew it was crumbling down around me. I lost a job I loved and might lose my house. My heart ached to think of giving it up. As a child, I was traumatized by my parent's separations and the subsequent moves. With my divorce, I had made damn sure Nate did not have to leave his home. During that difficult time, I wasn't about to cause him more damage. The divorce itself was painful enough.

I was starting to think that this time, I might not have a choice. I couldn't hold on to this symbol of security forever. It seemed that life was pushing me down another path, whether or not I was ready. Change did not come easy for me, but since my trip to Barcelona, there was a tiny glimmer of a vision—a life beyond the one I'd known.

My thoughts turned to Barcelona and I dared to dream. *Maybe… I can find a new life in Barcelona.* My brain raced at the thought. Pulling open the laptop again, I began searching job listings for Americans abroad. It didn't appear too likely—and certainly not an easy task—but my mind was opening up to possibilities.

The cell phone's text alert sounded, jolting me out of the research. My mood lightened immediately when I saw it was from Ethan. For the first time in days, I began to smile again

> Hey, just checking in on you. How did your day go? I know you were dreading today.

> It was about as bad as I expected, but I made it through day one. Now it will be a countdown to when I can find a way out of there. But thanks for the thought.

> Elena, you are in my thoughts every day. I'm sorry it's a rough time but hang in there. It's bound to get easier.

I'm thinking of you too. You're the only thing that's making me feel a bit better.

Oh, hon, I want to see you. I just got back to San Francisco, so I can come and take you to dinner after work on Thursday. Maybe I can brighten your mood a little.

That would definitely make my day.

Sweet and delicious thoughts of you until then...

I stared at the phone and released a heavy sigh. *In the midst of all this mess, he is my little island of bliss.*

Chapter Eighteen

THE NEXT FEW days were not much easier than the first, but I settled into a quiet state of resignation. As the week droned on, I confided in the few friends who I knew from my previous stint. As for the others, I remained silent and wore the facade of a pleasant demeanor. I spent every lunch hour and every evening, searching for a new job or some way out. An exit strategy was priority number one.

But on Thursday, there were different emotions stirring inside of me. Throughout the day, my mind drifted to thoughts of Ethan. As always, it was distracting when my body started to heat up when I visualized him. At five o'clock, I sprinted down the stairs and headed for home.

I've got forty-five minutes to freshen up and get dressed. I glanced at the clock, racing to get ready. *Oh god, what do I wear?* My bed became a pile of clothes, as per the usual pre-date routine. I pulled out one thing after the other and tossed the rejects. Finally, settling on a simple black dress and high heeled boots, I took a last look in the mirror and bolted out the door.

Ethan was waiting for me at the rapid transit terminal when I pulled up to the curbside pickup area.

"Need a lift?" I called out through the car window.

Ethan grinned back at me and shook his head. "You better be careful about picking up strangers, woman." He slid in the passenger seat and his hand grabbed the nape of my neck, planting a quick kiss on my lips.

"Look at you…" he held my shoulder and gave me the once over, examining me from arm's length. "You are so damn cute."

"What? You've forgotten what I looked like in four weeks?"

"God, has it been four weeks? I've been so busy."

"Well for me, these past weeks have been long and hellish ones. But tonight, I have a break. I'm thinking of a little Mediterranean restaurant on the border of Oakland and Berkeley. I think you will like it."

"Sounds good. I just want to be with you for a while. I know it's a work night for you."

A pang of disappointment struck me, knowing we wouldn't have a late night together. No more waltzing into work whenever I pleased. It was eight-thirty sharp or my paycheck could be docked.

"So, what are you going to do about your job situation?

I kept my eyes on the road and released a heavy sigh. "I have no idea. But it's not an option to stay. I've been there before, in this job. I escaped once, but this time I feel trapped."

Ethan reached behind my head and caressed my neck, instantly warming me.

"You can manage, babe. At least until you figure something out. What if…" his pause caught me by surprise.

"What?'

"What if this is an opportunity? You want to travel, and you loved Barcelona. Maybe this can be a time to try something new."

"Believe me, I've been thinking along those lines. But this work is all I've ever known."

"Hon, I haven't known you long, but long enough to see that you are one determined woman. We have that in common, and something else."

I pulled into the parking lot near College Avenue and turned to look at him. "What's that?"

"We don't settle for the average life. We are both adventurous. Clearly." A wry smile curved his lips and suggested more than his words revealed. "If I can help in any way, you can count on me."

My head fell against his neck and couldn't have been more grateful for those big broad shoulders to lean on.

As we walked into the dimly lit restaurant, I waved to George behind the bar. He responded with a friendly nod and a smile.

"Elena, table for two?" I nodded to the waitress and she escorted us through the small, cozy restaurant. The richly colored dark wood decor radiated simple elegance. The romance factor was enhanced by the glow of candle lights atop each table.

"I do like this place, the ambiance is special, and the food is excellent." My eyes glanced at the familiar surroundings.

"So, you come here often? It seems like they know you here."

"Yes, it's one of my favorites," I answered evasively. Ethan peered at me, an eyebrow arched with an implied question.

The truth was, it was a very popular place for first dates from online dating sites. I'd been there with countless guys, but I wasn't going to admit that to Ethan. Instead, I used one of his diversionary tactics.

"They have a good wine list here, I'll let you choose since you have a much better sense of wine than me."

As he examined the wine list, my mind wandered back to the first time we'd met at the wine event. I smiled at him across the table of our intimate booth.

"What?" He looked up and saw me beaming at him.

"I was just remembering the first time we drank wine together."

"*That...* was an interesting night. How crazy is it that we are sitting here now?" He interlaced his fingers with mine and gave a squeeze before withdrawing his hand.

It was so obvious. Ethan was always reserved when he was out in public with me. There were no public displays of affection. I learned the acronym PDA during my education on current dating practices. That one, along with many others I had to look up online. It was like learning a new language.

"So… I've been wondering something."

"Yes?" Ethan paused, holding the stem of his wine glass between his elegant fingers.

"You always seem so standoffish when we first see each other, and you never kiss me in public. Yet, you're so affectionate when we are in private. Is it me?"

"No, of course not," Ethan shifted uncomfortably in his chair and looked down as he answered. "It's just how I was raised. Growing up in the conservative South, well… it was different for me."

"Of course, and I can't begin to know what it feels like to grow up as a black man in the South, but how does that relate to PDA's?"

"You don't know how many times it was drilled into me that a guy just doesn't invite trouble. That my behavior had to be appropriate at all times," Ethan glanced out the window. "Look at those kids horsing around while the parents just stand there. I never would have gotten away with that when I was young. Children need to learn to behave when they are out in public."

"I don't get what you mean, they are just kids playing. That's what kids do. Their mission is to play, not act like little adults. They don't worry about how other people see them. We don't have that freedom anymore as grown-ups."

I rested my chin into the palm of my hand, "You really are a control freak, aren't you?"

"Oh, my sweet, you have no idea," his eyebrows twitched with a look of danger dazzling in his eyes. "I have a question for you now."

"Okay, what is it?" I peered up at him over the rim of my glass as I took a sip of wine.

"Are you one of those girls who are into the books that are so popular now? The ones on bondage, with submissive and dominant themes."

I coughed as the wine trickled down my throat and into my windpipe. "Wow, that was out of left field!" I hesitated, not sure if I should divulge my guilty pleasure.

"Actually… yes. They caught my attention." I looked into his eyes to judge his reaction and thought I saw a sparkle of interest.

"I haven't read them myself, but I know a lot of girls who love the books." Ethan propped his chin on a knuckled hand and leaned in. "I'm curious, what is it about the books that you like?"

"I started reading them when a friend told me about the bold sex scenes. At first, I was curious, then I got hooked on them." I felt a flush of heat rising to my face. "I found myself becoming interested in the world of sub/dom sex."

"Do you like the bondage thing?"

The force of his direct question flattened my back against the seat. He wasn't going to let me off with a vague answer. I weighed the risks of revealing my fantasies.

"I haven't really had experience with it, and I can't say I would be into the aspect of pain. However, I am intrigued by the idea of surrendering power to someone I trust. That is of course, if sexual pleasure is the intent."

Did I divulge too much? I scanned his face for a reaction.

"And how about you? Have you had some experience with this?"

Ethan averted his eyes, "Only superficially, but I think there is a certain excitement and freedom in giving up control, for me too. In the right circumstances, of course."

I cocked my head to one side, caught his gaze and asked, "So you wouldn't be opposed to taking control, or maybe being the one to surrender control?"

A sliver of a smile crossed his face and I saw the facade of power slip away for a moment. "Elena, I am always in control, but maybe it would be nice to let go of that sometimes. It is tiring." Then he straightened in the chair as if buttoning his shirt to the neck and tightening a tie. Once again composed, the thin veneer in place.

"Dessert? He asked as the waiter appeared at our table.

"I'm good," I shot him a seductive smile, "I'm more than good right now."

"Oh really? Hmmm, I wish I could take advantage of that tonight. But I will save it for this Sunday."

I sighed with resignation. "Okay, *vamos.*"

The street was nearly deserted when we made our way to the car. It was only around eleven o'clock, but this was life in the suburbs. We strolled side by side down the street when suddenly, Ethan hooked an arm around my waist and pulled me into the dark doorway of a storefront. Fisting his hands in my hair, he swiftly brought his lips to my mouth in a ravenous kiss. A kiss that took my breath away. His body pinned me against the glass doors. He bent his knees and sent his erection sliding against my cleft. Instantly my body responded, and I rocked my hips, the friction stimulating my cleft.

He broke away just as abruptly, leaving me with a gaping mouth and my chest heaving for air. "Well, finally!" I gasped, trying to regain composure.

The corners of his lips turned up in a sexy grin, and his eyes narrowed as he viewed the effect he had on me.

"I'd love to seduce you right here, right now. But you need your sleep."

I looked at him with a sideways glance and shook my head.

"What?" he asked.

"Nothing. Just… You. You never cease to amaze me."

Our eyes locked in a heated gaze. "Ha! Likewise, my girl."

Chapter Nineteen

Time dragged in slow motion until our date on Sunday. As usual, I had no special plans for Friday or Saturday, in contrast with Ethan who seemed to have his evenings booked. My life had become mundane again since returning from Barcelona. With the stress of my job, I had little energy or motivation to even go dancing. Besides, after experiencing life in Europe, there was little that excited me anymore. That is, except for Ethan.

Waking on Sunday morning, the butterflies in my stomach alerted me to the anticipation of seeing Ethan again. He sent a text while I was still in bed, and then again in the afternoon, telling me how he couldn't wait to see me and planting suggestive ideas in my mind which made my arousal climb. With each text alert, I became wet, an automatic response to him.

I followed Ethan up the stairs to his second-story flat and emerged into the softly lit living room. "Wow, you certainly know how to set the mood." The room was aglow from the candles set upon the tables and window ledges. The lamps were dimmed, the sparkling lights of the city illuminating the room through the parted curtains of the bay windows.

"Thank you for coming over to my place again. It's been a crazy few weeks with my cousin's visit and work. I'm looking forward to being with you and relaxing at home for a change." Ethan pulled me into a gentle hug, towering over me by a foot, my head settled onto his chest.

As his body pressed against mine, the familiar heat began to replace the sense of unease I was feeling. *It's been a long four weeks. We've only been together once, I wonder… could it have been just a fluke?*

"Are you hungry? I have some tapas for us."

"I had a late lunch, but I could be tempted." With my arms still locked around his narrow waist, I flashed him one of my seductive smiles.

His eyes widened and a flicker of excitement crossed his face. The palm of his hand slapped against my ass, making me squeal.

"C'mon," he said sternly. He took my hand and led the way to the kitchen.

Walking a step behind, I was rewarded with a view of his backside, clad in dark blue fleece pants that hung low on his hip bones. My eyes fixated on the perfection of his round, muscular buttocks and long legs that looked as good in sweatpants as they did in a pair of tailored slacks. The form-fitting dark t-shirt softly hung against the outline of his exquisitely cut frame. *Jeez, this guy can pull off the casual comfy look and still be sexy as hell.*

I perched on a stool at the wooden counter across from Ethan. Food wasn't really enticing me at that moment, but he had made the effort.

"*Hmm*, what have you got here?"

"I'm keeping the theme going." He pointed to the plate he had prepared. "Spanish cheese, serrano ham, and olives."

"And of course, red wine," he said, opening a bottle of Cabernet

Sauvignon. *"Salud."* He raised a glass, his eyes piercing into mine. Sparks flew as our glasses touched. *Yep, it's still there.*

As we ate our late supper, tapas style, I began to feel more at ease. The jittery feeling subsided when I talked about my rough week at work, though I wasn't really sure how much he was listening. His eyes raked over me, and I saw the fire ignite as he glanced subtly at my cleavage emerging from atop the tight sweater I wore. My choice of clothing wasn't accidental.

"Let's move this party to the living room." Ethan carried the glasses, leading the way. "You up for a movie?"

"If it's not bloody, violent or too crazy. I'm in need of serious de-stress time."

"Yeah, it doesn't sound like your week has gone well. Let's see what we can do about that."

Ethan lifted a blanket off the chair and released my hand when we arrived at the large, overstuffed couch. "Lay down," he directed.

I took the cue, kicked off my shoes, and plopped onto the soft cushions, landing on my back. My mind reflected back to the last time I was on this couch, but somehow, he was different. I couldn't quite put my finger on it, but he was looking at me with warmth—not just lust or flirtation.

"Don't want you getting cold," he said, and he tenderly covered me with the soft chenille blanket.

What? He's taking care of me. Unfamiliar emotions washed over me. *No one has taken care of me... since... I can't remember.*

Ethan stood back and gazed down at my prone figure. "Comfy?"

I pulled the blanket up to my chin, nodded my head and smiled up at him. *Jesus, I feel like a kid at Christmas.*

"Good. Now, can I get in next to you? Make room, woman."

Ethan leaped onto the couch feet first, sinking into the cushions and rocking my body as he fell to my side. Sliding one arm under my shoulder, he snuggled next to me under the blanket.

"Mmm," I purred. Cradled in his arms, the thumping of his

heartbeat filled me with contentment as I laid my head on his chest. The scent of him drew me in, naturally sweet with a hint of freshly washed linen. His chin nuzzled my face, the stubble of his beard rubbed against my forehead when he spoke.

"So, what movie do you want to watch?" With his free hand, he scrolled through the list of movies on the cable channel.

My mood was quickly shifting from *let's get cozy* to something a little more stimulating. *There is no way we are going to get through this movie.* All the neurons in my body were on fire. Our bodies were in full contact and I was pretty sure I wasn't the only one feeling the energy exploding between us.

"Have you seen this one? It just came out. It has good reviews."

I snuggled in closer, my arm draped across his cut abdomen. "Nope. Let's give it a go." The truth was, I could've cared less about what was on the television.

The movie seemed benign enough to tolerate, but the sex scene which began unfolding on the screen made my breath quicken. I was already halfway there, fantasizing about ripping his clothes off when his body shifted under me.

With the subtlety of a teenager on a date in a movie theatre, Ethan slowly reached his hand past my shoulder and cupped my breast. I put my hand on top of his as he gave it a squeeze. Arching my neck to look up, my lips pursed in a teasing smile. "You are distracting me from the movie, you know."

"Am I now? Let's see how distractible you are."

Easily lifting me in the air with his hands on the sides of my torso, he moved my body on top of his. "Arms up." I didn't hesitate as he removed my sweater and then covered me with the blanket.

As I lay face up on his chest, his fingers slid down my bra, my nipples visible as erect points under the cover. His large and sinewy hands began their caress of my heavy breasts, kneading them in a rhythmic motion. I arched my back to raise my chest into his skillful touch.

His long, graceful fingers expertly teased my tender nipples. He pinched the knobs between his thumb and middle finger. With his index finger, he brushed the tips gently in a circular motion. His touch sent waves of electricity through my body, reverberating between my legs. My lips parted to accommodate my heavy breaths, arousal pulsing in my sex. I lost all control when he dipped his fingers in a glass of wine, spreading the liquid on the hypersensitive nerve endings. As he kneaded and pulled on the long erect nipples, he sent air from his lips, accentuating the delicious cool sensation from the moisture.

I lay helpless against his body, my chest heaving. Eyes closed, the sound of voices from the TV faded into the background. I vaguely registered the sound of my own voice, whimpering as my hips churned and rose, in an agonizing need to feel him inside. Dazed by the power he possessed to make me wild, I became lost under his touch.

My breaths came in jagged rasps, "Baby—what are you doing to me?" My body begged for more as his relentless stimulation drove me higher and higher toward a climax in record time—and he was nowhere near my sex. Never in my life had I come so close to an orgasm this way. My core clenched, spasming with his flicks and pull on my nipples.

His voice whispered in my ear. "*Ah,* my sweet... yes... you are getting close, aren't you? Your nipples are incredible, so beautiful. Look how they respond." He rolled the plump, erect knobs between his fingers. Rocking his hips upward in a rhythmic motion, his thick erection flexed against the crease of my bottom.

I gasped, "*yes...*" My hands dug into his muscular thighs and gripped the fabric of his pants. My clit throbbed, so desperate for touch. I reached between my legs and felt the heat rising from under the soaked panties. I stroked the length of my finger between the lips of my sex, craving a release from the sweet tension mounting in my core.

"I need you... inside me," I pleaded, craving him beyond reason.

Ethan rolled me to his side, the length of his body pinned me to the back of the couch. His hands clutched my hair and he brought his lips to my mouth with a powerful desire that rocked me backward. I kissed him back, hungrily devouring his lips, darting my tongue against his.

My hands clawed at his body, wildly maneuvering over his flexed biceps, the hard muscles in his strong back, and down to the firm roundness of his perfect ass. I thrust my hands inside his sweatpants and dug my fingers into his silky skin, forcing his hips forward against my pelvis. Desperate to relieve the burning need, I rocked my sex against the hard ridges of his cock.

"Wait," I cried out, my hands pushing against the tight muscles of his chest, forcing him back. I knew what I needed to do at that moment. It was what I had wanted to do since the first night we met. "Those sweatpants have got to go." Grabbing a hold of the waistband, I tugged the pants down past his groin. Ethan lifted his hips and his engorged cock sprang from under the fabric. He had gone commando, and I didn't take my eyes away from his perfect organ as I wildly stripped off his pants. Seizing the hem of his t-shirt, I slid my hands upward against his sculpted chest and slipped it off over his head. "Better." My breath caught in my throat. *My God, I could worship this body.*

Ethan caught me by the waist and his lips curled into an amused smile. "You amaze me. I love seeing you so excited," he lunged at my mouth in a deep and passionate kiss. "You… are so sexy—so free with me." Tugging the waistband of my skirt, his hands tore at the last remnants of my clothes, freeing my body to press into his flesh.

"I want you, Elena." This time, there wasn't even a hint of doubt in his voice.

He pushed my legs open wide and knelt in the space he made. Open and exposed. I was more than ready. *He can take me any way he wants—just so long as he takes me **now**.*

Wrapping his hand around the base of his cock, he slid the plush crown along the slickness between my outer lips. It reached my engorged clit and I cried out as he flicked it against the tender bundle of nerves. The softness of the head glided along my slick arousal, sending waves of ecstasy with each thrust.

"Jesus… that feels so good… yes… that's perfect." Moving my hips in sync with his rhythm, I tilted my pelvis to bring the strokes to my clit, crying out each time his carved cleft reached the pearl.

Ethan drew in a sharp breath, his eyes gazed down to watch as he guided his cock. His other hand grabbed hold of my breast, his fingers tormenting the sensitive nipples.

I felt my core tightening as the ferocious tension built inside me. He made me desperate enough to beg him shamelessly. "Please... fuck me now."

"Oh, my baby." His eyes locked onto mine. His pupils were dilated and dark. They were like a window and I glimpsed the intense, smoldering place inside him. Within him lay such power, the power to make me beg for him with uncontrollable need. And he knew it, relished it. I could see it in the way he looked at me, the way he skillfully aroused my body until I became a slave to my urges for him.

The weight of his large frame sank onto me. His lips pressed into mine, the softness of his lips and the wild lashing of his tongue sent me spiraling into a mindless frenzy. The crown of his cock aligned with the slick entrance of my body and he pushed into me slowly, each inch of him straining into my walls. My cry reverberated against his lips as he filled the aching emptiness inside. The muscles in my abdomen tightened and clenched around his hardness. "Yes," I hissed, "I need you right there." My arms clutched at his strong back in a feverish desire to hold him close.

"God... Elena," he gasped. "You're so tight... you are driving me crazy." He pressed in further until the full length of him was engulfed.

Writhing my hips under him, the long shaft rubbed against my needy clit with each thrust. Pleasure rippled through me in a rush; my eyelids closed while I absorbed every luscious stroke. The heady mix of the scents that emanated from our heated bodies filled the air. The smell of sex—our combined pheromones combusting.

His breath hissed out between clenched teeth. Pushing my knees up against my chest, he steadied himself for a moment, attempting to gain control. His eyes grew wide—dark and foreboding. The muscles in his face drew tight across his strong jaw. He exhaled deeply, quieting his arousal for a moment. "Not yet."

My chest expanded with the force of each breath. I stilled with him, teetering on the brink. His hands clutched at my breasts, his mouth parted, then poured over each one, sucking and pulling at the tips as if he could never get enough. His hunger flowed over me in a rush. "I… love… your… breasts," he uttered, in words punctuated by the 'pop' of his mouth each time his lips released my swollen nipples.

My muscles clenched around his erection. I couldn't stay still any longer. The deep pulls of his mouth echoed in my core until I thought I would burst. "Please," I begged, and lifted my hips against his pelvis in an agonizing need for friction.

Ethan let out a low deep growl that resonated on my tender flesh. He pounded into me so hard I cried out, partly from the force against my soft walls—but what moved me, was his passion. His desire for me was a powerful aphrodisiac.

Holding onto my raised knee with one hand, he managed a deep but steady pace. The other hand was at my cleft, the pad of his thumb stroking and circling my clit. He watched my face as my mouth parted in sharp pants.

"I want you to come for me. Look at me, baby… look at me when you come."

My eyelids longed to close, but I couldn't tear my gaze away from him, from the searing connection I saw in his face.

"Ah… you're so deep. Don't stop…" My body took him in, exquisitely stretching me to the limit.

The look in his eyes beckoned to me, inviting my release. Rocking my hips, I rode the circling of his thumb and each slide of his cock brought me closer to the edge.

Possessed by his stare, my body convulsed, ravaged by the climax tearing through me. A scream emanated from the very depths, I had lost all control or sense of shame. In wild abandon, my hips met his thrusts and my fingers ripped at his flesh as the waves hit my body over and over.

"Oh, baby… you look so good. I love watching you come for me." He exhaled sharply and his penis jerked as my muscles spasmed around it. His thrusts quickened as he pounded his hips into mine. I could feel him lengthening, becoming more engorged. "Fuck... Fuck!" he yelled as his powerful body stiffened, racing toward his climax.

He growled out my name as he reached the peak, spurting hotly inside me. The sound of his voice, so ragged and erotic, radiated to my core. A convulsive shudder racked his powerful body, the orgasm rolling through him in waves until he sunk heavily on my chest. Sweat misted on his skin and I breathed in the sweet scent of him. Holding me by the nape of the neck, he kissed me softly.

I purred through the kisses. "That... was... nice."

"Nice? Ha!" he snorted. "Nice is a walk in the park. That... was like a megawatt lightning storm."

The TV was dark, somewhere in the process of losing my mind under his touch, he must have switched it off.

"I guess I'm going to have to rent that movie if I want to see the ending," I laughed.

"You were very distractible," he mumbled into my neck. "Not my fault."

My belly bounced against his as I let out a giggle.

"Come." He took my hand and led me into the shower. The warm water stung a bit on my battered sex as he soaped me up. I moaned out a sound of pleasure as his hand began to ignite my arousal again. My hands trailed down his cut abdomen, following the trickle of water until they landed on his erection, still half hard. *Impressive...* I resisted the impulse to stiffen him once more and followed him out of the shower.

He handed over a fresh towel, and we stood in the bathroom mirroring each other while drying off.

"Come here, you're still wet." I took the towel and dried his back. He turned to meet my lips with a quick, hard kiss. "Thanks."

My mind was racing ahead. I wasn't accustomed to staying for a sleepover, and I had no idea what he expected next. Usually, I ran for the safety and solitude of my own bed. Staying the night meant there was intimacy beyond the sex act. This was rare. But with Ethan, I had no desire to leave.

When he headed for the bedroom and said, "Come, let's go to bed," I didn't hesitate. Wrapped in a towel, I followed him into his room, pausing to look at the dresser which showcased the little things that made him real. Small frames held photos of friends and relatives. Cologne bottles with brand names lined up in a row, and natural stone beads laid in a basket.

"What are you thinking?" he asked, seeing me bent over and scanning his stuff.

Flustered, I answered, "Just curious, that's all."

With a cute grin lifting his cheeks, he pulled back the covers, beckoning me into the empty side of the bed and folding his arms around me. Snuggling into his chest, I was filled with a rush of contentment.

I hesitated to ask the burning question that had been on my mind since our first moment of intimacy. But I needed to know. I tentatively spoke, though afraid of what I might learn.

"Hey, just wondering. You didn't sleep with Beth, did you?" I asked with trepidation.

"No," he answered without hesitation. I felt the relief sweep through me.

"What the hell happened that night anyway? I saw her kissing you."

"Oh god, I don't remember much. We were so wasted. But I remember looking over and saw some guy kissing you." Ethan's eyes flashed a sideways glance at me. *So, he was keeping an eye on me that night?*

"I wasn't into him, I was just dancing with him because you had gone off with Beth, and he seized the moment to kiss me. What happened to you, why…?"

"I don't know." He placed a folded arm over his forehead. "Was she a good friend? Because she sure didn't act like it."

"What, did she trash me?"

Ethan was deliberately a little vague. "Well, she wasn't singing your praises. She said something like, 'Who do you want, me—or… her?'"

"Oh." I knew exactly what he meant. Beth had played the age card. That stung, especially because he hadn't chosen me. But how could I blame him? I wasn't the logical choice.

"Anyway… I am very glad that in the end, I am with you." Ethan had the grace to smile and kiss my forehead, wrapping me tightly in his arms. Yet my insecurities about our age difference bubbled to the surface.

He took my hand and placed it on his semi-erection.

"What? You ready for round two? Already?"

He aligned our bodies and pressed his hardening cock against my pelvis, his lips nipping along my neck. His mouth drew me in, meeting mine in a sensuous kiss. My arousal mounted with the lengthening of his erection against my skin.

"I can't help it. With you, I can't get enough."

My eyes squinted in the bright light of the morning as I left Ethan's apartment. Sunshine in the city was a welcome sight. San Francisco was so gorgeous when it was sunny, but I hated those dark, damp days when the fog laid over everything like a dull blanket. On this crisp day, the brilliance of the light bounced off the glass of the tall modern buildings. From atop the steep street, I had a view of the gleaming water and the Bay Bridge, the strong steel structure which connected San Francisco to the East Bay. The ferries were running their usual routes, and sailboats dotted the blue ocean.

"God, it really can be beautiful here," I sighed, reluctant to leave Ethan, but it was a workday for him. I had arranged for a sick day and having slept very little last night, it was a relief that I didn't have to rush into the office.

As I rounded the corner, the smell of coffee drew me into a small cafe. I indulged in the simple luxury of lingering to have breakfast and enjoy the ambiance of the city. Halfway through my bagel and cream cheese sandwich, a text came in from Ethan.

> Hi, hon, thinking of you. You are proving to be a distraction in my workday.

Warmth rushed through me at the sight of his message, and my lips curved into a grin I couldn't contain. I'd seen that giddy grin on girls' faces, staring at their phone with a dreamy-eyed look.

> I think I already distracted you enough. Round three this morning was delicious, but I'm surprised you have any energy left to work.

> Ha. I am fighting the urge to go back to bed. Have you left the city yet?

> No, I'm having a coffee and some food to wake me up before making the drive. But don't get any ideas, I can barely walk today.

> I would love to have the chance to put you in that condition again, very soon, I hope. Last night was... well, it was quite special.

I was sure my face must have lit up like a whole damn Christmas tree. It was just what I needed to hear.

> It was for me too. Never had a night—and morning—like that.

> I'm smiling... Kisses, baby. Drive safe.

I had not felt so happy in a very long time. Now I knew there would be no more waiting anxiously the morning after. Ethan was in. Last night was proof it would just keep getting better. He put a smile on my face that would last for days.

Chapter Twenty

Smiling was not something that came easily once I entered my cubicle and tethered myself to a headset. The following day, I begged to start answering the phones rather than continue pointlessly listening to other's calls as a trainee. And so, the mind-numbing work began.

Making a break for it at exactly one-thirty, I drove down the street for a lunch break at the local Starbucks, perched at the edge of the estuary. Accessing the WiFi, I searched the web for potential jobs. None of which were conveniently located ten minutes from my house. I questioned if I could handle a two-hour commute. Torture. Maybe take a room in a house during the week and come home on weekends? Would I be able to move to Los Angeles? Where the landscape consisted of strip malls and wall to wall traffic? But there was no way I would go back on the front lines of social work with the high stress and lower pay. I drew the line there.

I finished an online application for a management position as a clinical supervisor for the Department of Children and Families, Los Angeles County. I hit "send." Groaning at the prospect, I looked up and saw Gerald, who had escaped at lunch to enjoy the view of the harbor while catching up on his latest book. I caught his eye just as he picked up his latte at the counter.

"Hey, kiddo, fancy meeting you here. Fifty minutes of freedom, right?"

Gerald had become one of my favorite new co-workers. He complained about the job as much as I did. He trudged heavily past my desk numerous times a day to retrieve the print-outs from each call and deposit them in the appropriate basket. I think it was his only source of exercise, except for the brisk walk as he entered the office somewhere between eight-thirty-five and eight-forty-five and made a dash for his desk. Each time he rounded the cubicle dividers, I heard him mumble, "Ah marone." His limited fluency of the Italian language included this useful phrase. My best guess of the translation was, "Damn it." The fact that he verbalized what I was thinking caused me to chuckle every time.

"Yep, Gerald, I am having fantasies of a prison break. Think we can dig out with these plastic spoons?

With a book tucked under his arm and a coffee cup in one hand, he motioned to the empty chair at my table, "Mind if I join you?"

I nodded and closed my laptop. "Please, have a seat."

Gerald took a sip of his hot coffee, momentarily wincing at the burn. "I have another seven years until I can retire and a kid to put through school, or believe me, I'd already have made a break for it. I have no idea how I'm going to make it through."

"Well, I'm not waiting. I've already applied for jobs all over the state. But management positions aren't easy to come by. I know how the system works. They're required to post the position but in actuality, they'll hire from within."

"How'd you end up here anyway? I mean, we needed another clinician. We've been short-staffed for months, but I'm getting that you didn't exactly come back because you missed the work."

"Long story and I only have forty minutes to get back in the door and clock in. In a nutshell, it was political, and I got caught in the fallout. Political correctness is not one of my strong suits. Middle management is like holding the rope in the center in a game of tug-of-war. Supporting my staff meant that I was pulling for the wrong team, at least in the eyes of my dictator boss. In the end, I had two choices. Lose my employment or come back to work here. It was a hell of a shock, believe me."

"Jesus, no wonder you came in scowling. I feel you though. I came in thinking this would be a cakewalk to retirement after burning out in social services. The job was brutal, but at least I had my autonomy. I did whatever the hell I wanted, no one was looking over my shoulder. Now I'm chained to a friggin desk and a system that monitors my every move." He shook his head and used a few Italian hand signals which weren't hard to interpret. "I really didn't know what I was getting myself into. The monotony is a killer, I've lost all motivation. But I find little ways to rebel," he said with a smirk and a glint in his eyes that confirmed my impression that we had a lot in common.

"So, what's your plan?" Gerald had a way of dragging out the vowel sound revealing his Bostonian roots.

"My *plaaan…* is to get the hell outta this place, but I haven't put in enough years to the retirement plan. That's why I am looking for jobs in the public sector so I can keep accruing. I'm chained to this job by the 'golden handcuffs.' Just like everyone else, I'm sticking it out for the pension. What I really want to do is run away from home."

"What, like join the army or something?" He chuckled, "I don't think they are recruiting women of your particular age. Uh, I mean thirty-five-year-olds."

I shot him a look that said, "Don't even go there," but I was already accustomed to his playful jokes.

"No, I want to run away to Europe, Barcelona exactly. I went a few months ago and fell in love with the city. It's a completely different lifestyle there. They don't live to work, like people here. They only work to be able to live. Socialization is a high priority, part of daily life. People are in the plazas for a two-hour lunch in the afternoon and again late into the evening. Drinking wine, talking—instead of being stuck in front of a TV screen after a long-ass commute and even longer workday. It's all about the quality of life, not about material things."

"Oh c'mon, you'd leave your lovely three-walled cubicle and

time clock to drink wine all afternoon in Spain instead of an hour at Starbucks?" Gerald gave me a wink, his arms splayed out in an obvious sarcastic gesture. "Sounds like a dream, but what would you do there? Retire?"

"I have no idea, yet. It's too early for retirement. But I feel like time is slipping away. There's so much of the world I want to see and experience."

"Tell me about it," he scoffed, "We aren't getting any younger."

"I suppose I could sell the house, take the money and run, but I still need an income. I don't know any other work. This has been my life since I was in college. However, this job has obliterated my love for the profession." Sipping the last of my coffee, I gazed out the large windows to the view of the waterway. "Right now, I'm feeling pretty lost, but desperation is a great motivator."

"Well, if you figure it out, clue me in on the secret would ya? For me, it would be Italy. God, it's so picturesque there. I took the family to Florence last year on vacation and I hated to leave. Give me a nice villa in the hills of Tuscany, a view of the vineyards and a fully stocked wine cellar—now *that's* heaven." Gerald's eyes became distant, almost wistful, as he talked about visiting the places where his ancestors lived. "I've thought about taking a year or two leave-of-absence and settling in one of the small villages, but close enough to drive into Florence. However, I don't think the wife will go for it, her career is here.

"How about you? Do you have anything tying you here? Except for the job of course," he said, the haze of the daydream slipping away.

"Actually, not really. My mom is here, but my brother lives right next to her so he can help out. My dad and stepmom are in Northern California. And as for my son, he's on his own, living with his girlfriend." I shrugged my shoulders, "So when I think about it, there's nothing holding me here. It's just that I've lived in the Bay Area all my life. I never expected to ever leave, but life threw me this curveball, so it's got me thinking outside the box."

"Atta' girl, keep the dream alive." He glanced at his watch and groaned, "Crap, it's time to get back to the chain gang." We tossed the cups in the trash and made a dash to our cars.

Though Barcelona was always on my mind, I had been using every spare moment to search for another job and submit applications online. It seemed like the only practical thing to do, given that I'd been working almost my whole life.

Job interviews were challenging. Hell, I hadn't looked for a job in years. So much prep work was involved, even PowerPoint presentations were expected in the modern age of technology. The competition was fierce, and I noticed many younger applicants in the waiting room beside me. The odds were stacked against me. Though I had the experience, the bottom line was that it cost the agencies far less money to hire someone younger. While ageism wasn't legal, it sure was alive and well in the workplace. Having been on the other side of the interview table, I knew the considerations that were discussed but never documented anywhere.

The days droned on, and the lull between calls gave me time to think. What options were there for a woman caught somewhere between midlife and retirement? Staying stuck in the job wasn't an option I'd consider—yet finding new employment at this point in life that would fit my professional goals was not looking good. I couldn't go near any potential jobs in an agency that would put me in the wide-reaching realm of my previous boss. She had effectively locked me out of my career.

"You're scowling again," Jackie said, as she whisked down the hallway, stopping at my desk.

"I am not, it's the look of my perfectly sunny disposition I wear every day when I step into this office." My mouth formed into a forced, toothy smile.

I appreciated Jackie's laugh at my sarcasm, as well as her bubbly nature. Though just as frustrated as the rest of our gang, her cheery voice filled the room, giving me a smile when I needed it the most.

"How do you do it? I mean, you've been here a long time and you still manage to sound like you give a damn when you are on a call."

"Oh, honey, I am counting the days until I can retire and if I didn't have a team of some good people to work with, I think I'd lose it. Some days are harder than others, but I really have no choice. I have a family depending on me. But I chose to be here, your story is entirely different."

The ring of my phone interrupted our conversation. I rolled my eyes and Jackie sprinted back to her cubicle.

"Good afternoon, my name is Elena. How can I help you?"

A worker from social services barked her request, asking me to process yet another referral for an abusive parent whose four children had been removed from her custody.

"Each child needs their own referral for therapy as well as the mother," she stated.

I asked all the relevant questions and looked up the history in my database.

"These referrals have been processed three times already and they have never actually made it to a therapy office. The last expired three months ago."

"That's why I'm calling, I know they've expired, and the judge has extended the order." Her voice resonated with annoyance—probably with the system but at that moment it was with *me*—for questioning *her*. All I could think about was the time it was going to take to process those referrals again. A pointless, useless task. I didn't care anymore. Not about the work, not about the clients. They were anonymous and disembodied. Mere names and data on multiple forms. I used to actually help people, but I no longer felt any purpose in the work I was doing.

The realization came crashing down on me, so weary from the battle to hold onto what was familiar. My identity was wrapped up in my profession, and I was losing everything that defined me. I had to face it—no longer did I have the same motivation to practice in my beloved field. The enthusiasm that propelled my career when I was young, had dissipated over the years. Ultimately, it died a mortal death with the transfer.

The realization was a rude awakening. I was a professional woman without a direction at a point in time when I should be cruising to retirement. There was never a doubt in my mind about what I would do with my life, but at this point, I had hit a wall and had no idea what was on the other side. When I was happily secure in the management position, I didn't foresee that I would be faced with the challenge of reinventing myself while others were counting the days until they could collect a pension. But at that moment, it felt right to call it. Game over. I was done.

Barcelona had changed me. At once it dawned on me, if I had to reinvent myself, why not go big? I searched the web looking for ideas on becoming an expat in Europe. I had so many questions. Was it even possible for me as an American to live abroad? Living in a place where I could barely speak the language seemed daunting. I wondered if I could really leave all that was familiar. It was boring as hell, but my safety-net was in California. It was all I'd ever known. But something was driving me head-on, into the unknown. Ethan had called it. I needed more.

He traveled to Europe frequently, straddling the two worlds. If anyone knew how it could be done, it would be him. I decided to pick his brain for information. It was in the middle of his workday, but I hoped he wouldn't mind an email. After all, he did say I could count on him for help.

Hey, babe, I'm drowning here in boredom. There doesn't appear to be a lot of options for me, so I've been thinking more about how I can live in Barcelona, at least part time. I have to get out of here. What's the deal with living abroad, how do you manage to go in and out of the country so much?
Ps; the other night with you put a smile on my face for days.

No sooner had I placed my phone on the desk, I heard the ping of his response.

Hi, hon, nice timing. I was just thinking about you. Very stimulating thoughts… But as for your question, you can be in the Schengen countries for 3 months, then you have to be out for 3 months before you can go back. I go in and out of non-Schengen countries, so the time doesn't count. But you can apply for a visa to live there, I'm just not sure of the process. You are really thinking about it?
Ps; our last time together was incredible, even better than the first!

> *Yes, I'm seriously thinking about it, but not sure yet how I will make it happen. You've inspired me about Barcelona - and in other ways as well ;-) Thinking about you always stimulates me, which is inconvenient since I'm at work.*

Oh, baby... I wish you were here right now. You're making me hard, and I have to go into a meeting. Damn. You have this effect on me. I have some ideas for when we see each other. Are you free this Saturday?

> *There's no one else I'd rather be with. I can't wait until Saturday. Until then, sweet and lascivious thoughts of you…*

Ethan left me with a kissy-face emoji, a serious throb between my legs, and once again, the grin I was grateful to have radiating on *my* face.

Chapter Twenty-One

I woke late on Saturday morning with a smile and languished under the soft down comforter with vague recollections of a dream about Ethan. Bits and pieces floated into consciousness. His warm skin pressed against my back, cuddling me in a spooning position. Except for Ethan, there had been no one to cuddle with for a very long time. My bed wore the one-sided indentation of a single woman. I always felt as if I was rolling up a steep hill if I ever ventured to the other side of the king-size bed. My only companion was the tiny, spaniel mix pup, who slept nestled against my leg. A part-time pet who spent weekdays with my ex. Nate had come up with the idea to adopt another dog, long after the divorce. He meant well, but a dog was not the companion I needed on those lonely nights. Toby looked up at me with eyes that shimmered like dark pools, seemingly too big for his tiny face. While he stretched in his version of downward facing dog, I got the hint. It was time to get up.

Scooping him in my arms, I rubbed my cheek against his soft golden fur. "You, my pup, are going to your Dad's today. I have a date with Ethan and he definitely beats spending another weekend at home on dog duty. No offense." Toby cocked his tiny head and raised an eyebrow as if he registered my words.

A sweeping view of the bay waters came into sight from my vantage point on the bridge, the drive into the city only marred by the annoyance of sitting in traffic. Weekends and commute times were the worst, as thousands of cars hit the road and jammed their way into the main conduit to San Francisco from the East Bay. After I managed to squeeze my four-door sedan into a parking space that was clearly meant for a compact car, Ethan texted me to wait for him, a taxi was on the way to pick us up.

It was a perfect afternoon to be in the city, and I had been looking forward to this day all week. As we made our way by taxi to the seafront, I was again taken with the beauty of the city. The sun's rays blanketed San Francisco with a brilliance that made even the dingiest of buildings look lovely. The air had the crystal clarity of a crisp December day. We got out near Fisherman's Wharf and leisurely walked toward the piers along the seafront. Fishermen unloaded their catch, and Dungeness crabs were piled in stacks, awaiting their fate in the boiling pots. The smell of steamy crustaceans and the salty sea hung heavy in the air, despite the brisk sea breeze.

As we made our way to the Ferry Building, the famous clock tower loomed tall from the center. The building's long corridors bustled with locals and tourists who came for the farmer's market or the many shops and seafood restaurants. This day, the sun's rays shimmered through the glass on the high vaulted ceilings. We landed in an oyster bar at Ethan's suggestion. It was brightly lit with light shining through the floor to ceiling windows, and we had a front-row view of the bay. The rectangular bar made of stainless steel gleamed in the bright spotlights set in tracks on the high ceiling. We ordered a dozen to start, of all different kinds. Along with a bottle of wine and sourdough French bread, I was in heaven.

Ethan's leg nuzzled against my thigh under the table while we watched the chef wield a large knife, separating the mollusks from their shell. The white linen tablecloth hid the view of this simple sign of intimacy.

"I can't believe you've never had raw oysters before!"

"Another first, with you. You seem to be introducing me to a lot of adventures." I looked up at him through my eyelashes and found him grinning back at me.

I tipped my head back as I brought the oyster to my mouth and tilted the shell in one swift movement, sending the slippery delicacy onto my waiting tongue. I licked the salty taste from my lips and Ethan's mouth parted as he drank in the sight of my pleasure.

"Yum, you're right, they're delicious." I proceeded to plunge the tips of each finger in my mouth, slowly, one by one as I sucked the juices that had spilled. The look on Ethan's face as he watched was priceless.

"Do you remember the conversation we had about bondage? Ethan jolted me with the sudden change in conversation.

"Yes, at the restaurant. We were talking about the book."

"I've been thinking of some ideas, for us. If you are willing, of course."

"So, what are you trying to say? You are asking me to be your submissive?

Ethan raised his hand while making a *shushing* sound. He scanned the other patrons seated close by to make sure we weren't being overheard. But everyone seemed to be chattering in conversations.

"Not exactly, no." He looked away and paused, his brow furrowed as he calculated his words. "It's about you, letting go, and trusting me to pleasure you. I want to explore all your desires." His gaze was piercing and hot as he confided, "It's you. I'm stunned at how free you are with me, at how I feel when I'm with you. There are no limits with us."

I squirmed in my seat, arousal brewing. Ethan's desire for me was intoxicating. My mind flashed to the times we had been intimate. How his power and force had ignited something in me. Something I had never experienced before. With him, I relished being taken, possessed, dominated. The idea of being restrained just magnified by a thousand the anticipation of what the evening might bring.

"Okay, you have piqued my interest." I felt flushed already from my body's involuntary response to him. "But no crazy stuff, like degrading or pain. Well, a little pain is okay." My eyes cast down with inexplicable embarrassment, "I did like when you spanked me," I said in a soft voice.

I looked up and saw the warmth of a smile radiating on his face. The back of his fingers stroked the side of my cheek and I tilted my head, leaning into the caress. "My girl, you are so willing with me. I love it. I'm going to make you come so hard," he whispered in my ear in a deep, seductive voice that rippled through my body. "I want you bound, wet and quivering when I touch you."

"You've already made me wet, so one down," I said, as a breath hitched in my throat.

The ride back to his place was, thankfully, short. Sparks flew with a simple brush of his pant leg against my calf. I saw the acknowledgment in his face as he turned to look at me, his lips formed a suggestive smile when he ran his fingers through my hair. Ethan hurriedly paid the taxi driver and with a brusk "Thanks, man," we were through the front door of his apartment and up the stairs.

Freed from the public eye, Ethan scooped me into a fierce embrace. Holding me by the nape, his soft lips began their seduction as his tongue danced playfully in my mouth. His kisses made my knees buckle, my hands held onto the back of his head, gliding along the stubble of the parts recently shaved. Abruptly, I broke away, my lips wet and softened from his kisses. "Now what?"

Ethan smirked and ran a hand across his hair. "Always so impatient."

At once, I realized that he needed to be in charge. Nerves compelled *my* need to be in control. My thoughts raced, *how is this ever going to work? We both want the power, how do I let go of that?* I stepped back from him a few paces as the realization set in. It took about a nanosecond for him to sense what I was thinking. Taking my hand, he interlaced his fingers in mine. His eyes softened as he gazed at my uncertain face.

"Elena, do you think I would ever hurt you or make you do anything you didn't want to? I won't push you past what you can handle. We'll take it slow."

I looked up from under lowered lids, and nodded, "I trust you."

With dark eyes, slowly, he moved toward me and pinned me to the wall, imprisoning me with his body. I felt the force of his grip as his fingers tightened around my wrist. First one and then the other, binding them together above my head with one hand. The other hand found the soft skin of my belly and slid inside my jeans, his mouth pouring over mine, hungrily invading me with his tongue. His fingers hit their target. There was no concealing that my excitement had already built. He made long, sensuous strokes along the slick sensitive tissues, inserting one finger inside while his thumb brushed rapidly over my clit.

My breathing quickened and I moaned into his mouth, darting my tongue to meet the lashing of his. The seduction was made more intense by my immobility—there was no denying it. I melted into him. No thoughts, just delicious sensations driving me higher and higher, my hips thrusting into his hand.

He already knew my body well. When he felt the tissues of my sex swell with the impending climax… he stopped.

"No, please," I panted. My body begged for the release from the aching tightness inside me.

"Not yet. I will arouse you in every way I can think of to pleasure you before I let you come."

Slumping into his arms, I was already spent from the exhilaration— every muscle in my body clenched in preparation.

Ethan guided me into his bedroom. "Get undressed, I'm going to get something, and I'll be right back." It was more than a request. The demand in his tone told me that we were heading into new territory.

He arrived as I removed the last of my clothes, holding a chair from the dining room and a long, white rope, appearing to be a half-inch thick.

"Sit here," he commanded. My bare feet skimmed the hardwood floor as I self-consciously moved across the room before him. My naked bottom found the seat he had covered with a towel, which quickly became noticeably darkened by the wetness he had generated just moments before. Desire replaced uncertainty, but the anticipation was driving me crazy. It occurred to me, that it was all a part of his plan.

Ethan pulled my hands to the back of the chair and twisted the ropes, tying my wrists together. He worked swiftly, and in moments, I couldn't move. While I was focused on my hands, he moved to the front of the chair and bound each ankle to the chair legs. Ethan stood back to admire his handiwork. Arms crossed, his lips formed a satisfied smile as he scanned my body.

"How do you feel?"

"The rope is soft enough, so it doesn't really hurt, but damn, you know how to tie knots. I can't budge."

He leaned in and kissed me gently. "That is the point, my girl."

Ethan dimmed the lights, ignited candles around the room, and chose some soft ethereal music.

"I'll be back in a second."

"What? Where are you going? You're just going to leave me here like this?"

I heard his velvet laughter coming from the kitchen. He reappeared with a glass of red wine, placing the rim of the glass on my lip. A few drops spilled as I drank, cascading down my neck and onto my breast. His eyes followed the trail. Without hesitation, he bent his head to my breast, and his broad tongue ran against my flesh from nipple to neck, soaking in the wine. I arched into his mouth, the warmth of his tongue igniting the fire within me once again.

Slowly, precisely, he undressed. Just out of reach, he stood a few feet in front of my bound body, revealing his perfect form and mouth-watering chocolate brown skin I had come to adore. He raised the soft knit sweater up over his head, teasing me with a view of the defined muscles rippling against his t-shirt. Spellbound, my eyes traced the outline of his etched form, from his broad shoulders down to the bulging biceps. His jeans hung low on his hips, and as he removed his shirt, my eyes drifted to the V that was his waist and the cut edges of the muscle at the hip bones. A sudden breath hitched in my throat as he unbuttoned his jeans and I fixed my eyes on the outline of his long erection, pressing sideways against his black boxer briefs. I gazed down to his equally muscular thighs and calves, as he stripped off his pants. Watching the show before me, my lips parted, and my breath left me in a shaky exhalation. His thumbs slid under the waistband of his briefs, slowly forcing them down, revealing his narrow hips and freeing his steeled organ to spring out in all its glory. *"Mmm,"* I purred, *he is a sight to behold.* The look on his face told me that he knew exactly the effect he had on me.

"You're doing this to torture me, aren't you? Since I am sitting here, unable to touch you." My expression must have looked somewhere between a pout and a grin, so frustrated and aroused at the same time.

"Shush… close your eyes," Ethan instructed. As my lids closed, a chill ran down my spine. Vulnerability and anticipation coursed through me with a rush, making my palms sweat and my heart race. And then, I sensed him on my skin. I felt his warm breath on my cheek as he brushed his stubbled chin from my face down to my chest. His body moved in closer, cupping my heavy breasts in each hand, squeezing hard. I heard his knees strike the floor with a *thud.* My breath came in a sudden inhalation as his mouth began the assault, warm and wet on my skin. He devoured each breast, one and then the other, with lips that sucked on the roundness of my flesh.

"Ah, my girls," he breathed, claiming each one with audible delight. His mouth puckered, and drew in the sensitive nipples, making a popping sound as he released. In that moment, I relinquished all control. My head rolled back against the chair, surrendering to the ecstasy. Each suck, nip, and bite on my tender flesh sent waves of pleasure to my core. With eyes shut tight, I focused on the sound of him, his low growl tingling my flesh. I loved the way he took such pleasure from my body—owning me, as I sat bound.

I gasped, as I felt the tip of his finger reach my waiting clit, so desperate for his touch. I longed to open my eyes to look at him, to see what he was feeling. Instead, I kept them closed, anticipating the next sensation.

The bite of his teeth stung my tender nipples, making me clench at the touch of his finger, gliding past the slick opening of my sex. An involuntary moan escaped from my lips as he rhythmically massaged that sweet spot, deep inside. My bottom writhed in the chair—the combination of pain mixed with pleasure driving me higher. His mouth was relentless, alternately biting and teasing my nipple with quick lashes of his tongue. My breaths came in shallow gasps, signaling to Ethan that I was on the brink again. He stopped short.

"*No*, not again!" I opened my eyes to see him standing in front of me, his eyes smoldering and hot.

"Savor it, baby... patience."

Planting himself a foot away from me, his thick cock was rock hard and just out of reach. I ran my tongue seductively over each parched lip and peered up at him, my steamy eyes enticing him to enter my mouth.

Silently, he closed the gap between us, his legs parted as his feet planted on either side of the chair. The plush crown of his cock teased at my lips. Grabbing a handful of my hair, he guided his erection into my hungry mouth. He moved his hips slowly at first, gliding past my lips while I used my tongue to dart and stroke with every penetration.

I lapped at the ridges, the bulging veins. Greedily devouring him as he pounded faster and faster, I heard my reward in the ragged sound of his voice as he became more engorged. "Jesus... Elena... ah." He pushed deep to the back of my throat and my mouth engulfed him down to the root. I came up gasping for air when he released his hold on my head, but I wasn't done. He was close, I tasted the salty liquid pouring from the slit. I puckered around the plush head, sucking him in. With a sharp cry, he pulled away. A look of amazement spread across his face as he gazed down at me. Cupping my cheeks in his hands, his eyes warmed.

"My girl." He pressed his forehead against mine and relaxed into me with sweet tenderness. The contrast stunned me. In one moment, he moved from powerful lust to pure intimacy. With a deep sigh, he kissed my forehead before releasing me. "Let's get you out of this chair, I need you." His fingers worked quickly to untie the slip knots, and in a moment, I was free. I curled into his strong arms as he lifted me easily out of the chair and carried me to the bed.

Tenderly, his graceful hands moved over my body, soothing the soreness. One finger tipped up my chin to meet his face. "Thank you... for trusting me." My smile met his lips in a soft kiss. "Only for you, baby... only you," I said, tracing his cheek with the back of my finger.

Something had changed, I felt a shift rippling between us. A door had been opened and there was no telling what was on the other side.

"I need to take care of my girl," Ethan said, as he pulled my ankles apart and brought his head between my legs. "Hold your arms above your head and don't move them." I complied without hesitation, sprawled out naked, quivering with need. His broad tongue lapped at the wetness of my sex and teased the length of the fleshy tissue inside the slit. With a low growl that reverberated through my body, he greedily sank his tongue inside me, sending waves of exquisite pleasure against the hypersensitive nerve endings.

Mindlessly, I whimpered soft cries as my hips churned and raised off the bed to meet his mouth. The laps of hot velvet flicked and circled across my swollen clit. I was lost to the magic of his mouth, my fingers twisting in the sheets as I held them above my head.

"Oh baby, your pussy is so wet and swollen, do you want to come?" His voice lilted with the erotic tease. He was in control. He could leave me on the edge or give me what I needed with a flick of his tongue.

"Oh God, yes..." I hissed, my eyelids pressed tight, "I need to come." Every muscle was clenched and aching for release.

He nudged the knob with the tip of his tongue and puckered his lips, swirling and sucking until it sent me to that sweet precipice. "Please... don't stop..." The intensity of the orgasm jolted through me like an explosion, built from his diabolical teasing. A tangle of emotions left me both screaming and crying simultaneously as I found my release. His tongue thrust relentlessly inside, prolonging the climax to roll on and on. My body wildly convulsed as his mouth rode the spasms.

Tears tracked down my cheeks, overwhelmed by the pleasure and the freedom that I felt with Ethan alone. This man rocked my world.

I felt myself helplessly falling for him, tumbling down a hill out of control. The exhilaration was matched equally by the terror.

My breaths came in jagged gasps, pleading, "Come here, now, I need you."

Pulling me hard to the edge of the bed, he possessed my body. His eyes blazed down at me, leaning in, his mouth poured over mine. He kissed me with a hunger that made me crazy with desire. Cradling his head in my hands, I could taste the subtle scent of my arousal on his face as his tongue darted in my mouth.

With one swift motion, his body flattened over mine, his steely erection easily sliding into me, along the slickness of my flesh. A whimper escaped me in a rush of air as he filled me with the connection I craved. I wrapped my legs around his hips, inviting his hard thrusts. The orgasm still reverberating, my tissues swollen and hot, I thrashed my hips wildly to bring him deeper. Ethan's breath gusted on my neck each time he reached the end of me. I cried out when his teeth bit hard against my throat. The moan he sent into my skin made me quiver.

"No, not yet," he rasped, his body rigid—pulsing in an agonizing battle to delay his ascension.

In measured strokes, he slowed his pace. He withdrew, the crown poised at the entrance to my body, quieting for a moment. Then with his eyes blazing at mine, he speared into me, sinking deeper than before. His face pulled taut over his rugged jawline, sucking in air through gritted teeth with each plunge. Over and over, he held himself steady and paused before torturing me with his thick, rigid cock. Each time, I cried out from his withdrawal and the rush of penetration as the silky head pushed past my entrance into the depths. My whimpers and his low guttural moans filled the room. Nothing else in the world existed in those moments, apart from the heady feeling of each luscious stroke along my slick walls.

At once, his pace quickened into a steady, relentless tempo. His eyes grew wild with fierce abandon he raced toward the edge. With one hand, he seized my breast. The other was at my neck, gripping me with a firm hold and pressing me to the bed. His possession of my body ignited something deep within me. My eyes did not move from his steady gaze. I arched my hips higher to meet his heavy surge, urging him on. Just when I felt him swell, I tightened around his lengthening cock. My flesh began to burn with the heat of another orgasm building.

"Elena… ah… it's too good… I can't stop. You are pulling it out of me. Baby… you are going to make me come so hard."

His eyes widened, wild with need. He shifted, clutching my hands above my head. With our fingers laced, he pounded hard, slamming against my clit and sending me over the edge. The orgasm jolted me into uncontrollable spasms. I came with a sharp cry and he was right there with me. His cock jerked, and the climax shuddered through his body. "Oh—Elena… *Fuck!*" his voice bellowed in a primal scream as he spilled into me. The satisfaction was mine. Hearing the powerful orgasm overtake him, I knew that in that moment, he was as much mine as I was his.

I don't know how long we lay wrapped in each other's arms, our breathing slowly returning to normal. "Jesus," he groaned, his body heavy as he rolled and splayed out on the bed. "My God, woman." His arm hooked my waist and brought me to his side. Resting my chin on his chest, I felt so complete, so satiated.

I hated to break from his grasp, but I stood on wobbly legs and zigzagged to the bathroom. Standing in front of the mirror, I caught sight of my breasts. *Holy crap!* They were marked with numerous bruises—hickeys everywhere his lips had sucked on the round flesh. Sliding back into bed, I held my breasts in front of his face and pointed to the marks.

"Just look! You marked me and made me yours, didn't you now?" His face broke out in a wide smile, and he pulled me down on top of him. Stroking my hair, he leaned in to kiss me. "You are mine, Elena."

My eyes flickered open as the morning light streamed in through the almost sheer blue curtains. The other side of the bed was cool to the touch. My fingers felt their way across the sheets even before I could register that Ethan was not in his place next to me. The bedroom door was closed, and the sound of classical music drifted through the apartment. I wobbled to my feet and grasped my head with both hands. *Oh... way too much wine last night.* I pulled out a black satin robe from my backpack and wrapped it around me as I moved toward the door. Turning the knob slowly, I peeked down the hallway and heard the melodic sound of stringed music emanating from the living room.

Following the sound of the chords, my bare feet padded down the hall. I silently watched Ethan, his godlike body clad only in his underwear, he held a violin against his chin. His eyes were closed, playing the notes from memory. Those long, sinewy fingers moved in graceful motion along the neck of the instrument. He looked as stunning as the sound of the music he created, his face reflecting the emotion of the piece. A stark contrast from the mask he wore to the world of confidence and command. Sensing my presence, he stopped short.

"That was lovely, what is the piece called?"

"Bach Partita in E. Sorry if I woke you, I didn't mean to. You were sleeping so peacefully."

"Do you usually play first thing in the morning?"

"Sometimes, when I need to quiet my mind. It relaxes me." Ethan turned to place the instrument in its case.

"So, you have something on your mind?"

Ethan wrapped his arms around me and sighed heavily, murmuring out a low sound. He buried his face in my hair. "You, Elena. You are on my mind," he breathed, nuzzling a stubbled cheek against mine.

"What are you doing to me, Elena? I don't know what it is, but I can't leave you alone. It just feels so right with you."

There was something in his voice that was different. It was solemn, needy even. He was struggling and I wanted to know why, so I waited. Instead of an explanation, I felt his erection building, pressing into my pelvis. The tone of his voice changed in an instant. I heard the familiar low growl of seduction against my ear.

"Speaking of... now that you're awake, let's take advantage of the time we have. I've got a soccer game this afternoon."

Ethan untied my robe and his fingertips caressed my skin, making a path from my neck to my nipples. They puckered, the long points becoming round and firm under his touch. He scooped me in his arms, and I laid my cheek on his chest as he carried me to the bed. Conversation could wait, I already knew that he would discuss things when he felt ready.

I emerged from the shower and pulled on a pair of jeans and a t-shirt. The smell of food cooking drew me to the kitchen where I found Ethan standing over the gas stove, spatula and frypan in hand.

"Good morning," he said, puckering his full lips on mine in a quick kiss.

"God I'm hungry. What's for breakfast?"

Ethan slid an omelette onto a plate and placed it in my hands then carried his plate to the high table. Patting the stool, he motioned me to join him.

Perched on bar stools in the sun-drenched kitchen, we devoured our breakfast. I stopped between bites, "You... are a man of many talents. I've been pleasured all night and morning, serenaded with the violin and now treated to breakfast. What more could a girl ask for?" I teased him with a smile as my hand caressed his thigh.

"I wanted last night to be special." Ethan looked down and avoided my eyes. "I'm going back to Barcelona this week. I have a wedding to go to, some friends are getting married."

My mood instantly took a nosedive. "Oh. How long will you be gone?"

"Not sure, probably about three weeks. I'll make my rounds to see friends in Sweden, Belgium, and travel a bit. I have some business in London, and I'd like to see Venice."

He moved his fork aimlessly around his plate and shifted a little on the stool. "Some of my friends are already married and having kids. I'm not sure what's wrong with me, I've never even been engaged. I mean, I've had long term relationships, but I've just never been motivated." Ethan glanced up from his plate. His face softened, and his eyes warmed with a melancholy sweetness.

"Except... you came into my life. I've never been so motivated to be with someone. But..."

His unfinished sentence hung heavy in the air between us.

"You want kids though, right?" My face fell into a neutral expression, belying the anxiety raging within me.

"Yes, I think three kids. But at the rate I'm going, I'm not sure I'll get there."

"Well, you have plenty of time." Suddenly my appetite had evaporated. I hopped off the stool and carried my dish to the sink. The bubble we had been encased in burst open, and I felt reality like a hard slap across my face. Pushing back the thoughts that would release the dam of emotions, I escaped down the hall into the bedroom and packed up my overnight bag.

We stood in the doorway, our arms locked around each other. Ethan nuzzled his face in my hair before tipping my head back to plant a soft kiss on my lips. His index finger pushed back the strands of hair from my face and he looked at me with solemn eyes.

"I will miss you in Barcelona. Believe me, I wish that we could be there together."

I blinked to stop my eyes from the inevitable flow. "I will miss you too. It's going to be so hard to be here when you are back there."

Ethan saw the look in my eyes and shifted to a more positive tone.

"Hey, soon you will be back there too, and besides, I will keep in contact." He took my face in his hands. "I'll be back in a few weeks to see you."

I held it together until I reached the car. Opening the door handle released the flood. Our time together was limited. I had pushed that back into the recesses of my mind, but his words had forced it front and center. I'd selfishly hoped that our closeness had changed him, given him a new direction with me. But he was on his own journey, one which couldn't include me. In an instant, everything could change. I could choose to walk away and avoid diving into the deep end of the pool where the pain would surely drown me. But playing it safe would rob me of the time we could share. Making the choice to stay the course, keep rolling the dice, and leaving my fate to chance was not the smartest decision. The power was not mine unless I picked up my chips and cashed in. Leaving the table with a win. But like a reckless gambler, I would stay in the game. If he only knew, he didn't need ropes. I was already bound by him.

As best I could, I prepared myself for the inevitable, steeling myself not only for three weeks without him, but for what the future would hold.

Chapter Twenty-Two

December's cold was not the only thing that chilled me to the bone. Our last conversation reverberated in my mind on a daily basis. I wondered about what Ethan was doing while he was in Europe, or more specifically, who he was seeing. *Was he still dating that girl I saw him with?* We had no binding contract, though it was clear he wanted to claim me. But he was as impossible to pin down as a wild horse.

So, I did what I had to do to keep myself from being that *needy girl,* the kind who sits at home waiting for the text or email. It wasn't that I didn't have the urge to email him a dozen times a day, but I curtailed my impulse. I needed a diversion.

I left my profile up on the dating sites and continued to search for guys within an *age-appropriate* range. But there was no denying I was already hooked on that stallion. How could anything or anyone compare?

My dating life in the suburbs had consisted of countless tedious first dates from online sites. Most often the first date was the last. It was an entirely different world than the one I'd left before getting married. Online sites had changed the dating scene. It was like placing an order on Amazon. What looked good from the description, turned out to be something completely different when the package arrived. So, back it went on the shelf since there were always twenty or more like it to try. I had learned to be thick-skinned in the disposable world of dating, but the learning curve had been painful.

Before I had met Ethan, there were a couple of guys who were on my occasional date circuit. I called them BTNs. Better than nothing. We enjoyed each other's company and the sex was decent, but there was something missing. I wondered if I was the problem, always attracted to wild ones—the alpha males. Like a moth to a flame, it was unavoidable, and it always combusted. I had little interest in the nice, average, suburban, American male. But when John called to invite me out, I accepted. It seemed better than sitting home alone thinking about Ethan.

I drove the familiar highway to his house on a Friday evening, deep in the heart of California suburbia. The upscale town reeked of money. The status symbols of expensive cars and ridiculously large opulent homes were the norm. As he held open the door of his Porsche for me, he gave me a quick kiss.

"It's good to see you again. You look gorgeous, as always." His bright eyes sparkled at me. I smiled and returned the compliment. John really did look handsome. At fifty-something, he was in great shape, always dressed well, and smelled good. My physical attraction for him may have been diminished by his lack of height, but he had all the qualities on most women's checklists.

"I would love to hear about your trip to Barcelona. From your Facebook posts, it looked fantastic."

I hesitated before answering, censuring my words. "It was an amazing city with so much to do and see. You would have loved the architecture and artwork. It was so exciting to be back in Europe again and honestly, it's hard to return here to the same old thing."

"Well, I hope that comment doesn't reflect on spending the evening with me." He smiled and gave me a sideways glance while he drove with one hand on the wheel, the other on my knee.

"No, of course not. I always have a good time with you. But you have to admit, the Bay Area can be a bit dull at times. Don't you get tired of going to the same bars and restaurants year after year?"

"It's home, my friends and family are here, but I'd like to have more time to travel abroad, no doubt."

"So, what have you been up to?" I asked, deliberately changing the subject.

"Oh, you know, the same old thing," John laughed. "But I have joined the campaign to support the Republican candidate for the Senate race," he informed me, grinning when he saw the look on my face. "Bet you didn't see that coming."

It was useless to hide my surprise, but then I thought about how it fit for him. Our political differences were roadblocks in developing a serious relationship. Me, passionate about my liberal views and him, quite serious in his conservative beliefs. His character was impeccable, but we were not an easy fit.

John held my hand as we walked through the town's Christmas Fair. I couldn't help noticing that there were a lot of women stopping to greet him. He was clearly one of the most popular bachelors in town.

We followed the crowds to one of the favorite pubs on Main Street. Live rock and roll music was blaring in the tiny space. John edged his way to the bar and came back with our drinks.

Placing a cocktail in my hand he asked, "Do you want to dance?"

I cringed. "I can try, but this music is not my thing."

"I know, it's not salsa music." He gave me a wink and put his arm around my shoulder. "We can go after you finish your drink."

We both knew I'd come back to his house at the end of the evening. He had been a gentleman when we met. It had taken a handful of dates before he had brought me to his bed. Since then, sex had been a part of our routine. But he surprised me with his seduction on this night, undressing me in the kitchen, kissing me from my neck all the way down to my sex, before bending me over the sink and taking me from behind.

We finished in his king-size, elegantly decorated bed. But first, he had to remove the ten color-coordinated pillows. I had trouble with the idea of dating a guy who kept an immaculately clean home, and whose sense of decor was far better than mine. He had skills in the bedroom though, and I never left unsatisfied. But the ingredients that made for passion just never materialized. And as we made love, all I could think about was Ethan. When I closed my eyes, I imagined how excited he made me with just a touch. How he'd drive me wild with desire, the passion overcoming us both. And when I reached my orgasm, it was Ethan's name I was screaming in my head.

John caressed my skin and settled in beside me to sleep. He invited me to stay the night, but as always, I dressed and kissed him goodbye. On the drive home I realized that nothing would ever be the same since Ethan. *I'm ruined. What the hell am I going to do?*

Ethan had taken me to new heights, but there was no telling how long he would be in my life. I loved how free I could be, only with him. It seemed pointless to be with anyone else.

OVER A WEEK went by without hearing a word from him. Finally, I couldn't resist sending an email to make sure everything was okay. I kept it simple.

> *Hey, how are you and how's your trip going?*

I stared at the computer more intently every day, as if willing it to produce a response from him. A few days went by and my anxiety was building. I had fallen into the needy trap, dammit.

His response appeared one night while I was at home working on my laptop, giving me the relief I needed.

> *Hey, girl! I just got back to civilization from a rustic house in the north of Spain and now have reception. I thought of you, as well. I can't wait to be with you again. You have ruined it for the rest of them…*
> *I'm coming over soon after I get back. What would you like*

to do? Let's plan a date. I'm off to Italy tomorrow. Talk soon.
Going to watch a Barca game now!
Bye, hon. Be good.

My response time did not fit the standard dating protocol. That is, wait—don't appear too anxious. I fired off a message and hit 'send.'

> *Hey, hon, so glad you are fine and I'm on your mind. So, I ruined it for the rest of them huh? Good! I will admit you've had the same effect on me, without a doubt. You'd better be over when you return... jet lag or not.*
> *Regarding our date, I have some ideas... You, under the Christmas tree. That would be a memorable present.*
> *Bye, babe, be good too*
> *(yours truly,*
> *in restraints)*

His emails came more frequently, keeping me posted on the highlights of his trip. I opened my browser at least ten times a day, anxiously anticipating any communication that would validate he was really coming back to me. He was my crack cocaine. I was addicted and going through withdrawals. His next email fueled my addiction.

Was in The Born today looking at apartments to buy.
   Thought of my girl...

"*My girl...*" My heart warmed, and I thought it might glow right through my skin. *Was I his girl? Was he mine? And what did he mean "be good?" Did he expect fidelity? And what about him, who else was he sleeping with?*

This was torture. It was both exhilarating and exhausting. Standing on the edge of a cliff, I felt more alive than I had in a very long time. I was on fire just thinking about him. It drove me to do something rare, for me at least. Admittedly, a deliberate move to keep his interest focused in the same direction. The selfie I sent of his beloved *girls* did the trick. His response was swift.

OMG! They are so perfect. That pic is creating an obvious effect on me. Can't wait to see you, I've really missed you.

In the world of this new dating game, I'd learned quickly that men are visual creatures. His words did it for me, I hung on every sentiment of adoration like clinging to a rope he cast. But for him, a picture was worth more than a thousand words. It would be the first in our virtual love affair, separated by thousands of miles.

Despite the fact that we were at different places in our lives, it seemed that neither one of us found it conceivable to let go. I wasn't yet sure which one of us was at greater risk in this game, but I was betting it was me. I had written in my journal after the first date, "I've found the quintessential lover—but he's young, so I need to just enjoy the time we have together and guard my heart." Unfortunately, my brain had long since lost the battle to stay in control. My body was hot with the anticipation of his return. And my heart... it was opening like a flower in Spring.

Chapter Twenty-Three

My phone sounded an email alert and instinctively I knew it was him.

Hon, I am flying in on Saturday. When can we see each other that isn't the same day? Saturday will be my 'hate the world day'. Missing you…

I shot back a response right away, reining in my excitement.

> *Well, let's see. I have work, house cleaning, laundry, and the yard. But I think I can squeeze you in on Sunday.*

I had to laugh at his surprised response.

What?

> *I'm teasing, silly. Get yourself over here as soon as you get a little sleep. You will need to be rested.*

I'm looking forward to it, babe. Kisses.

I EYED THE door of the restaurant while keeping watch on my cell phone which lay within striking distance on the table. The second Ethan walked through the door my pulse quickened, and I jumped up to greet him with a hug.

"Hey, you made it, thanks for coming over to my side of the bay."

Ethan's brown eyes beamed at me, as he wrapped his dark muscular arm around my waist, drawing me close. "Oh, babe, you look so good. I've missed you." His voice had a rich, silky tone, like chocolate and a full-bodied cabernet. "My beautiful girl." He brushed the long brunette locks away from my face with his fingers and kissed me sweetly on the forehead.

"Ah yes, no obvious PDAs. I know." I shot him a pouty look.

Rolling his eyes, he said, "Let's eat, I'm starving. For some food, to start with." His eyebrows raised above the menu and he wore a mischievous grin. "I brought something special for tonight," Ethan announced.

I replied, let me guess... the ropes?" My body immediately responded as I recalled our last time together. I shifted a little in my chair. "I have a few surprises for you too." I pulled my chair closer to his and seized his hand under the table. Placing his hand on my leg, I scanned the restaurant to make sure no one was looking. I guided his long fingers over one of my stockings until it met with the garter belt.

"Oh! My sweet girl, what have you done?"

I cocked my head to the side and provocatively looked into his eyes. I nodded, "Go ahead, more... that's it." I moaned with an audible purr of satisfaction as he ran his hand up to the apex between my legs. He had unrestricted access, his index finger skimmed between the lips of my sex.

"You exceed my expectations again." Holding my gaze, he brought the finger to his mouth and tasted my excitement. He let out a low, sexy growl, "I could taste you all night."

I couldn't pull away from his stare, his eyes blazing and excited. "Oh, you could, huh? I dare you." I perched my chin on my hand, moving closer. "Let's eat and get out of here."

He parked his car behind mine as we arrived at my home, grabbing his bag from the trunk, he followed through the door behind me. I moved quickly to the thermostat and turned on the heat, avoiding his eyes which were scanning the entry room. *Why am I so nervous?*

"Come, I'll give you the tour. It's short, the house isn't that big." We settled in the small, galley shaped kitchen.

"Nice house, I like the layout. When was it built?"

"Originally, around the 1920s, it is a typical Bungalow style they were building at that time. Glad you like it, I think it's pretty cozy."

"What would you like? I opened a cupboard door and scanned my supplies. "I have wine, beer, and *ooooh*, here is some tequila. Shall we do a shot?"

"By all means, sure." Ethan stood close with his arms crossed. I could feel him watching me as I stretched up with my arm and balanced on my tiptoes.

"Here, let me help." He easily pulled the bottle from the top shelf. He kissed me on the top of the head. "Shorty."

"Hey, who are you calling shorty?" I called back over my shoulder.

He moved against my body, pulling me into him from behind, his arms binding at my waist.

"I was thinking about my girl while I was away. Barcelona reminds me of you now," he whispered low into my ear. My heart swelled. It was exactly what I longed to hear.

His face nuzzled in my hair, the warmth of his breath on my cheek gave me goosebumps. The mouthwatering scent of him sent waves of heat down to my core.

"I missed you... a lot. I couldn't stop thinking about you." A low moan of satisfaction came from deep in his throat, radiating in my ear.

"*Hmm*, lots of good fantasies?"

"You do inspire me, babe," he said.

He hardened within the confines of his jeans, the erection pressed against the cleft of my behind. I tilted my head to the side, my eyelids lowered while he trailed kisses down my neck. "That feels so nice,"

I purred. He flipped me around, engulfing me in an embrace. "You know, you've ruined me for all the rest."

The stubble of his beard scratched as my face grinned against his cheek. "You did mention that in an email. I'm not sure who *all the rest* is, but I love hearing it from you."

"I've never met anyone like you." He held me by the shoulders and looked into my eyes. "*You*, Elena, have some kind of hold on me."

Abruptly, he changed the subject. "Let's have that drink. Better yet, let's take it with us, I can't wait any longer." As we moved through the dining room, he picked up a chair and carried it into the bedroom.

"Oh my," I exclaimed, spinning around to face him, "We're going *there?*"

"I think it's your turn to surprise me." He hooked his arm around me, tumbling both of us onto the bed. His hand fisted in my hair and brought my lips to his.

"So, I get to tie you up and have my way with you?"

"*Uh-huh*, if you would like. I trust you, Elena."

"I've been waiting for this," I cooed, my voice laced with seduction.

Without hesitation, I reached for the sleep mask in my nightstand and placed it over his eyes. He was mine, to take and pleasure. Slanting my head over his full lips, I pressed into him with a deep kiss, my tongue invading his mouth.

"Surrender to me, baby," I whispered against his ear. A low moan rumbled in his throat and coaxed me on. I reached for a box under my bed and pulled out a pair of soft handcuffs. Thankfully, he didn't ask any questions when I took his wrists and one by one, fastened the Velcro straps, then clipped them together over his head. After our last adventure with the ropes, I had made a trip to the sex toy store and bought the fabric handcuffs on an impulse.

"These are handcuffs? I could get out of these," he laughed.

"Yes, but you won't. It's my turn now, so let me do my thing," I insisted, surprising myself with how bossy I sounded.

My hands tore at his shirt and fumbled with the buttons on his fly.

His muscular frame shifted on the bed, cooperating with my clumsy attempts to strip him of his clothes until his godlike body lay naked before me.

With my knees on either side of his hips, I leaned in and began my slow seduction. My lips made a trail of soft kisses from his neck down to his rock-hard pecs. He drew in a sharp breath through his teeth as my tongue fluttered across his nipples, moving from one to the other. My eyes feasted on his body, my fingers traced their way over his hard abdomen and gripped the base of his erection. With my head resting on his thigh, I lingered to admire every inch of his gorgeous penis. I was in control and planned to take my sweet time, indulging myself in him.

The muscles in his buttocks flexed and raised from the bed to meet the touch of my fingers as the tips lightly teased the head of his cock. My tongue lashed once, surrounding the curved rim.

"Jesus," he cried out, his neck arched into the pillow.

"Oh, baby, I love how you respond to me."

My lips skimmed along the inside of his muscular thighs until they met the heavy sack resting between his legs. The flick of my tongue across the rippled skin drew the jewels close to his body. One by one, I sucked them into my mouth, my tongue circling over the round spheres. With a sudden gasp, his carved buttocks strained off the bed, the bands of muscles in his abdomen tightening.

"What a view I have, my God you have a gorgeous body."

From between his legs, I watched every etched muscle tense and flex under the sweep of my tongue as I worked my way up the long rigid shaft.

Leaving him pleading for more, my arms tugged him over on his stomach. In a bold move, I mounted him, straddling his perfect ass. Rocking my hips at just the right angle, I stroked my sex against him, gliding my clit along the silky skin between his cheeks. The wetness of my arousal spilled onto him, softening the path. He heard the sound of my breaths quicken.

"You're enjoying being the dom, aren't you?"

"Yep. That one was for me." The weight of my body sank onto his back. Flattening my breasts against his skin, I soaked in his warmth.

He moaned in that familiar sexy tone, "I love the feeling of your breasts like this, so warm, so full."

His arms held high above his head, my body was dwarfed in comparison to his large frame.

I hated to move away, but I had plans for him.

Raising up, my arm came down hard as I planted a slap on his ass. "Turn over now." I caught the smile on his face as he rolled and lay face up.

Positioning my body over him, I drew my breasts across his chest, the crisp hairs teased and tightened my nipples. My fingers slipped off the mask and released the Velcro on the handcuffs. I looked into his smoldering hot eyes, wondering if he was pleased.

"I never... My god woman..." His fingers slipped into my hair and cradled my head. His lips pressed into mine, kissing me with a slow swirl of his tongue.

Breathless with excitement, I broke away. The corners of my lips curved into a satisfied smile. "I'm just getting started, now, where are those ropes?"

His strength was no match for me, but I pulled at his arm and struggled with the weight of his large frame. "Up now, please."

Shaking his head, he said, "I'm seeing a whole new side of you. What have I unleashed?"

He raised himself from the bed, and in a few long strides, he'd snatched his backpack from the corner. Rummaging through, he produced the coil of long white rope. The same one he'd used on me.

Amusement lit his eyes and curved his mouth into a grin. "Here, it's all yours, darlin'."

"What are you smiling at?"

"You're so damn cute, you're getting into this."

"Yes, I am. So, sit your fine ass down, and let me figure out how to tie you to the chair."

Ethan cooperated, and I fumbled with the knots, which were not nearly as effective as his.

"You know, I can still move."

"*Shush*, I'm trying. There, that should work." Hands on my hips, I stood inches in front of him with a sense of pride. "I think I've got this. Babe, you look so hot," I gushed, my eyes scanning his elegant body held captive in the chair, selfishly drinking in every inch of him.

Placing my knees on the sides of his legs, I climbed his torso and wrapped my arms around his neck, pulling him into a kiss.

The heat pulsated from between my legs, I needed to feel him inside me. Steadying myself on his broad shoulders, I raised up on my knees and positioned the crown of his long shaft against the saturated folds of my cleft. Slowly, I lowered myself down, his wide cock exquisitely stretching me.

"Wait… You're going there already?"

"Hey, I'm in control now. You can relax, I'll take care of you. Jeez, even tied up you want to call the shots."

Inch by inch, I took him in deeper, pushing past the discomfort until all I felt was the warmth of him filling my walls. "Ah, yes," I hissed, holding him deep.

His low guttural moan vibrated against the skin on the crest of my breast. "Your pussy feels so warm, so tight."

I didn't move, except for the involuntary clenching of my muscles deep in my core. This was going to be slow and easy, to start.

Pressing hard on his shoulders, I raised my hips and freed him from my body, his erection glistening from my arousal. I stood without touching him, allowing him to feel the void. His eyes burned into mine—waiting.

Slowly I sank, my knees hitting the carpeted floor. Gazing up at him with a devilish grin, I possessed his cock with both hands. This time, I would show no mercy. I drove him into my mouth, sucking hard while my tongue flattened against the broad shaft. Air poured hard into his lungs and his chest heaved with quick breaths.

My mouth rose and fell, over and over, tonguing the bulging veins and ridges of his thick cock. I registered his voice, building to a feverish pitch, cursing and gasping out my name.

Wrapping my lips around the plush head, I paused and licked the entire length. Looking up into his eyes, I let my tongue flutter and tease at the cleft. I licked the moisture from the tip and purred, "I love the taste of you."

"Gorgeous." His chest expanded with a sudden breath, his eyes fixed on mine. "You look so damn sexy like that." I saw the flash of white teeth as his face lit up in a smile—a smile that was singed with amazement.

I beamed with satisfaction, relishing how I could drive him wild with pleasure. Hearing his voice cry out in sweet agony was my reward as my mouth engulfed him in deep rhythmic motions. Gripping him tightly, my hands stroked with intensity, followed by my lips. He swelled in my mouth and I released him as suddenly as I began, leaving him teetering on the brink.

"*Ah*, no! Baby that was so good."

"*Shush*, I'll take care of you. Remember? Savor it, slow and easy."

I placed my feet on the chair, stepping carefully on the edges at either side of his hips and raised to stand, my groin strategically aimed at his face.

A smile crossed his lips, "You know exactly what you're doing, don't you?"

Without answering, I pressed my sex to his waiting mouth. He growled softly as his tongue lapped at the folds and relentlessly circled my clit. I clung my hands on his head as he drove me higher. A whimper escaped my lips as the intense pleasure overwhelmed me, but I forced myself away from his mouth. I had other plans in mind. Carefully turning my body around, I boldly placed my backside in front of his face and leaned forward. His surprise was exactly the response I had hoped for.

"Oh my God, you are amazing, I can't believe you. Babe, you look so delicious from this angle."

His tongue reached for the sensitive opening and I obliged him by moving closer. My legs trembled as his velvet tongue licked and tickled at the rim of my bottom, sending shockwaves of pleasure to my sex. The exquisite feeling was unlike any other. Gasping in waves of air, my knees almost buckled from under me. I steadied myself on his shoulders as I turned to face him and slid down his body, hovering just over the wide crest.

"I could get used to this, I kinda like calling the shots. But I haven't finished taking care of you."

I kissed him, and his mouth poured over mine. The nip of his teeth on my lip showed me his power was very much intact.

My fingers wrapped around his cock and placed the crown between the lips of my sex, sliding it against the slickness of my arousal. Slowly, I lowered onto him, feeling the roundness of the carved head and every nuance of the steely shaft, then held him just above the deepest point. My hands cupped the weight of my breasts—raising them to his mouth, feeding him. First one and then the other.

In wild abandon, his mouth sucked on my nipples, flicking the tips with his tongue. Waves of pleasure rippled through me, fueling the fire deep in my core. I climbed higher, the sounds of his desire spurring me on.

"Yes baby, let yourself go," I muttered, as my head tipped back and I took him in down to the root, straining to accommodate the length of him.

My heart swelled at the intense connection—at the freedom we felt with each other. This powerful man trusted me. He had given me much more than just his body, and I loved taking control of his pleasure. This one was for him.

Riding him, I commanded the pace, sliding up and down on his cock. Each time my buttocks slapped against his hard thighs, I watched him unravel. Defying the burn in my thighs, I pounded my hips faster, driving him to finish. He uttered my praises and sounds of passion, his breath gusting on my neck.

"Elena, you are going to make me come, I can't stop it. Do you want me to come? Tell me, baby," he panted. His face winced as he tried to hold back the force welling within him.

"Yes, I want you to come. Come hard for me, let it go, babe." I tightened around him, milking his cock with each ferocious pump of my hips. Sweat misted on his skin and the air was thick with the heady scent of him. Steadying myself with one hand on his shoulder, I reached behind my buttocks and cupped his balls. My hand gently squeezed the sac. With my index finger, I massaged the rippled skin just below, feeling the pressure mounting.

"Yes, just like that... There it is!" His voice roared as the orgasm overtook him and he poured into me. His body tightened and convulsed with the release until his head fell helplessly against my breasts.

My arms wrapped tight around him, holding him as his breaths gusted against my chest. Muttering against my skin, he sighed, "Elena, that was incredible. What you do to me... only you."

"It's you. You inspire me," I leaned in and kissed his brow. "Now that I've had my way with you, let's get you out of these ropes."

Slowly I rose, hesitantly disconnecting our bodies. Freeing his hands, he took control again. Lifting me into the air by my waist, he toppled me onto the bed. I lay on my back, my eyes fixed on his tall frame standing between my legs.

"It's my turn to take care of you." His voice was firm and determined.

I watched as he stroked his semi-hard penis into a full erection. He looked so damn sexy. His gorgeous body loomed above me and seeing him masturbate that thick hard cock drove me crazy with desire. I mirrored him, running my index finger in circles over my clit as my hips rose off the mattress and the muscles deep in my core tightened.

The weight of his body descended onto mine and he guided the crown to the precipice. His powerful hands took hold of my hips, slamming me against the thrusts. Our eyes locked in a heated gaze, I climbed higher, driven by the undeniable passion that drew us both into a frenzy. I slid the pad of my finger over the engorged knob, circling faster and faster, while he maintained a steady rhythm of deep strokes. Air hissed out through my lips, begging him not to stop. Everything tightened, on the brink of the impending explosion I so desperately craved. It came with a force that violently shook my body. A wild scream escaped me in a rush of ecstasy as the orgasm rolled on and on, until I whimpered from the repeating spasms that pulled at my core.

Ethan covered my mouth in a deep kiss, cementing the bond between us. I could sense his excitement build, his cock twitching against my clenched walls. With a look of hot determination, he grabbed my wrists, pinning my hands above my head. His biceps bulged but never wavered as he held himself over my body, the dom again. My sex wet and softened from his orgasm and mine, took in all of his thick, long erection. Wrapping my legs around his back, he sunk deeper with every thrust. My voice rasped out in a cry, calling out his name and claiming his release. His pace quickened and with a feral roar, he came again, his powerful body stiffening as the orgasm tore through him. In a ragged breath, he said my name and gusted against my neck in an agonized sound.

With a sudden heave, he flung his body and landed on his back next to me. His arm bent over his eyes, his chest rose and fell with heavy breaths.

"What's wrong?"

"Sometimes I'm just stunned at how we are together," he sighed in the rush of his exhale.

"Believe me, so am I," I snorted. "But there's something else, I can tell."

"I can't find the words... It was a first for me, letting go like that."

"How did it feel? To not be the one in control?"

He uncovered his eyes and I saw a look of vulnerability.

"I don't quite understand it, but what you bring out in me... I've never felt this way before. I feel... safe with you."

"It's the same for me, you know, but..."

I curled my body around him, enveloping myself in his warmth and soothing his worried brow with a caress of my fingers, acutely aware of the conflict between desire and fear.

He turned to look at me. "But what?"

My chest burned with a heavy breath. "Nothing. We have each other right now and that's all that matters." Soothing him as much as me, the flat of my hand stroked rhythmically across his chest. With eyelids drawn tight, his arm curled around my hip, binding me tight against his side.

"Thank you, for trusting *me* this time." I tilted my head and grinned up at him. "That… was so much fun—it was another first for me."

Ethan chuckled, "You are a natural, my girl."

He pulled me on top of him, one hand on the cleft of my ass, the other caressed my hair as my cheek laid in the curve of his neck.

"Again?" I asked. My need for him was insatiable.

"Ha! Give me a minute. Let's take a break, have a cigarette and a shot."

Ethan followed me to the kitchen. I stood shamelessly naked in front of him, too engrossed in him to be worried about the bright lights. "So, what's next for us? Have we hit our peak of daring adventures or have you got more surprises in store?"

He cupped my face and stroked his thumb along my cheek, "My girl, with you, there will always be more."

Chapter Twenty-Four

CHRISTMAS AND NEW Year's Eve. Dreaded holidays for singles, and for all intents and purposes, I was still single despite the intensity that had built with Ethan. We had one last night together in San Francisco before he left to be with family for Christmas. They were scattered over the South, so he would be traveling again.

Each time I was with him, the passion and intimacy were more amazing than the last. He held me in his arms before falling asleep and whispered, "I will miss you while I'm away." Clasping my hand in his, I returned the sentiment. I couldn't help but wish that somehow, we could share the holidays together. But I had to settle for the moments we could steal from time. Besides, I couldn't imagine a scenario in which he would be bringing me home to meet his parents. I lay awake listening to his soft snores, nestled under his arm, and soaking in the warmth of his body pressed against mine. It was always bittersweet, knowing that it would be a while before I saw him again, but Ethan gave me something to look forward to. A promise of a weekend getaway on the coast the first of the new year softened the sting.

Without Ethan in town, San Francisco felt empty when I went to meet Anna for a girl's night out. We joined up in Union Square where the giant Christmas tree glowed with thousands of lights, illuminating the holiday displays. The city was bustling with people who came to see SF at its finest, brimming with holiday spirit. It had been a tradition in my family to make the trip to the big city just before Christmas to see the lights and window displays. I had vivid memories of peering in the Macy's windows to view the animated dolls and vintage scenes.

Anna and I bypassed much of the sightseeing and headed to the top of the Sir Francis Drake Hotel, the Starlight Room. It was one of the few places in San Francisco we could go dance and have a drink and not feel like we were somebody's mother. Most of the clubs and even the lounges were packed with twenty or thirty-year-olds after 10:00 PM—or, couples. We had tried them all, even the "Meetups" at various bars. They were designed to bring out the baby boomers, a place where we, *old folks* (anyone over forty) could socialize and ultimately find a partner. But there were always more women than men at the events, and the men… well, they tended to be the ones who lacked the social skills to hunt outside the relatively safe structure of a group.

Even the music was geared to the older generation, the DJ playing 70s and 80s music. Anna and I preferred reggaeton and hip hop and could get down with the best of the *kids,* but this left us bumping booties with the younger crowd. And, with Anna around, that usually left us with trouble. The way she could shimmy her ass left a trail of young erections begging for more.

We got off the elevator on the twenty-first floor, the opulent bar already packed. Anna scanned the room before we headed to the coat check.

"I see them already, the stags on the hunt."

I rolled my eyes at Anna, "Here we go again."

"Well, at least we're out, it's better than staying at home. Let's try to have a good time."

"I guess," I said, lacking enthusiasm." Let's get a drink anyway and find a seat." I eyed her with a sideways glance while we waited in line. "You're looking sexy tonight, as always."

Anna had on a skin-tight animal print dress, hugging the curves men drooled over. Her figure resembled that of Marilyn Monroe, an hourglass shape. She stood a little shorter than my five foot four inches, but she made up for it with five-inch stiletto heels. The kind that made my feet scream just looking at them. The deep red tone of her shoulder-length hair made her stand out in the crowd of blondes and brunettes. Anna oozed sexuality, and the two of us together were sexy multiplied.

"Thanks, and you're looking hot yourself in that steamy black dress. Didn't you wear that in Vegas?"

"Yep. And I think I did the *walk of shame* in it the morning after. I can't remember which hotel I ended up in. Or for that matter, which one you landed in."

Anna's red lips broke out in an impetuous grin, and her giggle was infectious. "We have had some wild times, haven't we?"

"That we have, but my wild times have been limited to Ethan for a while now. I'm trying to be sensible and keep my options open, but all I can think about is him—which sucks because he's away a lot of the time."

"You know my opinion on that one. You can't count on him—he's young and wild. Just enjoy him when you can, but don't lose your heart to him."

"Ha! That's easy to say, but how long is it now that you've been hung up on the married guy?"

Anna shrugged and took a long pull on her cocktail. "It's been eight years with Kevin. He'll never leave his wife and kids and I keep trying to find someone else, but he has a hold on me. There's something about him I can't resist."

"You mean besides his big black dick and skills in the bedroom?" My lips curved into a wry grin. She was never shy about sharing the details of her love life with me.

Anna snickered out a laugh through her nose. "*That* is definitely a good part of the appeal, but he's got that alpha male personality too. Which also means he can manipulate the hell out of me. That's why I can speak from experience. I see Ethan doing that with you. You think he's what you want, but is he really what you need?"

"Girl, we both need *and* want the same thing, but we don't seem to be able to find it encompassed in one, reliable man. Passion, love, chemistry with a guy who is reliable, *age-appropriate*, and treats us well? At our age, the odds of finding that are about the same as meeting a magic unicorn," I snorted.

"We aren't likely to find *him* here tonight, that's for sure. These guys are probably staying at the hotel and are on the prowl. But let's go dance and have some fun anyway."

"Agreed." I slugged down the rest of my drink, we hooked arms and headed to the dance floor.

At least the music was a decent mix. Anna and I got our moves on amidst the crowd and before long, we each had dance partners. From the dance floor, we had a stunning view of the city. The large windows overlooked the bay from a dizzying height. In the dark night sky, San Francisco shined bright with colored lights and skyscrapers. But after an hour of heated bodies dancing the night away, the windows became clouded by the rising steam. By 1:00 AM we'd had enough of being groped, fondled and propositioned. I grabbed Anna by the arm, and we made our escape to the bathroom. The lady's room was a haven for women who needed a good excuse to break away.

"You ready to go?" I asked.

"Sure, I'm over it."

"Well, another fun night out in our town," I muttered, with a heavy dose of sarcasm. "God, I'm so sick of the same old thing. I really can't take it anymore. You definitely have to come to Barcelona with me sometime. It's different there—there's no age limitation on going out and having fun. In most places, people of all ages are out all night dancing and there's such a variety of things to do."

"I really want to see what it's like there. I'm feeling the same way you are—stuck and stagnant here."

I couldn't stop talking about Barcelona while I drove Anna home, and the night left me more convinced I needed a change.

HOSTING CHRISTMAS FOR the family at my house kept me busy at least, and my mind occupied. Since I didn't have the seniority in my new position to get the day off on Christmas Eve, it took a significant amount of planning and help from my son to pull off hosting a big dinner when I couldn't get away from work until five o'clock.

Ron became my pseudo-partner for the holiday. Since he had placed me in the friend zone, he had adopted my family and showed up for holiday dinners. I guess I had spoiled him when I'd tried to lure him back with my award-winning turkey meals. He did like my cooking, so he came back for the food—not me. But it provided a little solace, having someone next to me during the festivities who wasn't a blood relative. Our family had become accustomed to the mix of exes for special events. My mother and stepmom had become good friends, and my ex-husband was always amongst the group of this modern-day family constellation.

I thought about how nice it would feel to have Ethan there with me, although I knew it wasn't realistic, he'd always be with his relatives. Though I hadn't kept him a secret from my family, it wasn't a topic I liked to discuss. It wasn't an issue of race, even though the older generation was rooted in conservatism—there had been interracial marriages introduced into the constellation and I was happy to see the acceptance of diversity. It was more a matter of the age difference.

My Mom would provide her unsolicited motherly advice. Completely logical advice, even though she knew I always followed my heart. My son certainly didn't want to hear about his mother's lover, but Dana did pull me aside to ask me how it was going. She was always wise, but gentle, taking care not to trample on my dreams. They all just wanted me to be happy, having seen me lonely and sad for so long. Obviously, they had their doubts about the direction I was heading with Ethan, knowing how young he was, and I preferred not to face reality—not just yet.

When all the guests had departed, I was left alone sitting in the living room, staring at the lights on the Christmas tree. The room looked like a bomb had gone off, the remnants of paper and bows littering the carpet. Settling in with the familiarity of the ghosts of Christmas past, I turned the lights off and curled up on the couch with a glass of wine and a blanket. It had been a very long time since I had someone to cuddle up with on my favorite holiday, and the sadness began to creep in.

I reached for my phone and saw an email from Ethan, sent several hours earlier. Just knowing he was thinking of me brightened my mood.

Merry Christmas sweetie, hope you are having a good one with your family. I miss you so much! The ladies cooked up a feast here. I ate way too much and I can't get off the couch.

He attached a photo of himself, sprawled out on the sofa with the family dog at his side. God, I missed him too. His message gave me a reason to smile. It would be late there, but I sent back an email for him to see in the morning.

Aww, babe, I miss you too. Merry Christmas! It's been a hectic one here but I pulled off another turkey dinner in my minuscule kitchen. Love the pic, send more when you can. Kisses.

Hating selfies, I attached a photo of my brightly lit Christmas tree.

In the next few days, I gathered the courage to ask him about his plans for New Year's Eve. I knew it was going to get dicey and my heart pounded as I fired off the message. He was evasive but finally wrote that he was hosting a small party with friends. I wondered if it had occurred to him to invite me. But he had not introduced me to his friends, and NYE dates were for couples. My experiences in the dating world had taught me that men usually move slowly into making that kind of statement. My relationship with Ethan was made more complicated by its unconventional nature—according to his standards. I wasn't concerned about how society would view us, but I sensed that he couldn't break free from those pressures.

So, there it was, I would be alone and searching yet again for an event where I would feel comfortable as a single woman on one of the two most dreaded holidays. It was second only to Valentine's day. When it came to NYE, getting a date was tantamount to a marriage proposal. Ron clued me in. As my friend, he always felt free to give me dating advice. A NYE date signified a guy was serious and headed for a real relationship. I had hoped for an invitation from one of the men I occasionally dated, but they chose to celebrate flying solo. No strings attached and on the hunt.

Texts and phone calls with single friends were flying during the days before the big night. A last-minute decision was made to join up with a house party down the peninsula, deep in the heart of the Silicon Valley. It was either that, or stay home alone, but the party ranked low on the scale of the vision I had for the holiday.

The countdown rang out and the plastic horns sounded the end of another year. In place of being lip-locked with a lover at midnight, our group of lonely singles all reached for our phones and texted "Happy New Year" to loved ones. One of mine was to Ethan, but he didn't respond. I imagined him partying the night away with his friends and felt the sting pierce through me.

There was an upside—my friends agreed the party was a bust and since we had carpooled down into the valley of the bored and restless, we made our escape shortly past midnight.

With the last of the dreaded holidays out of the way, life turned back into its regular state of dull normalcy. Except that the new year would bring Ethan back to me. Our plans were set for the next weekend, an overnight on the coast of Monterey. It would be my first mini-vacation with a man since I was married. He couldn't begin to comprehend how much this meant to me.

Chapter Twenty-Five

THE DRIVE TO Monterey always flooded me with memories. The two-hour trip from Oakland gave me plenty of time to reflect. I got on the road early on Saturday, looking forward to some time on my own, since Ethan couldn't join me until the afternoon.

When I reached San Jose, I recalled the place where I lived as a child, up until the time my parents separated, and I was painfully dragged away from all that was familiar. Some of the landmarks had changed and it had been grossly developed. Strip malls and apartment buildings marred the landscape which was once filled with walnut trees. I drove past the exit to the home I'd bought together with my first husband in Morgan Hill. The urban sprawl had pushed its way thirty miles out of the main city, in a continuous stream of tract homes. Unsettling memories of my first divorce bubbled to the surface. He was such a good man, probably the best I'd known. But at age twenty-three, three years into the marriage and probably four years after my heart knew, I had to finally admit it to myself. I had fallen out of my teenage love.

I fell into the arms of a man in the next town down the highway. It was where I found the adventure I had craved. Working in a counseling center right out of college I met the most extraordinary man, the most gifted therapist I had ever known. He'd never lost the strong muscular frame developed in earlier years as a military man, but he was anything but traditional. Almost twenty years my senior, this Spanish/Puerto Rican rogue swept me into a world of sexuality and fiery passion that I never imagined was possible. My adventurous, wild side was forever unleashed. It was a mutual decision to part, and luckily, we'd managed to sustain a loving friendship through the years.

As I drove along the coast of the Monterey Peninsula, the rugged, windswept beauty stunned my senses once again. It had been some years since I had ventured there but I knew the area well from my many visits dating back to high school. The scenic route took me past Monterey Bay, the harbor filled with fishing boats, the wind heavy with the smell of the sea and freshly caught fish. Snapshots flashed as memories of the times I'd been there in my life—with husbands, lovers, family. We came for the award-winning clam chowder and a view of the sea lions perched on the wooden docks, barking well into the night.

The two-lane road followed the edge of the coastline, merging next to the footpath with a view of the wild Pacific Ocean crashing over craggy reefs. Opposite the ocean, seaside homes caught the salty mist driven by gusts of air and fog. I passed by the highly rated, boutique Green Gables Inn where I had spent the post-wedding nights with my second husband. To say it was a honeymoon would be overrating the occasion. It was more of a family vacation since he'd invited his family along. Unfortunately, this was not my first clue the marriage was doomed. Though he married me, I never occupied the place of top priority in his life. My propensity for blindly following my heart was like a video set on loop mode, dating back as far as my recollections would allow.

The room was ready by the time I parked at the aptly named Lovers Point Hotel. Situated one block from the coast in Pacific Grove, I had a view of the deep blue waters of the ocean through a grove of cypress trees. The room itself was basic but the bed large and comfortable. And the setting, it couldn't have been more perfect. Arriving before Ethan gave me the chance to reflect as I set out to explore some of my favorite places. The awe-inspiring beauty brought back a rush of memories with every turn of the road from Pacific Grove to the charming village of Carmel.

I arrived back to the hotel room in time to take a quick shower, and within moments of getting dressed, Ethan texted his arrival. I opened the door and watched as he sprinted up the stairs, swooping me into an embrace when I opened the door.

"I've missed you," he said, holding me by the nape and giving me a head to toe glance. "You look great. Sorry I'm a bit late, I rented a car to make the drive. The motorcycle doesn't make for a fun ride during the winter. It comes in handy in the city though, since there's never any place to park."

I beamed up at him, "I'm just glad you're here. The effort you've made to get here…" I paused as a lump formed in my throat. "This is the first overnight away I've had with any man since my divorce." My watery eyes threatened to reveal the sadness that had built through the years.

"Seriously?" The incredulous look on his face gave me pause, *should I have revealed how lame my life has been?*

Burying my face in his chest, I hid from his penetrating gaze and wrapped my arms around his waist. He pulled me in tighter, and bending his head, he kissed my forehead.

"You up for taking a drive? Let's go explore and catch the sunset." His diversion pulled me from the edge of dipping into an emotional moment. He always sensed when I might go *there*, and he always used a diversionary tactic to make things light. I quickly shifted my mood, appreciating that he could read me so well.

The sun's rays reflected on the deep blue ocean as we drove along miles of rugged coastline. Waves crashed and sprayed over the rock formations jutting out of the sea.

A long sigh of delight escaped me, "I love being here, I've always felt so alive in this place. It's beyond spectacular." I glanced at Ethan, easily maneuvering the sporty car around the windy turns. His face lit up with a smile and he reached for my leg, stroking my thigh while the other hand held the steering wheel.

"This is one of my favorite places too. This, and Big Sur. I've been here quite a few times to shoot photos. But being here with you... is special." A hum of pleasure warmed me from within. His smile, his touch, his words—simple gestures, yet with Ethan, they meant everything.

"Do you mind if we go exploring? I brought my camera along and the sun looks like it's about to set soon."

"Sure, but I'm getting bundled up, it's friggin freezing out there."

Blasts of cold salty air bit at my skin as I stepped out of the car. I heard the sound of his throaty laugh, standing in front of me as I zipped up my knee-length puff coat and pulled the hood over my head. "Look at you! It's like you're dressed for the arctic."

Clad in sneakers, jeans, and a coat that made me appear twice my size wasn't the most attractive attire. He still looked damn fine in his slightly insulated jacket and jeans, apparently immune to the cold.

I pouted my lips, frantically brushing the strands of hair whipping across my face. Ethan moved into me, silencing my lips with a soft kiss. Cupping my face in his hands, he warmed me with his smile. "You look adorable."

He clenched his fingers in mine and led me to a place where the beach met a pathway to a large rock formation. The water ebbed and flowed where the tide was blocked, our feet carefully stepping from each jagged rock to the other until we reached the ascent.

"You good?" he asked.

I nodded and shot him a thumbs up.

"Follow me," he shouted over the roar of the surf. He found the footholds and my shoes struggled to grip the slippery surface as I followed his steps. Each time he climbed a few feet ahead, he turned, reaching one hand in back to steady me. "You got this, girl. You're doing great."

"Yeah I am." Though I loved the way he took care of me, I needed to prove that I could be as athletic as any of my younger counterparts.

The sun tipped at the horizon as we reached the top, radiating hues of orange and red across the sky. Ethan positioned the camera against his eye, rotating 360 degrees to capture every angle.

"Wait here for me," he instructed.

I watched as he navigated down and around the craggy rocks with skill and ease. He captured images of the waves crashing on the shore, the spray of foam flying off the top of the highest point, and of me—silhouetted against the darkening sky. I shuddered to think how that would look.

His breath was heavy when he reached me at the top. "The sky was brilliant, but I think I lost some light on the other shots."

"Come here, my adorable perfectionist," I hugged him at his waist, feeling the chill on his lips as I pulled him into a quick kiss.

In one swift move, his powerful arms spun me around and wrapped me in a hold against my back. He swung the camera over his shoulder, hanging on its lanyard, and buried his chilled nose on my neck. We stood on the precipice of the highest point our bodies locked as we watched the last of the glow dip below the horizon. A shiver trembled through my body, but despite the cold, I couldn't have felt more content.

"Baby, you're chilled, aren't you? Let's get you back in the car and crank up the heater."

We made it down the same way we came, Ethan leading the way. There was a sweetness in the way he took care of me, a look in his eyes I hadn't seen before.

I felt it as we drove back to the hotel and in the way he looked at me while I fixed my hair and makeup, getting ready for the evening. Over my shoulder, I saw his reflection in the mirror, watching me while he reclined on the bed. It felt so odd. I had never gotten ready for a date, in front of my *date*. Not since I was married.

The mirror gave me a view of him, his tall lean frame striding across the room and sliding in behind me, binding me at my hip. "You look so fine, babe," he said, pressing his cheek against mine while together we faced our reflection. My arms folded over his, holding his embrace.

"Me? I still have that windblown look and the fog turned my hair to frizz. But *you*, don't have that problem. You always look good—more than good. Do you know how much I love looking at your gorgeous face?"

His expression scoffed at me. "You give me too much credit, but I'm lucky that you like what you see."

A bulge formed in his pants, his hips circled and pressed into the cleft of my behind. My head rolled back against his shoulder. I moaned, my eyelids closing as temptation trickled through me. "If we start now," I moaned, "We will never make it to dinner."

"I know... but you feel so good." He made a sensuous sound against my neck that drove me crazy for him. At once, he slapped me hard on the ass, grabbing a handful of my cheek before he let me go. "Okay, let's get out of here. The sooner we eat, the sooner I can get you back in this room. I need you," he said, in a tone that trembled through my body and weakened my resolve. I needed him, craved him, with every breath I took. His hands fisted in my hair, his mouth slanted over mine, his tongue dipping and swirling across my lips.

My breath left me in a shaky exhalation when he released me. "Okay then," I stuttered, "let's get the hell out of here before I lock us both in this room."

If he only knew how much self-control it took to wait, but with Ethan, every moment we spent together was delicious foreplay.

Chapter Twenty-Six

"Do you know where we are going?" I asked, pulling on a black wool coat over my tight-fitting sweater-dress.

"Of course, I do," he said with his usual authority, "I checked an app on my phone and booked us a table at a great seafood and steak restaurant. Luckily, it's not far." A dark brow rose, his eyes glinting in that way that seduced me with just his look.

A bottle of red accompanied our feast. Both of us starving after our climb and the fresh air, we weren't shy about finishing every last morsel on our plates. With cocktails replacing desert, I filled him in on some of my adventures along the Monterey coastline. A bellow of laughter burst from his chest, "He *actually* brought his family along on your honeymoon?"

"Yep. And my first honeymoon was in Carmel. We were so tired, we ordered room service and watched a movie. That's *all* we did," I snorted. "So… I'm looking forward to a very different kind of night, with you." I held my glass up for a toast and shot him a hot look. At once, he called the waiter for the check.

After one quick stop at a liquor store for a bottle of his favorite Italian *digestif* and a pack of cigarettes, we closed the hotel room door behind us. "Finally!" we said in unison. I threw my coat on a chair and set up a track of slow hip hop music on my computer, while he poured the drink into two round glasses set next to a wine bucket. Dimming the lights, I lit a candle and set it on a nightstand near the bed.

Ethan walked toward me with slow, deliberate steps. My heartbeat quickened at the sight of him. Like a lion closing in on his prey, his gait was dangerous and determined.

"*Salud*. To... this amazing setting, and... sharing it together." Our glasses *clinked* and I took a hesitant sip of the clear liquid. Predictably, my face scrunched with the bitter taste scorching its way down my throat. "God, I do *not* understand why you like this stuff." Shaking his head, he said, "Drink up, it's good for the digestion."

He brought his mouth to mine, forcing me to taste the liquor once again from his tongue. With one hand, he cupped my behind, swiftly capturing me in his wickedly strong arm. The passion shot between us in a flash, my mouth no longer tasted the bitter, only the sweetness of his tongue as he possessed my mouth, invading it with delicious darts and swirls.

The pounding rhythm of the music moved my hips. With the right beat, they were unstoppable.

"Dance with me, please?" I knew I would have to beg, he wasn't one for whom dance came freely. It wasn't that he *couldn't* dance, I had seen his moves. But for some reason, he restrained himself. Like everything else about him, it fit when I considered his need to be perfect at whatever he did—multiplied by the compelling force to remain in control.

I set my glass on the table with the intention of seducing him senseless. Placing my arms around his neck, I rocked my hips, pumping against his pelvis. My body snaked against his hard chest—then I dropped my booty to the floor, body-rolling up his stomach and groin as I raised. He rocked in time with the music, his hips thrusting with my every move. He drew in a sharp breath, inhaling through clenched teeth as I grinded on his body, and my hands gripped the firm roundness of his ass.

"Damn, woman! You could put a black girl to shame with your dancing."

Spurred on by the high compliment, I grew bolder. I nipped at his neck while my fingers opened the buttons on his shirt, giving me access to his perfect chest. I let my hands run across the rock-hard pecs and down the muscles of his finely cut abdomen, then dropped down in perfect timing with the beat, perching in a squat. The outline of his erection strained against his jeans, my fingers ran the length from the base to the tip and tugged open his belt. Ethan shifted, absently moving his hips to meet my touch and I lost balance, teetering on my heels. With swift reflexes, his hands caught me under my arms, saving me from landing on my ass.

Tucking me under his arm, he walked us to the edge of the bed. His eyes warmed with affection, "Let me help you," he said. I watched as he kicked off his shoes, pulled off his shirt and pants, throwing them over a chair.

My breath caught at the sight of his naked body. "You know, I could never get tired of seeing you like this." He saw the hungry look on my face and cupped me under my buttocks with his long arm, the other hand rounding over my breast with a possessive growl.

I denied him with a sudden impulse to press my hands against his chest, sending him down onto the bed. Perching his fine bottom on the edge of the mattress, he watched as I slowly stripped for him, sending each piece of clothing to the floor.

His eyes smoldered, his long erection laid high on his belly as his arms stretched back and supported the weight of his large frame. "I am in awe of you."

I flushed, feeling triumphant in my art of seduction.

I fell into his open arms and the warmth of his lips. He swept me into the magic of his touch, his hands caressing along my back, and then I remembered—there was more to my plan.

With my hands pressed against his chest, I pulled away from his embrace, leaving him sitting on the edge of the bed, his naked body barely illuminated by the candlelight.

"Wait, I have something for us." I turned to the laptop placed nearby.

I pressed the arrow to start the music I had chosen especially for this moment. The first time I heard the song "Ride" by SoMo, I was jolted. *This is us, this is the way we make love.* The melody reminded me of our pace. Slow, sensuous and seductive—never hurried, the timing perfect. We rose with passionate surges, and slowed again, only to return to the peak. The lyrics spoke to me, as if they were his words, coaxing me, comforting me and then taking control of my body—bringing me to new heights of pleasure, and beyond the boundaries of just sex.

As the first notes of the piano sounded through the speakers, I returned to the heat of his body, my lips pressed against the fold of his ear. "I want you to make love to me." I climbed his torso, straddling him above his hips. Steadying myself with one hand on his broad shoulder, I grasped his erection in my other, guiding the crest along the slick tissues between the lips of my sex. His hands cupped my heavy breasts and brought the erect nipples to his mouth, a low moan rippling onto my flesh. The seductive voice sang out commands that moved our bodies in a slow, rhythmic tempo. The singular notes of the piano, punctuated by the sound of two fingers snapping, primed us for the build.

In perfect timing with the powerful ascension of the melody, my back arched into him, my head falling back as his lips kissed and sucked on the delicate flesh of my neck. The heat rose in my belly and up into my chest with a rush, so overcome by desire and emotion I felt—only for him.

The mood set by the song—the lyrics, the silky tone of the male voice, and the soulful melody—propelled us into a mindless state of sensuality. We merged into one, driven by the passion swelling between us.

His fingers traced a line down the curve of my spine, relaxing into the slow pace. Then clutching his arms around the curve of my bottom, he raised up, toppling me on my back. In one fluid movement, he flattened his body on mine. Interlacing our fingers, he raised his hips at the perfect angle, and the crown of his cock slid effortlessly into me. The music rang in our ears as we devoured each other in deep, luxurious kisses. Slowly, he descended deeper into my clenching walls. A cry escaped me, yielding to the heavy surge of his cock filling the aching emptiness.

The music enveloped us, drawing us into new depths of intimacy. It moved me to give this man my heart, my soul, my body. His hands fisted in my hair holding me in place, teasing me with velvet licks along the rim of my lips. For a moment, he was still, his eyes flickered, and he breathed one word, "You…" He slanted over my mouth and kissed me with a hunger that claimed me with the undeniable force of his desire.

Our bodies moved in harmony as he flexed his hips, pumping into me, keeping a steady rhythm. The visceral sounds of his excitement resounded in my ear. Sounds that rose and softened, echoing the tempo in the song.

The music built into a pounding crescendo, sending his body into a frenzy. He arched and slammed hard against my pelvis, once-twice-three times. My breath gusted each time he hit the end of me—and then, he stilled. My gaze poured over his rock-hard body, every muscle rigid and bulging as he perched over me. His neck arched back, and I heard his voice bellow through parted lips. My heart hitched at the agonized look on his face. It was as if he was fighting something deep within him.

As the last of the slow, evocative notes of the piano solo faded into silence, he folded over my body and his muscles softened. Stilling inside me, he cradled my head and gazed at me with an adoring look in his eyes. The depth of his emotion swept over me—the excruciating clarity rocked my very core. Stripped of all barriers, we were both split open and vulnerable.

One seductive R&B song rolled into another, sustaining the mood. Slowly, softly he took great care in pleasuring every inch of my body. I knew he would make sure I was satisfied before he found his release. His kisses, sweet and tender, moved from my lips and trailed down to the breasts he loved before finding the sweet spot at my apex. His tongue darted inside, then circled my clit. Our fingers laced, my hands turned white from lack of blood, tight in his grip. I arched my hips into his skillful mouth. His lips puckered and sucked at the engorged tissues, drinking in my arousal. My entire body tightened, straining and climbing toward the release I craved. "Babe, what you do to me," I whimpered.

He pulled his mouth away from my swollen clit, leaving me gasping for air. He uttered sweet words of praise that formed half sentences, then darted his tongue again, bringing me to the edge. And then I heard those words—the words I was dying to cry out but didn't dare.

"Elena... I love..." he paused, "I love you. I love being with you."

My heart thrummed in my chest, and I struggled to comprehend the muffled sound of his voice. *Did he really just say what I think he said? He couldn't have.*

His full lips glistening, hovering between my legs, I could only see his silhouette in the darkness. I strained to hear the whisper of his voice over the music. "I want to be with you.... Elena, I want to take care of you."

Slayed, I couldn't find my words. I breathed "Oh, baby," and a soft sob escaped me.

Given the alcohol we'd both drank and the euphoria of the moment I knew instinctively it wasn't a true declaration. We were both caught up in a swirl of emotions. And yet... it felt real. He'd laid himself bare before me.

The desperate longing in his voice and the relentless flickering of his tongue sent me over the edge and crying out his name. My body spasmed through wave after wave of the orgasm *he* owned. His power to bring me to such heights was overwhelming, exquisite, and frightening as hell.

We made love all through the night, Ethan spilling into me three times—each time the climax claimed him as powerfully as the first— and brought me with him. With the last shudder, he clutched me against his chest, whispering barely audible words of adoration. We fell asleep in a tangle of arms and legs, neither of us noticing when the music ended.

My eyes opened gingerly in the morning light. Ethan was curled against my side, his arm draped across my belly and his mouth slightly parted with the slow easy breaths of sleep. I loved waking up with him, his face looked so tender, so handsome. I thought of how I must look after a night being ravaged by our sex and cringed, running a hand through my tangled hair. Carefully, I slipped out of bed. Thankfully, he didn't wake as his arm sunk onto the mattress.

The mirror confirmed that it was going to take more than a brush to get me looking presentable. My body ached, muscles sore from the nights' workout. Craving the relief of a bath, I ran hot water and sunk into the tub. In the quiet, my mind played back the tape of the night and reflected on more than the incredible sex. It was the intense intimacy that touched my heart. The bond between us had been magnified into something new. So powerful—so… *loving*. The sound of his voice rang in my mind, his words of love had poured out with desperate emotion. His feelings for me were real, my core resonated with the truth, but I knew it was just a moment—he would retreat. He wasn't supposed to fall in love with me. And I wasn't supposed to fall in love with him— but I did. The night had sealed him indelibly in my heart, there was no escape. I didn't have the luxury of basking in the love, of hoping for more that would fill my every need and desire. With every ounce of strength I had, I boxed up my feelings and tied it tightly with ribbon.

The creak of the door startled me. Ethan peeked his head around the corner, rubbing the sleep out of his eyes.

"There you are. I woke up and you were gone."

"*Aww*, did you miss me? I said, with a tease in my voice, disguising the pain coursing through my blood.

"Yes, as a matter of fact, I did." My heart melted at his response.

"What are you doing in the tub?" he chuckled.

"Why does that amuse you?" I shifted my head against the side of the tub to get the full view of him. "Girls like baths, in case you didn't know. Besides, I'm recovering from last night. I'm not sure where this bruise came from," I pointed to a purple spot on my ribs. "Did you elbow me in your sleep?"

"Sorry about that, but it doesn't look like those are the only marks

I left," he said, with a fixed stare at my breasts. "Stay there, like that, I want to photograph you."

"No! I look a mess," I hid my face behind my hands. "My makeup is off, and my hair is a wreck."

He gazed down at me, "Babe, you look beautiful. Natural and perfect." He began snapping pics of me in the water. Despite his compliment, I felt self-conscious.

"Okay, enough, let me get cleaned up and we can get some breakfast."

"Let's have a little morning shower play first."

"Are you serious? You are insatiable."

"For you—always." He jumped in the bath with me, pulled the plug on the tub and turned on the showerhead. Soaping up my delicate parts stung, but seeing his gorgeous thick organ emerge to full length sent me past any lingering soreness.

As we left the hotel, Ethan asked me if I didn't mind taking a drive down the coast. He didn't explain, but he wanted to find a beach, one he'd been to long ago. We pulled into a parking spot and our shoes sunk into the sand as we walked close to the water's edge. We stood on the beach side-by-side without touching, quietly gazing at the waves crashing on the shore. Ethan's mood was pensive. Deep in thought, his eyes stared out to the sea. I didn't ask what he was thinking, and he didn't reveal. In stark contrast to me, his inner world was a private fortress. We stood in silence until his hand clasped mine, reconnecting once more.

"Thank you for giving me that moment," he paused, sighing heavily.

"Now, I'm starving, and you must be too," he said, his mood shifting. "Let's head out to find some breakfast."

"Well, the trick will be to find breakfast at one o'clock but let's give it a try."

After checking several restaurants in Pacific Grove, we finally settled in a booth, hungering for eggs, pancakes, and sausage. Waiting for our order, he took more photos of me but when he presented the images in his camera I cringed. "Delete!" When a twenty or thirty-year-old wakes up after a night of too much booze, little sleep and a whole lot of sex— she manages to fare out okay the next day. What I saw in my photos was the image of a woman whose eyelids drooped and a face that had succumbed to gravity overnight. The photos were unsettling evidence that I might be able to pull it off in the dim lights of a bedroom but not in the glaring light of day.

Facing each other in the hotel parking lot, an awkward uneasiness fell over us as he prepared to leave.

"Are you going to stay here a while or get on the road?" Ethan asked.

I knew I needed to take some time for myself to think. "I'm going to stay for a while, but I'll text you later."

Ethan pulled me into an embrace and saw the misty look in my eyes as the time had come to part. He exhaled a long sigh, and his body stiffened in my arms. I looked up to see his eyes were steeled and distant. I felt him pulling away from me, the distance growing between us. I imagined him boxing up his feelings too, retreating from the danger of getting in too deep.

"Alright, drive safe, and text me when you get home." He turned without meeting my gaze and opened the car door.

I watched his car drive away and headed for a walk down the coastal path. A heavy wave of fatigue washed over me, but it wasn't just from the lack of sleep. The feelings between us were stronger than ever, yet I knew that nothing could come of it. I had as much power over our destiny as I did over the waves that crashed on the shore. There was no other choice but to tread water. To ride on the ebb and flow of the tide. And I had an ominous feeling that the tide was about to recede.

Chapter Twenty-Seven

Ethan texted later how special our weekend had been. But he also informed me that he would be traveling again, back to Barcelona and other countries, not sure of the date of his return. Since he was returning so soon after the last trip, my gut told me there was a reason. And that reason must be a girl. It cut me to the core, especially after the things he said the last time we were together. My fears were substantiated. I wasn't a part of his travel plans, but I wondered who was.

My spirits were tanking, and I knew a girl's night was in order. Lena was one of my besties, but she didn't often have time to meet up. Her job and family kept her busy, but she always kept in touch. When she heard the sound of my voice on the phone, she dropped the kids at home and raced to meet me for Happy Hour. My cell alerted me to her text.

Tell me where to meet you.

Jack London Square. Kincaid's has a good happy hour. And aren't you driving? Stop texting.

Shut up, it's Bluetooth activated. See you in a few. Hugs.

She found me with a drink already in hand, facing the large glass windows with a view of the estuary, and bent to give me a hug.

"You look cute," I said. Her dance training prompted a slight curtsey before she settled into the cushioned chair next to mine. Lena always looked good. We were both in the same situation. Battling the forces of time and dancing our butts off trying to keep slim.

Her keen eyes zeroed in on me, surveying my face. "What's that?"

"What am I drinking?" I held up the martini glass. "Lemon drop martini. A chick drink," I said dryly.

"Oh, it's that kind of day is it." It was more of a statement than a question. My face wore the obvious signs. We all knew the look when a woman was torn up over a man.

Lena knew all about Ethan, I had nothing to hide. Though I wasn't sure Ethan had told anyone about me.

"What happened after your weekend together?"

"He left, traveling again. But this time he's not communicating much. It's been weeks and I've barely heard from him. The last time we were together it was pretty intense, and I know he's pulling away. He answers my emails, but they are *friendly*, more than anything. And the worst thing is, I feel like there is someone else."

I raised the martini glass to my lips, licking the sugared rim before gulping down a fair portion of the drink. A handsome waiter appeared at our table to take our order.

"I'll have a caipirinha please," Lena gave him one of her charming smiles and cocked her head, causing her long blond curls to cascade over her shoulder. She swatted my leg once he'd left. "He's cute, right?"

"Yeah, I guess," I said flatly.

"Wow, you must be down if you can't get a twinge from looking at that hottie."

"I wish I could, but Ethan has got me wrapped. He's emailed me from different places, I guess he's having fun."

"Why do you think there's someone else?"

"I can feel it. He has been distant, and not just because of the miles between us. I don't know, maybe he's just been too occupied with his friends." My fingers rubbed my temples and I let out a growl of frustration. "I just need to stop obsessing about him. Whatever happens, it's out of my control."

I pulled out my phone and scrolled through the messages.

"He emailed me from Columbia finally. He knows I dance," I shoved the phone in front of her face, and she read out loud.

"Chica! I'm in Columbia with four friends. You should be here dancing salsa with these guys 'cause I sure can't. I miss you. I'm coming back soon and want to see you."

She looked up at me over the rim of her glasses. "That should make you feel better, right?"

"I guess so. It certainly got my attention and raised my hopes, but it doesn't change things. He's off leading his own life and I should be too. And who knows what *soon* means. It could still be a while."

Lena put her hand on my knee and her eyes softened. "I'm worried about you. You haven't been the same since you met Ethan. Yes, you've had crazy highs, but the lows are concerning. You and I both know that you cannot count on a wild thirty-five-year-old. Get out there and date at least, have some male company. And seriously, you've got enough to worry about with that job of yours."

I nodded, "Yep, I know you're right. I can give you all the reasons why I can't stop with him, but you make a good point. And where is that waiter? I sure as hell need another drink."

"I need some advice," Lena said with a sheepish grin.

"What's up?"

"I'm trying to spice things up with my boyfriend. He's a little traditional, and me... well..." Lena paused, her eyes cast down. "I would like to make things a little more interesting. It's not something I'd talk about, but you've shared some things about your sex life, and it has me curious."

"*Leeena*," I drawled out in exasperation, "Why wouldn't you talk about sex? Just because we aren't twenty-something doesn't mean we have to lock our libido in the closet. We haven't lost it, yet – far from it."

"Well, I'm not a ball of hormones anymore, I'm more discriminating now. If I'm going to have sex, I want it to be great, not mediocre," she said with a swish of her hand, causing her glass to tip precariously in my direction. Lena had a tipsy grin on her face, and I knew things were about to get fun. So, I pressed on with the girl talk.

"I remember when I was in my twenties… I had no clue how unsatisfied I was in the bedroom. I mean, I knew I was frustrated, but I figured that was the extent of what I could expect." Crossing my legs, I shifted in my seat at the thought of the mind-blowing orgasms I never failed to experience when I was with Ethan.

For a moment, she was quiet, and I stared into my martini glass as if it were a pool of erotic memories.

"It's about that elusive chemistry, it lights everything on fire." When I looked up, my eyes met her stare. "Ethan lights *me* on fire and I love the way I can be my passionate self with him." I shrugged my shoulders and admitted, "Even if I can't have the whole package, the moments with him have been some of the best in my life. I don't want to give him up."

Sliding her palms against the jean fabric on her thighs, she leaned forward and asked, "So, what does he do to 'light you on fire'?" Her face exploded into a wide grin, looking like she was going to burst with curiosity.

I didn't even try to stifle a laugh, then I felt the heat rising in my cheeks. "Girlfriend, he does it *all*. But he adds some extra spice. He's on board with bringing sex toys into our play, and there's more." Lowering my voice to a whisper I added, "I like it when he restrains me, there's something powerfully sexy about a strong man taking control and pleasuring me senseless."

Instantaneously her spine straightened, and her eyelids fluttered as an idea shot through her like an electric jolt. "Ooh," she breathed out, "Bondage? That does take play to another level. What does Ethan use with you?"

"His specialty is ropes. I don't know where he learned it, but he can tie knots like a sailor," I chuckled. "Just go down the sex shop and bring your guy along. Bondage is trendy now so there are handcuffs and a wide array of toys. Vibrators, whips and even costumes."

Lena's face lit up. "I like the idea of adding toys, but I don't know if he would set foot in a sex shop."

"Girl, it's mainstream now, not like it used to be when the shops were tucked away in some sleazy part of town. The one I go to has great customer service. It's hysterical to see people of all ages testing the vibrators. The place buzzes with the sound and everybody acts like it's totally normal to be checking out the kinkiest of toys."

"I need to get over the idea that there's something taboo in talking about sex in a public place, it's a generational thing, I guess. But I need something to make our sex life a little kinky. Vanilla gets boring after a while," she said.

"I agree, and I'm quite sure we are not unusual. I'd like to go with Ethan. That is, if we are still seeing each other when he gets back."

We ordered a few more rounds and carried on the girl talk well after happy hour. Making our way to the parking garage, she wrapped me into a hug as we reached our cars.

"As for Ethan, I just want the best for you. I know you're crazy about him but please take care of yourself. I love you," she said gently.

I brushed her curly hair from my face and smiled against her cheek.

"I know, I love you too. I will try my best, and thanks."

IN THE COMING weeks, I took Lena's advice. I tried to keep busy and date other men. That did not prove to be easy since all I could think about was Ethan. He kept in touch by email, giving me snippets of his travel experiences, but often only after I reached out to him first. It began to look like he would be gone for several months, and although he told me he missed me, hope was plummeting along with my mood.

I made some desperate efforts to move things forward with a couple of men I had been casually dating, but it completely bombed. As I suspected, *casual* was as far as they wanted things to go. Online dating was one disaster after another, but then, my motivation just wasn't there.

I forced my thoughts away from Ethan and focused on building a strategy, a new life plan. I imagined myself working on a cruise ship out of Barcelona or starting over as a flight attendant. The only problem was, I was prone to seasickness and my legs had begun to swell from long air travel. I was becoming increasingly depressed by the daily drudgery of my job, and the only spot of clarity in the morass of my life was that I needed a big escape. The biggest one of my life. A giant leap into something new.

Future security was central in my mind though, I couldn't leap without a safety net. That's when I found the key to the 'golden handcuffs.'

Turned out, I could *buy* some retirement time. I had worked for the government program before, but in those days, I was part-time and not eligible. But as a full-timer, I could now benefit from those precious years. I kicked myself for not doing it sooner, many of my co-workers had jumped on that opportunity—doing anything to speed up the release of retirement. As usual, nothing was simple in a bureaucracy, but perseverance paid off. I'd hit the magic ten-year mark and then some—one year over what I needed to be vested. Freedom seemed to be within reach. But freedom wasn't going to be cheap, I would need more than a pension to pay the bills.

Sitting at my kitchen table with a calculator, a notebook and a pen, I ran some numbers. I tugged at my scalp with both hands in frustration. *How can I manage this? There must be a way to at least go part-time at work? And there is no way in hell I'm making it another year there.*

I gazed out the window to my backyard as my thoughts ran in circles. I rubbed my temples, trying to relieve the colossal headache that was developing. The leaves from the towering elm trees rained down in the wind and piled on the roof of the old garage structure which sat at the back of the property. Built in the 1920's, it stood apart from the house, accessible by the remnants of an old driveway that extended to the street.

It had been partially remodeled into a workspace when my ex-husband was around, but he never finished the project. Sheetrocked walls over redwood framing was as far as he got before setting up shop. Vines were growing through the cracks, and spiders took advantage of the many entry points. The old cement foundation was filthy, and mold was growing where the roof had leaked. It was a dumping ground for yard tools, plastic boxes filled with Christmas decorations and my son's childhood books.

I had begun a project to fix it up, mostly because I hated to enter the rat and spider-infested space every time I needed garden supplies. Maybe it was the desperate mood I was in, but when I looked out from my kitchen table, I saw beyond a dilapidated garage. I saw freedom.

This five hundred square foot space could be transformed into an income-producing cottage. With the rents skyrocketing in San Francisco, workers were looking for a more reasonable cost of living in the neighboring communities. Oakland was just across the Bay Bridge, a relatively short commute by car or mass transit to the city. With rental income, I could go part-time at work, and that alone would transform my life into something bearable. Then I could have more time to formulate an escape plan. But this would be no easy task.

"So, DO YOU think you can do it?" I asked.

Dan stood in the middle of the old garage and surveyed the broken-down structure.

"Sure thing, but it's a big project. I can't do it alone but I know a guy who has done a lot of construction and he needs the work. But there's one thing you should know about him."

"Knowing you and the friends you hang with I'm afraid to ask."

Dan shot me a dirty look but didn't argue. "This guy is an ex-con, he did some time."

"Why am I not surprised. Is he safe to be around and is he using?"

"There won't be any problems, I'll make sure of that. He's clean, as far as I know. He's good at what he does, has a lot of experience."

My head fell against my neck with a groan. "Well, beggars can't be choosy. I have a very limited budget for this project and a short timeline, so I just need you guys to be dependable."

"When do you want it completed?"

"Ideally, in four to five months."

Dan laughed and rolled his eyes at me. "We might need a bigger team."

"I have a plumber coming in to assess and hopefully he will take on the job. And I will be helping out with the work." I turned to Dan, "There's another thing. I will be directing the job."

"So, you are the acting general contractor? With no experience?" he chuckled.

"Yep. I can't afford a professional to come in here with a team, so we are going to pull this off together."

"Well, you're the boss," he said, shaking his head.

I didn't divulge to him that I was in way over my head. I was hurtling into a construction project with a rag-tag team. Dan was my handyman, jack of all trades but master of none. A short dark-skinned man born with a Spanish heritage, he'd learned to do a wide array of jobs over fifty years or so. He was a hard worker—when he showed up. He overestimated his skills and always left a colossal mess at the end of each job. Any money I paid him quickly disappeared as he gambled it away. I could pretty much bet that he would be at the casino instead of on the job after payday. But he was loyal, and he wanted to see this project through to the end. He cared about my dream.

The fate of the project rested on one crucial element. That shit would flow downstream, literally. That's where George the plumber came in. He was highly recommended and lived just up the street, but his expertise came at the cost of my sanity. Before any work could be started, I called him over for a consultation and an estimate.

"Hey, doll. Wow, you're a cutie. What can I help you with?" George winked at me as I greeted him at the door.

Seriously? I thought, *Is he for real?* I ignored his comments and showed him the structure while explaining the plans.

He examined the old garage and crawled under the main house to identify the sewer pipeline, all the while rambling like a hyperactive child with absolutely no filter between his random thoughts and what came out of his mouth. I could barely get a word in, and my jaw began to tighten in frustration. He finally verbalized his assessment.

"See here? This is where the main line is, and the new pipes have to reach all the way to the back of the yard. There is a minimum level of drop we need to make sure the shit flows downhill. There's about fifty feet, and the pitch has to drop at ¼ inch per foot. It's very tight because the land slopes downward here—the wrong direction. I am ninety percent sure I can make it work. But if anyone can do it, I can. I'm the best in the business, just ask anyone. I'm the best at a lot of things, just ask my ex-girlfriend." His eyebrows twitched suggestively. "Hey, gotta run. Have to get to the gym, I have a workout schedule to keep." He rolled up the sleeves on his t-shirt and flexed his biceps.

It was all I could do to keep my eyes from rolling in response, and I blocked my thoughts from turning into words that might sabotage his taking the job. He was enough of an arrogant rogue to attempt this kind of challenge, mostly to satisfy his own ego.

"Wait, are you going to give me a bid?" I asked as he headed toward the door.

"I will email it to you by tomorrow. This kind of job would cost you a lot of money, but I will give you a discount. After all, we are neighbors." He swatted me on the ass as he left.

"Hey, there will be none of that," I yelled after him, but he just smiled and waved with the back of his hand as he headed for his truck.

He left me psychologically drained and fuming mad. I knew this was going to be the pattern with him, just another part of the job I would learn to manage.

For the next few months, I sat on the floor of the developing cottage night after night, often with only a flashlight as I measured, visualized, and sketched out the design and listed out the plan for the workers as they came in the next day. More often than not, something went wrong and supervising from my day job was increasing my stress level exponentially. I remembered my mother's adage, "What doesn't kill you, makes you stronger." *Ha,* I thought, *this could go either way.*

Evenings and weekends turned into hard but rewarding labor, with multiple trips to the local big box hardware store, helping to load and unload the truck, and cleaning up the daily mess well into the night. Sometimes my only company was the salsa music I loved and my small, adorable, but highly neurotic rescue pup. He wouldn't let me out of his sight, so he chose to come to work in the cottage and curled up on the bed I set out for him.

I often thought to myself if someone had told me a year ago that I would be designing a house, learning the intricacies of construction, and end each day battling with a sexually harassing plumber, I would have thought they were crazy. But these were desperate times and I worked tirelessly at my goal.

It cost me, my stress levels were off the charts. But I was determined to be out of there and into a new chapter of life. So, while I envisioned the completed perfect little cottage home, I also dreamt of what life would be like in my new city. Every day I scoured the internet apartment rental sites in Barcelona, not only to learn about what was available on the market, but also to keep the dream alive. I imagined living in one of those quaint little apartments with high ceilings, with balcony doors opened to a view of the gothic-inspired architecture. It was a matter of survival.

There was nothing else in my life, having given up on dating entirely. I waited for Ethan's return and wondered if there would still be anything left between us. He'd erected the barrier, but I couldn't let go. It was my damn pattern of persistence. Once I was hooked, I held on until the bitter end. But then, he hadn't let go either. He held me with his emails and desire from a distance. I would soon find out if he still felt anything, or if we were done. Only seeing him in person would give me the answer.

Chapter Twenty-Eight

I THINK MY CO-WORKERS must have had a collective bet on how long I was going to last at the job. It was no secret that I was looking for a way out, and most were supportive.

Though I was making new friends there, my restlessness was evident. I longed to be back in Barcelona, thinking it might provide inspiration for a solution or at the very least a break from the monotony. And since Ethan was spending more time abroad than twenty minutes away, maybe I'd actually see him. It was the beginning of Spring and Ethan had still not made a plan to meet. He had traveled for months and then entertained guests once he was back home. Despite the texts and emails, he wasn't rushing back into my arms.

I put my plans in motion for a second trip back in May, first to Barcelona for a week of language school. I was on a mission to learn Spanish and my skills had not improved much by using Spanish language apps. I researched the schools that provided a one week Spanish intensive and narrowed it down to one convenient option. There were student apartments situated above the floors which held the classrooms. It seemed the only way I was going to make it to a class that started at the brutal hour of 9:00 AM. Barcelona came alive at night, and so did I. The early morning classes would be torture, but at least I'd have the afternoons free.

The second part of my trip would be spent in Florence for five days. Firenze held fond memories; I'd been there twice in my twenties. I had found Florence to be my favorite place in Italy, it wasn't a bustling city like Barcelona, but it held a unique charm and beauty. Florence was only an hour by plane. While I wanted to take advantage of the opportunity to travel since I was in Europe, I wasn't so keen on going alone. I dared to fantasize about being there with Ethan amidst the romantic backdrop of Tuscany. It was a long shot, but I emailed him with the idea.

> *Hey, I was wondering if you might be in Europe in the next month or so. I'm planning on being in Barcelona and heading over to Florence for a few days. What do you think about the idea of joining me there?*

I waited nervously for his response. Luckily, he didn't keep me waiting long.

Hi, how are you anyway? I will probably be over there, so I might be able to meet up with you. I haven't been to Florence and I'm a little overdosed on Spain. Let's talk.

By "talk" he usually meant text, and that wasn't going to cut it. I needed a face-to-face.

> *Great! I'll be coming to the city tomorrow. Do you have some time?*

How about 2:00? Late lunch at a restaurant by the bay, I'll text you the address. Looking forward to seeing you...

I was surprised at his willingness but held back my excitement. With Ethan, things had turned into "maybe" and vague possibilities.

The crisp sunny day in the city did not lessen my anxiety as I parked and walked to find Ethan at the restaurant near the marina. As always, my heart raced when I laid eyes on him. Nothing had changed, for me at least.

Sitting across the table from him, I felt the awkward tension between us. It had been almost three months since we'd been together on that magical weekend in Pacific Grove. We pushed through the pleasantries of catching up, and he filled me in on his travels.

"What have you been up to?" he asked.

"Mostly job hunting without much success. So, I changed my plan. I'm aiming to leave my job—to what, I don't know just yet. I've been working on an income-producing project that will help get me out of there. I think I emailed you about it.

"Yes, I remember that, how's it going?"

"Ha! Don't ask. Right now, it feels like "The Money Pit." You can't imagine how many things have gone wrong. It's been a challenge, but it's coming along. All my time has been going to the project, but I did get a break. I went to Santa Barbara to see my son and visit a friend. I needed to get away."

"A friend? What kind of friend?"

I was surprised by his inquisitiveness but knew exactly what he was getting at. Hesitating for a moment, I decided not to hide anything from him.

"A guy who lives down south. We went out on a couple of dates when he was in Oakland last year, so I thought I'd connect with him."

His eyes widened before casting a glance at the bay. He paused and I waited for the reaction.

"Did you sleep with him?"

In an instant, I weighed my options. What right did he have to know? I wasn't asking him who he'd slept with during the past several months. But he seemed to care, and I wanted to know how much.

"Yes, I did. Why? Does it matter?" I said with indignation. "You left me alone for almost three months. Why shouldn't I sleep with him?"

Biting his lower lip, he leaned heavily against the back of his chair as if my words had forced him away.

"Was it good? Was the sex good?" His eyes blazed at me.

My back flattened against the chair and I took a deep breath.

"Yes. I'm not going to lie, even though that question is pretty intrusive. Technically speaking, he was a good lover but there was something missing." I stammered when he turned away from me. I saw the muscles tighten in his face, pulling at his hard-set jaw.

"The missing piece was his heart. I couldn't feel it, there was no connection. It's not like it is with us, the passion between us moves me. It's deep and it's real." I leaned forward, afraid he had put even more distance between us.

"Why did you stay away?" I asked.

"You know I was traveling, and hosting visitors. Then I had to catch up on work."

"Bullshit."

He looked at me in surprise. Feeling emboldened by a burst of anger I stood my ground.

"You heard me. Bullshit. When a man really wants to see a woman, he finds a way."

A flicker of a smile crossed his lips as he acquiesced. "This is true, you have a point."

"So?"

"It's just that things change when people have sex. There's expectations, you know, the relationship talk is next." His eyes wandered everywhere but at me.

"Look, I recognize what happened. The last time we were together was powerful. You got in way further than you intended and said some things."

"What things?"

"You said you loved me, but I didn't take it seriously since at that moment you may have been directing the declaration to my pussy, not me," I said flippantly.

He looked down at his lap and said quietly, "I believe what I said was, that I loved being with you. And I do."

"I heard both, but seriously, don't worry. I didn't see it as a binding contract. But there was something else. You said you wanted to take care of me."

Ethan froze in his chair, suddenly deep in thought. A look of recognition flashed in his eyes. We sat for moments without saying a word, and the empty space made it more unbearable. I was already churning from the mix of emotions, my vulnerability bubbling to the surface. Finally, he broke the silence.

"It's not that I don't want to be with you. I love so many things about you, and our time together. You make me laugh, even when you're not trying. The way you get excited about seeing the world, I love that we share that passion. We have so much fun together… it's truly the best I've ever had in my life." He paused, then his chest rose and fell with a heavy breath. "What we have is so real, so intense, and it's not just about adventurous sex. When we make love, it's like a meeting of our souls. I think about you every day."

His eyes squeezed shut and his head bowed on his chest. "That's what makes it so difficult. It's just that I see myself on a different path, you know, with kids."

Hearing that again did not hurt any less than before. Especially since he'd confirmed how great it was, only to leave me feeling empty.

"Well, I guess I should go." I wanted to run or at least be capable of having a poker face. "It's not like I didn't see this coming anyway." I raised out of the chair, throwing my napkin on the table.

"Sit down," he said. His fingers wrapped around my wrist as I prepared to bolt. "Don't go, please. I've missed you." The muscles in his clenched jaw loosened and his eyes softened. The steely veil lowered. I saw vulnerability—need in his eyes. The pleading look on his face stopped me cold, I couldn't step away. I fell back into the seat, so weary from the emotional roller coaster that was *us*.

He ran his hand across the top of his hair, as I'd seen him do when he was frustrated. "Come back to the apartment with me, please? I have some time before my next appointment."

"Why? Where is this going? As you've just reminded me, it can't go very far." I was on the brink of tears and couldn't let him see me break down.

"Because I need to be with you. And I think you need to be with me right now too."

Any resolve to be tough evaporated with his declaration. Making love was the way we connected, the way we felt each other's hearts. I needed him more than I needed to protect myself and so I folded. The reunion was different than our previous lovemaking though. It was laced with apprehension, maybe fear, but it brought us back to a place that we recognized. We were becoming intimate again in that tenuous place of an undefined relationship. Without a promise of exclusivity, without a future. All we could do was steal moments in time.

Chapter Twenty-Nine

"Happy birthday to you, happy birthday to you..." he sang in a low and sultry tone. Ethan's voice trailed off into his voice recorded message. "Hope you are having a good start to your day, hon. Just want to let you know I might be ahead of schedule. I'm excited to meet up with you, could you text me the address of the hotel again? Kisses, see you soon, babe."

I played the message several times, just to hear the sound of his voice. It rippled through me, stopping first at my heart then moving south as I felt that tingling of excitement. *God, what that man does to me. Just the sound of his voice makes me hot.*

I dreaded birthdays. They just reminded me of the inevitable clock ticking the years toward the end of life as I knew it. Particularly my dating life. Sliding down the slope of age, when each year brought body parts closer to the ground, pulled by the irrefutable force of gravity. There was a time limit, a shelf life to my looks and the ability to attract the men I would want to be with.

It was also a reminder that with each passing year, I had no one special to celebrate with. No one to wake up with who might roll over and whisper with morning breath, "Good morning sweetie, happy birthday. Today is going to be your day."

But as I packed my overnight bag, all I could think about was how this birthday would be very different from the rest. The last several weeks had been amazing with Ethan since we hashed things out at lunch in the city. I was surprised at how we flowed back together again, like we'd never been apart. We had always talked about a weekend up the coast in Northern California, so I took advantage of my birthday to plan something special. I was prepared to go alone, but it would not have been a pretty picture. Me, sitting all by myself, surrounded by couples in an idyllic retreat. He relieved me of that agony, in fact, he was thrilled about the idea.

I had reserved a small hotel set on a bluff overlooking the ocean. The windswept beaches, sprinkled with tall pine trees, stretched for miles. It didn't matter if there were few restaurants or places to explore nearby. This year, all that mattered was hunkering down in a hotel room for two days with the only person who could turn my birthday into something I looked forward to.

Ethan's text popped up only minutes after his sweet voice message.

> Hey, I have to work this morning, so I'll take my motorcycle up the coast this afternoon. Do you want to ride with me or meet up there?

Not relishing the idea of a long motorcycle ride, arriving sore and windswept, I opted to drive. I knew it took some preparation to get ready for our time together, not to mention a reserve of energy.

> Thanks for the offer, I'd love to take a ride with you sometime. But you know me... I'll be bringing more than a backpack. I think I'll meet you there. I'll text you my arrival. Hopefully, I'll have access to a signal, it's pretty remote.

As it turned out, the drive was long and grueling through miles of hairpin turns. I was relieved to finally arrive ahead of him and have an opportunity to relax.

Checking in at the desk, I got the keys and lugged my bags upstairs. The room was perfect, just as I had imagined. The walls and ceiling were made of wood beams and in the center stood a gas fireplace. A king-sized bed was situated near the glass doors that opened onto a private balcony. Laying down on the bed, I gazed out at the expansive view of the ocean. I thought about how perfect it was going to be with him there. It was the ultimate romantic setting.

Changing into a t-shirt and yoga pants, I curled up in a chair on the sun-drenched balcony perched directly over the sea. I opened the bottle of wine I'd packed and poured myself a glass. *Let the party begin, Happy Birthday to me.* I raised my glass to the clear blue skies and sunk into the tranquility of the magnificent surroundings. The view of the rugged coastline was spectacular, the vast ocean and surf crashing hard against the sand below. Damp ocean mist drifted in all directions driven by the wind, and in the air hung the smell of the salty sea. The combination of the wine, the sun, and the power of the ocean were already sending me into a state of sensual bliss.

I visualized Ethan, naked and on top of me, or taking me from behind. *Hmm… I wonder if he is bringing the ropes…* My body instantly responded, and a shiver of excitement pricked my skin. *Damn. How does just the thought of him makes me so turned on? God, he is taking his sweet time getting here, I thought he'd be here by now.* It was an hour past his estimated time of arrival, so I pulled out my phone and hoped the text would reach him.

Where are you?

Hey, I just stopped for a break… It is taking a really long time to get there. I think I will arrive by 5:00. It's a killer bike ride, so it's a good thing you didn't come with me.

Glancing at the phone, I groaned a feeble protest. Patience was never easy for me, and it looked like it would be another hour of waiting. Pacing the floor wasn't going to help. So, I poured another glass of wine and propped my feet up on the chair.

Finally, I heard the rumble of a motorcycle and just then, he texted his arrival.

I hurried to the railing overlooking the parking lot and waved, *"Hey, I'm up here."* Excitement replaced impatience as I waited at the top of the stairs. I watched in awe as he dismounted the racing bike. It was a beauty, Italian, I guessed, and hot red. *Yep, that suits him well. Sexy, hot and dangerous.*

His tall frame stumbled through the door, clad in a full jumpsuit and helmet. Cold and windblown, he burst into the room and flung his body face down on the floor.

"Are you okay? What happened?"

"That was a hell of a ride," he said, with an agonized laugh. "I didn't know whether to hate you or thank you as I made my way up that wild coast, though I stopped and got some great shots along the way. I had to keep taking breaks. It was such a strenuous road, it took a lot of concentration." He struggled to squeeze himself out of the helmet.

"But Maps said it would only take you an hour and a half from San Francisco, what happened?"

"Well… I think I put in the wrong route on my GPS and instead of coming up the inland road, I took Highway 1 all the way."

I attempted to stifle a laugh, unsuccessfully, "Seriously, dude? You went up that windy coast highway, practically hanging off the cliff? Let's get you out of this crazy suit. Your hands and face are freezing cold."

I tugged at his hand, trying to pry him from the floor. He staggered to his feet and pulled me into an embrace. "Happy birthday, baby, thank you for inviting me." His soft gaze was filled with tenderness, the warmth flowing through my skin and melting me into his arms. He brushed his thumb along my bottom lip and then lifted my chin. Softly, his full lips moved over mine in a sweet kiss.

"Out of all the people you know, you chose me to be here and I'm really touched."

Does he really not know how important he is to me?

I shrugged my shoulders. "There is no one else I would rather be with on this day, you are the only one."

He paused, sinking into my gaze with familiarity. He had a way of seeing right into my soul. "I'm very glad to hear that, my sweet."

He grazed my lips with a kiss, then stripped off his racing suit and layers of clothing as I watched.

"I need a hot shower first, do you mind?"

"Not at all, be my guest." I gestured to the small shower strangely situated in the middle of the bedroom, then flopped down on the bed to take in the sight of his fine body.

"God, this feels good. I really needed to thaw out." Steam billowed into the room and I couldn't help reflecting back on the time he asked to use my shower in Barcelona. But this time, instead of only seeing his half-naked body covered with a shower curtain, I had the full view. I loved watching him as the water trickled down the lines of his etched form.

"You're enjoying this, aren't you?" His smile was an invitation I couldn't resist.

"Yes, I most certainly am."

Jumping off the bed, I opened the shower door long enough to run my hands over his wet, slippery body, tracing a trail from his chest down to his thick penis. My lips parted. "Ah... you are so delicious." Taking a firm grip, I stroked him slowly—my hand running up and down the long shaft made slick by the soapy water that poured down to his groin.

A breath rasped from deep in his throat as I coaxed his erection to full length. He moaned, the sound of his voice so erotic it made my sex tremble. "You better watch out, or I will pull you in here, clothes and all."

I withdrew my hand and closed the door. "That was just a tease. I'm saving the rest for later."

"We may not get out of this room all night, you know," he called out as if it was a warning.

"We have a dinner reservation at six-thirty, should I call to change it?"

"I'm starving, so let's try to make it. Be out in a moment."

Ethan dried off and tucked a towel around his waist, then moved toward me with a dangerous look in his eyes. His hands reached my waist and lifted me into the air. Letting out a squeal of surprise, I landed hard on the mattress. He scanned my body sprawled out before him, clothed only in a bra and panties.

"Ah, you little temptress! You make it very difficult to wait."

"I was trying to change into some nice clothes until you *rudely* interrupted me. I thought you were hungry. We don't want to miss dinner." The towel slipped away, and I rolled my eyes at him, pretending not to notice the glorious package between his legs.

"How can I wait?" His hands tugged at my bra, exposing my breasts. "When I have you right here in front of me?" His hands splayed open, gesturing at my half-naked body, his eyes blazing. "Look at you, you're so hot."

In one swift move, the weight of his body pinned me to the bed. He pressed his rock-hard cock between my legs, straining at thin lace which blocked his entrance.

"I need you right now." Stripping off my panties, he stood at the edge of the bed and held my legs in the air. Moving his hips into the space he made, his erection slid against the soft, fleshy tissues, already wet with desire. An involuntary moan escaped me as the full length of his cock deepened inside me, making me wince from the sudden fullness against my walls. The muscles tightening in his abdomen was the only warning I had before he slammed into me with hard thrusts.

"Oh my God, you feel so good." His head tipped back, his etched jaw pulled tight.

I sucked in a deep breath, feeling exquisitely stretched, and curved my hips to send the long strokes at just the right angle. Abruptly, he withdrew, leaving me empty and needy.

He kissed me swiftly before abandoning my body. "I don't want to come now, let's save it for later."

Left reeling and hungry for him, my breaths slowly quieted.

"Well, I guess I had that coming. Turnabout is fair play, huh?"

Ethan landed a hard slap on my ass when I bent to find my underwear and looked at me with a devilish grin.

"Get ready, woman. Let's go eat and celebrate your birthday."

Dinner was a sumptuous feast for the senses. Seated at a table with an expansive view of the sea at sunset, Ethan treated me to wine, one of Napa Valley's best, a meal of shellfish and steak and topped it off with dessert. I couldn't figure out when he had tipped off the waiter, but my chocolate coulant arrived with a single lit candle. Thank God, it was without a staff of singing waiters. He planted a single kiss on my neck and whispered in my ear, "Happy birthday, baby, make a wish." He breathed out the song, slowly, in his deep sexy voice, making my skin tingle with goosebumps.

With my hand on his knee, I pressed my eyelids shut and scrunched my forehead before I finalized my wish and blew. It was more than a wish—it was a plea and a prayer. When I opened my eyes, his gaze caught me.

My brows raised. "I'm not telling you what I wished for, so don't even ask."

He laughed and threw his palms in the air. "I'm not even going there, so don't worry."

"By the way, when are we meeting up in Florence? I gave up trying to track the date changes in your emails." He rolled his eyes at me, but I couldn't blame him.

"Yeah… sorry about that, I've been juggling dates because I'm trying to use airline miles plus negotiate the vacation schedule with my boss. I will send you the precise itinerary, but I take off for Barcelona in about a month, at the end of May."

"I'll join you after I get back from Turkey. My friends made the plans a while ago, so I'm locked in, but I think it will work."

I threw my arms around his neck. "I'm so excited! I can't wait to be back in Barcelona with you. I hope we can be there for a day at least, and I'm really looking forward to Florence. I'm keeping my fingers crossed the timing all works out. I know you tend to leave your schedule a little open-ended when you travel."

Ethan shrugged, "I'm not much of a planner, you know that, but I would like to go with you to Florence. Anyway, I'll see you again before you leave so we can talk more. Right now, let's move this party to the patio. I see some empty seats by the firepit."

We stepped outside to sit by the roaring fire. There, away from the city lights, the stars covered the night sky like a million shimmering diamonds. The ambiance couldn't have been more perfect if I'd scripted it. Listening to the surf crashing on the rocks below, we sat by the warmth of the open flames—but it was not a private romantic moment. Three other couples joined in and pulled their chairs closer to the fire.

Ethan flagged the waiter to order cocktails, and by the time the drinks arrived, he had already jumped into a conversation with the young couple sitting beside us.

"Yeah, really crazy drive up here," the man agreed with Ethan, "but we were here before and it's so spectacular that we decided to make it back here this year. We came up from the Bay Area." His wife nodded in agreement and added, "Where do you guys live?"

Maybe they think we are a couple, that we live together. Instantly, I was flooded with those desires I had felt for so long, to be someone's girlfriend—to be Ethan's girlfriend. There was a pause, and Ethan's answer dispelled the illusion, giving away that we lived in different towns. Even so, I held onto the fantasy, because for this night, we were a couple. I settled back in my chair and enjoyed the precious moments.

Ethan was a master at generating conversation, and while I considered myself good in social situations, I was in awe at how easily this came to him. He cracked a few jokes and had us all laughing. There was something so comfortable about the night. So normal for most people, I thought, as we talked with the other couple. But for us, this was outside the norm.

Ethan never brought me into his circle of friends. It was a painful trade-off I had come to accept. I was socially unacceptable in his world, and he seemed to care what his friends thought. But if our ages were reversed, and he was a fifty-three-year-old man with a hot thirty-five-year-old on his arm, no one would raise an eyebrow. In fact, guys would be envious. I wasn't the only woman struggling with this issue. Many of my girlfriends were also dating younger guys. Societal norms had not adjusted to fit what was becoming the new normal and it enraged me—but not enough to challenge the one man who mattered.

He looked at me with a private nod, and I knew it was time. When we finished our drinks, he leaned in and whispered, "You ready to go?"

I hated to give up the rare moment we were having, socializing with other people as a couple. But the twinkle in his eyes easily seduced me with the promise that he had some very special moments planned for us.

Chapter Thirty

Ethan ignited the gas fireplace and turned down the lights. The glow from the fire radiated through the room, creating a golden light and giving off its warmth on the cold night.

"This is so cool, having our own fireplace." I rubbed my hands together and held them near the glass. "Oh, wait, I almost forgot, there's something I can do to set the mood too." I went to my computer and clicked on the music station, locating a perfect genre to set the ambiance. The sounds of soft, romantic, acoustic guitar music filled the room.

Before I could turn, Ethan captured me from behind, his arms folded around me, and he buried his face in my hair. "This is perfect, you know. You picked a great spot for us. I love the room, the view—everything. I love being here with you."

I tugged his arms tightly around me. "I'm so happy you are here, it's seriously my best birthday ever. It means a lot that you came here to be with me."

"Ever?"

"Well, I probably had some good ones when I was a kid, but it's hard to remember. For a very long time, birthdays have been pretty routine. This is anything but routine."

Ethan spun me around to face him and a smile lit his eyes. His hands cupped my face, his look turning seductive in a flash. "I'm going to take very good care of you tonight."

Slowly and deliberately, he undressed me with the finesse I had become accustomed to until I stood naked in front of him. His hands cupped my breasts while his thumbs flicked across my nipples, coaxing them erect. When he took a hardened tip in his mouth, I cried out from the waves of pleasure arrowing to my core. He kneaded and sucked one and then the other, greedily feasting on their fullness.

His lips made a languid trail downward, lowering himself to his knees until he reached the apex between my legs. I watched as his full lips engulfed my sex, and his tongue fluttered along the slit. Moaning with pleasure, I laced my fingers at the back of his head and pressed into his mouth. Abruptly interrupting my ascension, his hands gripped my hips and flipped my body around. The force of his hard chest first rippled against my buttocks, then my back, as he raised to stand and wrapped me in his arms. I arched my neck to reach his lips and felt his steely cock pressed between my thighs.

We stood naked in the center of the room, bodies pressed together, his arms wrapped around my waist. "See that," Ethan said, "There, in the mirror," he motioned. "God that looks so hot, the way we look together in the firelight. I wish I could capture this with the camera."

I leaned my head against his chest and laced my fingers with his. The image of us was stunning. I had never seen our reflection together. The glow erased any differences between our ages that my eyes might have pinpointed. We looked like a perfect fit.

"Wait right here, don't move," Ethan commanded. I caught sight of the rope in his hands as he strode across the room.

"Do you trust me?" He held me by the shoulders, his eyes blazing hot.

I nodded, "Yes, of course I do."

With a look of hot determination, he unraveled the rope. The power he exuded was palpable. I knew what was coming. This time, I trusted him completely and craved his dominance.

"Down, on your knees." I obeyed automatically and knelt on the carpeted floor, grateful for the cushioning.

Ethan manipulated the rope around my body, lacing it between my legs, across my back, up to the shoulders. Wrapping it around to my waist and then my chest, he encased my breasts in the rope until they protruded, squeezed into bulbous points. He pressed me downward until my forehead touched the floor. Finally, he tied my hands together behind my back. I was completely bound, unable to move. He stood back to admire his handiwork and said, "Oh, Elena, do you know how amazing you look? My god, I love your body. You are mine," he said, with a firm, possessive voice that made my core clench.

I sensed him circling, his bare feet making a path around me. The electricity of his body permeated my skin. The way he'd imprisoned me, possessed me, drove me mindless with erotic fantasies. Arousal shot through my body until I thought I might come from the slightest touch.

"I want to fuck you so badly right now, but there is something I need to do first. I want to photograph you like this. Stay completely still."

I heard the click of the shutter over and over again as he moved around me. I held steady, the ropes biting into my skin.

"The fire glow is doing amazing things to the shadows on your body. It's perfect for the photos."

His shadow was the only warning that he was poised behind me. Sounds from the camera stopped and I heard the subtle whistling in the air before I felt it. Strands of soft leather slowly grazed my back.

"I will start slow and easy. Tell me if you want me to stop, okay?"

I had fantasized about a whip, but in that moment, desire and fear threatened to unravel me. I knelt helplessly before him, bent over from my knees and unsteady without the use of my hands.

The strands fanned across my buttocks as he began the blows in a slow, steady rhythm. I inhaled sharply when the leather moved through my legs, snapping against my sex. The sting reverberated on my clit leaving me craving more.

"*Yes,*" I hissed, and he flicked the whip faster, sending blows to the hypersensitive nerve endings. The muscles in my core clenched with the sting on my ass, and the flicks that reached the outer lips of my sex. Delicious sensations of pain and pleasure sent me higher, my arousal flowing onto the soft leather.

I waited... surrendering to the new sensations. My breath hitched when the strands fanned across my breasts. He sent another blow, and another. My nipples drew into tight points. Each flick bit with unexpected intensity, waves of exquisite heat rolled through me. My body was on fire, every nerve ending pulsing, waiting for the next blow to come.

Ethan coaxed me on with his adoring words until all inhibition disappeared. I felt completely free to push the limits of my sexuality, held bound before him. His excitement fueled mine, the electricity of his passion extending through the whip.

The low, seductive sound in his voice made me quiver. "*Ahh*, Elena, I want to take you, right here, right now." He pressed a finger into me. "My girl, you are soaking wet. And your ass is a pretty shade of pink." His lips gentled the tender skin, kissing the spots where it had colored from the whip while his finger primed me. My clit throbbed as the flat of his finger made circles around the engorged bundle of nerves.

My voice rasped out a plea, "Yes, please, don't stop." The sweet tension was building in my core. His wide crown pressed at the entrance to my body, gliding along the slickness of my desire. Heated breaths filled my lungs, as the long shaft pushed into me.

"Steady, baby," he said, his voice low and foreboding. His hands moved to pull at my hips, forcing me back against his pounding thrusts. A primitive growl escaped him each time his brutally hard cock slammed and hit the end of me. With each thrust, I felt him claiming me, possessing me. I whimpered as my body struggled to accommodate the length of him. He slowed at the pained sound in my voice, and reached his fingers to my clit again, circling with light strokes.

"*Shush,* my sweet, I'll take care of you." Pleasure rippled through me, softening my walls. I took more of him, letting him in deeper. Pressing into the fullness, I climbed higher, my body igniting under his touch and the sweet sound of his voice. Needy, helpless sounds spilled from my throat. I was barely able to register the tip of his finger tracing the line down the curve of my back until it reached the cleft between my round cheeks.

Ethan knew my body well, how to make me crazy under his touch. He teased the ridged opening of my bottom with the pad of his finger, making me squirm. Even with the ropes holding me in place, I arched into his touch. Slowly he pressed into me and began rhythmically sliding his finger. The intense combination sent me into a frenzy.

"Yes, oh yes," I cried out. With each thrust, I wildly rocked my hips back to take him in to the root.

Bound, I closed my eyes to focus on each slide of his cock and the feeling of his fingers tormenting my nerve laden tissues. Taken from behind, distractions disappeared—there was only the primal bond between us.

"You're so close, aren't you? you're so swollen, so hot." My only response came as a whimper between ragged breaths. "Come for me baby, I've got you... let it go."

At the command of his voice, the slow heated roll pulled at my core, sending me over the ledge as the delicious explosion began its ascent. My muscles clenched around his cock, my body consumed by spasms as the climax rolled through me. Straining against the confines of the ropes, I bucked my hips with each thrust he sent into me, screaming out in curse words and agonized sounds of pleasure. I shuddered again and again, my belly clenching in the aftershocks.

"Oh, baby... I need you," I sobbed, so lost in the intensity and overwhelmed by emotion. My eyes opened in surprise at the sound of my own voice.

I didn't know if Ethan heard me, but he stilled, deep inside, and folded over me. His arms encircled me, and his hands caressed each breast. His engorged cock pulsated as my walls spasmed around it.

Sweeping my hair aside, he buried his face in the back of my neck. "Ah, my baby… my sweet Elena…" he said softly, then slowly raised himself. "Let's get you out of these ropes."

He skillfully untied every complicated knot in just a few moments. Just as I stood, my legs buckled. Ethan caught me in his arms and carried me to the bed. He scanned my body, his hands tenderly massaging the places the ropes had chafed. His lips bathed my sore breasts with kisses, while I lay dazed, slowly returning to the reality of time and place.

He murmured tenderly, "My sweet girl, you didn't tell me to stop. I would never want to hurt you. Was that too much?" His gentle voice warmed me from the inside. I looked at him from under heavy eyelids and ran a caressing hand over the back of his head.

"I'm fine… just a bit overcome. How can you overpower me and make me feel so free at the same time? I don't understand it, but damn, that was one hell of an orgasm." My lips curved into a blissful smile, and I saw relief softening his tight jaw. He held my gaze, shifted, and lowered onto me, his belly flattening against mine.

My hands moved to cradle his face at his etched jawline. I stroked my thumbs along the stubble of his beard.

"Ah, yes, baby…" I whispered, feeling the weight of his body pressing me to the bed. "This is where you belong."

I lifted my hips to meet the crown of his cock as he slid into me and sealed his mouth over my lips in a deep kiss. The velvet sides of his tongue swirled around mine, pulling me into him with increasingly hot flicks—devouring me. My senses were drenched in him, his scent, his taste—the euphoria of *him*.

I could have kissed him for hours, soaking in the shallow dips as his cock stroked against my walls, when Ethan shifted his head, leaving my lips parted and wet. My lids pried open and the look in his eyes made my pulse stutter. The shield was down, the depth of his emotion penetrated my heart. He looked at me with longing, and something more—something I was afraid to wish for. The tip of his finger brushed the hair from my damp forehead, I melted at his tender touch.

He breathed in long and deep, then lowered his head on my neck and began rocking his hips. The muscles in his firm buttocks flexed, pressing against my thighs in a steady rhythm.

The intensity grew with each delicious stroke, I felt him merge into me with body and soul. Buried deep inside me, he paused.

"Oh, my girl," he groaned out. "I am so close, but I want to last. I want to stay inside of you."

His lips nibbled and kissed along my neck, sending shivers of pleasure as goosebumps rose on my skin.

"Yes, please stay..." My voice pleading, I stilled, my hands clutched at hard muscles of his back.

"I need you too, you know," he whispered. His chest expanded with a sudden breath and he slammed into me, arching his back. A desperate growl poured from his throat. His muscles tensed and rippled under his silky skin as he flexed into me—enveloping himself in the depths of me.

Tears tracked down my temples. He had the power to move me like no other. I wrapped my legs around his hips and rode the wave of emotion and ecstasy. Ethan's hands clutched under my bottom, as he drove his cock into me with a ferocious need, frantically racing toward his release. I clenched my muscles around him, and he exploded into me with hot bursts of semen.

"Ah... Elena" he cried out, sobbing my name. His arms held me in a grip so tight, I could barely breathe. After the last of the tremors subsided, his body relaxed onto mine, his muscles lengthening. Slow, warm breaths grazed my neck while he absently weaved his fingers in my hair. When he finally lifted his head, I saw the dazed look in his eyes. He kissed me deeply, sealing our intimate bond.

With a long sigh, he rolled and pulled me on top of him. In the perfect afterglow, we lay silently, listening to the crackle of the fire and the rhythmic surge of the ocean. After the intensity, I was grateful for the peaceful sound of his steady heartbeat, my head resting heavily on his chest.

"I'm going to want you again, you know," he said, finally breaking the silence.

"Of course, I know, babe. I counted on it." I smiled and ran a finger against his cheek.

With a slap on my ass, he pulled me off the bed and into the shower. I ran my soapy hands over his broad chest and followed a trail to his ripped stomach, ending at his groin. My hands lathered and stroked his cock, still only half softened.

"How are you still hard?"

"It's you, babes, only you. It's never enough when I'm with you."

Pinning my wrists above my head with his powerful hand, he took the soap and ran it between my legs. I yelped as his soapy fingers reached behind, in between my cheeks.

"I have plans for this sweet bottom." He ran a finger in circles across the sensitive pucker.

"Oh, you do, huh?" I smirked at him. I knew there was no use playing hard to get.

Wrapped up in towels, I followed Ethan to the balcony.

"Damn, it's so hot in here," Ethan said, opening the doors.

"Hmm, I wonder why?" I teased.

We stepped out into the cool night air. Ethan wrapped his arms around me, holding me from behind as we took in the spectacle of the sea and star-filled sky. In the darkness, the white caps of waves glowed as they pounded against the shore.

I breathed in the cool, salty air and sighed. *"Ah*, this is incredible, our own private balcony. It's so beautiful here."

"You... are... so... beautiful..." Ethan whispered as he kissed his way down my neck. His cock lengthened and pressed at the seam of my butt.

"Already? Jesus, you are insatiable."

His only reply was a purring sound, it poured over my skin and sent shivers of desire down to my sex. He stirred me with his hand as it grazed between my legs, and a finger stroked the length of my slit.

I moaned a sigh of satisfaction, my head falling back on his chest, "This is heaven."

In a bold, wildly sexy moment, Ethan ripped the towel from my body, then loosened his own and let it fall to the floor. With his hand pressed at my back, he bent me over the balcony and lunged his hips, his erection pushing upward between my legs. He slid in easily, on the slippery trail of his release. His cock was no less hard from the first orgasm, and I knew it wouldn't take him long to come again.

It was so raw, so primal. With the power of the ocean below and only the waves to muffle the sounds of my moans, he pumped his hips into me in a measured tempo. I raised to my toes, giving him room to angle at the sweet spot inside me and clung to the railing. Even over the noise of the surf, I heard his ragged breaths and sounds of pleasure as he relished each slide against my tight walls.

Our naked bodies were illuminated only by the moonlight. My head tipped up to the dark sky and I tried to wrap my mind around how crazy hot it was between us. I imagined how it must have looked if someone were to see us. His naked body ravaging me, consumed with a primitive force. The thought of being so exposed was more than a little titillating.

Ethan sucked in a long breath through clenched teeth and stilled, bringing himself back from the edge. His long cock glistened in the moonlight, hanging heavy as he pulled away from me.

"Come here, birthday girl." He took my hand, and I didn't question him when he pulled me back to the bed. I laid my head down on the pillows, waiting. My pulse thrummed with heated anticipation. With Ethan, I could never be sure of his next move.

His eyes darted around the room, then found their target. Taking my vibrator from the nightstand, he clicked the "on" button. He ran the tip over my clit in circles while his tongue lapped at the folds. Instantly every muscle clenched, sending my hips off the bed, my thighs quivering against the stubble of his head. An orgasm brewed like a storm inside me, the delicious rush threatened to send me over the edge. "*Ah*, I'm so close," I cried.

He pulled away from my clenching sex, depriving me, holding me captive and needy. His strong arms lifted and maneuvered my body so effortlessly, flipping me over and lifting my ass in the air. I found myself face down, on my knees.

"Oh, babe, do you know how I love looking at you from this angle? Gorgeous!" Ethan moved his mouth low so that his tongue reached my sex, and then flicked his tongue over the sensitive nerve endings of my anus.

"*Ah*, that feels so good," I whimpered. The feeling of his soft, wet tongue *there,* sent delicious waves of pleasure coursing through my body. My arms trembled against the bed and my belly drew in tight.

I collapsed on the mattress when he stopped, crying out a needy protest, so weak and spent from the torment of my spasms and the desperate need to relieve the burn in my core.

"Don't worry, baby, savor it, I'll let you come," he cooed, in command of my body—my pleasure.

He propped my bottom in the air once more and placed the vibrator in my hand before he moved in behind me. Knowing what was next, I was grateful he was so attuned to my needs. The wide crest pushed at the precipice of the tender pucker he'd primed with his tongue.

"Slowly, slowly, please" I cried out. With gentle pressure, he inched the crown past the entrance. I brought the vibrator to my clit and the clenching muscles began to relax, letting him in a fraction more. They tensed again as he penetrated past the tightness. I cried out, half in pain and half in pleasure. He slid in, slowly, until I took all of him.

My cries turned into moans of pleasure. "*Ah*, you are so deep." I pushed back and churned against his hips.

"You feel so soft, so warm—baby, I can't hold it, you're so tight," he rasped. His hands dug into the flesh on my hips, rocking me back against his pelvis with a pounding force.

I sobbed out incoherently into the pillow, "yes… please don't stop… baby…." The sweet tension burned in my core as I chased another climax. The combination of sensations overwhelmed me, it was almost more than I could bear. I cried out in screams and jagged whimpers as I gave in to the explosion of pleasure and emotion. The orgasm hit me like a wave, building and spreading until it crashed over my body.

My muscles tightened around his cock and he growled out a feral sound, driving into me once, twice. His powerful body shook as the orgasm tore through him. He bellowed out in ferocious sounds that melted into a sob as he succumbed to the intensity of the climax.

Collapsing on my back, he tucked his arms around me, his chest heaving with each breath. Sweat dampened and limp, I flattened against the bed, unable to catch my breath.

"I don't think I have ever had such intense screaming orgasms in my life. I come so hard with you," I panted in jagged breaths.

He rolled me to his side, and held me close, softening his lips in tender kisses. "Oh, my girl. You have no idea what you do to me. I get lost in you." He clasped my hands together and kissed the tips of my fingers. His eyes bored into me, and for a moment, I saw beyond the barriers into the deep place inside of him.

"I *am* lost in you," I said in a soft voice. Tears pooled in my eyes as I held his gaze, my heart bursting from his words and the depth of our intimacy. He pulled me into an embrace, wrapping me into the warmth of him. I felt his powerful body settle heavily into the bed, his breaths softening against my neck as he drifted.

I eased away from the tangle of arms and legs, careful not to waken him. Returning from the bathroom, I was struck by how gorgeous he looked as he lay naked and asleep on the bed. His dark, luxurious body was bathed in the gold light of the fire. His chest slowly rose and fell from each breath, his full lips slightly parted.

Standing in the middle of the room, I took in the scene before me. The room was still filled with the scent of our sex, and the bedding had fallen to the floor. Clothes were scattered everywhere, and the rope lay in the corner.

Ethan had done as he promised. He had taken very good care of me on this birthday. I felt completely fulfilled by him—it was everything I wanted... desired... hoped for.

As I watched him lay there draped across the length of the bed, that familiar ache in my chest became a sharp pain arrowing into my heart. *How I love this man. God help me because I know he will go away again.*

I climbed back in bed and snuggled next to his skin. It felt so reassuring to have him beside me, for the moment. I drifted off to sleep, hearing the sound of the surf and Ethan's soft snores.

Chapter Thirty-One

T HE MINUTE I stepped off the plane, I could feel Barcelona in the air. Her warm breezes, fresh with Spring rain and a scent that was somehow unique. I tilted my head to breathe it in and whispered, "I'm home." All my senses came alive again as I returned to the city I fell in love with.

The only thing missing was Ethan. Despite his efforts to coordinate with my schedule, we'd only have a day, maybe two in Barcelona before we left for Florence. I shoved away the pangs of disappointment, determined not to let his absence deter me from the thrill of being back. I told myself it didn't matter, that we would have Florence. But looking out the window, memories of the time we spent together in Barcelona came flooding back. I felt the emptiness carving its way through my reunion with the city where we began our adventure.

The taxi driver dropped me off at a building on the left side of Eixample, an area of Barcelona I had not yet explored. It wasn't far from the center, but it embodied a different ambiance. The streets, wide and tree-lined, were buzzing with traffic, but there appeared to be more locals than tourists on the sidewalks.

The sign above the door read *Camino Barcelona*. I pulled my bags to the front desk and thankfully, the receptionist spoke English. She showed me to my apartment on the top floor. It had three bedrooms, which meant I would have at least one roommate. The school had promised to match me with someone who would be a good fit. While I wheeled my suitcases into the bedroom with an en suite bath, I couldn't help but wonder how a match was possible. They would be kids, not anywhere near my age. That would make me the dorm mother. Lovely.

The whistle of the tea kettle in the kitchen rang out at the same moment I heard my new roommate's entrance. "Hello… *hola…* is anybody here?"

As soon as I saw her, I knew the school matchmakers were on point. She was an adorable girl in her early thirties, with a black pixie hairstyle and infectious smile.

She extended her hand, "Hi, I'm Katrin. Should we be speaking Spanish? They told me you were American." Her German accent was evident, but she spoke perfect English.

"I'm Elena, and my Spanish is not that good, so English works just fine for me. Would you like some tea?"

"That would be perfect, thanks." She perched on a bar stool while I opened cupboards in search of cups. "Where are you from?"

"I live in California, near San Francisco."

She squealed with excitement, "I've always wanted to go to the United States, and California looks so lovely in the movies."

"It is nice, but I prefer it here, in Barcelona."

"Is that why you are in language school? Do you come here a lot?"

"It's only my second time, but I want to come back more often." I hesitated, "It would be my dream to live here though."

"Why? Do you know people here? Oh! Do you have a boyfriend here?"

I felt my face scrunching into something like a lopsided wince as I contemplated how to answer that complicated question. "Well… not really, but I am involved with a guy from San Francisco who comes here very often. In fact, he should be here within the week."

Her curiosity and gentle eyes invited me to tell my story. Over two pots of tea, we shared the details of our respective dating lives. She listened with her heart and gave me sage advice, most of which was hard to hear. Sizing me up as a sensitive woman with an open heart, she worried I was at risk of having it broken. I appreciated her concern, but I found it embarrassing that a thirty-two-year-old had more sense than I possessed. But then, since I had been out of the dating pool until just a few years ago, it felt like I was starting over from where I left off as a teenager. The underlying difference laid in our personalities. I chased adventure. I always had.

As we accompanied each other throughout the week, she was a serious student, while I overslept classes. She went to bed early, and I stayed out at the bars until closing. She was sensible and took relationships slowly. I, on the other hand, leaped and threw caution to the wind. As it turned out, I needn't have been concerned that *I* would feel like my roommate's mother. If anything, it was the other way around.

While I was distracted by school and thrilled to be back in Barcelona, it seemed empty without Ethan. His email came a day after I arrived and helped to take the edge off the disappointment.

Hey babe, I can't wait to see you in Barcelona. I made it to Turkey and will be back just before we take off for Florence. I might have to meet with my realtor so I may come a day after you. Not sure about how much I will be on the cell but will email when I can. See you soon, kisses.

> *I can't wait to see you too! I've booked us a cute apartment in the center of Florence. The ambiance looks perfectly romantic. Five days with you, that will be a first. But I really hope we can meet up in Barcelona.*

I was filled with anticipation at the chance to sightsee with him or just spend five glorious days in bed gazing out the window at the rooftops of Florence. It would be a dream come true.

Language school nearly cracked my brain. My head hurt after four hours of grueling classes each morning. Afternoons were filled with school field trips, which broadened my cultural knowledge of

Barcelona, and every day there were activities planned. I was grateful for the company and busy schedule to take my mind off Ethan.

As each day passed that I didn't hear from him, my anxiety grew, but I modified my emails to hide the worry. He must have access to WiFi, so his lack of communication made for suspicion. I had this nagging voice invading my thoughts that screamed louder through the week. *There is something that doesn't feel right. If he really wanted to be with me, he would be here in Barcelona instead of running off to Turkey.*

The last time he disappeared on me was after our weekend in Pacific Grove. My birthday weekend was equally as intense with him, possibly more. Even though we had seen each other a few times after that, I feared that he would again retreat from the powerful intimacy. He always sought balance, and I had no doubt that when he was with me, his equilibrium was decimated.

Living with the unspoken assumption that he was probably dating someone in Europe was chipping away at my sense of security, making me doubt myself as much as I doubted him. But the choice was mine to accept the uncertainty, knowing that he could find his future bride at any time. The times we spent together were intoxicating and he was the one drug I couldn't resist. I ran headlong toward the dream of experiencing the world with him, ignoring the looming cliff beneath my feet.

The fall came sooner than expected, but it wasn't that I didn't see the signs.

I'm stuck in Turkey and won't be back to Barcelona today. Not sure when I will be there. Go on to Florence, I will see if I can meet you.

His message came in a day before I expected him to arrive. I couldn't believe what I was reading. Flooded with disappointment and unbearable despair, I fired off emails laced with the emotions that had been brewing all week.

You aren't meeting me in Barcelona? And you probably won't make it to Florence. I knew something had changed when you

didn't communicate. I can't believe you are bailing on me after
we talked for so long about these plans. But it wouldn't be the
first time you disappeared on me.
What the hell happened? Even if you are late getting back here,
can't you still make it to Florence?

His response came a few hours later.

I haven't booked my flight to Florence yet, and the way you are
reacting does not exactly make me want to join you. C'mon,
hon, you're being overly emotional.

Overly emotional? I planned this trip for months and he bails on me
without even an explanation or an apology? And what did he mean, he
didn't have a flight to Florence? I know he's a last-minute kind of guy, but
what if he never really intended to come?

Enraged and hurt, I paced the floor of the small student apartment.
My temper wasn't easily ignited, but when it was, I could stomp and
slam doors with the fury of a woman scorned.

In the back of my mind, I knew my reaction had inflamed the
situation. I had rushed to my assumptions before I let him explain. He
saw me as a hysterical female, and just like my ex-husband, he didn't
handle a woman's emotions very well. Maybe I should have given him
another chance, but I was tired of being—*nice.* Accepting what he was
able to give me without complaint.

Besides, I imagined him changing his plans and staying in Turkey
with his friends, or maybe even a girlfriend. I couldn't comprehend
why he would do this to me, and worse, that it didn't seem to matter
to him. This should have been our reunion in Europe, after all, hadn't
he told me he wished I was with him when he'd made those trips back
to Barcelona?

With the flight and the Airbnb already booked, I had no choice but
to go on without him. I packed up my suitcase and went out for one
last drink with Katrin. She didn't think I was being "overly emotional."
She got it. At least she didn't hit me with an "I told you so," instead,
she was supportive. Katrin gave me the girl's pep talk, "You deserve so

much better than that kind of treatment. Find a man who really cares about you." I knew she was right, but it didn't make leaving Barcelona on my own any easier.

Fighting back the tears, I boarded a plane bound for Italy, alone. The taxi driver brought me to cobblestone piazza and pointed the way to the apartment. My feet trudged heavily with the weight of my fatigued body as I wheeled my suitcase along the uneven edges of the stoned street. I pushed my way through the crowd of people who congregated in the sun-drenched square in front of my building, dark sunglasses hiding my red and swollen eyes.

The manager asked me if I would need another set of keys to the apartment since I had listed two guests on the rental. Casting my gaze downward, I shook my head and answered, "No, it will be just me." With his departure, I flung myself on the big double bed and sunk into the sadness. Once the flood of tears began, it seemed impossible to stop. For two days I barely left the apartment except to buy take-out food. The loft bed afforded me a view of the red-tiled rooftops set against the lush landscaped hills of Tuscany. It was the perfect pictur-esque, romantic setting. All I could think about was how wonderful it would have been to be making love with Ethan, snuggled in his arms as we watched the orange hues of dusk wash over the hills together. The accumulation of so many years living alone accentuated the bitter loss of the dream.

I lay on the bed, gazing out the window hour after hour. The bells from the small cathedral reminded me of time passing. The courtyard below was alive with the passion of Italian voices, but I couldn't find the strength to mingle and deal with the language barrier all by myself.

Day three, I ventured out to explore the Florence I remembered. I made my way through the throngs of tourists at the Piazza del Duomo to view the Gothic Cathedral. It was just as majestic as the first time I saw it during the European escapades of my twenties, but I lacked the enthusiasm to be impressed.

GPS led me through the ancient streets lined with shops to the most picturesque spot in all of Florence. Memories flooded back as I came to Ponte Vecchio, the medieval stone arched bridge, set over the

Arno river. I captured images on my camera as the boats drifted under its arches and the last rays of sun cast a glow gleaming off the waters. There was something about this bridge at sunset that felt so serene, the brown stones taking on a golden hue against the darkening sky. But the beauty of this place did little to improve my mood, and neither did dining alone on pasta and chianti while couples all around me chatted over candlelit tables. *Perfect,* I thought. *This is exactly why I need to order take-out.*

Desperately trying to climb out of the deep hole I was in, I booked tours for the last days. The first was to the hill villages in Tuscany. I stared blankly out the window of the bus as we passed vineyards and olive tree groves. Medieval stone farmhouses and cottages dotted the green hills. I sat alone, surrounded by couples and families on vacation. My dark mood persisted despite the tranquil beauty of the Italian countryside, or maybe because of it. The sparsely populated ancient landscape oozed melancholy, and I was in the unfortunate mood to absorb it.

The tour ended at a small family-owned winery, where we were offered wine tastings and a chance to explore the vineyards. Venturing off from the group, I walked a dirt pathway into the quiet serenity of the rolling hills. I was transported back to the 10th century in the place that had always had the power to capture hearts with its wistful charm. But all I could feel was the ache piercing through my heart, the solitude crashing over me. The silence was punctuated by the chirping of birds as they darted through the cypress trees. I watched in absolute awe as the sky cast a golden hue at sunset, softening the landscape into a picture-perfect postcard view. The call sounded that the bus was ready to leave so I trudged back to my seat and was lulled into a fitful sleep as the bus returned to Florence.

As soon as I stepped on the bus for the tour to Cinque Terre, I knew my final day held some promise for an improved state of mind. The tour guide was lively, and his sense of humor made me laugh. Finally, I was able to smile again. As we headed toward the sea, the bus made an unexpected stop along the road in Lucca. A woman hurriedly crossed the dangerous highway and hopped aboard the bus, taking the empty seat next to me. Slightly out of breath, her round face broke into a smile and her eyes gleamed at me with a greeting.

"*Buongiorno.*"

"Hello," I said, not sure which language I should attempt. She did not look at all Italian.

"My name is Aida Digat, where are you from?" She answered in English with a thick Spanish accent.

"I'm Elena Vidal, from California near San Francisco."

"Oh, me too! But I live in Los Angeles, originally from Cuba. I am staying in Lucca with my aunt, but she didn't feel up to a trip today. Are you traveling alone?"

My eyes averted. "Yes. Well, a guy was supposed to have joined me, but he didn't make it. I'm staying in Florence alone."

"Ah, I am in love with Florence! I've been there several times. You are brave my dear. I travel all around the world, but I always find a friend or family member to come with me."

"I didn't have much of a choice. I had everything booked and at the last minute, he canceled on me. This was supposed to be a romantic vacation in Tuscany."

Tears pooled again in my eyes, prompting her to question what had happened. The long bus ride gave me time to tell my story, backtracking to how Ethan and I met and ending with the pit of despair that I fell into. I couldn't believe I was pouring my heart out to a perfect stranger, but I needed the therapy that came with talking it out and she was a willing listener.

"Oh, *cariño*, I'm sorry for what has happened to you, but it is better to know how this man is before you go any further."

Her warm-hearted nature brought unexpected comfort, but her voice became stern as she raised her index finger and pointed it at my face to emphasize her point.

"Listen to me, I'm older than you and experience has taught me a few things. Men can trouble for soft-hearted women. Don't get me wrong, I love men, but I've learned to enjoy them in the same way they enjoy us." She looked at me with compassion, like she was talking to a sister, instead of a complete stranger.

"Have sex with this guy all you want, but don't give him your heart. Don't let him have the power to make you feel so sad. You are a beautiful, sexy woman, and you can have many men. For me, I decide when I want a man. I like my independence, no one is going to tell me what I can or cannot do."

Her features hardened into a determined expression, and I knew this was a woman who'd learned some life lessons, ones that had taught her to be tough. "I don't need all those messy complications of the heart. After sex, I don't want a guy bothering me with texts or phone calls. For too many years I had a husband trying to control me. Now, I don't want to answer to any man."

"For me it's different. I've been alone a very long time, and besides, this one is not so easy to just have casual sex with. What we have is too powerful. It's like the difference between having dinner at a fast food place, verses a five-course meal at a Michelin star restaurant that lasts for hours."

"Ah yes, I had one like that, I would think about him all the time. Even when I was with other men, I would fantasize that I was with him. We lived on opposite sides of the country, but when we were together it was heaven. Then one day I learned that he had fallen in love with a young woman in Cuba. That was it for me. I stopped all my feelings for him and never opened my heart again. But I can see in your eyes that you have much pain from this man. I ask you, is it worth it?"

"Aida, I don't know how to close my heart, but I know the pain I'm in for with him—*if* I ever see him again. All I know right now is that I don't deserve to be treated so rudely."

As we sat talking on the bus, my strength began to return. After stewing in my own emotions for four days, it was a relief to feel the bonding that only a sisterhood heart-to-heart could bring.

The bus dropped us off in the port town of La Spezia, where we boarded a small local train to visit four of the five seaside villages known as the Cinque Terre, beginning with Riomaggiore. When I laid eyes on the magnificent beauty of the rugged Italian Riviera coast, I came to life with a rush of enthusiasm. Each one had its own unique charm. Being far from posh, the centuries-old buildings were home to the local fishermen. The harbors were full of unpretentious vessels, bobbing on the gentle sea. Smaller fishing boats rested on their hull against the cobblestone streets, dry-docked along the row of tourist shops. Brightly colored houses clung to the steeply terraced hillsides and cliffs along the sea. The sweeping vistas from atop the cliffs of Manarola were breathtaking. Rock formations rose from the azure waters below where swimmers perched before plunging into the pools.

Aida and I explored the villages together, stopping at the souvenir shops and taking a cappuccino break at a seaside cafe. Boarding a small tourist ferry from Vernazza to Monterosso, the splendor of rugged and colorful coastline came into full view. I was awestruck. Never had I seen this mix of antiquity and colors set against the blue Mediterranean with its jagged coast. The unassuming beauty was enhanced by lush vegetation, olive groves, and vineyards.

After snapping loads of pictures, Aida and I stepped off the boat and set foot on land again in Monterosso, a small resort town with a sandy beach. Lunch was served at seaside trattoria. As a rule, tour group meals tend to be mass-produced fixed menus where the restaurant benefits by the number of customers, and for the diner, it's less than satisfying. But the pesto pasta and fresh seafood served at this family-owned trattoria did not disappoint. Carafes of delicious white and red wine flowed endlessly, as did conversations around the table in multiple languages.

Aida nodded to me from across the table. "You're smiling now, my dear, are you having a good time?"

"The best." The wine was definitely helping, I tipped the glass to my mouth then leaned in, resting my arm on the table. "This is what I want, Aida, to share experiences like this and meet new people and see such amazing places. I don't want to leave Europe," I rambled, bubbling like an excited teenager.

Aida chuckled, "Why do you think I save all year so I can travel the world? I get it—if it wasn't for my grandkids, I'd move over here in a heartbeat. But you can do it, there's nothing stopping you is there?"

"Certainly not my job, although there is that little issue of an income."

Our tour guide was circling the table, checking in with the guests and he stopped by my side. "How was the food? Are you enjoying the tour?"

I'd noticed him zeroing in on me starting with the bus ride, his dark eyes beaming at me. Marco, a short, dark Middle Eastern man who had rebranded himself as Italian. In my slightly buzzed euphoria, I accepted his invitation for a tour through the town. We stopped at the top of a hill with a magnificent vista of the jagged rocks and the sea below.

"I'm so grateful to be here in this spectacular setting." Leaning against the iron railing, my eyes fixed on the waves crashing on the shore. "It has a peaceful feeling like Tuscany, but so much more vibrant."

Marco reached for his cell and said, "Let me get a photo of you here; the background is perfect." I smiled for the camera, and as the shutter clicked, he said, "It's a joy for me to come to work every day and bring people here. Yes, it's a job, but it never feels like work," he gestured to the sea and added, "I never get tired of this view. And... I get to meet beautiful people." He gave me a wink and a suggestive smile.

I let his not-so-subtle advance pass right by me but used the opportunity to talk about my dreams. "I don't want to leave Europe. I want to live over here and get out of the States. There is so much I want to see and experience."

"Well, why don't you?"

"It's not that simple," I sighed in frustration. "How would I earn a living? I would love to travel and take people to experience this kind of beauty, like you, but I don't have the language skills."

"You don't have to speak the language. You can organize tourists from the States and bring them here. There are a lot of tour companies and they would be happy to have the business. You would earn a percentage of what the customers pay. You can even get paid by the restaurants by bringing groups. For today's lunch, the owner pays me a percentage of the cost just for bringing people here."

As I stood on top of the hillside, looking out in amazement at the scenery before me, the gears in my brain started to whirl and I felt everything click into place as an idea transformed into a decision. I never conceived of changing careers but going into the tourism industry would fit perfectly with the life I envisioned. Unlike Ethan, I loved planning travel and I was good at it. I'd organized all the family trips and even helped my friends with their vacation plans. Why not do it for strangers?

"I can do this," I said, with a clarity that took me by surprise. "I am going to find a way to make it happen. As soon as I get back to the States, I will start the research and put a plan into motion."

In my excitement, I threw my arms around that man and hugged him tight. "Thank you, Marco. You and the Cinque Terre have just changed my life!"

Marco seized me in his arms, only releasing me when I agreed to a dinner date, with the promise he could give me more tips about the tour business.

I don't know if the pizza was *actually* the best I'd ever eaten, or if my exuberance for Italy made it seem that way. I tugged off bites of the cheesy slices, pausing to fire off questions and jot notes on a paper napkin.

In the genuine spirit of Italy, Marco insisted on walking me home and made his true intentions known. It was a challenge to escape his octopus-like grip on me, but finally, I was alone with my thoughts. It seemed that there was a purpose in my solo visit to Florence after all. If Ethan had been with me, I might never have stumbled on to a decision that had the potential to free me from a life and career that I was ready to leave behind.

Aida's words rang in my ears as I prepared to leave for Rome and my flight back to the US. I began to wonder, was it worth it? My feelings for Ethan would not define the path I was on. I wanted to move to Barcelona, with or without him in my life. He'd had the chance to see me, and he had made his choice. It didn't matter that he'd sent texts telling me how much he missed me, since he was staying in Barcelona through the summer and I was headed back to the States. Again, we were separated by distance. But more than that, something had broken between us and I didn't have much hope that he would try to repair it. I didn't think I had it left in me to try again anyway. The mantra played repeatedly in my mind: *Let him go, it's time.*

Chapter Thirty-Two

"Hey, Gerald." I leaned over the top of his cubicle, grinning at him.

"Hi, kiddo, you look happy. How was your trip? Did you like Florence?"

Shutting my eyelids, I winced momentarily. "Florence was a bit of a disaster, but in Cinque Terra, I found the answer."

"What answer? The relevance is lost if I don't know the question," he said with a wry smile.

"Oh God, short term memory loss is the first sign of aging." I ignored his well-timed Italian hand gesture. "The answer to getting out of here, at least for me. I'm going into the travel business, planning group tours in Europe."

"Oh really, you run off to Italy and just like that you have a new profession?"

"Well... those Italian tour guides can be very helpful." I winked at him and headed back to my desk, leaving Gerald with a perplexed expression.

Gerald shuffled along the carpet as he followed me to my cubicle.

"So, you're just going to leave me hanging on that innuendo? What's your plan?"

"I'm taking an online course and the concept is designing small group specialized tours. I would go along as a coordinator, so I'd get to travel while making money. Planning travel is something I do well anyway. I would just have to find the hotels, plan the activities and contract with the tour operators. The main caveat is building the customer base."

"If you want my opinion—and no, you didn't ask for it, but I'm putting my two cents in anyway—I think you need to carve out a niche market. There are a million travel companies out there, and you can't compete with the big guys."

"Opinion duly noted. And I think you're right, I just have to narrow it down to a demographic population and a couple places in Europe. There's so much to think about though. I have to develop a website, an email account and buy domain names. But first, a business name has to be established, one that hasn't already been taken. And honestly, I would like your help."

"You got it, Elena, anything I can do to further the cause, I'm in."

By the end of the day, I had a two-page list of ideas, most of which were scratched off because the domain was already in use. I presented the list to Gerald, and he reached for his reading glasses to scan the papers.

"A lot of these are just too long, you have to make it easy for people to remember."

"I know, but I've researched the hell out of this and most of the good names are taken. I need to keep it generic for now, since I haven't nailed down a specific niche market. I think I'll go with this one to begin."

Gerald's eyes followed my finger, pointing to the highlighted name.

"RedHotTravels.com?" Gerald read the name out loud, "Sounds catchy and it's not too long, but what's the significance?"

"For one, it contains three strong words that might come up on a Google search. And, I have this concept of the baby boomers and singles as being in a "red hot" time of their life, ready for adventure. It came to me during a hot flash," I said, fanning myself with my notebook. My face conveniently flushed to illustrate my point.

Gerald shot a glance at me, then turned his eyes to Joanne, who was hanging her head halfway out the window in front of his desk to catch the breeze.

"*Ah*, I get it now. Not a bad idea, are you going to run with it?"

"I have to just pick something and get started."

"Damn, you are impatient."

"You aren't the first one to tell me that. Patience has never been one of my virtues."

Gerald peered up at me over the top of his glasses. "From what I hear, there might be a few other *virtues* you go light on."

"Hey, stop eavesdropping on my conversations," I said, my index finger wagging at him. But I knew full well that I never hid my less than angelic reputation. As I headed back to my desk, Gerald called after me, "Have you done any real job-related work today?"

"You're one to talk!"

The excitement of finally having a new direction and goal in place kept me working late every night. It also served as a distraction from the void I felt with Ethan's absence. I'd emailed him one of my long-winded letters explaining how much it had disappointed me that he had not met me in Europe as we'd planned, but as I expected, his only answer was short and unyielding.

This topic warrants a conversation, not an email. As usual, you are taking things too seriously. Relax, sweetie, things are fine.

I knew he wasn't fond of texting or emailing and usually didn't write more than a few lines. Besides, he never wanted to engage in a conversation that involved serious emotions. *Typical male*, I thought, and yet it didn't stop me from using that female part of my brain. Words were the only way I knew to express myself, even if I knew it would be a one-sided conversation.

The only way I could cope was to stay focused on my new project. Using my son's technical expertise, we created a professional-looking website with scenic photos of Barcelona. Choosing the best images from my own gallery, I promoted my new biz on social media. The Red Hot Travels became a Facebook page. Teaching me about Instagram and Twitter, my son learned a lesson in patience. But not before I reminded him how many times he'd worn out *my* patience.

The tech learning curve was as almost as challenging as figuring out a business plan. I sat at the kitchen table, papers strewn everywhere, as I made multiple stabs at writing a coherent business plan. Pouring over online tutorials, my index finger tortured a lock of hair, curling it around and around. *What the hell do I know about creating a business plan? I only know my goal—make money, quit my job and get the hell out of here.*

Overwhelmed and confused, I struggled to find my way through the morass of vague ideas and began to turn them into concrete steps. It was far from a linear process. I needed help, a sounding board at least. Ron seemed like the best candidate. He'd launched several businesses and was a whiz at marketing. He never seemed to be short on advice for me (at least on the topic of dating), so it wasn't difficult to get him to meet for coffee the following Saturday.

I drove to the valley to meet him, my old stomping grounds. We met up at his local Starbucks. When he leaned in to give me a platonic hug, I inhaled the familiar scent of his cologne. His aroma always stimulated my sensory memories, and I felt the rush sweep over me.

"What do you need? Where are you stuck?" Ron got right down to business. Though it had been several years since I was love-struck with him, I always felt the attraction. At forty-six, he still looked hotter than ever, with his thick jet-black hair and handsome face, he appeared younger than his years. Blessed with that flawless brown Indian skin combined with his ever-youthful attitude, he never appeared to age. He carried his 5 '11 muscular frame with a confident stride but it was his bad-boy-with-game and brilliant mind that always got to me. Underneath it all, he had a good heart and that, more than anything, made me fall for him.

"I need a business plan. I'm going around and around in circles. For starters, which niche should I focus on?"

"No, I think you should start by figuring out your target demographic. Who has the money to travel?"

"I'm thinking the baby boomers or the early retirees. They have the earning power or the most money saved, and travel is a priority."

"I would agree, and what kind of travel are they most interested in?"

"That's where I get stuck. Wine and food seem popular, based on my online search, but it may be an oversaturated market. I'm reading about a trend for unique travel experiences that include a cultural component. An opportunity for learning, perhaps."

"Good, you've done your market research. If you are going to stand out from the major companies, you have to offer something more unique as a small business. Zero in more tightly on a target. What connections do you have?"

"Singles, I suppose, I've certainly made it my personal research project to search out singles groups. There are a lot of us who want to travel but hesitate to travel alone." Leaning my elbows on the table, I propped my face heavily into my hands. "I still have no idea how I'm going to manage this while I transition from my current job, except to use all my stored vacation time to start."

"Maybe your goal should be to do a trial of one or two trips and then quit your job. Go balls-out and take a risk."

"That sounds scary as hell, but it's the direction I'm heading. God, I hope I can make this work. I really need a change. My ace in the hole is the cottage. When I finish and get it rented out, I'll have a source of income to work with."

"You aren't just a pretty face, Elena. You've got an impressive brain and we both know how persistent you can be when you have a goal in mind." A bemused grin fixed on his lips. He made a fair point. I had pursued him far past the time he had called it quits with us, always holding onto hope.

"Thanks... I think. I know I can be a bit delusional on occasion, but hopefully my persistence pays off this time," I said, mirroring his smart-ass grin.

"By the way, speaking of persistence, how's the cottage going?" Ron asked.

"See these bags and dark circles under my eyes? When I'm not at my job or working on plans for the new business, I am doing construction work nights and weekends."

"Yeah you do kinda' look like shit, but I wasn't going to say." He winked at me and I gave him a playful slap on the head.

"Thanks, I can always count on you to give me a boost." I raised an eyebrow and twisted my lips into a fake kiss.

"It's cool what you're doing, honestly. It's a smart plan."

"It seemed like a good idea at the time. I keep hiring and firing construction guys. Do you know how crazy unreliable these guys can be?"

I slumped over the table almost knocking over my coffee.

"Okay, hold up there, we are getting off track. I was just asking to be polite but that's enough details."

I held up my hands in resignation. If I didn't know Ron, I might have been offended. He could be blunt and to the point. People either gravitated toward his personality or ran the other way.

"So, what's your vision? All business plans have to start with a vision statement," he said more seriously.

"I don't know if I can formulate it into a statement just yet, but I want to take people to experience the culture the way I did in Barcelona—feeling its pulse and getting to know a city outside of its major tourist attractions. Unhurried, focusing on one or two locations. Budget and options are important to me, and I think that's the case for a lot of people. I want to appeal to those who don't want to travel alone but also want the freedom of choice lacking in big-bus tours.

"I like your concept. I think it's solid and stands out. Now, what's your action plan? What are your first steps?"

"I'm at the point where I have to generate a client base. I'm already in the process of planning the first tour. I have the hotels and itinerary, but no potential travelers. I started my own travel Meetup group, which will hopefully be a major source of clients, and soon I'm going to business networking events."

"In-person client searches are effective because you are the best salesperson for your product. But it's limited because you have to do email blasts and learn about SEO."

"What's that?"

"Search engine optimization. Embedding keywords to make you visible to your target population on Google search."

Rob began talking in a tech language that was Greek to me, but he was an expert. I took copious notes and formulated a to-do list for later. This was my least favorite part of the work, mundane compared with trip planning. But I didn't have the budget to contract it out, so it would be next on my learning curve.

I left our conversation on a high note. Ron's support meant a lot to me and he gave me the push I needed.

Self-doubt had a way of creeping back in though, particularly on those long lonely nights. Spurring me on, were the frequent night-mares I had of being imprisoned in a job I hated. Earning a living doing exactly what I longed for, being in Europe and traveling... it would be like a dream come true. If only I could make it work.

The day I picked up my order at Office Depot—the optimistically large box of new business cards—I *actually* danced in the aisles. As Marc Antony's song, *"I Need To Know"* resounded through the store, I couldn't resist breaking out in a solo cha-cha. A Latino clerk cheered me on, as my enthusiasm outweighed my sense of dignity. It suddenly seemed real, I must be legit, armed with a two-sided, full-color business card proclaiming my mission.

Within two months, my plan was in place, and I was in full networking mode. San Francisco's Network After Work monthly meetings served a dual purpose. While not a singles event, many of the Bay Area's finest suits showed up giving me an open playing field. Getting into the city at rush hour and finding a parking space, always took its toll on my nerves. Making it worse were the memories of Ethan and the anticipation I always felt as I drove across the Bay Bridge on my way to his apartment. *God, I miss him.* Everything about the city reminded me of him. I assumed he was still in Europe, but I fought the impulse to do a drive-by just to check. I told myself that it would be pointless. What would I do even if I saw him?

The large club on Franklin street was transformed into an event venue. Instead of dancers and colored lights, there were buffet tables surrounded by professionals with cocktails in hand.

Scanning the already packed room, I couldn't help but remember Ethan's face appearing in the crowd when we met at the wine event. But this time, I had a different mission. My hand brushed nervously against the wrinkled fabric on my black pencil skirt. This wasn't my work attire. Jeans and a t-shirt were the extent of the dress code where I worked. Isolated in a cubicle all day, there was no one to judge my professionalism based on appearance. I felt like a fraud dressing up in a blazer, a slim knee-length skirt, and a red satin blouse—opened to cleavage level. My feet rebelled at the change in pitch as I tried to keep steady in the impossible stiletto heels, but I planned to take full advantage of the attention my presentation might earn.

Color-coded badges that listed names and professions were adhered to lapels. It was helpful during introductions, however, my target demographic included most everyone in the room. First stop was the bar for some liquid courage, working a room did not come natural to me. Conversation starters were simple, people were there to talk about their work. Armed with a rehearsed spiel, I forced myself to mingle with everyone from techies to marketing specialists. Even the teachers and health care workers were potential clients.

"Hi, I'm Elena, I am a travel specialist... What do I do exactly? I make people's travel dreams come true." Happily, I found that in this overworked society, people's faces lit up when I mentioned vacation and travel. They wanted to talk about their fantasy vacation, but more importantly, they got excited about what I had to offer.

Stephanie in marketing was looking to change companies, but I got her sidetracked on the idea of taking some time in-between jobs to travel in Europe.

"I have been dying to go to Spain and travel in Europe, but I don't like traveling alone," she said. "What's it like?"

"It's amazing, the history, the culture—so different than anything in the US. I like to wander the cobblestone streets, finding treasures around every corner in the midst of the Gothic architecture. It's a social culture, a high priority is placed on enjoying life. Friends gather on terraces for a glass of wine and leisurely conversations, often in the afternoon, or well into the night. They wouldn't think of taking a coffee to go and racing through life. The pace is different, the priorities are different. They work to *live*—not like here, where we live to *work*."

Stephanie looked mesmerized as I described my experiences—the sights and sounds that filled the streets. "Your enthusiasm is infectious. I can see it on your face, you love it there. When you talk about Barcelona, it makes me feel as if I were there with you. Please, take me away with you!"

I realized instantly that I had found my selling strategy. It was so easy because I came alive when I told my story. Barcelona was not tough to sell.

"I have an upcoming tour planned, a small group. The group provides the security of a support system when you are far away from home, but at the same time, you aren't glued to it. You can choose from activities, and most importantly, you have time to get to know the culture, not just the touristic sights."

"Sounds perfect, just what I'm looking for, but when is it?"

"I have a tour planned in two months. September is a perfect time to visit during the off-peak season. Ten days will include Barcelona and the Cote D'Azur. Nice is another popular destination. It's a short flight from Barcelona and would give you a glimpse of French culture." When I told her the price, her face lit up in excitement.

"Really? That's reasonable, well within my budget. But here's the problem, if I get a job offer, I won't be able to leave."

My heart dropped. I thought I had one solid customer, but Stephanie hung in there with me, saying she wanted to learn more and stay in touch.

I collected at least twenty-five business cards that night and followed up with emails. But what I learned was disheartening. The hard-working folks in the Bay Area were slaves to their jobs, with vacation time running from zero to a couple weeks. If they were changing jobs, and many were, they wouldn't be able to get away for at least six months. The techies had the money and vacation time but were working twelve-hour days. The work ethic of the culture didn't support taking time away from the job.

The obstacle seemed insurmountable, considering I was promoting travel abroad to a customer base in the Bay. Though I had left with lots of contacts, I had no solid leads. Feeling discouraged, I began to doubt whether my plan was going to work.

Not only had I struck out with clients, I didn't encounter any potential dates. Ethan was still indelibly ingrained in my cells. Body, brain, and heart had not gotten the message that we weren't seeing each other anymore. My desire for him had not decreased in the slightest. I rationalized that celibacy was a catalyst for keeping me on track with the crucial goals at hand. The course of my life depended on moving forward through the obstacles.

THE SETTING I chose for my first Meetup event in honor of my newly formed travel group, was the restaurant B44. The Catalan restaurant in San Francisco where Ethan took me on our first date after our return from Barcelona. It seemed fitting since the main theme of the tour was Barcelona, but the second I stepped through the door a stream of memories overwhelmed me. The familiar sound of Latin music filled the air, as did the smell of Spanish cuisine being prepared in the kitchen. That night had marked the beginning of something so powerful, an addiction I couldn't cure. The void in my life without him was unbearable. My stomach lurched as I glanced at the table where we had sat over dinner, the sparks flying between us even before he touched me.

I struggled to push away the thoughts and prepare for the guests. Since I was hosting, I had to be on my game. Ten people had signed up, and as new meetups go, it wasn't a bad number.

Posting a sign on the table with the name of our group, The Red Hot Travelers, I opened my laptop to the intro of the slide presentation I'd prepared. One by one, people found the table, and I served glasses of sangria to welcome them. Anna came for support and to help me co-host, so there was at least one familiar face. When Stephanie walked in, I felt a sense of relief that there would be an enthusiastic member among the unknowns.

After the introductions, I launched into the slide show, pitching the tour I'd carefully planned. I hoped that it would suit the single traveler, even the seasoned ones who might want a small group tour with plenty of ways to individualize their experience. The itinerary included nightlife tours of Barcelona (something I was most interested in), cooking classes, Spanish wine tastings, and culture walks. Side trips to nearby towns, as well as the usual major attractions, were among the optional add-ons.

My hands shook as I pressed the computer keys to reveal the slides, and I fought the nerves that threatened to muddle my thoughts. The confidence I had mustered was slowly torn away by the comments that followed.

"*The tour sounds great, but I already have my travel planned out through next year.*"

"*A tour in two months? I need to plan far in advance to get vacation time from work.*"

"*I do travel planning too, maybe I can work for you and travel for free.*"

"*I have some other ideas for tours, maybe I can pitch one to the group.*"

"*I prefer to travel alone, that way I can do as I please.*"

"*I've already been to Barcelona and Nice, I'm more interested in other foreign destinations.*"

With each comment, I shrunk in my seat, demoralized. I hadn't considered the level of expertise that seasoned travelers might bring. Not to mention that everyone had a different idea about where they wanted to go. Even as we attempted to sort out the bill for the food, I caught a glimpse of the difficulties inherent in group travel. The thought of managing a variety of personalities on a ten-day trip made my stomach twist into a knot. After everyone had left, Anna and I debriefed.

"Well that was disappointing," I lamented, with my head hanging heavy and my arms splayed out on the table.

"Maybe it's just not feasible to expect that people can do a tour on such short notice. I think this is going to take more long-term planning," Anna replied.

"But I don't have the time to wait, I *need* to get out of this job, and I was counting on this plan."

"I really think it's viable and it sounds great to me. I've signed on to go, but it looks like this will be a test run." Anna tried to sound encouraging but I left the restaurant in a state of despair. One last look back inside didn't make it any easier. I visualized Ethan's face the way I'd seen him that night, and my heart sank. *Will I ever see him again*?

Chapter Thirty-Three

"Dammit, it's raining, get the buckets," I barked at Dan. "Why do I have another emergency with the cottage right now? Really bad timing, I'm flying out in the morning."

"Don't stress, I've got this. I'll throw a tarp over the roof and it will hold till I can seal it."

"Too late, I'm already stressed." The sum total of pressures had broken me down. God, I was looking forward to getting away from it all and back to Barcelona. I realized that it had been a year since my first trip to Spain last September.

"Just go on your trip, relax and don't worry. I'll get the work done while you're gone." Dan's voice was calm, like he was trying to talk me off a ledge.

"I've written out all the instructions, the goals for completion while I'm away, and I expect to see the progress when I get back." I handed him the piece of paper with handwritten notes. "You should have all the materials, but if you need something, keep the receipts and I'll pay you later."

Dan read over the sheet, pointing to each line with the stub of his index finger. Luckily, he hadn't lost the tip on my job, but somewhere along the line in his years of work in construction, a table saw had gotten in his way.

"Yes, boss, it will get done." When he finished reading, he mocked me with a salute.

I had an uneasy feeling as I trudged back into my house. Something always went wrong, and I wouldn't be there to sort it out. I had to let it go because I was going to crash and burn if I didn't get away from things for a while.

THE SHUTTLE ROUNDED the corner and crept through the traffic until we reached the curb drop off zone. I wheeled my suitcases inside the busy San Francisco terminal. Anna texted me she'd arrived at the airport and then found me at the check-in counter.

"Are you ready for our big adventure?" She was grinning from ear-to-ear and fist-pumping the sky. "I'm so excited, I've never been to Europe. After all you've told me about Barcelona, I can't wait."

I hooked my left arm around her elbow and pulled my cabin bag with the right hand. "I can't wait to show you Barcelona. We are going to have so much fun!" I glanced sideways to check out her travel outfit. She was dressed in tight jeans which hugged her curvy figure, and a teal blue sweater which popped against her magenta hair.

"You look cute, but I don't understand how you can sit in those jeans for over twelve hours.

"What? They're stretchy." Her fingers tugged at the denim.

"Well, my *girl* needs to breathe." I pointed an index finger downward. "Take note of the long skirt, nice and airy. It's not unlike the one I wore on my first trip to Barcelona and I remember that one brought me good luck."

"Ahem," Anna coughed out. "Well if it's anything like what you are wearing now, it might have something to do with your almost sheer chiffon blouse. Showcases the girls pretty well."

"Oh dear. Do you think it's too much?"

"I'd say it's just right." She gave my arm a squeeze. "Do you think you will see Ethan there? Does he even know we are coming?"

I scanned for the gate numbers as we rolled through the terminal, dodging the onslaught of recent arrivals.

"Elena?" Anna tugged my arm until my body jerked around to face her.

"What? I don't know how to answer that. I sent him some emails about the new business plan and attached a flyer that gave information about this so-called tour."

"And, how did he react?"

"He just gave me encouragement. Said, "Sounds great" and "Good job." Things I could have heard from anyone, but I'd hoped for a bit more from him. Who knows if he paid attention to the fact that I was coming." I shrugged my shoulders and lowered my butt into a chair at the gate. "Anyway, let's change the subject."

"You got it." She settled in the seat next to me, turning her attention to the large tinted windows and the aircraft waiting for us to board. "Okay, tell me about the itinerary again?"

I heard the flight attendant announce the boarding call for our group on the loudspeaker.

"It's time to go, let's talk on the plane."

The engine's roar reached a crescendo and the ascent forced my back into the seat. *Off to another adventure. I wonder what awaits me this time.*

THE TAXI ROUNDED the fountains of Plaza Catalunya and headed up the main avenue of Rambla Catalunya. This time, I had booked a central Airbnb slightly uptown, in a district of Eixample. Burnt orange leaves blew in the warm autumn breeze, raining down from the trees that lined the busy thoroughfare. Plenty of tourists frequented the street, but it was wider than in the older Gothic area, and terrace restaurants lined a center strip of land. Lacey iron-railed balconies hung from each floor of the majestic facades.

"How beautiful," Anna exclaimed, her head flinging from right to left, trying to take in all the sights through the limited view of the taxi windows. "The architecture is like nothing I've ever seen, so much character. And it seems so alive. Look at all the people on the streets."

"Just wait, each neighborhood has its own unique character and the social life is off the chain here. There's no problem finding plenty of nightlife in Barcelona."

Our apartment was somewhat less impressive. Simply furnished with unbearably hard beds, but it had two balconies and that was all the luxury I needed. Stepping out onto the small rectangular slabs of stone, Anna and I had a view of the action from above the treetops. The sea was almost visible through the buildings in the distance where Las Ramblas descended to the port.

After a much-needed siesta, I took Anna on a tour of the old Gothic area and my beloved Born. Stepping into El Copetin, the gorgeous bartender remembered me at first sight.

"*Hola, como estas princesa? Bienvenida*!

It warmed my heart and another region as well, to know that this was my place. A bar where I was remembered and welcomed each time I came back to town. Especially by this muscle-bound Argentinian hunk. I introduced Anna in my best attempt at Spanish. She looked at me and her eyebrows twitched in recognition of the hottie.

Bending his muscular torso over the top of the bar, he greeted Anna with a kiss on both cheeks. She used the intro to fire up a conversation in Spanish. I was lucky to have her along this time because she was a fluent Spanish speaker—thanks to an earlier marriage to a South American immigrant.

The bartender mixed our drinks with flare, throwing the ice behind his back and capturing the cubes fluidly in the glasses. It was early evening at around eleven, so we had all his attention until the throngs of people started pouring in around twelve-thirty. Latin music stirred us, and we tipped off our stools on slightly buzzed legs. We got our dance moves on, weaving around the sea of bodies competing for space.

"I love this place!" Anna shouted over the sound of the Shakira song, "La Bicicleta."

"Me too, it's my happy place. So glad you are here with me, Anna, it's not as fun when I come by myself," I cupped my hand and yelled into her ear.

We closed the bar at around three o'clock, and almost fell asleep on the taxi ride home. I had no problem with the schedule, but it was good to spend the first evening breaking in Anna to the rhythm of Barcelona.

"What time is it?" Anna asked when her eyes opened to sunlight streaming into the bedroom we shared.

I squinted at my phone. "It's eleven, glad we managed to sleep late."

"Seriously? I never sleep this late."

"Welcome to Barcelona life, girlfriend. Let's hit the shower and head downstairs for some breakfast. We can plan out our itinerary."

My eyes squinted in the glare of the sun and I opened my purse to fish for my sunglasses.

"There's hardly anyone here, it must be between breakfast and lunchtime. We have our choice of tables," I said.

The waitress appeared in moments after we found our chairs on the edge of the terrace nearest to the sidewalk where people watching was at its best. Relaxed by the warmth of the sun, we sipped our cappuccinos and soaked up the ambiance. Suddenly, a young man startled us out of our blissful morning. Out of nowhere, he appeared at our table flashing a piece of paper on which he had written something in Spanish. His speech was frantic, begging for money I assumed, though I couldn't understand most of what he said. Anna and I both tried to cut him off with a stern "No," but he persisted and flashed the paper close to my face. I waved the back of my hand at him saying "*Basta,*" enough, then turned toward Anna to continue our conversation. He was in Anna's line of sight and she watched as he turned and walked down the street.

"What was that all about?" she asked.

"I guess he was a gypsy, they are famous for begging and stealing in Barcelona. You have to be really careful with your purse here."

At that moment I thought to check my purse which I had carefully placed on my lap for safe-keeping. My hand dipped inside, and I remembered that I'd unzipped it to find the sunglasses.

"Oh my God!" I shouted. "My phone is gone. I'm positive it was here before because I checked the time when we sat down."

"Are you sure? Here, let me help you check." Anna dug her hands in my bag and came up empty-handed.

"That guy must have lifted it, but how did he manage? I didn't feel a thing and you were looking right at him the whole time."

Adrenaline coursed through my veins and panic struck me. The cell was my lifeline, I had everything stored there. Besides, I couldn't find my way around the block without GPS. At that moment the waitress appeared, and Anna explained in Spanish what had happened.

I understood most of her response, though she spoke in rapid questions and phrases while she looked up and down the street for the perpetrator. Her expression was sympathetic, explaining that this was a frequent crime in Barcelona and the gypsies were very skillful at extracting valuables from tourists. There was no use making a police report, the guy would be long gone, and he'd likely have passed it off to one of his compatriots anyway.

"Is your phone locked?" Anna asked.

"Yes, of course. I don't know what good it is to them."

"I guess they find a way. You better call the phone company and let them know to turn off the service and do a data wipe. Let's go up and you can use my phone. I don't seem to have service here, but we can use the WiFi in the apartment."

My mind blurred with panic. I struggled to think about how I'd even find the contact number but then remembered that I brought along a tablet. Connecting it to the WiFi, I found my contacts and felt relieved that I wasn't totally unplugged from technology.

"Now what are we going to do?" I said, after calling the phone company. "We can't go through the rest of the trip without a phone. Are you sure you can't get service here?"

"I called my cell carrier before I left and tried to get a roaming plan here. They said it would be activated, but I've tried, and something must be wrong. I can only get on with WiFi."

"I guess I'm going to have to buy some kind of smartphone here, but I have no idea where." In freak-out mode, it was difficult to think straight, and I needed help. My thoughts turned to Ethan and how he was probably still in Barcelona. It was one of those helpless female moments and there were no other strong male arms I would rather fold into but his. A feeling of desperation washed over me, overshadowing my pride. He hadn't reached out to me in a while, so I wasn't going to chase him. But I convinced myself this was different; after all, he'd help out a friend, wouldn't he?

I pulled the tablet onto my lap and using the one-fingered method, I laboriously typed out an email message on the screen and hit 'send.' I shifted restlessly on the bed, but relaxing was impossible, so I paced the hardwood floor while my fingers pulled on the stretchy bracelet around my wrist.

I heard the ping of an incoming message within a few minutes. My chest tightened.

So sorry, how did it happen?

My pulse raced, stunned by his quick reply. I gave him the short version of the day's disaster and made my plea.

> *Can you come over and help me sort this out? Maybe install WhatsApp on my tablet? I have to figure out where to buy a new phone too.*

Sure, I'll meet you for lunch. Where are you?

> *I am at 52 Rambla Catalunya. Meet you downstairs at MasQMenos.*

I'll be there in thirty.

"Anna, you are not going to believe this. He's actually coming." She looked up from her phone and raised her palm in a high-five.

"That's great! But you don't exactly look excited to see him."

"That's because I'm nervous as hell."

"Just play it cool, don't let him see you rattled. Guys hate that."

"I'll try, but I suck at hiding my emotions. Anyway, I've got thirty minutes to put on something that makes him remember he used to think I was cute. And by the way, you are coming with me. It's about time you two met."

"I'd like to see this guy in person. All I've seen are his pictures and most of them don't include his face."

I chuckled, "Oops, I guess I did overshare a bit."

Chapter Thirty-Four

The sound of an incoming email alerted me that he'd arrived at the restaurant. I stepped carefully down four flights of stairs in heels that were way too high for the rugged stoned streets. My legs appeared longer than they really were in the short black flared skirt. The black and white summer crop top stretched across my breasts and met the high waistband, giving me the tiny torso look I knew he loved.

His tall frame raised from where he was seated at a table, and I took in the sight of him. He was dressed in fitted jeans and a t-shirt that tightened over the muscles in his chest as he moved in to greet me with a quick hug. With Anna at my side, I made the introduction.

"Oh, I didn't realize you were here with Anna. Good to meet you, Elena has told me so much about you."

The corners of her mouth curved in a mischievous grin. "It's good to finally meet you too. Elena might have mentioned you a time or two as well." She shot him a playful wink.

I found a seat close to Anna, facing Ethan at a safe distance. Ethan seemed at ease, there was no way to read him. He was always capable of playing it cool in a way I never could.

"So sorry to hear about your phone. Unfortunately, it happens all the time here. As for your tablet, I don't think we can set up the WhatsApp application on it. I checked online and it seems the app is not compatible with tablets. Anyway, you are going to need a new phone, but they aren't as cheap here as in the States."

"Damn, not great news. This day has been pretty messed up. I was hoping to show Anna the sights."

"I'd try FNAC on the other side of Plaza Catalunya. They have a big selection, though the place is a zoo. It's packed, and the lines are long. Get an unlocked phone and a sim card that you can recharge."

"Anna, can you jot that in your phone notes? We can head over later. Luckily Anna speaks Spanish, otherwise, I don't know how I'd manage with something so technical." I'd hoped that he would take us over there, but he didn't offer. And the brief hug didn't satisfy my need to fall into his strong arms, but I took Anna's advice and didn't flinch. *Cool as a cucumber,* I thought to myself.

"So, how long have you two been friends and how did you meet?" Ethan leaned back in the chair, his elegant fingers linked across his tight abs and his long legs stretched out in front. He looked at us with that inquisitive expression I'd seen before, a subtle smile curving his lips.

I turned to Anna. "It's been about three years I think?" Anna nodded in agreement. "We met salsa dancing and found we had a lot in common. We've been best friends ever since." Anna's lips pressed into a sly grin and I knew she was about to burst out laughing. My foot inched over to kick her ankle. Ethan's keen perception never ceased to amaze me. He didn't miss a thing.

"What's up with you two? Anna looks like she's about to swallow her tongue."

I could feel my face turning some shade of red. "I guess you could say we've had a unique kind of friendship. We share everything and are always up for some girl talk, but we also found that we both have an adventurous spirit." I glanced over at Anna who was trying to hold a poker-face. "She's a great wing-woman and has a knack for getting us into trouble." I poked my tongue against the side of my cheek to stop myself from spilling out any more information.

Ethan scrutinized our faces, looking from one to the other. "I see. So, you two are trouble. Anna?" Ethan looked at her with an implied question. She flashed him her palms and pursed her lips tight. I could see she was struggling to hold herself back, so I offered him the tidbit of information he was looking for.

"Well, there was that time in the Dominican Republic." I turned to Anna. "You approached those guys for help getting a cell signal and came back with that hunk. The linebacker with dreads."

Anna finally released a breath. "Yes, and he went after you. I got the older boring one who went to sleep. You guys were trying to get it on in our hotel room and I had to pretend to be asleep in the next bed. I was so horny it was killing me. God, he was built."

Ethan's eyes steeled, but he wore a fixed smile. It was possible that I spilled the story to make him jealous. I hated to admit it, but I wasn't above playing the game.

Anna used the awkward moment to make her escape and give us some time alone. "If you don't mind, I'm going to go back up to the room. I promised my guy I'd check in with him. Considering the time difference, he should be awake by now and getting ready for work."

She stretched out her hand to Ethan, "It was great meeting you. I hope to see you again."

"Nice to meet you too, Anna."

Turning his attention to me, Ethan asked, "Do you want to take a walk? I know this cool restaurant not far from here where we can get better food than this place offers."

"Sure, I'm hungry too." The conversation with Anna present had made me feel more confident. Maybe even emboldened, which is just what I needed to be in order to face him. The unexpected encounter with him gave me the opportunity I'd been waiting for. I needed some answers to questions that had been burning in me since my last time in Barcelona.

As usual, I was impressed with his taste. We walked into the posh restaurant, Boca Grande, and I was awestruck by its elegant interior. Tones of gold and brown leather dominated the decor, accentuated by tasteful metallic and glass lighting which dimly glowed in amber hues.

Settling in the intimate booth, we sat next to each other on the leather bench with enough space between us to maintain distance but close enough to talk over the subtle Latin music set low in the background.

"Wow, the prices here are not typical of Barcelona," I remarked, scanning the menu.

"I didn't remember this place being so expensive, but what the hell, let's order some oysters and cava."

I looked up from the menu at him, remembering our taste of oysters in San Francisco, right before he introduced the ropes for the first time. His brow arched, hinting he had the same thought.

"So how have you been?" he asked.

"I've been okay, I guess. Working hard on developing a new business in travel planning. In fact, I planned this trip as a tour, and I generated a lot of interest, but it was too last minute. Anna was the only one who signed up."

"That's great that you're doing this, do you think it looks viable?"

"It's too early to tell, but I have put a lot of work into it already, and it looks like I could be successful if I can get a client base. What about you? Life going well?"

"I'm still looking for a place to buy. But I'm renting for the summer here, I've had a lot of visitors."

"Of course you have. Everyone wants to come to Barcelona." I suppressed the urge to roll my eyes since it seemed that he *always* had visitors. Knowing him, he had probably been sharing a bed with one of them.

Every neuron in my body was exploding. I breathed in the mouth-watering scent of him and steadied my hands on the rolled leather seat for balance. Finally, I was sitting next to him again and the sexual tension crackled in the air between us. But it was different. This time the chasm of time and pain formed a wall, keeping us guarded. As always, I needed to talk about it, but I knew that was the last thing he wanted. I had to risk it. There was nothing to lose.

"Look, there is no use going on with small talk. You know we have to clear the air, don't you?"

"Elena, I don't want to get into a heavy conversation right here, right now," he said, holding the flute glass between his long fingers and raising it to his lips.

"You never want to go there, but it is important. The last time I saw you we were going to spend a romantic vacation in Florence. A trip you agreed to and then you bailed. I need to know why."

"Actually, it's kind of embarrassing. I booked the wrong flight out of Turkey. My friends all left, and I was stuck there alone. It wasn't what I wanted. I couldn't get a flight out for days."

"So why didn't you just tell me that? It would have helped me to understand."

Just then, the waitress delivered our order, interrupting the conversation. When she was out of earshot, I eyed him, waiting for an answer.

"You were acting entitled, like I had to answer to you. You didn't have the right to impose those expectations on me. And it didn't help when you attacked me before I had the chance to explain." He avoided my eyes, but my stare finally forced him to face me.

"You mean that, because I wasn't technically your girlfriend, you didn't owe me anything?"

He was silent, but the look in his eyes affirmed my statement.

"So that's how insignificant I am to you? Even a friend deserves better than that. You wouldn't bail on a friend without an explanation and an apology, would you?" Tremors shook my body. I was unraveling, but I resisted the urge to run away, determined to face the demons that had haunted me.

"You are right, no doubt. I guess I have some triggers around expectations where a woman is concerned. But I apologize, it wasn't right."

His long slender fingers pressed against his eyelids and the muscles of his face clenched in a look of pained frustration, "Elena, I'm just trying to figure out my life, it isn't easy. Believe me, I wanted to see you."

My defenses were eroding with his honesty, but his words did little to stop the emotional avalanche.

"So, what am I? Just some chick to fuck? That's not what I want to be to you." My voice cracked, betraying my vulnerability. I turned my face away from him to hide the tears pooling in my eyes.

He pulled me into an embrace, holding me against his chest, comforting me. "I know… I know. I am truly sorry I hurt you. I do care about you… you have no idea how much." The self-assured veneer he wore lowered for a split second. "Sometimes, I don't know what to do… about us."

"Ethan you have the power to hurt me, like no one else. I wish it wasn't true, but I can't change that."

My body convulsed as I tried to hold back the sobs that so violently threatened to escape. He held me tight, but the heady feeling of being in his arms made my heart burst, releasing a torrent of emotions. I pushed my hands against his hard chest, breaking away from his hold, and wiped the tears from my face.

"I was there, in romantic Tuscany, alone. I wanted so badly for us to be there together. There has been no one since you."

"Really? No Italian man tried to sweep you off your feet?"

"Well, a few tried, but I was in no mood for another lover. And how about you? Have you been dating?"

"Elena, it's been four months since I last saw you," Ethan squirmed in his chair and evaded my eyes. "I don't know what you want me to say. I'm not going to lie to you."

My body stiffened and I had an overwhelming urge to run out of the restaurant.

"Oh. I guess that's it, then. There's someone else." *How could I be so stupid, of course he's moved on and been dating. But then, there's always been someone else. He was probably with 'her' when he was supposed to be with me in Florence. God, I'm an idiot.*

"I've dated, that's all. Haven't you?"

"I've been too busy. I have a full-time job and my nights have been spent working on building a new business on top of the cottage construction. I haven't had the motivation to go out with anyone. Not since Florence." My eyes fixed on my hands, knotted on my lap. I didn't want to admit how I'd given up on men, how I couldn't risk getting hurt again, how I only craved him.

"Elena, I'm sorry. I didn't realize how important that was to you. If you will let me, I'll try to make things better with us. I want to see you again, would that be okay?"

"I'll think about it." The tension in my body was raging and I needed to get far away from him. I would have left in a heartbeat, but since he had led the way to the restaurant, I wasn't entirely sure I could find my way back on my own. The last thing I wanted was to be dependent on him at that moment, but there was no way I could trust my lousy sense of direction.

"Can we go now? I really need to leave."

He walked me back to my apartment and I maintained my distance from him. Keeping my eyes fixed straight ahead, I asked, "Did you remember I was going to be here now?"

"Of course. I read your emails," he replied coolly. I felt his gaze, his head shifting briefly in my direction. "I'd planned on seeing you here, I just didn't know when the time would be right. If it means anything to you, I've never stopped thinking of you. How could I ever forget you?" He stopped and turned to face me, halting me in my tracks. We stood in front of my apartment building without touching, Ethan's hands tucked in the front pockets of his jeans. His face softened, but his eyes were solemn. "I could never forget the best thing that ever came into my life."

I watched as he turned and walked down the busy sidewalk until he disappeared in the crowd. He must have seen the shock on my face. I hadn't dared to say a word, for fear of collapsing into his arms and falling apart. *That* was not the time or place, I needed to keep my guard up.

When I saw Anna, I released the dam of emotions that had been threatening to erupt. She listened sympathetically and asked, "So is it done?"

"I don't know," I choked out through my tears. "He wants to see me again, and God help me, I won't be able to resist him. But right now, I can't see past the hurt."

"I get that. Damn men, they throw us away and then want us back."

"I know, Anna, at least you can relate."

I grabbed another tissue and blew my nose. "Let's get out of here, I need to walk. The beach always makes me feel better."

Sipping sangria at a beach *chiringuito,* I kicked off my sandals and my bare feet curled in the soft sand. I sat in silence, listening to the waves gently rolling to the shore, the tangle of emotions swirling in my mind when I heard my tablet's email alert. Remembering I'd connected to the restaurant's WiFi, I checked the inbox.

I turned to Anna. "It's Ethan. He is suggesting that we all meet tonight in the Born. Should we go?"

"It's entirely up to you. Do you think you can handle it?"

"He apologized at least, so that's a start. I want to make it right if that's possible, but not tonight. I feel shattered and if I see him, I need to be more in control." I wrote to Ethan that I'd be up for meeting, but not till the next night. His response came in an instant.

"Anna, he's not happy about having to wait but has agreed. I think that's a first."

"A first what?"

"The first time I haven't been available when he wanted to see me, and the first time he has shown me how much he wanted it."

Chapter Thirty-Five

THE FOLLOWING DAY was busy, thankfully I had distractions. With each hour that passed, the fluttering in my stomach grew until my whole body trembled, my brain barely able to focus. Thoughts of him invaded my mind and flooded my body, making my pulse race.

Ethan was right, the lines were long at the electronics store, but with Anna's help, I finally managed to buy a small smartphone and get it activated. I texted Ethan my new number and confirmed that we'd meet after dinner.

It gave me the afternoon to show Anna more of the city and some of my favorite places in the Gothic Quarter. Since it was last minute, we couldn't get tickets for her to tour the Sagrada Familia Cathedral, but I took her to view it from the outside. When we exited the metro, I said, "Look up," and waited for the usual reaction.

"Is that it? It's beyond magnificent!" she exclaimed with her eyes wide in amazement. "The architecture is so unique, so stunning."

Standing just outside the metro exit in the park across the street, the spectacle that was Gaudi's greatest work filled our view with its awe-inspiring magnificence. I'd been there twice in the last year, and each time I saw it, there was something new to marvel at. Construction of the cathedral had not stopped with his death. Builders continued the work, following Gaudi's original design.

As the work had begun in 1882, its architecture was modernistic, unlike Gothic cathedrals. For me, it was Gaudi's vision and symbolism, his use of color and light, that was so unique. Anna was duly impressed just by the facade and agreed that next time she'd take the tour.

In the evening, Anna and I had time to walk in the Born and stop for dinner before meeting up with Ethan. The rain came in a sudden downpour and we made a run for the inside of the bar, located only a few doors from El Copetin. I never noted it by name, instead I easily located it by the word "BAR" lit up in red neon letters. I scanned the dimly lit room, but there was no sign of him.

Making a dash to grab one of the few empty tables, we secured three empty chairs and waited. I crossed my legs, then uncrossed them but my thighs wouldn't stop jittering, my toes bouncing off the floor. My eyes were fixed on the door, on the lookout for him to appear. His approach sent my heart leaping in my chest.

"Anna, so good to see you again." He bent to give her a hug and then turned to me. "And you too, Elena, thanks for coming out." The sincere look he gave me softened my defenses.

His coat was soaking wet, droplets fell on my face as his torso folded and he wrapped his arms around my shoulders.

"Damn, you are soaked, dude."

"Yep. I ran all the way here through the rain. Couldn't get a taxi, but that happens here when it rains." Setting his coat on a chair, he joined us at the table. Slowly, the tension from our previous conversation began to melt away.

Ethan flagged the waitress, "*Tres mojitos, por favor.*"

"So, Anna, this is your first trip to Barcelona?"

"Yes, so far I'm impressed but there's not much time to see everything. We will be headed to France in a couple of days."

"I had a tour all planned out, so this is a test run with just the two of us. I will be checking out local tours and hotels for the next one, maybe schedule it in a year," I explained.

Ethan raised a dark brow and shot me a wry look with those steely brown eyes. "Well if I know you two, I'm sure you will be having a lot of fun along the way."

Anna saved me from responding to his innuendo. "I doubt we will be having that kind of 'fun.' Look, Ethan, do me a favor."

"What's that?" he asked.

"Would you please just make love to her, because you are the only guy she wants."

Ethan looked stunned. His lips parted but he didn't utter a word.

"Seriously, all she ever talks about is you, and she's driving me crazy. She's not getting laid, and no one is going to make her happy except for you. I don't understand it, because from where I sit, you keep hurting her. But apparently, there is something you two have together." She paused and shrewdly studied the look of surprise on his face. "She's happy when she's with you. I would like to see my friend happy, so get your head on straight and realize how lucky you are to have this amazing woman."

Anna was always bold, but even this shocked me. My wing-woman was trying to reunite us, but she'd exposed me. I leaned forward in my chair and ducked my face into my hands, hiding my vulnerability behind my fingers.

"Elena." I heard him gently call my name. I peeked out between split fingers and saw his questioning eyes.

"Is this true?"

I met his piercing stare and simply nodded. My back straightened against the chair and I squared myself to face him.

"I didn't put her up to this, in case you're wondering, and I will kick her later for outing me."

Ethan paused, and I held my breath, waiting for his response.

"Elena, you know what I said, I've missed... us. But I need to know what *you* want."

My heart lurched in my chest. His glistening eyes penetrated me. The look I was defenseless to resist. The cool facade I wore was eroding, torn down by my undeniable longing for him.

"I've missed *us* too. There's never been a doubt, I want *you*."

He beamed a wide smile, his gorgeous face lit up, and I melted at the sight of him. Stretching out his long legs, he nuzzled against my calf, sensuously stroking my ankle with the top of his leather shoe.

I broke away from his gaze and eyed the way he stroked me. It was a small sign of affection, but one he could tolerate in the public eye.

Ethan rotated in his seat to face Anna. "I have an idea. There's something I've always wanted to do, and your being here seems like the perfect opportunity."

Anna looked at him with trepidation. "What is it, Ethan?"

"I'd like to do a photo shoot of the two of us," he said, glancing in my direction. "When we're together it's a powerful experience and I want to capture it. So, would you be willing to act as the photographer? I can't think of anyone else who could do this for us. I can teach you to use my camera."

Anna looked at me to gauge my reaction.

"Elena, you trust Anna, right? Would you consider this proposal?" Ethan interjected before I could answer Anna's unspoken question.

My eyes darted from Ethan to Anna, their faces poised for my answer. Ethan wore that dangerous seductive look. The one I recognized so well, and it held the promise of a night I would never forget. My barriers crumbled under his gaze and I slipped into an onslaught of sensory memories. The thought was titillating. He was drawing me into another adventure. I grabbed onto the invisible rope he cast as he reeled me in.

"I'll consider it after I talk with Anna."

"Okay, fair enough."

Our eyes locked in an unwavering stare, frozen in our chairs as Latin music and voices filled the air. The people around us became a blur. In a sea of faces, it was as if we were the only two in the room. I traced his muscular body with smoldering eyes, undressing and seducing him with a dexterity that only *he* knew I was capable of. The electricity shot between us in pulsating waves and without uttering a word, we were inexorably connected again.

With his eyes still transfixed on mine, Ethan questioned Anna, "Do you see this? Can you feel what's going on between us?"

"Yes. I'm watching you two and I've never seen anything like it." I heard her voice emerge from beside me, becoming aware again of her presence. "The energy between you is powerful. I already feel like a voyeur watching you make love."

I laughed, "Just wait, you haven't seen anything yet." Ethan nodded and a smile flashed across his face. He lowered his eyes and drew in a deep breath, breaking our trance.

"You and Anna discuss it and let me know. Either way, can I see you tomorrow night?"

I didn't hesitate. "Yes, I'd like to see you, especially since it will be my last night here."

His body pressed against mine as we parted, pulling me into a full-body embrace. I felt his erection bulging through the fabric of his jeans. The steamy look in his eyes as we parted gave me all I needed to know. The fire was still there. He wanted me as much as I wanted him, and I felt a sense of female triumph, that I could elicit such desire in him—still. I knew I had a formidable sexual hold on him, but I'd felt his heart before too. The question ran through my mind, would his heart be there again?

Opening the door of the taxi, I felt the pressure mounting. I had to make the decision—Anna too.

"What do you think?" I turned to Anna.

"It's up to you," she shrugged. "You know me, I'm not shy. It sounds like it could be fun. Something new on my resume." She raised her hand in the air as if she was writing a new title for herself. "Porno photographer," she giggled. I hoped the taxi driver didn't understand English.

"Please... sensuous erotica. It sounds a whole lot classier." I paused and considered the idea. "It does intrigue me."

"You mean it makes you hot?"

I smirked at her. She knew me too well. "Yes. Exactly. I'll text him and let him know we're in," I said, shaking my head at the adventure that was Ethan.

Chapter Thirty-Six

"How do you feel?" Anna asked as we climbed the wide marble staircase to Ethan's flat.

"Nervous. I haven't been with him for so long, and I've never done a photo shoot. What if I look horrible naked, in unflattering poses, without the benefit of a rose-colored filter?"

"No need to worry about that, you look great. Besides, he has editing skills," she said with a wink that made me laugh.

"Well if anyone can help me relax, it's you. Let's do this."

No sooner than I rang the bell, Ethan opened the door. He was shirtless, his fine chiseled torso tormented me at first glance. His jeans hung low, clinging to his narrow hips with teasing innuendo.

"Welcome, come in," he invited, pulling each of us into a quick hug. An awkward tension hung in the air. I stammered out a conversation starter, following Ethan's lead into the living room.

"This place is gorgeous and large, by Barcelona standards," I commented, distracted momentarily from my racing heartbeat. The grand living room opened onto a large balcony overlooking a wide street and the treetops laced the corners of the railing. With my arms propped on the stone ledge of the balcony, I took in the sight of the city

I loved and attempted to quiet my nerves. The *pop* of a cork leaving a wine bottle diverted my attention. I turned to find Ethan filling three glasses and motioning me to come in.

"A toast, to reuniting in Barcelona—and welcoming Anna to our city."

As we took our first sips of the red, I couldn't help wondering if he felt at all nervous, but Ethan appeared coolly collected. He exuded confidence, one of his traits I found sexy as hell and at times, exasperating.

"Bring your glasses, I'll take you on a tour. I had to find a large flat, as it seems like I've been hosting visitors all summer."

"Three bedrooms and two bathrooms in a choice area of Eixample? This must have set you back several grand."

"Three thousand five hundred a month to be exact. The going rate for a well-appointed place during the summer."

As usual, Ethan's tastes were evident. The furnishings comfortable and modern, the art stunning and dramatic.

Ethan led the way to the master suite. I inhaled sharply as I surveyed the room. He had dimmed the lights and candles glowed from every surface, bathing the room in a warm hue. Soft music was set low in the background, seducing my senses with memories of *us*.

I flopped down on the king-sized bed and exhaled a sigh of contentment. "I'm so jealous, you have this memory foam bed while I've been sleeping on a twin-size concrete slab." The look in Ethan's eyes was mischievous as he watched me splayed out on his bed. Like a nervous teenager, I jumped up and walked to the second balcony, situated only feet from the bed. The warm September breeze lifted strands of hair from my face as I gazed out at the view, the lights of Sagrada Família's spires danced in the night sky.

I sensed his presence behind me even before I felt his body pressed against mine. He folded his arms around my shoulders and nuzzled his face against my neck, delivering delicate kisses that sent shivers down my spine. I drank in the familiar scent of him. *He's back,* I thought, hardly able to comprehend that so much time had passed. His touch ignited me, the familiarity drawing me back to him. In an instant, memories of our intimacy flashed through my mind and traveled to every cell in my body.

He pulled me around to face him, his soft lips melted onto mine in a sweet, delicious kiss. "My girl," he said, stroking my face with the side of his finger. There it was. I purred and leaned into his touch, so relieved to feel his tenderness again. It gave promise that his heart was still engaged as much as his libido.

Taking my hand, he led me back to Anna who was standing in the middle of the room, waiting and watching our reconnection. Her eyes shone bright, and she gave me an inconspicuous nod of approval.

"Here's the camera, Anna, let me give you a tutorial on how it works. I'll make this easy for you." She listened attentively and took a couple of practice shots.

"I've got this," she said with confidence. "This is going to be fun!"

With that, Ethan turned his attention to me. "You look so beautiful tonight," he said, holding my hands at arm's length while his eyes raked over me from head to toe. I had dressed for seduction, wearing his favorite color of blue. The knit dress clung to the soft curves of my body, dipping low in a V in the front, revealing the fullness of my breasts.

His eyes sparkled with excitement as he ran his index finger from my neck down to the line of cleavage between the mounds of soft flesh. He lightly traced along the curves of exposed skin revealed by the plunging neckline.

"Ah, my girls. How I've missed them." Before I knew it, he was down on one knee, his head buried in reverence against my breasts, his arms wrapped around my waist. My hands held his head steady, but my knees began to buckle.

"I've got you," he said, taking hold of my trembling legs in each of his strong hands. He caressed my calves and slowly inched upward to my thighs, lifting my dress with a final slide of his hands. Pushing the fabric up to my waist, his mouth found the mound between my legs. An involuntary moan escaped me at the feel of his warm breath on my apex, his teeth tugging on the satin of my panties. I longed to feel his tongue gliding between my lips, but he tortured me with soft nips and licks through the fabric, until I begged for more.

"Slowly, love, savor it," he soothed and raised my dress over my head. He stood back to take in the sight of me, shaking his head and murmuring sweet words, telling me how much he loved my body. Unwrapping me, he adeptly unfastened my bra with one hand and stepped me out of the panties, leaving me standing in nothing but my high heels. I watched as he unbuttoned his jeans and slid them down his long legs.

God, I loved looking at him—his body, so perfect, so masculine. Every muscle rippled as he moved. Already rock-hard, his penis strained against the boxer briefs as an undeniable declaration of his excitement for me.

Holding me from behind, he pressed his silky skin against my back, and his hands wrapped around to cup each breast. A violent shudder of arousal moved through me. My head arched back to meet his mouth, hungering for his kiss. Anna moved in circles around us, snapping pictures from every angle. "You two look so good together," she whispered. Oddly, her presence wasn't a distraction. Ethan had my full attention.

He bent and scooped me in his arms, effortlessly carrying me to the bed. There was no doubt he was in control when he slid me down his torso and onto his lap. I landed on my knees, straddling his thighs with his arm binding me tightly around my waist, but it was his gaze that held me captive.

"I love that you are here. Thank you," he whispered. With a low, needy groan, he sealed his mouth over mine, darting and stroking his tongue in a lush, deep kiss. The force of his hunger rocked me to the core, his mouth frantically moved from my lips to my breasts, devouring each one, then capturing my lips once again. He kissed me as if he was starved for the taste of me.

A low growl emanated from deep in his chest, one arm fiercely clutched around my bottom, and the other hand squeezed my breast into a point. His mouth locked onto my nipple, his tongue flicking the hypersensitive nerve endings, the deep pulls echoing in my core.

Suddenly feeling dizzy, I steadied my hands on his shoulders for balance. After four months apart, I was desperate to soak in every ounce of pleasure that only he could give me, yet the intensity was overwhelming. His mouth was relentless, and I could only whimper at the sweet torture, arching into him until my head rolled back. Only Ethan could bring me to the brink of a nipple orgasm. I heard the click of the camera, capturing the image I'd always carried in my memories. It was so *us,* our bodies locked in the intimate embrace.

Just then, he moved from my breast, his piercing gaze was laced with a look of sweet agony. "My God, woman, do you know what you do to me?" His arms tightened around my torso, crushing me to him in a sudden wave of emotion. He buried his face in the cleft between my breasts as if he was clinging to the warm familiarity. My hands cradled his head, tugging him tight against my chest. I was lost again—swept away by his desire for me.

I wanted him with every breath I took, impatience spurred me into a feverish pitch. "I need you... *all* of you." I pushed at his chest forcing him back on the pillows and tugged off his briefs. A breath escaped my lips in a gush of air. "*Ah,* such a beautiful sight to behold." I wrapped my hand around his erect cock. "Do you know how much I've missed this?"

His teeth flashed white in a wide smile. "It's only my dick you've missed?"

I smiled wryly, "I may have missed a few other things."

The muscles tightened across his abdomen as he raised and cupped my face in his hands, lavishing kisses on my lips.

"Come here," he took my hand, pulling me upright and leading me to the small candlelit table. I didn't question him. I knew his style. I loved the way he maneuvered us between passionate moments and pauses, prolonging our delicious dance. Refilling our wine glasses, he placed one in my hand. As he sipped from his glass, his eyes held the provocative gaze which never failed to seduce me. I took a long pull of wine and set the glass on the table. Matching him, I shot him a delib-erate heated look and dropped to my knees. My mouth watered at the sight of him. The heaviness of his full erection was in my hands, my fingers encircled him with a firm hold as I took control of pleasuring him, placing the perfectly carved head at my mouth. Slowly I wrapped my lips around it, my tongue lapping at the sensitive cleft. I heard him suck in air through a clenched jaw and curse, as my mouth began to engulf him.

"Baby... baby... *yes,*" he hissed out. The weight of his large hand gently pressed on the back of my head, and I complied, straining to take all of him, down to the root. My eyelids pressed shut and I inched my way deeper, sucking and lapping my tongue along the thick shaft. His hand brushed the hair from the side of my face, and a sliver of Anna's shadow came into view. *This must make for one hell of a shot.*

I felt him swell in my mouth, and my lips popped against the plush head as I released him. Holding him firmly at the base, the point of my tongue lapped at the tip, catching the sweet drops of liquid in my mouth. Teasing him with a devilish grin, I looked up at him. "You taste so good but savor it, baby."

The muscles in his face tightened over a clenched jaw. "You do make it difficult to hold back, as always."

He hooked his hands under my arms and lifted me upright, capturing me at his chest. My arm wrapped around his waist as he guided me to the bed. I fell back with the force of his hands on my ankles, raising my legs in the air and spreading them wide. Uttering a fierce guttural sound, he lunged forward, driving his mouth between my legs. Pulling apart the outer lips of my sex, the tip of his tongue quivered against my cleft, sending my back arching off the bed, every muscle in my body clenched. My head fell back against the mattress, succumbing to the way he aroused me. His tongue felt like silk, licking and sucking my throbbing clit, then bobbing into the clenching entrance to my body. His skillful mouth brought me to the brink. It had been so long since I'd felt those delicious sensations, I climbed with an uncontrollable urgency. Hearing the sound of his voice as he took greedy pleasure in my body sent me over the edge. I held the sides of his head and shamelessly churned my trembling sex into his mouth,

Everything inside me tightened, just before I exploded in a blinding orgasm that swept over me like a lightning bolt. I lost all control, eyes clenched tight, I screamed out—mindless of how my voice would carry through the open doors of the balcony. Ethan tongued my quivering flesh until the last of the tremors faded.

When I opened my eyes, I saw his gorgeous face, smoldering with lust. He climbed my torso and perched his powerful body above mine. I loved watching him mount me, seeing the hunger on his face and his skin taut against the rippling muscles of his arms. He pressed the wide crown against my slit, swollen and wet from my orgasm.

My mouth parted, longing for him. This was the sweet spot—the moment of anticipation as he paused at the precipice of our ultimate connection. I raised my hips, pressing against the plush head, aching for him to fill me. He slid against the tight walls, all the breath leaving his chest as he reached the depths of me. He began a steady rhythm, spearing me, then pulling out until the crest was at my opening. He paused each time, before sinking into me once again.

Anna appeared at the side of the bed, leaning in to capture our faces, but our eyes stayed locked in a heated gaze. At once, I was overcome with emotion. I wanted to tell him, to shout it out. I loved him, there was no denying it. But instead, with every stroke of penetration, I chanted in a whisper, "I love how you feel inside me." I said it on my exhale and again as I breathed in. "I love how you feel inside me." Again, I repeated the words in a hypnotic mantra, with each thrust of his hips. He paused, poised to slide into me. Ethan cocked his head to the side—those sharp brown eyes probing into me. I saw a look of recognition flash across his face. He knew. He returned a glance, so warm and tender it made my heart burst.

Flattening his body on top of me, he slid deep into our most intimate bond. With one hand fisted in my hair, he met my lips in a gentle kiss, slowly deepening as his tongue swirled and flicked against mine. I cried out in a whimper, the sound tangling in our kiss. His hips responded to my needy pleas, rocking steadily into me, then building to a feverish pace.

"Ah… my girl, my sweet…" Ethan cried out. His jaw clenched tight, a pained expression formed on his upturned face. Wildly clutching his hand on my breast, he slammed inside me with a primitive growl, then stilled. It seemed as if time stopped, the distant sound of a camera's click was the only reminder of a world outside of those precious moments where only Ethan and I existed. I struggled to absorb all of him, the length of his steeled cock hit the back of me and filled me so completely. His large frame rigid and pulsing, it was as if he was desperate to merge into my soul as well as my body. My arms clung to his broad back misting with sweat, holding him close. "Yes, baby, right there. Stay with me," I cooed.

With a ravenous look in his eyes, he lunged for my lips again. His mouth devouring mine in an exquisite kiss; his groan reverberating through my body. He began again, thrusting with powerful strokes. Each slide along my slick walls brought him higher as he chased his release.

"Come again with me baby, please," he pleaded, his breath gusting hard against my cheek. But I couldn't find my release, I was absorbed in our connection, torn by the intense emotions. I wanted nothing more than to experience his pleasure of my body. I coaxed him in a whisper, telling him how good he felt, imploring him to come for me. Lifting my hips from the bed, I tightened around his engorged cock, milking him with every stroke. I was rewarded with the sound of his thunderous voice as he cried out my name and spilled into me. His body shuddered as the climax raged on until he stilled, and his head fell against my neck. It was only then that I became aware of the camera, Anna clicking away.

"There is nothing else like it… being with you," he uttered, breathing out the declaration in a long sigh.

When we finally looked up, Anna stood at the foot of the bed holding the camera. Her face was flushed, and she looked awestruck. "Wow. That was something. I've never seen anything as passionate in my life." She fanned herself with her hand, "That made me so hot. I hope I captured it on the camera, but honestly, my hands were shaking."

Ethan raised from the bed and wrapped a towel around his waist, nodding in Anna's direction with an incredulous look. "There is certainly no lack of chemistry between us." His hands pressed against his face and slid down against the stubble of his etched jaw. "It's... intense with us."

My rubbery legs barely supported me as I stood. Anna saw the expression on my face, somewhere between a laugh and a sob, and held her arms out to catch me. I whispered, "Now you know," and I folded into her embrace. "Yes... I get it now, why he has such a hold on you," she said soothingly.

Ethan poured the last of the wine into two glasses and placed them in our hands.

"I think the photographer has too many clothes on, considering we have bared all here."

Anna looked at me for approval and with my nod, she raised her dress over her head revealing her curvaceous figure. Ethan watched as she unfastened her bra and it fell to the floor, her full breasts exposed.

"There, that's better," his voice rasped out. "I'm headed for the shower. You girls want to join me?"

Anna shot me a look. I responded in a whisper, "It's okay, but it's up to you." She grabbed my hand and we followed Ethan's lead. I knew where this was headed, and I trusted her, my best friend, to understand what was at stake. My emotions were fragile, my heart wrapped around this man. Yet strangely, I wanted her to intimately experience what we had together.

Wine glasses clinked as we set them on the bathroom counter next to the lit candles. Anna removed the last of her clothes and climbed into the shower with us. Ethan lathered himself in soap and moved aside, the warm water cascaded down our bodies. His hand reached for my breasts, his fingers teasing my puckering nipples with the slickness of the soap. With his other hand, he lathered my sex, triggering my arousal yet again. Wrapping my arms around his neck, I sank into the bliss, falling back against the tiled wall.

Though I was lost in his touch, I knew Anna needed attention. I opened my eyes and looked from Ethan's eyes to Anna. He took the signal and moved one hand between her legs, pressing a long finger deep inside her. Anna braced herself with arms pressed against the cool tile. Droplets of water beaded on her nipples and Ethan bent his head, lapping his tongue against the wetness of her skin. She raised her chest into his mouth, and I watched as he sucked hard, drawing in the pink knobs, then circling with the tip of his tongue. Anna's moans reverberated against the bare walls, only muffled slightly by the rush of the water.

Instinctively, Ethan knew to reassure me, and he pressed his lips against mine in a slow, luxurious kiss. His expert fingers worked their magic, simultaneously pumping inside both of us. I reached out and found his thick cock growing hard again. It stiffened against my long, even strokes. My hand slid easily on the slippery trail of suds and he swelled within my grasp.

Steam wafted around us and in a haze, I heard Anna climax, Ethan's unrelenting hand pumping until she cried out a second time and the tremors slowly subsided. I gave Ethan a nod and he wrapped us both in his arms before pulling us under the stream of water.

"Wow," Anna said. It was the only word she uttered as she stepped out of the shower and wrapped herself in a towel. Her cheeks were flushed and there was a dazed expression in her eyes. I had the impulse to check in with her, but Ethan's arms caught me before I could move. Holding me close, I felt the fullness of his erection pressing against the precipice of my bottom, his muscular chest against my back.

"Elena," he whispered in my ear, "I need you, please stay."

"I'm not going anywhere. It's been a long time without you, and I don't know when we will be together again." My voice broke, it pained me to think of more time and distance between us.

"Are you okay with this? I mean, involving Anna?"

"Yes, because I know this is about us, first and foremost. If I didn't feel that, this wouldn't be happening."

"Alright then, let's go. I have some ideas for us."

I couldn't help but smile at the prospect.

"Did you bring the ropes?" I asked.

"No." He cast a backward glance at me as he led me from the shower. "You should be glad I didn't."

I knew exactly what he meant. That play was reserved for the two of us. Since he hadn't planned for us having sex, there was no need for him to have packed them along. I radiated with satisfaction, realizing that though we'd been apart, there was still something unique that only the two of us shared together. I believed what he had told me over and over again, that nothing compared to what we had. Still, my heart ached thinking of him inside someone else, but I shoved away the pain. This was our time, and I desperately needed him in that moment. Even if it would be just for the night.

Ethan wrapped a towel around me and gently patted me dry before taking my hand and leading me back to the king-sized bed.

"As for the ropes, we can improvise," he said.

He opened the drawer of the dresser and rifled through, producing two of his belts. Throwing one to Anna he instructed, "Take this and wrap it around her ankle. Watch, and follow what I do with the other foot."

Anna did as she was told while I laid on the bed, cooperating with anticipation. The blood rushed in my head, my heartbeat thumping in my ears. Ethan and Anna pulled my legs apart and the belts wrapped around my ankles, secured to the legs of the bed.

He was in control again, holding me captive so he could pleasure me as he saw fit. In the dim light, I saw his dark, sculpted body looming at the edge of the bed. His eyes raked over my small frame while I waited, the anticipation pulsing in my chest. I vaguely registered the sound of the camera, reminding me Anna was at work.

"Do you know how I love looking at you like this?"

He could have held me captive with just his voice—dangerous, steamy, possessive. The mattress dipped as he climbed my body, his knees straddling the sides of my hips. His hand moved between my legs and with the pad of his thumb at my cleft, he stroked my flesh in circles over my clit. I writhed and lifted my bottom off the sheets to press into his touch, my legs straining against the belts. Being held immobilized and spread wide for him only intensified the excitement. With unwavering trust, I submitted to him.

The pulsing sound in my ears was deafening, but I heard the sound of his low growl, "You are so amazing when you get excited. I love watching you quiver. Steady, my girl. I'm going to make you come."

A helpless moan escaped me in a rush of air. I thought I might come with just his words. He angled his hips over my sex, and guiding his cock with his hands, he rubbed the carved cleft between my lips. Every time the crest moved over my clit, I felt the explosion building. At once, he slid inside, spearing me so hard I cried out. The pad of his thumb flicked over my clit as he rocked into me. With each move, he pressed against that sweet spot he knew so well. My body was on fire, every synapse screaming and climbing toward a climax.

"That's it, my girl, get it, let it go for me."

My core clenched, and the slow heated roll surged through me. The climax hit me with a shattering jolt, leaving me screaming and shaking in its quake. When all the tremors had stopped, he flattened over me and sealed his mouth over mine in a deep kiss.

Stroking my forehead with his finger, the tender look in his eyes made my heart stutter. "I love watching you come," he whispered.

"What about you?" I asked.

"Where do you want me to come?"

I licked my lips and raised a brow.

He had no trouble interpreting my thoughts. Obliging me, he moved up my body until the plush head was at my lips. I plunged my mouth over the thick, long shaft and greedily sucked, my hand sliding in tandem with my lips. His hips ground into my face with increasing force and I heard his voice rise to a feverish pitch.

I primed him to come in my mouth. I craved him, the only man I had ever craved with such desire. And the only man whose juices I longed to taste.

I heard his voice cry out, "Baby, you are going to suck it right out of me."

I pumped my fist hard just under the swollen crown and felt his cock jerk. He bellowed out a deep, guttural moan, and the warm, sweet semen spurted into my mouth. I closed over the tip and sucked him dry, his powerful body spasmed and the muscles in his abdomen clenched with each tremor.

His back arched and he sighed audibly, running his hand over the stubble on his head. "Jesus... that was... mind-blowing. Then he bent, and laid his forehead against mine, sweeping the damp strands of hair from my face.

"Oh, baby," he breathed, and for a moment we lay there, absorbing the aftershocks.

"Are you okay?" he asked.

I nodded, "But the belts are hurting a bit."

He raised himself off the bed and bent to untie me. I had time to admire his fine ass as he headed to the bathroom before I noticed Anna in the background holding the camera, fully dressed. Somewhere in the middle of our frenzy she had put on her clothes and resumed her job as the photographer.

"I forgot about you, sorry about that."

She laughed, "No worries, that looked like one hell of an orgasm."

"It always is, with him. Did you shoot that?"

"I sure did, it's going to look awesome."

Ethan strode into the room wearing a towel around his waist, then settled next to my side on the bed, one hand skimming down my naked back. "You got some good shots, Anna?" Taking the camera from her, he scrolled through the pictures. His eyebrows arched and a look of delight spread across his face.

"These are amazing, but damn, you must have taken hundreds of pictures. It will be some job going through all of these when I transfer them to my computer."

"I thought that's what you wanted, to just keep snapping. You never know which ones will come out well."

"You are right, of course. I can't thank you enough, Anna." Ethan leaned in to give her a kiss on the cheek.

"And you, Elena." He scooped me in his arms, cradling me in his lap. The way he held me by the nape of the neck and looked into my eyes was enough to make my nipples hard. My desire for him was relentless.

"Thank you, my sweet, gorgeous girl. This was quite a gift."

I shifted on his lap, encouraging the bulge below my crotch to grow yet again. "Well, it is almost your birthday again. Consider it your present." I stroked the back of his stubbled head with my hand and beamed with a satisfied smile.

"I could go again, you know," he said.

"Believe me, I know." I looked at Anna and we traded glances. "But we have a flight in the morning, which is not very much time from now. I hate to leave, but…."

"Where are you flying to first?

"We are headed to Nice, then Paris and home."

The tip of his finger on my chin raised my mouth to his. "Kiss me," he breathed. My mouth slanted over his, I brushed his lips with mine before folding into his lush tongue. With his hands gripped in my hair, he pressed me into a deep kiss. Possessing me in a way only he could.

He released his hold, his fingers cupped my jaw and his look penetrated me. "Now that I have you again, I hate to let you go. I want to see you when we're back home."

A rush of emotion swept me into a euphoric haze yet doubt held me in check. I nodded into his hands and wrapped my arms around him one last time before we said goodbye.

He watched from the balcony until we were safely in a taxi. I paused and waved up at him, with an earnest attempt to appear cheerful. Anna turned to me and asked, "Are you okay?"

My lip quivered, exhaling in a shaky breath I tried to steady myself. "I don't know yet. Being with him tonight broke me wide open again. My emotions are all over the place. I can't stop with him—I love him."

Anna looked at me with compassion in her eyes and she clutched my hand. "I know, I can see it. But if it's any help, I can see it in his eyes too."

"You can? I wondered if it was just me projecting, you know how we girls can get delusional at times," I snorted.

Anna said quietly, "No, it's there. But what he chooses to do with his feelings is anybody's guess."

"Exactly," I sighed heavily.

Chapter Thirty-Seven

The sights of Nice and Paris were a welcome distraction from Ethan. I hadn't been to France since the escape of my twenties. The awe-inspiring beauty was just as I had remembered. Following the path I had planned as a tour, I got quite an education. Independent travel to destinations by public bus proved to be a nightmare. It left us missing our stop at Villefranche Sur Mer and climbing hillsides with no idea where we were going. I pulled out my guidebook and tried to follow the map, with obscure instructions like, "Turn left at the rock in the fork." "What the hell?" was a phrase I used often, followed by Anna breaking out in a fit of contagious laughter. This left me standing on the side of the road, hanging onto my friend's shoulder while I laughed so hard I had to press my thighs together in the bladder restraint position.

On the way to a medieval hill village, Saint Paul de Vence, we watched the bus pass by on the opposite side of the road. Unfortunately, we learned too late, that was *our* bus. It was another forty-five minutes before another came along. At that moment, I realized there was no other way but to hire a driver or buy a day tour if I was leading a group. I chalked it up to a valuable learning experience, but the sights I had planned were breathtaking, and I knew I had proved my research skills.

Paris proved to be a smorgasbord of men. They landed at our feet wherever we went. We had plenty of opportunities to have our way with the French men, but after reconnecting with Ethan in Barcelona, I had no desire to be with anyone else. Anna was also missing her man back home. She was in a similar boat, loving a man who couldn't—or wouldn't—commit solely to her. Neither one of us judged the other, we knew the pain of this kind of addiction, as well as the overwhelming highs.

While she was happy to be boarding the plane back home, I burst out in tears at the airport. The emotions crashed down on me, flooded with the anxiety of returning to face the job I hated, and an uphill battle to be free. Anna tried to be supportive, reminding me that Ethan would also be back home soon, but where he was concerned, I could never be sure.

The long flight home gave me plenty of time to think. The dread I felt at the prospect of going back haunted me, but it also gave me the push I needed to refocus on my goals. I got my notebook from the backpack and pulled out the tray table. Feverishly scribbling, I formulated a new timeline and plan. It took hours, but the time flew by. When I finished, I looked over at Anna, engrossed in a movie. I gave her a nudge on the shoulder.

"What's up?" she asked, removing her headphones.

"I can't face going back to my life and waiting another six months to a year before coming back to be in Europe. Every time I go there now, I don't want to leave. What if I can get the cottage rented out in the next month and I quit my job?"

Her eyebrows furrowed with concern, then she asked, "How could you quit your job when this new business isn't off the ground? What will you do?"

"I've been running some numbers, and I can get half of what I need from the rent of the cottage. The other half I'll take out of savings for now. I have some ideas about a new angle for the travel business, and if I'm not distracted by my job, I can go balls-out to make it happen."

Anna looked doubtful but I rambled on, maybe partly to convince myself. Saying it out loud made it real, instead of just a fantasy.

"When I get back, I will apply for a visa to live in Spain and I'm targeting to return early Spring for a couple of months. I can scope it out, get to know people and look for a place to live. While I'm gone, I can rent out my house to finance the trip. After that, it's just a guessing game as to when I will be approved and can actually move."

"What are the chances that you won't get a visa? And then what? I see a lot of risk in this plan of yours. Sorry, I don't mean to kill your dream, but you have to be realistic."

"Don't look so worried," I said, reaching for her hand and giving it a squeeze, "I have a safety net. I learned about an agency policy that allows me to return to my job if it's within a year from my departure. Believe me, the positions in my department don't get filled too quickly. Besides, if I have to, I can start drawing an early pension since I've put in the time into the retirement fund. Worst case scenario, I move into the cottage and collect rent on the house and the pension. That was always my back-up plan anyway."

"Wow, you are really going to do this, aren't you?"

"I sure as hell hope so." I slumped in my seat, worried about the *what ifs*. It was going to take more time before I might convince myself that this didn't all sound like a pipedream.

"And what about Ethan?"

"He's the wild card in all this. I have no control over my relationship with him. I can only work on what is within my control. Lord knows I would like to control what happens with him, but he's the ultimate control freak." I smiled and shook my head. I liked that he was powerful and in control. I probably wouldn't be attracted to him if he wasn't, but it also drove me crazy. "Anyway, we will see what happens when he gets back. It may be weeks before I see him—if at all."

It was midday when the long journey came to an end and the shuttle van dropped me off in front of my house. My body tensed when I laid eyes on Dan's truck in the driveway. It looked like there wouldn't be a private moment to sink back into the reality of my life.

I dropped my luggage inside the doorway, and with a sense of trepidation, I peered out at the cottage in the yard from my back steps.

"Hey! You're back. Did you have a good time?" Dan greeted me in the yard, which was covered with lumber, sheetrock, and an array of tools. *He* was covered in sawdust and white powder. His brown eyes appeared as peepholes against the white coating on his skin and his jet-black hair looked like a flocked Christmas tree. *What a colossal mess, but did I expect anything different?*

"I had an interesting time… it wasn't all relaxation, but it was good to get away." I skimmed right over the adventurous nature of the trip. "I hesitate to ask, considering how things look in the yard, but how did it go?"

His face scrunched into a cringe. "I have good news and not-so-good news."

Steeling myself, I held onto the railing of the back porch and battled the fatigue that made me ache all over. "Okay, give me the good news first."

"The plumbing seems to be working and the electrical system is up and running. I installed the bathroom fixtures and the toilet actually flushes." He shot a hand in the air giving me a thumbs up. "I've got the walls textured, but you will have to tell me if you think it's even. I'm a little snow blind by now."

"Oh, that explains why you look like a ghost. That spray gun makes a mess everywhere." This was not my first experience with Dan and his spray gun. I'd scraped the spackle off windows for weeks when he worked in the house.

"The wood flooring you ordered was delivered and so was the Ikea kitchen." He pointed to my dining room, which was filled with boxes stacked everywhere, including on my nice wood table.

"The bad news is that the old garage cement foundation was more uneven than I thought. It's going to need a lot more leveling compound before we can lay out the planks."

"Jesus, that stuff is about a hundred bucks a can and I'm already well over budget." A dull ache was forming in the pit of my stomach.

"And, I tried to put together the cabinets for the kitchen, but I just don't get the assembly instructions. Those diagrams look like Greek to me. I saw the measurements you left and since I put up the walls, it doesn't look like the lower cabinets are going to fit."

"Oh no, they are GOING to fit. I spent days planning, measuring to a fraction of an inch. I knew it would be tight, so you are just going to have to cut out a patch of sheetrock and squeeze that sucker in."

The challenge of this job was that we were working with the frame, walls, and flooring of a structure that was over eighty years old. Nothing was remotely level or straight.

"And another thing." There was that cringe again. "I turned on the shower to test it and there seems to be a leak in the pipe." Dan saw my face gaping at him and quickly added, "But don't worry, I can take apart the wall and fix it."

The palm of my hand pounded against my forehead and then I silently walked back into my house. Changing into a pair of old jeans and my painting t-shirt, I prepared to push through the jet lag and get to work. I had the weekend, but if I was going to meet my goal, we were going to need a lot more help and I already had a plan to call in sick with a horrible disease of some kind. There was no way I could go into work and leave this job unsupervised. Besides, I was a key member of the construction team.

Operating on a shoestring budget meant that I had to rely on semi-skilled labor. As the days rolled by, I realized that I probably hadn't saved much money in the end since the work often had to be re-done, wasting time and money. Realizing Dan's limits and mine, I finally used an app to find a worker to assemble the kitchen. But not before I struggled for days with the screwdriver, putting together pieces of the drawers and cabinets. A million parts were strewn all over my living room carpet along with the useless instruction sheets.

Each day, I found myself handing over my credit card to the clerk at the construction store. I began to know them by name and I simply gave them a weary smile when they quipped, "You're back again?" I did enjoy the design element—choosing the tile, the lighting, the paint colors. I even got excited when I found just the perfect style of molding among the vast lineup of ten, and twelve-foot planks.

Though we managed to find a few workers to help, each came with their own set of challenges. There were the hyperactive ones that couldn't stop their mouths from chattering all day—those who carried flasks which weren't functioning as a water bottle—and the guys whose car seemed to break down every time they were scheduled to be on the job. I lost count of the number I'd hired and fired over the course of the project.

My back ached from bending over the tiled floor I'd insisted on helping to lay. I learned how to install wood laminate flooring and even gave the spray gun a try. Dan almost wet himself laughing when I accidentally turned the nozzle on myself. Sawhorses filled the backyard and the plants turned a nice shade of beige when I attempted to use the jet-powered sprayer on the doors. Though slower, the paintbrush proved to be much easier to handle.

A calm spread through the cottage when the workers left on the last day, and I hummed to a tune by Marc Antony while I brushed on the finishing touches of paint. It had been a grueling three weeks, but it had finally all come together. I stood in the middle of what was now the living room, my clothes covered in all shades of paint, and I surveyed my accomplishment. The light birch colored wood floor gave way to a slate gray tiled entryway and a wood-framed glass door, which I had chosen to maximize a light and airy feel to the small structure. The old rafters had been removed, and the A-framed ceiling created the illusion of more space. A new ceiling fan hung from a support beam just under the skylight. At night, the moon's rays illuminated the ivory walls trimmed in white baseboards and molding.

The kitchen was my favorite. I slid open the drawers, feeling the way they smoothly glided on the tracks. Sleek and modern, the gray cabinets and chrome accessories provided the *pop* the little structure needed.

Though I'd economized by using faux-granite prefabricated slabs for the countertops, the blended color combination of black, beige, and gray resonated perfectly with the tones throughout the room which I had artfully coordinated. Admittedly, the kitchen was small, but every inch was planned to maximize storage space. The window above the sink gave a view of the private patio, divided from the main yard by a picket fence and decorated with pots of bougainvillea. I'd picked out a privacy window shade in a gray that perfectly matched the cabinets. Since the kitchen in the main house was only minimally updated from its original 1920's version, the design of the cottage kitchen was like a dream for me. It brought a smile to my face, knowing that I had pulled it all together.

A pocket door separated the living room from the step-down bedroom. Though it didn't slide perfectly on the tracks, it made the difference between calling it a "studio" versus a "one-bedroom" unit. The bedroom was constructed out of what was previously an enclosed patio. With three large windows giving view to the tree-laden backyard, a peaceful feeling of nature swept across the pale-yellow walls. The floor to ceiling beige pocket curtains softened the room, but they had been a nightmare to hem. The room was as bad as the "Mystery Spot," floors and walls sloped at crazy angles. As my bare feet padded over the carpet, I eyed the size of the room again. There would only be enough space for a double bed and a small dresser.

I stepped onto the cold tile of the en suite bathroom. While it didn't turn out as level as I'd hoped, the beige and browns of the flooring perfectly complemented the ebony brown sink stand, cabinets, and matching wood mirrors. I remembered how we argued about how to construct the bathroom. I'd insisted on installing a bathtub rather than just a shower, and the plumber insisted on placing the toilet in just the right place for drainage. In the end, we accomplished both. I polished the brushed chrome fixtures, took one last admiring look and shut off the light.

I headed for the front door, reached for the handle, then paused. I surveyed every detail and captured the image in my mind. Despite the countless problems along the way, the project had turned out as I had envisioned. The space was warm and cozy, with a lovely ambiance. Though not luxurious by any means, I could be comfortable living there, I thought. That is, if all else failed and I had to resort to Plan B. But in *my* mind, I was determined not to settle for Plan B. With the cottage project complete, I could see the end in sight.

Chapter Thirty-Eight

It was time. Time to own the plan and proclaim it as real. I walked into my office the next day with a burning need to tell someone, anyone, except my boss. I found Mary sitting at her desk, adjusting her headset and firing up the computer in preparation to begin the day's work. She was past the official retirement age, and although anxious to be rid of the job, the security of a paycheck kept her tethered.

I stood at her desk, heart pounding in my chest, fumbling for words.

"Good morning. What's up with you? You look like you're about to explode."

"I'm quitting the job and moving to Barcelona." I blurted the words out and wondered if they sounded ridiculous. "The cottage is finished, and I've listed it for rent, so I'm preparing to take a giant leap of faith."

I expected the look of shock on her face, but her response was a surprise.

"Good for you, it's about time," she exclaimed, her face beaming with genuine excitement. "Life is short, go live your dream. When are you giving notice?"

"I'm not sure but I think in two weeks. That'll give me time to make sure the cottage is rented and money will be coming into my bank account. So, don't say anything to management just yet."

"No, of course not. God, I envy you. I want to get out of here and travel the world, but I wanted to save more money first. You know, in the 401K, because the pension alone isn't going to pay the bills." She paused and looked pensively at the computer, then back at me. "But time is even shorter from where I sit, I could die tomorrow and then what? I would have wasted precious time saving money, tied to this job."

"Atta girl," I said, clapping my hands. "You can come to visit me in Barcelona."

"You've got me thinking now. I have family in Sweden and I'm planning a visit. But what if I can go and stay in Europe to travel around? *Hmm*, I also have friends in the UK." Her fingers thrummed on the desk as her mind ticked through the possibilities. "When do you think you might move?"

"I will be submitting my visa application soon, but from the information I've gathered, I should qualify and have it within three months. I plan to do a test run early Spring and check out the rental market. But I'm still in the process of figuring out my travel business. The group tours concept is going to take a while to build."

Just then, Gerald rounded the corner and sauntered to his desk across from Mary's. His rear thudded into the chair and he let out a heavy sigh. "Well, here we are again, folks."

"Nice of you to join us," Mary commented dryly.

"Hey, you know I could care less if I get here on time," he glanced at his wristwatch. "Let 'em try to fire me."

His reasonably astute power of perception clued him in that something was up. "What are you gals talking about? I can see the wheels turning and it's a fair bet you're not talking about work."

Mary and I traded glances. "I'm going to quit and move to Barcelona. It's time." Each time I said the words out loud, it became easier to believe.

"Dammit," Gerald pounded the desk with his fist, "I wanted

to be the next one outta here." His face softened into a kind smile. "Congratulations, kiddo, I knew you could do it."

"Thanks, but I have a few hurdles. One is developing another concept for my travel business."

"You know…" Gerald scrolled through the contacts on his phone, "The wife and I use a travel agent. I will forward you her contact. Maybe you can pick her brain. It's another avenue but related to what you want to do."

"You read my thoughts, Gerald, that's exactly the direction I had in mind. I've already looked into some online agent platforms and I can work from anywhere. No need for a brick and mortar office."

"If I know you, you will figure out a way to make it happen." He winked at me and then his head fell heavily on his chest at the sound of his phone ringing. "Ah *marone*, here we go."

I scooted across the carpet back to my desk, relieved at the support of my co-workers. Relieved that I had finally announced my commitment. There was no turning back now.

Setting up the online travel agency was easier than I thought it would be. I decided to work under a large travel agency as a parent company. There was a minimal startup fee and a decent commission structure. They had endless tutorials I could access and an easy website for purchase. It didn't require sophisticated technical skills to drag and drop my photos and agency information, so within hours, I had the ability to utilize all their database resources. However, it would take some time to learn the terminologies and the nuances of each travel supplier. Again, another learning curve, but I reasoned that I'd have the time to study once I was out of my day job. Marketing would also be the next step. I'd have to develop some savvy skills in all realms of social media. But in the meantime, I spread the news to friends, family, and co-workers that I could be of assistance with all their travel needs.

Of course, this included Ethan. We had exchanged emails since our time in Barcelona, but after his return to San Francisco, he was on a plane again. This time to see a buddy in Boston. Besides, I had been too preoccupied with finishing the cottage to worry about where and when he might turn up. Though it felt strange that since we had so powerfully reconnected in Barcelona, there was no specific plan as to when we'd meet again. Simply vague references to making a date when he was back in town. I was almost numb to the roller coaster ride with him. I'd grown accustomed to relinquishing expectations, but since his birthday was fast approaching at the end of October, I dared to suggest a celebration—as usual, by text.

> Hey, how'd your flight go? Are you back from Boston?

> Hi, sweetie, I got back a couple days ago. God, I'm so tired of traveling. How's your week been? Mine has been crazy busy, catching up on so much work, as you might imagine.

While I appreciated his quick response, I knew that "busy" usually meant he didn't have time for me. Still, my annoying persistent streak pressed me further.

> Mine has been hectic too, but I've finished with some projects and need some R&R. I will catch you up when I see you. Btw, since you gave me such an amazing birthday, I would be happy to return the favor. Just let me know when you want to celebrate.

> Babe, that's so sweet of you. Right now, I just don't know, I'm handling so many things and I can't say my schedule yet.

There it was again, the same old thing. His birthday was in a week and I was quite sure that his friends must have made some plans with him. But he couldn't plan with me. I'd had enough, I was done trying.

It had been a while since I'd had a break and I needed a night out.

I drove into the city and since Anna was busy, I went out solo. Maybe it was time again to try to meet someone new, a little male attention couldn't hurt. Especially if it diverted my thoughts from Ethan.

I located a restaurant that featured live jazz music on Wednesday nights and sat at the bar to order. When I went out alone, it was just too awkward to sit by myself at a table for two.

Next to me sat an older black gentleman, dressed in a suit and ordering a whiskey neat. By older, I mean senior citizen old. He glanced my way, then struck up a conversation. I learned he was the lead singer/sax player of the band. I also learned he was hitting on me, then I took note of the wedding ring on his right hand as he brought the tumbler to his mouth for a draw of the amber liquid. After the usual introductory questions and answers, and hearing a fair dose of his life's history, he politely became more personal. With all his southern charm, he was honest about his marriage. He'd made a promise for life, but they'd grown apart. There was a void in his life, and he was looking for a woman to fill him with joy.

"So, I need to ask you, if you don't mind... what is an attractive woman like you doing out all alone? You are charming and sweet, certainly sexy. How could you be single?"

God, I hated that question. I'd heard the same thing a million times and all I could think of was Ethan and the others before him who I'd fallen for, but yet—dammit—I was still out alone.

"It's complicated," I began, "There is a man in my life, but it's... complicated."

"You deserve a man who appreciates you, who treats you as his queen."

I raised my martini glass, "I'll toast to that."

I held my charming smile until he raised himself from the barstool and took his place on the stage. Releasing my facade for a moment, the sadness surfaced. I looked away as the muscles in my face became lax and tears threatened to pool in my eyes. I did deserve someone who really appreciated me, but I wasn't doing a very good job of loving myself enough to hold out for that. Not that I had any confidence I could find that guy, at least one that I might be attracted to.

I pulled the cell from my purse and ran through a cursory check for messages. My pulse stopped when I saw a text from Ethan. Checking the time stamp, I saw that it had been sent hours earlier.

> Hi Elena, how are you doing today?

My options were simple—don't respond and leave him alone or let him know I was in his territory and see what would happen. Since I'd already had a few drinks and my only prospect for the night seemed to be an elderly, married southern gentleman, I chose option number two.

> Hey Ethan, I didn't see your message before. I'm in the city tonight. Are you watching the soccer game?

My text was returned within a few minutes.

> You're in SF? What are you doing?

> I'm here having dinner and listening to some jazz on Ellis Street. And you?

> I'm out eating dinner. You're going to be here for a while?

> I don't know, it depends.

Against my better judgment, I left the door open, hoping for an invite.

Depends on what?

On whether you want to join me for a drink.

I waited anxiously for his answer, knowing he was at dinner, certainly not alone. I thought it might take a while. I tried to let the music distract me, but my focus was solely on the cell phone in my hands, waiting for the vibration of the alert. Within minutes, I jolted in my seat when I felt his response.

Don't go, wait for me to get home, please. I'm dead tired and will go to bed, but still, come over. We can sleep together.

I looked up when I heard the singer dedicating the next song to me, just in time to see him gesture in my direction. I smiled politely and wanted to sink into the floor. But I put my phone away and listened attentively. His fingers danced on the keys of the alto saxophone, each note perfectly executed. I believed him when he'd claimed over thirty years of experience with the instrument. After a few more tunes, I checked my phone.

Are you still here? Where are you?

Now he's interested—when it's convenient and I happen to be in town. The thought of even lying next to him, cradled in his arms overwhelmed any resolve to demand the respect of a scheduled date. Besides, I was horny as hell and if sex was all we had between us, well then, I would take advantage of the opportunity too. I just had to disengage my heart.

I'm still here. I'll be leaving in a moment.

Come to my house, I'll meet you.

I paid my bill and waved goodbye to the gentleman still on stage, then began the familiar drive to Ethan's flat. My phone dinged another alert.

Where are you? Are you on your way? Text me when you park, I'll come down.

Jeez, why is he so anxious to see me all of a sudden? This text was not five minutes from the last one.

When I arrived, he was waiting for me downstairs, his tall frame filling the space of the metal doorway. He'd already changed into his sweatpants and t-shirt, but as always, looked sexy as hell. I waved, and as I hurried across the street in the darkness, I caught his stare. There was an intensity in his eyes, that penetrating look he wore when we were deep in the throes of lovemaking. Just as I approached the front gate, he pulled me into a tight embrace, his nose buried in my hair.

"My girl, I'm so glad you're here."

His enthusiasm caught me off-guard. He was different. The texts he'd sent this week hadn't conveyed any particular interest. I'd expected ambivalence, but what I felt from him was warmth and something more, as though he *needed* me.

He held my hand while we climbed the stairs and then walked into the kitchen. The cork popped out of a fresh bottle of Cabernet. We sat side by side on barstools with wine glasses in hand, while he listened attentively to my latest news, and toasted my accomplishments.

"Your eyelids are getting heavy," I said.

"I've had a hard week, with travel and business meetings. I'm beat."

My hand caressed his head, over the smoothness of the recently shaved sides. He leaned into my touch, then planted a kiss on my palm. A simple gesture, proving again that he could be so tender, so sweet. Rising from the stool, he stepped in between my legs and lifted my chin with one finger, bringing me to his lips in a soft, gentle kiss. Tentatively, I swirled my tongue against the lush sides of his. He moaned in response, his tongue darting possessively in my mouth. The sudden build took me by surprise. At once, my sex clenched with a throbbing need to feel him inside.

He left me slack and panting when he abruptly broke away. "I'm going to take a quick shower, do you want to join me?"

"I just took one before I drove in tonight, but I'd be happy to watch you," I said, then pursed my lips together in a grin.

I stared unabashedly as he turned on the shower, steam filling the small bathroom. His eyes never diverted from mine as he slipped off his t-shirt and sweatpants, his every move a deliberate seduction. His effect on me was swift and predictable. My pulse quickened at the sight of him, scorching hot and exquisitely masculine.

Glancing my way, he slipped under the water and lathered himself in body wash. Even semi-flaccid, his thick penis hung long against his leg. My mouth watered as I imagined what I wanted to do to him.

I stripped off my clothes and waited for him, handing him a towel when he stepped from the shower. His sleek dark skin glistened under the beads of moisture. He eyed me, naked in front of him. I watched as his erection built, loving that just the sight of me could excite him.

Reaching out a strong arm, he hooked me around the waist, and in an instant, pinned me against his body. The crown of his cock pressed against my sex, teasing me but not entering.

"Wait, I thought you were tired, and we were going to sleep?"

He moved in fast and hard, ignoring my tease. His teeth nipped at the curve of my neck, growling into my flesh as his hand reached for my breast. Squeezing one and then the other, his mouth drew in each nipple, sucking hard before releasing them.

"I was tired, but you have a very stimulating effect on me." Cradling my face in his hands, his eyes pierced into mine with startling intensity. "I'm helpless to resist you, dammit."

"Unfortunately, you have the same effect on me."

Slowly, I lowered, sliding against his skin and trailing my hands over every sinewy muscle of his body until they wrapped around his hard cock. My mouth positioned at the crown, my tongue ran the length of him before I slowly engulfed him in my mouth. I tortured him with the strokes I knew would drive him crazy.

My eyes glanced upward at the sound of his voice and found him gazing down at me with a tenderness I didn't expect. His lips raised into a gentle smile and one hand caressed my hair as I sucked and stroked him.

"I love you... I—love—you," he said, his voice lilting with a sound of incredulity. He looked stunned and grateful, his eyes warm and tender.

I took it to mean nothing more than a testament to the pleasure I was bestowing on him. I reveled in his momentary adoration, releasing him from my mouth. Without a word, I reflected back the warmth, my face glowing up at him.

Ethan's hands reached under my arms and pulled me to my feet, thankfully relieving the ache of my knees against the hard tile. He led me down the hall and when I stepped into his bedroom, I drew in a deep breath. The scent of him, so familiar, so comforting, hung in the air. I folded against him, and he pulled the comforter over us, tucking me under his arm. It seemed like forever since I'd been in his bed. I snuggled into his chest with contentment, breathing in the sweet aroma that was *him*.

At once, he engulfed me in a tangle of arms and legs, clutching my body to him as if he couldn't get enough of me. The touch of his hand weakened any resolve to keep my inner guard intact. Running the smooth pads of his fingers against the satin skin along my inner thighs, he purred in delicious sounds, his voice seducing me. "I love this spot, right—here," he said, stroking my sensitive skin and stirring in me a desperate need to feel his touch at the apex between my legs. "So, so soft... and I love this spot, right—here," whispering as he obliged my desire and stroked the length of his finger along the inner lips of my sex, rounding over the throbbing bundle of nerves. "You're so wet for me, baby. You feel so good." I pushed my hips into his hand, my sex trembling with want.

My head rose on his chest when he drew in a sharp breath, releasing it in a slow, pained moan. With sudden urgency, he wrapped his arms around me, crushing me to his body. My breasts pressed against his skin as we lay on our sides in the tight embrace. There was an obvious shift in his mood and in my somewhat buzzed state, I struggled to comprehend what he was feeling. The sound of his rasped breaths filled the room and I watched as his lips parted and closed, as if he was struggling to form words. Uncertainty gripped my insides and froze my limbs. Then, dipping his head, he cupped my face in his hands and nuzzled the tip of his nose against mine. With one finger, he tilted my chin so that our eyes met. The brilliant depth of emotion in his glistening eyes was like nothing I'd seen before.

"I love you... *I love you*," he whispered in a voice so laced with feeling, it was almost a sob. "I've loved you for so long."

There was no mistaking it this time. It wasn't lust talking, it was his heart.

"I love you, and I know you love me too. Oh baby, baby," he cooed, capturing me in his arms once again. In a haze of his kisses, and hands that moved frantically over my face, and fingers that laced in my hair—I tried to register his words.

My mouth parted, but I couldn't find my voice. I'd expected indifference and prepared myself not to give a damn. I could hardly believe it, but when I heard the sounds he uttered against my ear, so ragged, so desperate, I knew it was true.

"I do love you," I said softly. Finally. I was able to say the words out loud. The words I'd kept bottled up inside.

In the brief empty space, my voice erupted in half sentences, spilling out the thoughts I had kept tied up in the box for so long. I rambled about how I had felt this way for so long, how he had taken care of me, how I'd seen the look in his eyes....

"Shush, baby...shush," he whispered, his breath warm on my cheek. Pressing his fingers against my lips, he silenced my voice. There was only stillness... a few seconds in time when nothing else existed except the stunning clarity of love that was reflected in our gaze. In the quiet

of this most poignant moment, his mouth poured over mine, kissing me long and deep. A kiss like I'd never felt with him before. A kiss that convinced me of his love.

In one pained motion, he threw himself on his back with a roar that ripped us from the intimate bond. With a draped arm over his forehead, he cursed out. Startled, I didn't move, my hand pressed against his chest. A breath caught in my throat.

He raised his head to look at me. "It's so fucked up… isn't it… well isn't it?" His eyes flashed at me in sheer frustration. His arms spread wide, his palms splayed up as if he wanted me to answer the question. But I had no answer. I knew exactly what he meant, and it scared me. My eyes widened, but I couldn't speak.

Lost in his own torment, he dug the wide pads of his hands into his eyes. "I finally find love and…" he sighed into his forearms in a gust of air, "it's so perfect with you, so real—more than I ever dreamed of. When I'm with you, I feel complete."

As sudden as he'd let go of me, he swept me up again and buried his head against my breasts, his breathing jagged and hot on my skin. I stroked his hair with a soothing touch, his heartbeat racing against my belly. With an upward lunge he possessed my mouth, kissing me again, but this time, I felt his desperation, his need to merge into me.

Moving his body on top of mine, he pushed the crown of his erection against the slickness of my sex and plunged into me. He rocked his hips rhythmically, each slide against my walls inexorably binding us together in a connection we were powerless to control. His arms wrapped around me, sealing me to him. Our bodies moved as one, my hips arched into every stroke, and my fingers clutched his back as if I could absorb him into my very skin.

I wanted him, needed him, loved him—with an intensity that took my breath away. Finally. I could freely give him my heart, my soul, my body. Tears spilled from my eyes and trickled down his temples, at the place where our faces joined.

The sound of his voice melted me. Beautiful, sweet sounds and soft whimpers each time he slid along the plush walls of my sex. I sensed his orgasm building. I clenched tightly around him, trying to hold him, trying to keep him inside me. Instinctively, I knew he craved a release, not just from the physical arousal, but a release of the emotional tension which tortured him. At once, his body stiffened and with one deep thrust, he poured into me, crying out my name.

The weight of his body sank onto mine as his tight muscles finally relaxed. I knew he was spent and needed to rest. Though I didn't have the chance to climax, it didn't matter. I had all that I needed.

His gaze was soft and tender on my face, propped on his elbows he leaned in and kissed me, punctuating the intimacy of our afterglow. Slumping into the fatigue, he rolled to his back, his tight grip pulling me to his side.

My head rested on his chest, listening to the slow thump of his heartbeat. His right arm wrapped around me at my waist, and with his left, he clasped my hand, interlacing our fingers. He kissed my forehead and whispered, "My girl, my love," in a sleep laden voice, then drifted off.

With eyes wide open, I lay nestled against him, unable to rest. I was stunned beyond belief and my brain was still trying to comprehend what had just happened. His words echoed in my mind and my thoughts raced. *Is this real?* I had dreamed about this moment for so long and I was struggling in a haze of blurred lines between fantasy and reality.

As he fell into a deep sleep, his chest roared with the sound of his snores. Still captured in his arms, I attempted to slip away, out of his hold so I could roll him onto his side and quell the noise. I knew the routine.

But in his deep slumber, his hand refused to let go. His arm reflexively gripped me tighter, binding me to his side. He clenched my fingers, tugging our clasped hands back to center on his belly.

Oh my God... he does love me! My heart swelled, and I thought it might burst from joy in that moment. I submitted to the hold he had on me, laid my head back down on his chest and rested on the rise and fall of his breath.

Chapter Thirty-Nine

Happy Birthday, baby. How's your day going? I texted Ethan the morning of his big day.

> Hey gorgeous, thank you! I'm working but will see some friends tonight for dinner. We are on for tomorrow night, right?

> Yep, and I have some surprises in store for you. BTW, what's your favorite flavor of ice cream?

> Cookies and cream, why?

> Never mind. I will see you tomorrow night. Kisses baby, until tomorrow. Have a good one.

> I can't wait...

As I had assumed, he had made plans with his friends for his birthday on Friday night. Since I only existed in his alternate life, the one he kept secret, I was not a part of the celebration. Nothing much had changed since he proclaimed his love for me, but then I knew he was wrestling with the dilemma. I felt it the next morning. After wild morning sex, I could tell he didn't quite know what to do with the new version of *us*. He was quieter than usual, pensive even.

I wondered if he might retreat again and I fought the urge to panic, though I had every reason to panic. Given that I was not able to bear the children he wanted, I was still the least likely candidate for girlfriend material. We loved each other, our declarations made it real. But did it change anything? The dilemma hadn't magically disappeared.

Yet, dopamine ruled my brain, and I was high on the drug. When you are high on love, anything seems possible, and reality fades into the deep, dark recesses.

Friday was girl's night out. I was invited to a birthday celebration held at a late-night club downtown. It wasn't the safest part of town and it had a reputation of being somewhat sleazy, but I needed the diversion since Ethan was going out with friends for his birthday. I slipped into a tight black dress and stiletto heels and set out for a night of dancing.

The hip hop music blared loud enough to obscure conversation, but after booty bumping with a new twenty-something gal pal, she was intrigued with me enough to start asking questions.

"You are an amazing dancer, how old are you?"

"You really don't want to know, and I hate saying it."

"But you are so cool, it doesn't matter how old you are. You are stunningly beautiful and so much fun. Don't you have a boyfriend?"

Oh God, here it goes again, I thought. The two questions I hated the most. But since I was drunk on love and several cocktails, I spilled the tale of Ethan. How fate brought us together, and we fell in love only to struggle with the ultimate dilemma.

"*Aww*, that's so sweet. You two belong together. Tell him I said you are a hottie and he is lucky to have you. And age doesn't matter if you have love."

Spoken like a bright-eyed, anything is possible, twenty-something. If only it were true.

"C'mon, let's take a pic together," she insisted.

I posed with a sexy, seductive smile. My eyes picturing Ethan behind the camera inspired a burning hot smoky look. I checked out the photo, and texted it to Ethan, along with the sage words of my new friend as soon as I arrived home. He responded within minutes.

> OMG, baby, you look so hot. I wish I was with you.

> Thanks, sweetie, wish I was with you too. Where are you?

> I'm out partying with my friends. Are you in the city?

> No, I was out in Oakland but I'm home now.

> Damn, I want to see you. I love you so much… I told my friends about you tonight…

I re-read the texts over and over again. He loved me, and this time it was in writing. Somehow that made it even more real. And telling his friends? It meant he was ready to introduce me into his life. It meant I mattered. Finally. Tears of happiness pooled in my eyes, my mascara running in black streaks down my face.

> Really? You told your friends? I can't tell you how happy that makes me. Baby, I love you so much. Kisses, until tomorrow.

I barely slept that night, so overwhelmed with emotion and missing him beside me. I spent Saturday preparing birthday surprises for him and headed across the Bay Bridge in the early evening. He threw open the gate to greet me and exclaimed, "What is all this?"

A delighted laugh boomed from his chest when he saw me standing in the doorway holding a large helium balloon with the words "HAPPY BIRTHDAY" written in bright colors, a large overnight case, and a shopping bag.

"Here, let me help you," he said, carrying the bags up the stairs and into the kitchen.

"I've got… cookies and cream cake AND ice cream," I said, pulling the items from the bag with a "TaDah" to emphasize the surprise. "And, I brought a bottle of your favorite Cab. The other surprises will have to wait until later," I said, grinning with the anticipation of what was to come.

"I couldn't think of what to get you for a present, so that will come later. What the hell do I get a guy who has his suits tailor-made, and can buy anything he wants?"

His gaze fell soft on my face, "All I need is you. And thank you for all of this, it's so sweet of you." With a roll of his eyes, he quipped, "It's way more than anyone else has done for me."

As he pulled me into a tight hug, I had the presence of mind to wonder who was "anyone else"? The look on his face had given me the hint that maybe there was a special "anyone else."

He held me at arm's length and looked me over, head to toe. I'd gift wrapped myself in a low cut, slinky blue dress, lacy undies with a garter belt and stockings, and finished the ensemble with matching stiletto heels.

"Holy crap, you look amazing, smoking hot, babe. Thank you."

He planted soft kisses on my lips, one for each word he spoke.

"YOU… are… my… best… present."

With arms locked around his narrow waist, I said, "Happy birthday, sweetie. Do you remember where we were last year on this same day?"

He responded without giving it thought. "Of course, it was our first date after Barcelona. We were at B44."

"We've been through a lot of ups and downs this year, but here we are..." I said, with a sentimental tone.

"Let me put the ice cream away before it melts, and we'll take this to the living room and have a toast to our one-year mark," Ethan said, releasing me from his grasp.

Soft music filled the candlelit room. I thought back to the first time he held me on the overstuffed couch. Where nervous anxiety used to be, I now found familiarity and comfort in his presence. We settled into that same sofa, propped against a pile of pillows. My back relaxed into his chest, cocooned in his arms. We sipped wine and shared the details of our week. Something so simple—normal even—but we'd had little normalcy and simple pleasures over the course of a year.

Ethan leaned and set his wine glass on the table, my head balancing on his chest as he moved.

"I'm so glad you're here," he declared, then engulfed me in his arms.

Feeling the warmth rush through my heart, I wrapped my arms around his neck and smiled into his stubbled cheek.

His low, seductive voice poured into my ear. "Can I open my *present* now?" He looked so damn cute, wearing a sexy grin singed with excitement.

"You are the birthday boy, darlin'. You can do anything you want with your present." I glanced up at him and saw his eyes light up in a wicked smile.

"Oh really?"

He started as he had done before, reaching his soft hand inside my bra to cup the fullness of my breast. Peeling away the material which separated him from my skin, I stood before him in a G-string and stockings, still in my heels.

"Wait." With a measure of restraint, I pulled myself from his touch. "I'm going to change into a sexy little thing. I'll let you know when you can come in."

My pointed heels ticked against the wood floor as I scrambled to the bedroom, grabbing my overnight bag along the way. A thrill rushed through me as I climbed into my outfit. I finished by covering the lamp with a dark red cloth, bathing the room in a seductive hue. I posed, lying on my side across the bed with one knee bent and my head propped against my hand.

"Okay, you can come in now," I called out.

My pulse quickened at the sound of his feet shuffling down the hallway and the creak of the door opening. The next sound was not what I expected.

"What are you wearing?" He erupted into a gut-busting burst of laughter.

Embarrassment replaced excitement and a blush warmed my face. "This was all I could find at the last minute. I wanted to try something erotic and playful," I said in a small voice.

He came to my side as he caught sight of my face falling. "Oh baby, I love it, I was just surprised, that's all." He ran his hand along the black fishnet bodystocking I wore, still looking shocked.

"You do look hot in this outfit, but... it may be a dumb question, but can we make love with you in this thing?"

It was my turn to chuckle. "Dude, note the cut-outs. This thing is fully functional to suit your needs." I pointed to the openings for my breasts, leaving them accessible to his touch. And to the crotch, slit from the front to the very back of me.

"Oh, now I see. I'm beginning to appreciate this get-up more and more," he said, his eyes flickering with that sexy look he always had just before he was ready to pounce on me.

"Come here," I commanded and pulled him to me by the waistband of his jeans. While I unbuttoned his fly, he slipped the pullover knit shirt over his head. His hardening cock sprung out of his boxer briefs as I tugged down his pants. I grabbed hold of him at the base, ran my fingers lightly over the length.

"God, I adore you," I said, with my eyes fixed on his beautiful organ.

With ease, as if I was as light as a feather, he flipped me on my stomach and lifted my hips high off the bed. He lowered himself behind me and the softness of his tongue poured over my sex.

I gasped in air, releasing my breath I whimpered, "Yes... oh... please... I love how you take care of me."

He paused, "Oh, my love, you always take such good care of me."

He plunged his thick tongue inside and between the folds, then flicked the tip across my cleft.

"I love the taste of you," he breathed, and his lips engulfed me again, his tongue sending waves of ecstasy to my core. A trembling moan left me, and he knew I was reaching my peak. His mouth broke away and I let out a soft sob.

"Hush, my sweet girl, I've got you."

He raised my hips with both hands and gripped me tight. The carved crown pushed along my swollen tissues as he slid into me from behind. I yelped as he sent a deep pounding stroke, hitting the end of me. "Easy, baby, easy. Let me get used to you."

He slowed his pace as I struggled to accommodate his heavy surge. I opened for him, pushing my hips back to meet his thrusts.

"*Ah...* yes... I love how you take all of it," he said with a low, sexy growl.

After only a handful of strokes, he stilled. "I want to wait. You drive me crazy, but I don't want to spill just yet." He pulled out and I rolled onto my back, my chest heaving with every gulp of air. My body was on fire. No one else had ever made me so turned on. No one else had ever made love to me this way. No one else had relished each moment. To him, I was like fine wine. Each sip to be savored and enjoyed.

Straddling over me, he held the heaviness of my breasts with his hands, squeezing and kneading them between his fingers until they puckered and swelled under his expert touch. Clamping a breast in each hand, his tongue fluttered over one nipple, and then the other with a ferocious need, arrowing waves of pleasure straight to my sex. My fingers stroked the back of his head, holding him close. I loved watching him take such pleasure from my body—almost as much as the feeling of his mouth on my nipples.

"Oh, my girls." He declared his possession with utmost reverence, then laid his cheek against my chest with a heavy sigh. The sound of his ragged voice reverberated on my skin. "I don't know what I would do without you."

My heart melted at his words and the tender look he gave me, his face buried against my breasts. "Oh, baby," I sobbed, "you are the only one I want."

I clenched him hard around his back, my spine bowed as I folded into him. His chin tipped and his mouth poured over mine, our tongues dipping and swirling with the force of a desperate hunger. It was as if we were more vulnerable than ever before, each of us in so deep, the risk was frightening. The power of our bond strong, yet fragile.

When he broke, it was like a tidal wave, his force and strength overpowering me. Tugging my hips to the edge of the bed, he held my ankles, drawing my legs upward and apart. He aimed the crown of his cock between the lips of my sex, slick with arousal. Slowly, he entered and slid into me with a steady rhythm. I cried out, lost in the primal connection between us. My eyelids pressed shut and I gripped the sheets, absorbing every delicious sensation as his hips rolled faster and faster. The circles he made with the pad of his thumb at my cleft sent me into a frenzy, wildly bucking my hips, urging him on.

In a haze, I heard his adoring words, "Ah my sweet, I love watching you."

He clutched at me, riding me hard and pulling my hips into him. I felt him swell inside me, just as his chiseled jaw tightened. His chest expanded with one gusting breath, and he pulled out, leaving my sex clenching at his absence.

With a dangerous, hot look in his eyes, he bent and dove his head between my legs. The luscious sensation of pleasure made me gasp— the heat of his mouth on my sex, his tongue relentlessly lapping at my clit while he pumped inside me with a long finger.

My muscles spasmed, the sweet tension spreading through my

body. I couldn't hold back any longer and when he nudged the hyper-sensitive knot with the tip of his tongue, he sent me over the edge. I climaxed with a thready cry, the rush of my orgasm jolting me to the core. Fueled by the passion I felt for this man, I came so hard it overwhelmed me as wave after wave shook my body.

Before I could recover, the weight of his body sank onto mine, his erection sliding easily against my slick tissues, and at once I felt the fullness I craved. My orgasm rolled on, with each pump of his hips.

Ethan called out my name, told me how good it felt to be inside me, how he never wanted to stop. His words and desire for me sent me higher once again.

Bellowing out a yell that I swear must have shaken the walls, his steeled cock jerked, and hotly spurted into me. I locked him in a tight embrace and clenched around his spasms that seemed to last forever. His sweat misted body collapsed on mine, my breasts pressed by the heaving of his chest.

A smile raised his cheek against my face.

"What?"

He lifted his head and stroked a sweaty lock of hair from my forehead. "I just can't believe how we are together. Never in my life..." his voice trailed off.

Rolling to my side, he clenched my hand and his chest raised with a heavy sigh.

I snuggled against him and kissed his cheek, but the netting on my body prevented the skin contact I loved.

"Babe, I've got to unwrap myself." I tugged a finger through the outfit and caught him choking back a snicker. "Okay, this thing is going in the garbage."

"Oh no it isn't, we might want to use it again. You can leave it here, just for safekeeping," he said with a hint of possessiveness.

"Here," I said, throwing him the wad of netting. "Now, I'm starving, it's time for a snack."

Ethan followed me to the refrigerator where I retrieved the cake and ice cream, while he reached in the cupboard for two plates. Wrapped in towels, we sat on barstools in the kitchen, the familiarity of the room filling me with a sense of contentment.

I broke out into a chorus of "Happy Birthday to You" and his creamy, cold lips thanked me with a kiss. There was something different about this night—*we* were different. I thought of how I felt more confident and playful. Holding him in that spot in my heart he had touched, I felt loved.

It was my goal to pleasure him through the night and into the next morning. As usual, he had no problem rising to the play I had in store for us. The soft handcuffs came in handy. I used them to restrain his hands above his head so my fingers and mouth could stimulate every erogenous zone on this body.

The cold and warm lubes intensified the sensations, as I stroked and sucked him right to the brink—breaking away to prolong his release. I reveled in the cacophony of primal sounds he made when he came. I loved watching him unravel with such intensity, his body straining and rigid, his gorgeous face ravaged by the fierce release.

When I had succeeded in fully satisfying him, he pulled my body to his and held me tight, spooning me from behind. Shivers rushed through me at the tenderness in his voice. "I love you," he sighed, the sound falling against my ear as he drifted off.

I woke to find his head buried between my legs, his tongue lapping against the folds. I propped my head on the pillow to watch as the sun illuminated the room in muted rays. *Jeez, what a beautiful sight.* It was so damn hot to see his full lips engulfing my sex and his tongue dancing on my clit.

My body draped on top of him, I shuddered with the last tremble of an orgasm. His slackening penis still inside me, I lay boneless and satiated from the sexual tidal wave that was Ethan. The soreness would be evident when I bathed, but I didn't want to tear myself away from the warmth of his body. I don't know how long we lay there, with his arms wrapped around me and the point of his finger absently tracing up and down the curve of my spine. He had almost lulled me back to sleep when I faintly heard his voice break the trance.

"My sweet girl, thank you for the wonderful birthday." He kissed the top of my head and I looked up to meet his gaze. "I hate to unlock our bodies, but I have to get showered."

My eyes widened in surprise. "Oh... I thought we would have some time together today. It's Sunday. Where do you have to go?"

His lips pursed together in silence, but his eyes didn't break away. He had something on his mind, I could see by his look. But the words did not come.

The realization flashed through me in an instant. My face grew taut. My eyes narrowed at him. "Oh no—don't tell me you have a *date* today?"

He stared blankly at me, his eyes conveyed an apologetic look and a cringe darted across his face.

"I don't fucking believe it! After everything—after last night?" Anger boiled up, coursing through my veins. "I thought things were different now, but I guess I was wrong."

My hands fisted on his chest, pushing myself away from him. I had one leg off the bed when his hand caught my arm. I whipped my eyes at him in a lethal glare.

"Elena please, don't do this. Don't make things worse."

"Worse? For who?" I spat.

His hand held its grip, but his other formed into a fist.

"Don't you think I want to be with you? You are the only one I want to be with, dammit." His eyes darted like a caged animal, frustrated and desperate. Don't you see the impossible situation we are in?"

His hand slackened and I tugged my arm free. I grabbed my clothes and ran into the bathroom, slamming the door behind me. Sobs threatened to rack my body, I held one arm across my stomach as I bent in half, the other over my mouth to prevent any sound from escaping. *STOP!* My voice reverberated in my head. I needed to keep it together, stay in control. The hell if I was going to let him see me as a hysterical female. But he was right, it was impossible. I'd known it from the start.

Air filled my lungs in a deep and quivering inhale. I stepped under the hot water and washed quickly, wincing when I soaped the raw place between my legs.

I fixed my makeup and hair with just enough effort to look presentable for my exit and the drive home. After pulling on a pair of jeans and a sweater, I gathered my courage. I stood up straight and came out of the bathroom. My body was rigid, and my face wore an impenetrable mask.

I didn't look at him as he passed me in the hall. My brain fuzzy and flushed with adrenaline, I went from room to room frantically gathering my things that were strewn all over the apartment. I stopped for a moment in his bedroom and a rush of memories flooded me. *Can I really walk out of here and out of his life?* I pushed back the emotions that threatened to derail my determination and hurried down the hallway.

He met me at the stairs, bags in hand and ready to bolt. My arms laid at my side as he pulled my stiff body into an embrace. His attempt to make things better fell flat.

He kissed my forehead and rubbed his stubbled cheek against mine. "I'm sorry about this," he said quietly.

The warmth of his body so close to me, the scent of him almost undid me. My emotions were torn, stretched apart between hurt and anger—but also by the love and desire I could not escape.

I started down the stairs. He waited until I'd reached the gate and called out, "Drive safe." I looked back at him for a moment.

"I'll see you soon Elena, okay?" I nodded and raised my hand in a silent gesture of good-bye, then turned and headed for my car. My mind was reeling, I needed the solitude of my home and a long hot bath. I already knew the decision I would have to make.

Chapter Forty

With bold strides, I walked into the office on Monday. Dark circles and bags hung under my eyes from lack of sleep. It seemed that my face had aged five years in a day, but through my misery and contemplation, I had emerged with decisions and new determination.

I knocked on my supervisor's door, only slightly ajar.

"Good morning, Elena." Jennifer's bright smile greeted me.

I sat down on the chair in front of her desk and attempted to return her smile, only managing to move the corners of my mouth a fraction of an inch.

"Good morning, Jennifer, I have something for you." I passed a typewritten paper across her desk.

"Oh my," she exclaimed, "you are giving two weeks' notice of resignation?" Her warm expression faded and gave way to a look of dismay. "Are you okay?" she questioned, looking confused.

"I'm fine, well, sort of," I stammered. "You know I haven't been happy here and I've talked about my plan to move to Barcelona since traveling there. The cottage is finished, and I have some good prospective renters. It should get finalized this week. I need time to build my business as a travel agent, so it's best if I leave and focus on a new direction."

I hadn't hidden anything from Jennifer. We'd compared notes on our respective construction projects, and I had filled her in on my sideline business.

"I knew you wouldn't stay here, but I just didn't expect that you would resign so soon." Her face relaxed in a sweet, compassionate expression. "I do wish you all the best, and I want you to know that you will be missed."

"Thank you, Jennifer, that means a lot. Though I need to move on, I have developed friendships here and I'd like to stay in touch."

She chuckled and said, "Yes, it was a rocky start when you came aboard, but you settled in very nicely with the team. Would you like to have a goodbye party? It's customary, of course, but it's up to you."

I paused and thought of the last time I left the job. I refused a party and simply packed up my things on the last day. I said goodbye to only a couple of people and made a hasty exit. This time was different. Many of the staff had supported me through my angst and efforts to be free. I had a good relationship with the administrative team and some of my co-workers had become friends.

"Yes, I think I'd like that. I'm okay with a short workplace party—since we can only be off the phones for break time—and then we can arrange something with whoever wants to meet up after work."

I closed the door behind me, feeling lighter than I had in a year. I had finally broken free from the shackles.

As I'd anticipated, by week's end, I had a lease signed for the cottage. A single woman in her thirties who was moving out of San Francisco due to the skyrocketing rents. The location of the house was perfect for public transportation and shared car-pooling. She loved the cottage, and it's fresh, modern look. It was "Like having her own little house," she said.

The pieces were finally all falling into place. In the next week, I booked a cruise for my first client. Debbie was a co-worker and sat across from my cubicle. She happened to mention that she wanted to go on a cruise with her family. Mindful of my years of social work training, I asked her key questions to gauge her true desires for the vacation. I learned her priorities and those she had for her family. I found her the best dates to travel—for the best price—on the cruise ship of her dreams. Due to my new connections with the global travel company, I was able to gift her with extra bonuses. She was excited and I was thrilled. I had found another profession in which I could use all my skills. It was fun, rewarding, and the commission would be deposited into my account within a few months. Not that I had given up on planning tours, but I reasoned that as a travel agent I could work with a wide range of people and earn income sooner rather than later.

"Hey there," Mary appeared in my cubicle. I startled and let out a yelp. She chuckled, "You seem a little jumpy today."

"You would think I'd be relaxed on my last day but there are so many details to finish up. Damn paperwork."

"Besides that, how do you feel?"

"Spoken like a die-hard therapist," I teased. "I feel good... a little scared, and maybe a lot nostalgic, but excited. I'm leaving behind my entire career, so there's the reason for the nostalgia. But I have no qualms about leaving this office—except for the friends I'm leaving behind."

"Well, I won't be far behind you." Her face lit up with excitement and her toes trotted on the carpet. "I handed in my resignation. I will be officially retired in a month. I wanted you to know how much you inspired me to follow my dreams."

"Oh, Mary, that's fantastic. I'm so happy for you." I jumped from my seat to give her a hug. She was radiant, having finalized her decision to set out on a new path of her own.

"It was you," she said, pointing her index finger in my direction, "your hard work and determination made me realize it was possible. I watched you through this entire process—from your nosedive when you arrived—to the end of your journey. Or should I say, the beginning of your new journey. You struggled through each challenge and never gave up. You are not only one strong, resourceful woman—you are incredibly brave." Her eyes shimmered and her cheeks formed bright rosy pouches as a smile brightened her face.

"I'm so touched," I squeaked, my voice cracking. "I can see this is going to be one hell of an emotional day."

"I will see you tonight at Quinn's after work. And... I will meet you in Barcelona," she said with a wink.

Quinn's was an iconic restaurant/pub. It had been around since 1984 but it was constructed inside an old lighthouse, circa 1903. It was a second home to many old sailors. Some nights you could stomp and swagger to the tunes of a live band playing old sea chantey music. But since it was situated across from government buildings, it was also a place to unwind after work for many of its employees.

I entered the restaurant and found the gang immediately, thanks to the raucous cacophony of voices cheering, "Yay, she's here," followed by instructions to take my place at the head of the huge wooden table. I had come to learn that my co-workers could be quite the party animals when they were let out of the cage at five o'clock sharp. As the drinks flowed, so did the laughter, the jokes and the warm camaraderie I had come to appreciate.

"Do you remember when you first came to work here? We thought, 'What the hell is up with this chick?' You wouldn't talk to anybody," Debbie remarked.

"I thought, this girl is trouble. And I was right." Gerald said with his tough Bostonian bravado. He shot me a wink and his face rounded into a wide smile.

"We didn't think you'd last a month, let alone a year. But you hung in there and we're really glad you did because we had the chance to get to know you," Becky said. Her cheerful smile and the sincerity in her eyes made my eyes well up. God, I didn't want the waterworks to start. Goodbyes made me feel sentimental and weepy.

The group of eight chanted, "Speech, speech," and I knew I was going to lose it, but I realized I did have something to say.

When the clinking of glasses subsided, I cleared my throat and put aside my fear of speaking in front of groups.

"I came into this workplace a total mess. I think all of you know the story by now. But each one of you has helped me along the way, with your support, your guidance, and most of all your friendship. I don't know how I would have made if I hadn't been able to confide in you all. The future is still an unknown, and I will admit it's a little scary, but wherever I go, I will take ya'll with me."

A round of cheers exploded across the table and Jill chimed in, "Oh please take me with you, I can't wait to get out of here. Spain is calling me too, so I'm coming to see you as soon as I can. I've got two more years to put in and I'm outta here."

Mary gave the group her good news and announced she'd be meeting me in Europe.

Terry pulled me aside and looked into my eyes with an earnest expression. "I think you are so brave to be doing this, I can't imagine having the courage to pick up and move to another country without knowing anyone." Terry and I had shared many midlife dating stories, being the only two who were single and looking. She knew about Ethan, but I hadn't told her the latest developments. "Look," she said quietly, "be careful with that one, I've seen the ups and downs you've been through and it doesn't seem like he's treating you right. You deserve someone who appreciates you."

"Yes, there seems to be a growing consensus on that opinion," I said dryly. She gave me a questioning look, but I brushed it off with a "Thanks" and, "Never mind, I'll tell you later."

When we called it a night, I hugged each one as they left, with a promise to stay in touch. I walked back to my car alone and stopped for a moment, staring up at the building which I'd labeled 'my prison' from the first day I was obliged to walk through the door. I realized that if the fates had gone a different way—if I had been placed in any other job—I probably would not have found liberation. I wouldn't have found Barcelona or Ethan. Both changed my course forever. A chill ran down my spine, but it wasn't from the cold night.

Now what? I gripped the handle of the car door and wondered where this new path would lead me. If I wasn't a full-time mom—a wife—a lover—a social worker—who was I? The thought was as exhilarating as it was unsettling.

There was one thing left to do. My heart raced as I took the phone from my purse and began a text to Ethan. He'd tried to contact me a few times during the week, but I put him off, telling him I was busy. Now was the time. I typed a few words, then erased. *It has to be short and to the point.*

My fingers hovering over the touch keys, I began again.

> Can you meet me tomorrow? We need to talk. I can come to the city.

His response came swiftly.

> Sure. I can get away later in the afternoon or early in the evening if you'd like. Meet at that restaurant in North Beach?

> I'll text tomorrow when I'm on my way.

Our messages, void of any endearing words left me feeling empty. My hand clutched my chest, painfully aware of the ache in my heart. I craved him, more now than ever. But he had the power to destroy me and I couldn't let that happen. I thought of the old southern gentleman. He was right—I deserved better.

Chapter Forty-One

I FINALLY PULLED INTO a parking space after making three attempts to parallel park on the steep San Francisco hill. The image of Coit Tower standing tall against the darkening sky haunted me. The place I had grown to love now kindled in me a deep sadness.

I trudged uphill until I reached a level stretch of street. North Beach was famous for its restaurants, but this one was special. And not because of its trendier decor. I had memories of Ethan and I dining there. I couldn't remember what dishes we ordered, but I did remember the touch of his fingers on my cheek, and the burning look in his eyes just before he kissed me.

I looked at the time on my phone. I was fifteen minutes early, but then, I had planned it that way. Heading to the back, I found the restroom and faced my image in the mirror. My hand shook as I applied a fresh coat of lipstick. I gripped the side of the sink and looked into my own eyes. They peered back at me with clarity and determination, but there was no hiding the sadness reflected in those green eyes Ethan had admired.

Luckily, the restaurant wasn't packed with people since it was still early, long before the after-work crowds descended. I settled into a private booth in the back where I could face the door. I pulled out my phone, nervously checking messages as a distraction. Suddenly, I sensed him. Tilting my head, I saw his tall frame come through the doorway. My heart pounded in my chest. A smile lit up his face when he saw me, but it didn't reach his eyes.

"You look good, really good," he complimented. As his eyes raked over me, I remembered all the times he gave me praise for the way I looked. And for the way I took charge of my life, overcoming challenges.

I dipped my head in a nod, squeaking out, "Thanks."

"Do you want to order something to eat?" he asked.

I shook my head. My hand flattened against my belly, churning with a sick feeling. "No, thanks, I'm not hungry. A glass of wine will do."

Ethan motioned to the waitress and ordered two glasses of our favorite Cabernet. We fell into an uncomfortable silence.

"So how is it going at work?" Ethan blurted.

"I quit. Yesterday was my last day." I straightened in my seat with a bold sense of pride. "It went well. I'm confident in my decision but still nervous about what's next."

"I'm proud of you, babe, you did it!" Ethan beamed a smile at me and asked, "So what's next?"

"I'll apply for a visa to live in Spain, and I'm making plans to give it a two-month trial while I wait for it to be approved."

Air whistled through my clenched nostrils on the inhale and rushed out through my lips. A deep cleansing breath, although it failed to lessen the raging tension.

"Ethan, this is hard for me, but the last time we were together made me realize something." I took a second breath, but it stopped in my throat. My fingers knotted in a vice grip on my lap. "I can't do this anymore. I can't do *us* anymore. Not like it has been."

The waitress appeared, delivering two glasses of wine, which gave me another moment to collect my thoughts and fortitude to go on.

"Do you know how bad I've felt being the girl in the shadows?" He shifted in his seat and dipped his head, his jaw tightening. "When you said you loved me, I thought things would be different. I thought you would finally bring me into your world, your life. I need to be a priority to you, not a lover on the side."

"I know," he whispered. Ethan shifted his gaze to his wine glass, his long graceful fingers twisting the stem.

"I won't share you with other girls. I can't. I love you too much." I snorted when I heard my own words. "It's not like I'm oblivious to the realities here, I know you've been dating. Your goal is to have a family. I can't give you that, but I had hoped…" my voice trembled out, "I had hoped that we'd have some time together as a couple before time forced us into different lanes. But I guess that's unrealistic. Better to end it now because it would be even harder down the line."

Ethan brought the glass to his lips and took a long pull of wine, his face growing more taught by the minute. My heart ached and I longed for his arms to fold around me and tell me everything would be okay, but I knew by the look on his face that everything was not okay.

"Elena, there is someone else." An unbearable pause hung in the air, and a breath caught in my throat. "I've been feeling torn apart. You have no idea how much. I've wrestled with the dilemma—what direction I should take."

The pained look in his eyes mirrored the agony shooting through my body. Finally hearing the truth did not bring the relief I had hoped for.

"I know it hasn't been fair to you. I've hurt you, and for that, I'm truly sorry. But I do love you. It's not just about the sex. I love *you*…"

He leaned back against the rolled leather seat and squared his shoulders. A long breath escaped through his lips, and for a moment, he was silent. I took a gulp of wine, steeling myself for what might come next.

"I divide my life into two parts. The one before I met you, and the one after." He raised the flat of his palms in the air, one and then the other. "You have changed my life forever. I am not the same." He raised a finger to my cheek, but halted in midair, grazing only the shadow of my face. "I've never met anyone like you. You're so sensuous, so loving and giving all at the same time. I've never had this kind of depth of emotion with any other woman, and probably never will again. It's perfect, with you." He paused, his eyes somber as he looked deep into mine. "I need you to know this, Elena, you are always in my thoughts."

The shock of his words paralyzed me, my lips parted in a silent gape. I watched as he struggled to formulate thoughts. Sounds stuttered in his throat but stopped. Fragments of sentences dangled in the air while his fingers thumped nervously against his strong thighs. He rarely expressed his feelings so directly. I closed my mouth and waited, hanging on his every word.

Finally, his words came tumbling out. "It's not just sex with us. I've had lovers who were adventurous, but it was just a performance. It always left me empty. But you and me—we connect on another level. With us, everything flows so naturally and feels so right. When we're together, it's like our souls are merging. Since I met you, the bar has been set to a level I didn't know existed."

His beautiful brown eyes bored into me like a lance. *Dammit.* Hot tears broke through my weak barrier.

"What I feel for you is so powerful… it's more than I ever dreamed it could be. It's everything I've ever wanted. *You* are everything I've ever wanted." He shook his head and his face lit up with the saddest of smiles.

My mind blurred with the words I wanted to say—the words I'd bit back so many times. I had wanted him to fight for me, to jump over mountains to be with me. But I pursed my lips, knowing it was too late.

"You don't know how many times I've wished time could stand still, so we could stay together. Believe me, I want to be with you. Except, I can't be with you casually, it's too intense." A wince crossed the face I loved, then he raised the glass to his lips before starting again. "In order to be with you, I need to be aligned in my body, heart, mind, and soul. That's what makes it so beautiful yet so hard because I'm always aware of the conflict inside me."

A waiter rushed by our table, balancing plates on the palms of his hands as Ethan watched. Balance. It's what Ethan craved. *I,* was not 'balance.'

"I think you know by now, I've been trying to figure out the course of my life. It hasn't been easy, but I'm at a place in time when I have to make decisions about my future, just like you."

A bolt of clarity broke through my stunned brain. This was the reason he hadn't brought me into his life or introduced me to his friends. I may have had his heart, soul, and body but there was someone else who occupied the role of girlfriend in his public life. In Barcelona, he had told me he was dating, and we'd been apart for four months. Loving me didn't change anything. I was not his future, not if he wanted a family. He deserved to have that chance. I'd had my shot at motherhood, and it was an experience I never would have wanted to miss.

I knew I shouldn't ask, and most likely it would be hard to hear, but I plunged ahead anyway.

"Who is she? Is she the same woman you were dating in Barcelona when we met?" As soon as the words left my mouth, it felt like I was freefalling off a cliff.

Ethan hesitated and averted his eyes, his brows furrowing. "No, she's not the same girl, that ended not long after I met you. But she's from Europe and I've known her for a long time." He bent his head, nervously shifting his gaze to the table. "At first, we were just friends, but then she began visiting me here. I didn't expect to like her, especially when I couldn't stop thinking of you, but…" His voice shook in a way I'd never heard.

I treaded lightly. "So, I'm guessing she's young and can give you a family?"

"Yes."

He stopped, and I didn't press him for more. I nodded and forced a smile. Though I cringed in pain, at least I knew that he wasn't walking away from me. He was stepping into his new life, someday as a father.

I slumped into resignation, but my heart was full. I knew what I had to do. Leaning in, I faced him and placed my hands firmly on the table.

"Destiny caused our paths to cross; we were meant to find each other. That, I'm sure of. You are everything I've ever wanted. With you, I have love, passion, excitement—if things were different, I could have the life with you I've always dreamed of. I wanted to travel the world with you." I shook my head, bowing it into my neck. "It's so ironic, now that I am free to plan a new kind of life and can go wherever I want, you won't be coming with me."

My heart stuttered in my chest and I fought to clear the clamor of emotions that threatened to derail my thoughts.

"Ethan, I've come to realize, you are not what I need."

His eyes widened and I saw the ghost of a wince in his gaze, but he didn't look away.

"I need to be with someone who can love me without reserve, without conflict. Whether or not I find this, I'm going to chase my dreams. Time is short from where I sit and I've no time to waste. I'll find passion in the next chapter of my life. It may not be in love, because I doubt that I will find anything close to what we have, but I'll find passion in discovering a new life. It's time for me to take care of myself."

It was heartbreaking to watch his face soften and see the loving look in his eyes.

"I understand. I don't want to let you go, but there doesn't seem to be any way around this situation." His fingers raked through his hair, his face wearing that frustrated look I'd seen before. But this time, it was singed with pain.

I ran my hands across my face to wipe the tears which had begun to trickle down my cheek and reached for a napkin to blow my nose.

"Goddammit, why do *we* have to be so complicated." I shifted my body toward him and pleaded, "Why do *you* have to be so complicated?" I choked out a tearful laugh, trying to break the tension raging through me.

Ethan reached his long arm and held my shoulder firmly in his grip.

"My girl, you wouldn't like me if I wasn't." His full lips lifted into a smile and his gaze locked on mine.

My mouth parted, ready to form words to argue his point, but I stopped. I felt my eyes soften in resignation. He was right. I complicated my life with complicated men. Always.

He lunged forward, wrapping his arms around me with a force that knocked me back. I could barely breathe with the pressure of his body pressed tightly against mine. He held me so long and hard, like he never wanted to let me go. When he did break, he kissed my lips with the same hard longing and then lifted me under my arms to stand. I saw the tender look in his eyes, the trace of tears glistening... just before he grabbed me into another fierce embrace, burying his head in my hair.

"I will always think of you," he rasped into my ear.

"And you will always be in my heart. I hope you find your dream," I choked out, my body trembling as I fought back the sobs that tore apart my chest.

Ethan broke away and reached into his pocket to throw down a twenty for the bill. He turned, and I watched as he walked out the door. Neither one of us could bear one more look into each other's eyes.

Chapter Forty-Two

8 months later

"Is this the last of the kitchen stuff that has to be packed?" Lena asked, crouching down with her head inside the cupboard.

Looking down from the step stool, I answered, "I just have to get this liquor cabinet cleaned out and we'll be done." Stretching my arm up to the top shelf, my fingertips grasped the bottle of tequila. It was the same one Ethan and I had drunk from a couple times. I still felt a twinge when little things reminded me of him. Maybe that would never change.

"Here, free booze. Take it to the next salsa party."

Lena took hold of the bottle and put it in a bag, along with the other things I was parting with as I emptied out my house.

She saw my face fall and asked, "Have you heard from him?"

"We've texted a few times. I needed some information about the visa process and picked his brain about neighborhoods in Barcelona when I was looking for apartments. It's impossible not to want to share with him the details of my big move."

I stepped down from the stool and plopped my bottom on the

floor. Anna peeked her head around the corner and started to give a report on the bedroom packing, but she stopped short when she saw the look on our faces.

"What's up?"

Lena nodded her head in my direction. "We're talking about Ethan."

Anna's mouth formed into an 'O' before pursing her lips tight.

"I was just saying that I'd been in touch with Ethan about the move. He was so excited when I got my visa approved to live in Spain." I paused, a shadow of a smile lifted the corners of my lips. "If it wasn't for him, I might never have set my sights on moving to Barcelona. He opened up my mind to the possibility of another kind of life, not to mention that Barcelona became a special place for me because of him."

Anna looked down at me with a reassuring smile. "Have you considered that maybe that's why fate brought you together? It wasn't supposed to last with him, but he brought you to a new place in your life. And look at you! You've made it happen. You are ready to walk through that door."

I snorted, "Yes, I am. I still don't know what's on the other side, but it's an opportunity I've always dreamed of. Travel and adventure await!" I shot one arm in the air, mustering the courage to sound bold. "I'm not going to lie, it's a little scary. I'm leaving everything and everyone behind and moving across the world to find myself. I'm starting over, alone."

"But you have friends there now, the ones you made last time you went back for two months. You'll have a support system in place. And besides, I'll be there soon to visit, so get that guest room ready!" Lena waved her arms in the air like a cheerleader.

Excitement began to peek through the fatigue that had made me feel so weary. "I've moved mountains to make this happen. If I can pull this off, I can do anything. I'm looking forward to setting up my new apartment. It's just as I imagined it would be—with a little balcony overlooking the streets of El Born."

I pulled out my phone from my pocket and found the photos. Lena and Anna gathered close to get a look at my new home.

"It's adorable," Anna exclaimed. "You are going to be so happy there."

Lena asked, "It's all set? You've signed the lease?"

"Yep. I paid a hefty chunk of euros to secure it. Luck intervened for me, because the rental market is brutally competitive there, and I don't have a job. The rental income from the house and the cottage was finally accepted by one owner. Others had turned me down."

"See, this was meant to be! What are you going to do with your time there?" Lena added.

"Besides getting my apartment ready, I'll do a lot of traveling at first. And of course, I will need to work on building my business remotely. But I need to find a new purpose in my life. One that isn't wrapped up in a man." My voice sounded determined, but yet, it felt daunting.

Anna giggled, "Knowing you, a lot of men will be chasing your tail. Have some fun anyway."

Her giggle always made me laugh, and she was right. It was about time for some new sexual adventures.

"Okay, girls, let's have a shot to celebrate." I rose to my feet and Lena grabbed the tequila while I found a few paper cups.

"To my best friends, I couldn't have done this without your undying support."

Tiny paper cups clinked and Lena chimed in with a toast, "To your leap of faith, may your new life bring you happiness."

Anna's eyes sparkled, "To new adventures and finding your passion."

We downed the shots in one gulp and smashed the flimsy cups on the counter. "I expect to see both of you visiting me regularly, and I'll be back, of course, a few times a year to check on you."

My arms folded around their necks and we huddled in a three-way hug, muttering how much we'd miss each other. Lingering in the kitchen, sharing precious memories of our friendship, made me nostalgic. Finally, I pulled myself out of the love-fest, in need of some private time to say good-bye to the life I was leaving behind.

"Thanks a million for the help. I've got it from here. The last of the furniture that sold will be picked up tomorrow. My flight is in two days and there are lots of details to finish up."

"That's right!" Anna exclaimed, "You are leaving on July Fourth. Independence Day."

I shot her a wry smile. "My departure date is not a coincidence. I see it as *my* independence day."

I stood in the doorway and watched Lena and Anna get into their cars. *What am I going to do without them?* My heart ached as I waved goodbye. When they drove away, I closed the door behind me and sank against the wood. "It's really happening," I sighed.

I walked from room to room, feeling the emptiness of a house void of all my worldly possessions. I had taken on the job of remodeling it so it would appeal to renters. I chuckled and spoke out loud, *I waited all those years to make the improvements. It looks great—and now I leave it.*

It was my safety net. I could come back if I needed to, there were boxes of my things piled in the basement and new storage shed. But deep in my heart, I knew I was leaving for good. This was my old life, and I was trading it in for something different. Soon enough, I would find out what that would look like.

In the quiet of the night, I climbed in the makeshift bed. An airbed I'd borrowed for the last two nights. It felt so strange to be lying in the middle of an empty room. Everything familiar was gone. It wasn't that I didn't expect waves of emotion to hit, but it was the exhaustion that made me feel so heavy as I lay there staring up at the patterns on the ceiling. The same swirls of plaster I'd looked at during so many phases over the last twenty years of my life.

Ethan always came to mind in those silent moments before sleep. When I told him of my impending move, he had cheered my success by text. He also said he loved me. I still loved him too, probably I always would.

I had no regrets. Ethan showed me I could love again, more power-fully than ever before. He opened the door to new sexual adventures I would never have known if not for him. Going forward, it was my task to learn to love myself—before giving that love to any man.

I ROLLED MY suitcases out the front door to meet the shuttle, the same way I had done the first time I went to Barcelona. This time, I had my whole life packed up in two 70-pound suitcases plus a carry-on. And this time, if I returned, someone else would be living in my house. I turned to look back at my home, and I knew that nothing would ever be the same. Thinking about what might lay ahead, I smiled and closed the front door behind me.

Acknowledgments

I SET OUT ALONE on this journey to become an author, but many dear friends back home and in Barcelona have accompanied me along the way. To all of you, thank you for believing in me, giving me the gift of your undying support, and listening to my story through its many renditions.

I want to give a special thanks to my test readers who've stuck with me through the innumerable versions and always encouraged my writing, from the painfully amateurish start to the polished end result. There were many along the way who guided me with their gentle feedback through those early stages.

Especially my dear Barbara, who read the first drafts and simply encouraged me to let my heart shine through. I will never forget the proud look on your face when you began reading the finished manuscript and threw your arms around me, exclaiming, "You ARE a writer!!! This is not the same book as before, THIS is good!"

And Maurizio, an avid reader of books miles from my genre, thank you for making pasta dinners while listening to me read the passages. It must have been the good Spanish wine that helped the chapters seem palatable.

My dear Alla, thank you for loving the book in all its forms and always being in my court. You are truly the sister I never had and have rescued my heart so many times along my journey.

To Yana and Adriana, who verified that this story resonates deeply in the hearts of my sisters in singledom.

And to my bestie, Lisa— my loving friend, my toughest critic and most diligent assistant throughout my journey—you made me strive to be better and never doubted that I could be.

My gratitude goes out to Aida Digat, who's real-life character appearance in the book was brief, but her undying friendship has lasted for years, bonded together in the sisterhood of midlife adventurers. I can't thank you enough for your support and for bringing me into your *familia*.

As for my entire family, your unwavering support kept the dream alive. As promised, I am making a redacted version for you all to read, the G-rated one. Thanks go to my stellar son, who thought it was a brilliant idea for me to write and supported me with his expertise as a film artist. Someday, I hope to be as good a writer as you are. And to his wife, for her professional and sage advice, always willing to lend a helping hand.

I honestly don't know what I would have done without the support and aid of my super team of professional readers and editors. Thank you to Marni MacRae and Whitney Baer for loving my story and taking such good care of my manuscript. When I read your comments and critiques, my heart soared. Your belief that my story was worthy of publishing gave me the confidence to press on, through all the hurdles.

And finally, I cannot forget to thank the man who inspired Ethan's character. It was truly fated in the stars. If not for you, this story would never have been written. The cord that binds us defies time and space. Maybe in the next life...

Since I have just returned from Bali,
brimming with the spirit of Ubud
and inspired to write the next part of Elena's journey,
I send all of you my thanks
I bow my head in humble gratitude
Namaste.

Printed in Great Britain
by Amazon